PASSION'S PRISONER

"Your hair is straight, and much too long for a civilized being." She examined the long, narrow braid amidst his hair, forgetting her critical intent.

"What are these?" She lifted her hand slowly, hesitating before touching him. Her fingers caught the bead-studded braid in his hair.

Her soft, wistful mood softened Seneca's resistance. When her shield lowered, the temptress emerged, even if she didn't realize it herself. "Shells from the Tremoring Sea. Our craftsmen form them into symbols," he said.

"They're pretty. What do they mean?"

"They mean I like this shade of blue." Seneca touched Nisa's cheek. "But here..." He gently circled Nisa's left eye with his finger. "And here..." He outlined the other, bending closer to her. "Here is blue so fair, so perfect, that no child of the Tremoring Sea compares."

His lips brushed hers, but Nisa didn't move. She leaned against him, her arms finding his waist. She started to pull away, then faltered. Instead, she pressed closer.

Seneca pressed a sensual kiss at the corner of her mouth. "Am I your prisoner...or are you mine?"

STOBIE PIEL

THE DAWN STAR

LOVE SPELL ◆ NEW YORK CITY

LOVE SPELL®

November 1996

Published by

Dorchester Publishing Co., Inc.
276 Fifth Avenue
New York, NY 10001

Printed in the United States of America.

To Neesa Hart, Sophia Voltin, and Toad of Toad Hall, for inspiring the creation of Nisa Calydon.

To Mickee Madden, Kathleen Morgan, and Anne Avery, because I sat with you guys at lunch at the Romantic Times convention in Nashville. Reading your wonderful, magical books inspired me to discover my own worlds, too. Thank you!

To Joyce Flaherty, for being the most wonderful, caring agent anyone ever had.

And yet, there is only
One great thing,
The only thing:
To live to see in huts and on journeys
The great day that dawns,
And the light that fills the world.

Eskimo song, from *In the Trail of the Wind*

Chapter One

Blood pounded through the warrior's veins, surging energy from his expanded lungs, forcing fire into his hardened limbs. The rough ground sped by beneath his long stride; his breaths came even and deep as he ran.

The darkness of night lifted, the first rays of the distant sun slanting through the drying leaves. The gray hues of the dying forest deepened, separating into faded green and brown and ashen white beneath the first light of morning.

Over rough ground, bounding across fallen trees and over sharp, narrow gorges, the warrior traveled an unseen path. His pace didn't slow as he left the tangled, dry trees behind. He crossed the rutted plateau, heading out toward the jagged-edged cliffs.

At the farthest edge of the cliff, Seneca stopped, his dark hair streaming in an upward gust of wind. Far below stretched the savanna lands. Cut into the savanna like a bowl rimmed with white trees lay the ancient village of the Akando. There the Clan of the Wind had lived for uncounted ages, hunting, gathering the meager harvest—living, not against their harsh world, but in accord with its rhythms.

Seneca turned his gaze upward. There, still bright in the morning sky, the Dawn Star glimmered. Though Seneca knew the distant light by another name, the people of Akando greeted the Dawn Star with ritual and honor. It spoke of eternity and permanence to a race that struggled to survive in a bitterly harsh environment . . . and endured.

From the shores of the Tremoring Sea, through the Undian Wastes, Seneca had proven his ability to survive, to conquer, and to endure. Through a trial that had claimed many lives before him, Seneca had reached the mountains beyond the Wastes. There, in a sacred grove, he found a sapling of the Lasting Trees.

He bore the treasured sapling back across the Wastes, knowing it symbolized his own future as well. Today he would plant the sapling in the eternal circle of the Lasting Trees. When its roots met the soil, his own roots would be transformed from his dark past to an Akandan future.

The planting of the sapling signified more to Seneca than the endurance of Akando. It meant freedom from the past. He had severed every root to his past but one. One clung tight to his heart, reminding him of what he had lost long ago.

But today Seneca would return to the village. In a ritual ceremony, the Akandan chief would release his hold on life and pass the leadership to Seneca. To receive, a man must give away. Seneca sighed heavily. He'd given away what he wanted most in another lifetime. What he had received in exchange was peace.

Today he would take the mate chosen for him; he would begin life anew. Today he would put the past to rest forever.

Seneca started down toward the valley, but a flash

of green and blue caught his eye. He squinted, but the flashing light disappeared. The light reminded him of something, something from another lifetime. *It can't be. I have been long away, long at the brink of endurance. My eyes deceive me.*

An unsettling tension descended around his heart. Seneca sensed a pursuit, an enemy closing in. But no beast . . . It was the past. The past he struggled to forget, its treachery, and more bitter still, its sweetness.

Seneca found the narrow, jagged path that skirted the sheer cliff walls. His tread disturbed no pebble, no stone. He moved with perfect precision, with perfect control. The mind-body training of Akando, the TiKay, had made him a creature of infinite control, of unmatched strength.

From the cliff's floor, Seneca ran with the wind's speed to the wide-rimmed bowl of opaque trees that sheltered Akando from the Undian Winds. Here, in the dry season, the Lasting Trees endured and thrived.

Through the trees, Seneca saw the village of Akando wake. Seneca's doubt dissipated. Fires sent smoke through the roofs of elongated huts; a few villagers appeared to begin the day. From a near hut, a young woman appeared: Elan. His mate.

Elan performed a ritual greeting toward the Dawn Star, then shouldered a large bushel of carth-wheat. No pride tarnished her nature, no treachery. Elan might not set his heart to flame, but Seneca had learned long ago how deadly love's fire could be.

"I have returned. Home."

Seneca started forward. A low hiss from the Lasting Trees stopped him. He knew every noise, every breath the wind took. This was no breath of wind. Every muscle in his body drew taut, held like a drawn bow.

The tree branches above Seneca's head quaked; the dry leaves fluttered and swirled to the earth. An oval shadow fell over the ground, darkening the sky above. Seneca whirled around and looked up. A narrow, gray vessel lowered above him, then stopped.

Seneca didn't consider flight. Instead he stood still as stone, his eyes closed as he allowed his senses to penetrate the hull. It contained vastly conflicting impulses. Human impulses, but primitive, unhoned. Deceit, evil ambition . . .

Seneca's primal force rose in resistance, forming a shield around him that nothing and no one could penetrate. As he closed himself to the outside, another presence made itself known within the floating hull. A sweet, probing presence; a presence he couldn't resist. A presence he knew.

Seneca's concentration wavered; his shield faded. Seneca left himself open to attack, to anything. Shocked, he opened his eyes. The vessel didn't move, just hovered as the tree branches quaked in its wind. A section of the hull slid aside and a woman appeared in the doorway.

The morning sun slanted through the tree limbs and reflected off the metallic hull. It pierced Seneca's eyes, shadowing the woman's figure as she crouched in the doorway. Seneca shaded his eyes, and her image became clear.

No . . .

The bright sun illuminated her golden hair, and sparkled on the cylindrical object she held in her hands. . . .

Seneca took a step toward her. A blast of light and energy shot toward him, consuming him, robbing him of his power. Seneca fell to the earth, but as his senses fled, he knew his trial had just begun.

"Got him?"

Nisa Calydon drew a tight, shuddering breath and nodded. "He seemed to disappear for a minute—must have been the sun. Bring him in here fast. He took so long gazing at that village that they're up and around already."

Three crew members lowered themselves on a ramp and dragged the Akandan's body toward their vessel. The men weren't used to physical labor; only with effort were they able to lift the large warrior onto the ramp.

The ramp closed, and Nisa turned to the helmsman. "We'll have to travel low until we're out of sight range. There's no need to disturb these people by a flight-ship sighting. Tranor, keep close to those cliffs, then pull up."

Nisa caught the navigator's veiled sigh at her abrupt, commanding manner. She refused to soften it. For one thing, she had earned her position as first lieutenant to Thorwal's councillor. But deeper inside, Nisa knew her own weakness demanded an authoritative manner. She'd learned at the expense of her heart how damaging femininity could be.

"I'll transmit the new position to the *Gordonia*," suggested the navigator as he coded in another program. Tranor eased the shuttle across the Akandan savanna toward the sheer cliff wall.

Nisa glanced at her unconscious victim. He lay motionless, stunned on the shuttle floor. His sculpted face appeared serene. Nisa had studied his image on the reflector screen before. She knew what he looked like—who he looked like. High cheekbones, a straight nose, firm lips to an angled, strong chin.

In person the Akandan warrior seemed more imposing. Less a specimen of a forgotten tribe, and more a man. A dangerous man. Even stunned, his lean physique radiated controlled power. With a slight alteration of attire, his resemblance to the rebel leader of Dakota would save Nisa's homeworld of Thorwal from disaster.

Fedor Mikaid entered the helm and studied the Akandan. "Shouldn't he be bound, Nisa?"

Nisa frowned, but she resisted the impulse to argue. Fedor was the councillor's main adviser. She knew

Helmar sent Fedor on this mission to watch over her, but the councillor's good intentions made the journey much more tiresome than it would have been otherwise.

"Put him on the gurney," she instructed her crewmen. "Strap him in, and secure the gurney to the wall."

The crewmen worked quickly, afraid the Akandan would wake and wreak havoc. They struggled again with the large warrior's unconscious body, heaving him onto the narrow gurney, then hurriedly strapping him down. The Akandan didn't stir.

The shuttlecraft lifted along the cliff walls. Nisa forced her attention from her captive and gazed out the window at the strange scenery. *Such an inhospitable land!*

"It's a wonder humanoids ever developed here." Tranor echoed Nisa's own thoughts. Tranor guided the shuttle up and over the cliffs, then above the jagged tree line through which the Akandan warrior had run at dawn.

"Yet they've lived here for millennia. Unchanging, constant." Nisa's voice faded. Something she didn't understand troubled her heart. Not with regret at the abduction. What she did, she did to avert a war.

Nisa's own people, the Thorwalians, had known change as their only constant. Yet they were the dominant race of the inner solar system. They were the builders, the leaders. Strange, though, that the intellectual, scientific inhabitants of Dakota should prove their worst adversaries.

"Not much chance for development down there," added Tranor as he gestured at the dwindling bowl village of Akando. "Not with environmental conditions like they've got."

Nisa gazed down at the planet's rugged surface. Akando's elliptical orbit around the Day Sun gave the planet harsh weather changes. From burning, desert summers to frozen winters that lasted a full half-cycle, only the strongest, most durable species of plant and animal survived.

Tranor completed his program for docking with the waiting Thorwalian transport craft, then sat back to study the Akandan. "He certainly looks like Motega, doesn't he? How do you suppose the Akandans and the Dakotans evolved to look so much alike? Got to be a connection somewhere."

"A connection seems likely, though it's never been proven conclusively. Motega thought so. . . ." Nisa stopped. Now the theory of her enemy would be used to correct his wrong.

"Well, if he's really going to fit in, he'll have to gain some weight." Tranor chuckled. "He's a little too lean, even for Motega."

The other crewmen laughed, too. The Dakotans were a sedentary race, opposed to exercising anything but their minds. Motega had been gifted with a powerful body, but he rarely used it more than was absolutely necessary.

No, Motega relied on the agility of his brain rather than his body. Nisa shuddered at the memory of his persuasive reasoning. He nearly persuaded her to betray her own world.

"The resemblance is amazing." Fedor studied the Akandan and shook his head. He leaned closer to examine the unconscious warrior. "Skin's darker than Motega's. I'd say he's a year or two older."

"It's been seven years since Motega died," Nisa reminded him. "He would have aged. No one will notice his skin color at this point." She allowed herself to assess her prisoner. A pang of forbidden longing gripped her heart. But for the skins he wore, his long hair, this man could be Motega's brother.

"Wonder if he's got Motega's gifts with women?" speculated Tranor. Fedor cast a quick, warning glance at the navigator, who paled. Nisa ignored them. What she had done, she had done as a young woman. A

17

woman who knew nothing.

Motega's handsome face and powerful body had attracted Thorwalian women like harem girls. He attracted even Nisa, niece of the Thorwalian councillor. Never had a Dakotan leader exuded such charisma. Curse him!

The minor planetoid of Dakota harbored an intellectual, passive race, long allies of the much-larger Thorwalian world. Since the two worlds discovered each other, they had worked together to future both cultures. While the Thorwalians excelled in technology, the Dakotans' brilliant science and research enabled both to accomplish swift progress.

The two worlds worked in unison for generations, though Dakota's government was subject to Thorwalian approval. The unison was shattered when a young research scientist seized control of the Dakotan government, accusing the former leader of subverting Dakota's interests.

Motega claimed the Thorwalian domination profited only Thorwal, to Dakota's detriment. He demanded equal representation in Thorwal's High Council, though Dakota's population was much less. He argued that Dakota's research formed the basis for Thorwal's fast-paced technology. He argued persuasively.

Nisa didn't want to remember Motega. His life had burdened her world, but his death threatened to destroy everything. A frown tightened her face as Tranor directed the shuttle up from the surface of Akando and through the layers of frigid atmosphere.

The surface blended and disappeared, but Nisa's gaze fixed below, lest she turn her memory too easily to the man who triggered a thousand regrets, a thousand pleasures. But she couldn't forget the Dakotan leader's touch, his kiss.

She remembered his sensual whispers as he urged her to remain in his chamber for a night of passion.

As his deft fingers peeled away her staid uniform . . .

Nisa banished the thought. Let people gossip, let them say she was the mistress of the most dangerous man Thorwal ever encountered. Motega had used her, plied her knowledge for his own ends. She would never be such a fool again.

"Should we drug him for the move?" asked Fedor. The shuttle jerked to the side as Tranor readied it for docking. Nisa braced herself against the helm, then eyed her adviser with distaste.

"Only if he becomes violent, Fedor. We want his co-operation; there's no need to frighten him."

"He's a primitive creature. He'll be terrified as it is."

Nisa glanced at the warrior. "He's already restrained. I see no need for anything more unless sufficiently warranted."

"He's going to be dangerous. We don't have the manpower to subdue him without drugs."

"If he's drugged, we'll have to wait a full cycle before applying the mind probe. We don't have time for delay. The Dakotans are demanding Motega's release. If they should learn, even suspect . . ."

Fedor nodded, but his pale eyes glittered. "If they learn Motega was murdered while imprisoned we'll be at war. A war we can win."

Nisa turned to Fedor, her expression knitted with distaste. "A war that will cost the lives of thousands."

"Maybe. But with our victory, we control all the research centers. Think, Nisa. . . ." Fedor leaned toward her, his eyes bright and demanding. His voice lowered. "You and I both know the Dakotan research stretches far beyond what they told us. They've designed a power cell capable of sending a vessel anywhere in this system. Maybe beyond. If they accomplish that, we'll be so far behind. . . ."

Nisa rolled her eyes. "Their designs may reach the outer rims of the galaxy, but they'll never build anything on their own. They don't have our resources. Just trees."

Fedor's fist clenched. "They can't build such a vessel. But we can."

"For what purpose? We have no need for such travel."

"Have you forgotten the Candor Moon?" Fedor's voice was a whisper, but it vibrated with repressed excitement. Nisa's face paled and she turned away.

"How could I forget?" she asked softly. "Because of that damned moon and its supposed riches, we now hover at the brink of war. And a man lost his life . . . because of me."

Nisa busied herself with her notes. She didn't want to grieve over Motega's death. The man had made her a fool. She had trusted him as if she were a heartsick child, and he betrayed her. She had enjoyed seeing him humbled in prison. But after his murder, she had wept bitter tears.

Seneca woke to find himself bound, flat on his back, laid out on a narrow pallet. Pulsing energy surrounded him, energy that obliterated the human impulses within. He fought the impulse to open his eyes, to struggle against his fate. Instead he held himself immobile, clearing his mind, hearing the voices of the wind. Hearing Akando.

A man is what he becomes over trial, through endurance. The past is no more than fleeting clouds on a fading horizon.

Seneca knew where he was—inside the floating craft. The energy he discerned before seemed more intense now. The sweet longing was muffled in a mass of conflicting impulses. Seneca heard beeping noises, like crickets, but devoid of song.

Seneca felt a surge of power; he felt the sudden calm as the vessel that carried him broke its hold to his world. With a sharp, painful grip on his heart, he felt himself ripped from the land of Akando.

No, Akando remained within him. No matter why they had taken him, how they had found him, he was Akandan now. Nothing, no one, could change that.

In his mind, Seneca saw his brother, Carack, laughing, waiting for him. He saw Elan waiting, too. His father, ready to depart life, now forced to endure for an unknown time. Until a new heir could pass the trial.

Seneca's jaw clenched. That bittersweet longing had robbed him of his life. But he also knew that with wisdom employed, he could find a way back.

A jarring, clanking noise disturbed the hull. The vessel lurched and the voices around Seneca intensified. A door hissed open. Without angling his head, Seneca's eyes turned toward the sound. He saw his abductor—her newborn's skin, her pale cream hair. Nothing offset the danger she presented.

Why didn't she speak to him? She seemed nervous, but not angry. It made no sense. She gave orders, which the men nervously obeyed. They treated him more like a captured animal than a man.

She held herself stiffly, as if relaxing in any way might cause her to shatter. She turned toward Seneca. Her face revealed nothing of the calm of his people, and all the mystery of the heavens.

She appeared startled to find him awake, but her small chin was raised. Still, she said nothing to him. She seemed uneasy, but she issued no accusations, no threats. Why? Seneca held her gaze. She seemed unnerved, and turned to the man behind her, gesturing at Seneca as she spoke. The man came forward with several others. But Seneca kept his eyes on her.

The men in her command unhooked Seneca's pallet from the wall, then rolled it toward the doorway. Seneca stood a full head taller than his light-haired captors. With little effort, he could win his freedom by combat.

Yet what then? He must learn the reason for his capture before seizing his advantage. The men seemed nervous around him. A small tube filled with fluid was clutched in one of the men's white-knuckled hands, a sharp point aimed at Seneca's arm.

They rolled the pallet into a shiny hallway, leaving the inside of the first craft, entering a much larger vessel. Seneca took in his surroundings without reaction. His sweet-faced abductor hurried along by his side, nervous, but refusing to show it.

As they progressed into the larger craft, Seneca felt a world of shocking diversity and conflicting purpose, a world never experienced in the rhythms of Akando. He kept his focus on his abductor. What he needed to know, he would learn from her alone.

Bright, unnatural lights flashed before his eyes as they passed along the myriad corridors. But all he saw was her small, determined face as she strode along beside him. She was trying not to look at him. Her eyes whisked to his face, and Seneca knew his gaze unnerved her. He fought an impulse to smile.

Another door slid open, and she gestured inside. She seemed to hesitate, but when the men guided Seneca inside the new room, she didn't follow.

Nisa watched the orderlies transport the Akandan into the holding quarters. The Akandan didn't fight. He looked around his new quarters with what seemed only mild interest. Tranor and the others scurried out of the room, leaving him alone. Tranor's hands shook when he set the locking grid into action.

"He's big," stammered Tranor as he eased back from the door.

Fedor glanced at the slight navigator scornfully. "So are Thorwalian subprimates, but we don't tremble in fear outside their cages."

Tranor absorbed the slight to his manhood, though Nisa saw his jaw clench. Fedor hadn't done much to endear himself on this venture.

"We need to get the probes hooked up right away. I want to start his initiation as soon as possible."

Fedor hesitated. "Don't expect too much, Nisa. We may alter his mind patterns enough to communicate in our language, but the advanced thought processes will be far beyond his capacity."

"Maybe. But we need this man on Dakota." Nisa hoped her determination was obvious in her tone. "What I can make him understand benefits us all."

"I've got serious doubts about this mission, Nisa."

Nisa drew a patient breath. "So you've said before. But we can't replace Motega with another Dakotan. The mind probe can control thought, it can alter thought, but its span isn't large enough to erase the entire memory of a Dakotan scientist. We had to find someone primitive enough to control."

Fedor sneered in distaste. "He's primitive, I'll say that."

Nisa watched as nervous technicians entered the Akandan's cell bearing the mind probe equipment. His expression never altered. Standing outside the door, she could study him at her leisure. Only once before had she seen a man so large, so innately threatening. Males on her world were little larger than the females, though Nisa still considered them more aggressive.

This man showed no signs of aggression, but the technicians still made wide berths around him. Nisa shook her head. Should this primitive man come to his senses, he would surely sense their fear. He might panic. Cooler minds were needed.

Nisa drew a breath and opened the cell door. "Set the gear beside the bed."

The Akandan's dark eyes met hers, never wavering. His bold stare unsettled her. In contrast, his thick, dark lashes lent him the impression of sweetness—an impression Nisa felt certain wasn't warranted.

She tried to smile, to reassure him. Her lips felt frozen, and the effort was lost. Nisa cleared her throat.

"Don't be afraid. This won't harm you." She knew he couldn't understand her, but she hoped the tone of her voice would be reassuring to him. No response.

The technicians hooked up the equipment, placing the probes at various points around the Akandan's skull. His eyes never left hers.

"This procedure is quick," Nisa informed her captive. "In moments, you'll understand our language." Would he? she wondered. He might understand, but could he speak? Used on Thorwalian subprimates in Dakotan research centers, the procedure had been successful, though the creatures generally had very limited response.

How would this primitive man react to knowledge of other worlds, of a culture so much more advanced than his own?

"Ready." The technician looked nervously at the Akandan. "It's bound to startle him. I suggest we all step back."

Seneca felt the first quivering impulses against his skull, and his shield rose. He closed his eyes and assessed his unseen assailant. Seneca felt the twitching waves as they invaded his thoughts, found their place, and offered the wisdom of speech.

Why were they seeking to instruct him in their language? Unless they didn't know. . . .

"Probes engaged and activated, Lieutenant."

The Thorwalian tongue had none of the rhythmic beauty of the Akandan language. Disjointed, unrelated patterns, subjective reasoning, often askew . . . Seneca wished he could banish the sound forever.

"What's taking so long? The whole transmission has slowed."

"I'm not sure." His abductor spoke softly, revealing a depth of emotions even she didn't know.

Another man answered her. His voice grated in Seneca's ear. "I warned you, Nisa. He's too primitive. It won't work."

Nisa. A tremor grazed across Seneca's heart. Her small, short name revealed no history, no tale of ancestors such as the name his father bestowed upon him. It was sturdy, yet fragile, like herself.

"Transmission complete."

"Thank you, Tranor. You may remove the probes now." Nisa's controlled speech began to irritate Seneca. This was a woman whose sense of control could destroy a man . . . or a world.

He turned to look at her. She smiled. A forced, superior smile. "Don't be frightened. We won't harm you. You're safe."

Seneca didn't respond. Right now he held the advantage. She wanted him to understand her speech; she wanted him to speak, too. Reason enough to maintain silence.

A quiet man learns more than one too eager for words. Seneca had learned that on Akando. Had the lesson been learned earlier, much devastation and loss might have been averted.

"Can you understand me?" Nisa appeared concerned. An element of doubt entered her expression. Her brows knit, and her lips curved to one side. Seneca ignored her question as he marveled at her smooth skin. The harsh climes of Akando didn't allow for such softness.

A tight braid kept her golden hair off her broad, intelligent forehead, framing wide cheekbones and a strong, determined chin. A wisp of hair brushed her cheek and she pushed it nervously back into its binding.

While she squirmed under his scrutiny, Seneca leisurely studied her features. Her small, straight nose gave her a pert, surprised appearance. Her lips formed an unusual bow that seemed as ready to curl with annoyance as to form a smile. Lips, Seneca imagined, more useful for kissing than for speech.

"I warned you, Nisa. These people aren't capable of advanced language patterns. I admire your ambitious plans, but it won't work."

Nisa drew a strained, irritated breath. Seneca knew at once that she disliked the man who spoke. "He's probably in shock."

Seneca found himself wondering what plans she had for an Akandan warrior. Impossible as it seemed, his capture seemed an arbitrary decision.

"He needs to be fed, to adjust himself to these surroundings. There are too many people in here," she added. "It might be best if I spoke to him alone, Fedor."

"I can't allow that," said Fedor.

"He's still restrained. This is my duty, and I will see to it now. Please direct the captain to set the headings for Thorwal."

Fedor shook his head, his jaw set in resistance. "You'll never have this man ready before we reach Thorwal."

"I will." That small chin rose even more than usual. The dark blue eyes sparkled. "We have no time to spare. He will cooperate. Everything depends on that."

Seneca considered Nisa's manner imperious, her tone that of a woman not to be trifled with. His immediate reaction was to do just that. A short, stilted nod sent the men from the room. She drew up a stool and seated herself at his bedside.

"I am called Nisa," she told him, drawing out her words and speaking slowly, as if to a child. "I know you must be frightened, but there's no need." Seneca maintained his frozen expression, revealing nothing. He waited.

Nisa checked his expression; she hesitated. Already rattled, Seneca thought with satisfaction. "The probes helped you to understand our language, but I know this must be very confusing for you."

Seneca didn't intend to react, but her patronizing tone grated. He knew his eyebrow arched slightly. He hoped she didn't notice.

"Can you understand me?" She leaned a little closer as she spoke, her face worried. "Nod your head if you can." Nisa nodded her head, slowly and deliberately, an encouraging look on her face.

Seneca considered his response. There seemed no harm in allowing her to know he understood her. Very slowly, and very deliberately, he nodded his head, too. He wondered if she sensed the sarcasm behind his action. Apparently not, because a bright smile lit her face.

Nisa looked young when she smiled. Her emotions seemed quick, close to the surface. Unhoned. Yet fresh. But beneath her youthful appearance and demeanor, Seneca sensed a guarded heart.

Nisa clapped her hands together. "Good! We need your help, you see." She paused. "Can you speak?"

Seneca fixed his eyes on hers. His lips remained firmly shut. *Not yet,* he said to himself. *Not until I know what you're up to.*

Nisa waited a moment for Seneca's response, received none, then continued her speech. "I am from another world, a world far away from yours. A world in the stars!"

She said this triumphantly, then waited for his shock. Seneca waited for her explanation to proceed to something he didn't know—such as why she abducted him, and what she wanted now.

Nisa's face fell; she appeared disappointed. "In my world, many wondrous things are possible. We can fly through space, and reach other worlds in the time it takes you to gather water."

Seneca longed to speak, to inform her she seemed capable of causing more damage in that time than he could, too, but he maintained his silence. He liked the way it unnerved her. She'd get to the point sooner or later.

"Many generations ago, my people made contact with those of a neighboring planet. A planet is what you live on, a world."

Nisa gave her descriptions much as an Akandan matron might when instructing small children. Very small children. Seneca's attention fixed on her lips as she spoke. He liked the way her lips curved around words, the way they twisted impatiently when he didn't respond. Her lips looked soft. If only the words emanating from them were briefer . . .

"By accident, the people of my world discovered a moon—which is like a small planet, generally without air, that orbits the larger planet—your world doesn't have a moon."

Seneca sighed. He couldn't help it. If Nisa started at the dawn of her world's history, he'd be listening a long while. She noticed his sigh, and her brow furrowed.

"Am I losing you? Do you understand so far?"

Seneca nodded. Once. He hoped she understood his exasperation with her long-winded explanations. Nisa seemed confused now, and she hesitated before continuing.

"Well, then. Good. You seem to understand. Anyway, the Dakotans—we call them Dakotans because they're from Dakota—learned about this moon. . . . By the way, my world is called Thorwal. I am a Thorwalian."

Seneca didn't want to smile; he pressed his lips together to stop himself. He cleared his throat while she watched him suspiciously. He restrained his impulse toward laughter, and waited, but he knew his eyes were glittering with amusement.

Nisa adjusted her hair, tucking a loose strand back into her braid. A nervous gesture. "Our two worlds have worked in unison—together—for ages. We developed science and technology. The Dakotans like to think and plan; we like to build. But when the Dakotan researchers learned about this moon, they wanted the riches for themselves."

Nisa seemed closer to the point. Two tribes had an interest in the same thing. Both wanted it, both had claim. This moon was at the heart of the matter.

Nisa took considerably longer getting to the same point, however. Long enough for Seneca to study and commit to memory every portion of her face: her straight brows, her intricately shaped nose, the light reflecting off the narrow braid of golden hair over her forehead. Wound from temple to temple, falling to one side beside her small ear . . .

Seneca's gaze traveled down her slender neck to the material covering her breasts. Ample and well-formed breasts, even beneath the shapeless attire she wore—the same attire worn by the Thorwalian men.

Seneca noticed that Nisa had fallen silent. He glanced back at her face. Her cheeks were pink. Apparently she'd noticed the direction of his gaze. He smiled faintly. Her cheeks flushed to a deep red.

"I think that's enough for now," she informed him hurriedly as she rose from her stool. "As I've told you, the Dakotans want to reach the Candor Moon, and take over our solar system. We . . . incarcerated their leader—a vile and greedy man—but they denied us access to their research centers."

Seneca's brow rose. He wondered what he'd missed while examining her breasts.

"So, naturally, we besieged their planet with our spaceships to keep them from crafting a vessel of their own."

Nisa paused, finally reaching the crux of the matter. "Unfortunately, the rebels raided one of our Dakotan outposts and stole several battleships. War is imminent. They're demanding their leader back, and unless they get him they'll begin attacking our technology ports. We had some . . . trouble with him, and we need you to help us. You resemble him, you see."

Seneca guessed his resemblance to the enemy leader explained his capture, which she would eventually disclose if he waited long enough. A strange twist of events. If true . . .

"I'll return later, once you've been fed, to begin your instruction. It's important that you're initiated into proper behavior before I present you to Helmar." Nisa started to leave, then turned back. "Helmar is my uncle, the high commander of the Thorwalian ministry. He's like a . . . chief."

Nisa darted from the room and Seneca stared after her. Dakota . . . Seneca closed his eyes, abandoning the Thorwalian craft. Abandoning everything Nisa told him. Here, in the primal clarity, he would discern the truth. Did she lie? Or was she really as guileless as she seemed?

Nisa stood outside the Akandan's door and took several deep breaths. A technician approached, appearing to be in a hurry, but Nisa recognized a tactic to avoid her orders.

"He needs to be fed," she told the technician, who sighed. "I'd like you to remove his restraints."

The technician's eyes widened. "Take a stun rifle with you," she added impatiently. "But don't use it unless you have to. He doesn't seem violent."

"I'll get Tranor to come with me," the technician decided. Nisa watched the man hurry away. A lilt-mouse would be tempted to chase him. What good the feeble Tranor would do against the powerful Akandan, she couldn't guess.

Nisa glanced into the holding cell. The Akandan lay immobile. Something about him disturbed her, though Nisa wasn't sure why. He made no threatening motions; he said nothing. Why did she still feel shaken after their encounter?

Was it his likeness to Motega that troubled her? Nisa considered this unlikely. True, the resemblance was strong, but the differences outweighed the similarities.

Motega had been much younger when she knew him, when he formed the center of her world. He was fairer-skinned than the Akandan, and lighter of build. He wasn't muscular and controlled—he was intense and far from calm.

The Akandan seemed hauntingly calm, considering his surroundings. The Dakotans were known for their high-strung, nervous manner. Nisa frowned. To impersonate Motega, the Akandan would have to develop a more outgoing manner. But first things first . . .

Nisa waited for the technicians to deliver the Akandan's meal. Perhaps the offer of food would appease his primitive resistance. Nisa tried to assess her success with her captive so far.

He understood her speech; that much was clear. Maybe the intricacies of her world were beyond him, but he seemed fairly attentive to her instruction. At least until his mind wandered . . . Nisa flushed with heat at the memory.

Men didn't look at her that way. They didn't dare. Only Motega had dared treat her as a woman. Nisa would never allow that to happen again. She forced her thoughts back to her captive. He seemed to be laughing at her. There was no getting around that fact. She amused him. He should be astonished, shocked, impressed. Instead he seemed amused.

How could that be?

Nisa pondered the matter awhile, then decided his reaction made no difference. She had to make him presentable before they reached Thorwal. She had to make him communicate, and prove he could pass for Motega, even on Dakota.

Tranor and the technician returned with a covered

plate of food. It was reconstituted, and Nisa wished they had something better to offer him. This looked like gruel.

Fedor joined them, though he waited outside while Tranor delivered the food to their prisoner. Both Tranor and the technician carried stun rifles. "I don't see much change in him," Fedor said.

"I haven't begun my instruction," Nisa replied wearily. "He understands me; he's no longer in shock. I have time."

"Not much," Fedor reminded her. "Not if you intend to make that barbaric hulk pass for Motega."

"The Dakotans need to see Motega, a Motega with a change of heart. It won't be difficult. It's been seven years, after all."

"Are you sure it's wise to release him?" asked Fedor.

"We'll soon see." Nisa watched as Tranor unbound the Akandan. She held her breath as the technician leaped back and headed for the door, as Tranor aimed his stun rifle at the warrior's head.

The Akandan sat up. He looked at Tranor. A slight smile touched his lips and he shook his head. As if he knew they were afraid of him, as if it amused him. He rose to his feet. Tranor seemed to shrink.

Nisa refused to let the Akandan's subtle intimidation go further. She entered the cell and calmly directed Tranor to leave.

"You may need this." Tranor thrust the stun rifle into Nisa's hands. The Akandan watched as the smaller man fled the room, leaving Nisa to deal with him alone.

Nisa tried to smile, but her face felt stiff. "That is your dinner." She pointed at the bowl of mush. "It's the best we can do on a transport craft, but you'll be fed wondrous meals once we reach Thorwal."

The Akandan eyed his platter and the bowl of tepid gruel. He made no motion toward it. Nisa gestured at a stool. "You sit here," she told him, tapping the seat.

She picked up a spoon. "You eat with this."

An amused twinkle appeared in the Akandan's dark eyes. Nisa lifted her chin. He seated himself obediently, however, and Nisa breathed a muted sigh of relief.

"It's important that you learn proper behavior. Motega might have been uncivilized in certain ways. . . ." Nisa paused. He had been a barbarian in certain ways. "But he had excellent manners."

The Akandan's expression told Nisa he had no interest in mimicking Motega's ways. Nisa wondered what he wanted. She had removed him from his world, true, but certainly he must see the change as for the better. Maybe he didn't realize how much better.

"Your world is much harsher than mine," she informed him. "Although we've certainly disrupted your lifestyle, such as it was, I think you'll find life among my people pleasant. If you're willing to learn."

The Akandan's firm, full mouth curved upward at one corner. Nisa felt certain she wasn't making headway. She considered another angle.

"It would be helpful if you could talk. Just a few words. If you try, I'll help you. Let's start with your name."

Nisa paused. No reaction. "I assume you have a name, some sort of title." The Akandan showed no interest in communication. "We'll save that for a later lesson, then."

Nisa seated herself across from him. "We've brought you a meal. I assume you're hungry?" She tried to smile again. Her lips felt a little strained, but she succeeded this time.

The Akandan eyed his bowl of gruel. Nisa endured a wave of embarrassment. "It's only barlit-meal, I'm afraid. Much of our food is grown on Dakota." Nisa paused. "My world, Thorwal, is cold all the time. Even in the warm season, snow covers the ground. Like your world during the cold season, perhaps."

The Akandan showed no interest in Nisa's world. She regretted telling him about Thorwal's frosty weather. "But it's beautiful there, much nicer than your world. We have subterranean lava flows which warm certain areas . . . molten rock that flows like a river. Even in our main city."

Still no sign of interest. Nisa sighed. "Since the rebels deprived us of their harvest lands, we've had to make do with less than our usual fare."

Nisa's expression hardened. "They have, you understand, wreaked havoc in the order of our world. We like order. It keeps our livelihood strong."

The Akandan cast a glance Nisa's way that told her he considered her fastidious attention to order extreme, then dipped his long, powerful forefinger into the gruel. He tasted it while Nisa watched. He made a face suggesting the gruel was as unappetizing as it looked, shrugged, then took a larger portion on the tips of his fingers.

Motega wouldn't eat with his fingers. Nisa seized the spoon and held it up. "You must use this to transport the food to your mouth." The Akandan glanced at the utensil, plainly considered it useless, then dipped his fingers in the mush again.

Nisa took a napkin, reached across the table, and grabbed his hand. His skin felt warm, his flesh hard. Currents of energy seemed to race within him, passing into her at the touch. Nisa imagined those hands touching her, his energy blending with hers. . . .

Nisa's eyes flashed to his. He appeared equally surprised at their contact. She snatched her hand away. Her pulse raced, and her breaths refused to deepen.

"Use the spoon," she commanded in a shaky voice.

The Akandan's head tilted to one side as he studied her, as if seeing her anew. He glanced down at the spoon, then picked it up, twirling it as it caught the reflection of the light replacer. With his attention diverted, his piercing dark eyes attending another subject, Nisa relaxed.

"I understand that such manners of decorum aren't necessary in your world." She settled back in her seat. "I don't know if you're aware of this, but the seasonal variations on your planet are due to its unusual oblong orbit. In your warm months, your planet draws as near to the sun as Dakota's."

The dark man looked at her for a moment, contemplating something Nisa couldn't guess. His gaze immediately unnerved her. "Your meal is getting cold." A slight elevation of his brow told her he doubted any change could make his dinner much worse.

"You're probably wondering how we knew about your people." Nisa waited, but he returned his attention to the spoon. To her growing annoyance, he seemed to be reflecting the light off her face. It flashed in her eyes. "Stop that!" Nisa's voice sounded unusually tense. Strident. She collected herself.

"We've known about your race for several generations, of course." Nisa tried not to notice that the Akandan abandoned the spoon and once again dipped his long fingers into the gruel. "But, quite frankly, you weren't of much interest to us. I realize your kind has little to do with building, with any kind of development."

Those long fingers swirled through the mush, thoughtfully. Nisa's jaw clenched. She had to remain calm, reasonable, in an effort to show him her patience, her civilized behavior, as a contrast to his own.

"Dakotan researchers began studying you several generations ago. Your race bears a striking likeness to the Dakotans. They found little of interest, no proof of a connection, but Motega—the Dakotan leader—renewed the study before the insurrection. I don't know why he cared. The Dakotans are far advanced from your race."

He smiled slightly. Nisa couldn't stand it. She

grabbed his spoon and jammed it into his hand, forcing his long fingers closed around it. She felt his warm, male energy again, but she ignored it. She looked him straight in the eye, daring him to defy her.

"No doubt the harsh realities of your life have made more complex achievement impossible."

The Akandan calmly set the spoon aside, dipped his fingers into the bowl, then flicked warm gruel into Nisa's face. Nisa's mouth dropped in astonishment. Her whole body tensed. She quivered. Her chin tightened into a ball.

"Don't you dare do that again! I'm trying to instruct you, you subterranean wortpig!" She emitted an angry sputtering noise, finding her insult insufficient for his crime. "Linger-worm!"

Nisa seized a napkin and wiped the gruel from her face. The Akandan just watched her, the faintest trace of a smile on his lips. He looked satisfied. Nisa struggled to compose herself, shocked at her outburst.

"I'm sorry. I don't know what came over me." Nisa stared at that dark, mocking face, then shook her head. She considered the matter. "We all have tempers. Of course, on Thorwal we have learned to control them. We become better persons for the control we practice."

Yes, this sounded good. After all, Thorwalian early history was riddled with violence. Small Thorwalian Ravager dolls were still popular with children, tokens of a wilder, unrestrained civilization. Remnants of a brave, barbaric people who relied on courage and strength, and scorned intellectual advancement.

"My ancestors overcame their violent tendencies," Nisa continued proudly. "As I'm sure yours will do when they've evolved to a greater extent." Nisa gazed thoughtfully at the ceiling.

"We turned our attention to technology, to creation, to the benefit of a greater good. We are, as you can see from your surroundings, beings of logic. We've lived without strife for at least seven generations. Until now, of course," she added as an afterthought. "Until the Dakotans' greed threatened us with war."

Nisa felt satisfied with herself. True, she'd lost her temper, but she was calm now. The Akandan would be impressed. She felt the corners of her lips tilt in a smile. She'd handled the situation well.

"You can learn from this, Akandan," she said with growing enthusiasm. "It's important to learn from our mistakes. You might benefit from my example—"

She didn't see it coming. A warm splatter of mush, square in the center of her face, even into her parted, speaking lips. Nisa's cool reason fled. She rose from her seat, trembling with fury. He was smiling. He licked his fingers, making small smacking noises.

Nisa leaped around the table and grabbed his hair, yanking his head to one side. A short laugh escaped him, though he obviously tried to control it. It was too much for Nisa.

"You will behave," she growled. He laughed harder. Nisa made a fist and slammed it into his shoulder. She didn't care that he was twice her size, that she endangered herself. She just wanted to wound, then subdue him.

He moved so fast, so smoothly, that Nisa barely realized what happened. In one swift motion, the Akandan flipped her onto her back and pinned her to the floor. Nisa stared up at him in astonishment, uncertain how she came to be in such a vulnerable position.

Nisa panicked, struggling wildly. "Release me!" she ordered. "Or I'll—" He clasped his hand over her mouth. Nisa fought like a wild creature.

Nisa's violent struggles intensified, to no effect. He loomed above her like a dark giant. She tried to reach the stun rifle, but he pinned her wrists to the floor above her head, holding her lower body still with the weight of his own.

Nisa's struggles ceased as she realized her danger.

Her fury turned to fear in the space of a second. His hair fell forward around his strong, angular face, and his dark eyes gleamed. She was powerless.

"Get off me." Nisa's voice quaked, but she tried to stare him down, to show him she wasn't afraid. She was terrified. "Now!"

His smile deepened. His eyes left hers and centered on her lips. For an instant Nisa saw the curiosity of a child on his face. Her breath held. He seemed to resist his own impulses. Then, very gently, he lowered his mouth to hers.

Nisa wanted to cry out for help, but she was paralyzed by his tenderness. The Akandan's lips brushed back and forth against hers. His tongue flicked out to taste her, but he didn't deepen the kiss. He seemed more interested in teasing her than in ravaging her.

Wild, forbidden currents surged through Nisa's body. Her lips softened beneath his; she was agonized by her own weakness. Nisa felt the large, taut body above her, holding her down without pressure.

With a shock she recognized the firm pressure of his male organ, large and hard against her thigh. This Akandan warrior would have no qualms about rape. . . .

Nisa heard footsteps outside the door. She twisted her head away from his, then opened her mouth to scream: "Help!"

The Akandan released her in one agile motion. He chuckled to himself, then seated himself at the table. Nisa leaped to her feet just as Tranor burst through the door.

"Nisa! Are you all right? What happened?" Tranor held a stun rifle in his shaking hands, but when he surveyed the scene, he appeared confused.

The Akandan picked up his spoon and ate calmly. Nisa stared at him in astonishment.

"Nisa?" questioned Tranor.

"I'm fine." Nisa struggled against the tremor infecting her voice. Her heart raced so fast she thought she might faint, but she wouldn't let Tranor know that. More important, she couldn't let the Akandan know how he unnerved her.

"If you're sure."

"It's nothing, Tranor. Just a . . . misunderstanding." The Akandan's dark brow lifted, but he continued his meal without further gestures.

Tranor looked between them, shrugged, and departed. Nisa wanted to follow, to leave this strange man's presence for good, but she had to regain the upper hand between them. It occurred to her suddenly that the "upper hand" might be something she had never really had to begin with.

"I'll leave you to your meal now," she said in as even a voice as she could muster. "I suggest you rest. We will continue with your instruction at the new cycle."

Nisa headed for the door, pressed the entry grid, and took a deep breath.

"Seneca."

He spoke. Low and even and perfectly calm. Nisa turned slowly to look at him. "What?" Her own voice was a whisper.

"I am called Seneca. You asked my name. I have given it."

Nisa stared, dumbfounded. Seneca pushed his bowl of mush aside, rose from his seat, and went to the bed. He lay on his back, his hands folded serenely at his chest. He closed his eyes, effectively dismissing her until their next encounter.

"I am called Nisa," she told him in a small, uncertain voice.

Seneca smiled, though he didn't open his eyes. "I know."

Chapter Two

Seneca waited until he heard Nisa's footsteps departing down the corridor, then rose from his bedding. His stoic expression softened when he saw her discarded stun rifle.

Beings of logic? Seneca lifted the device and examined it. Its purpose would be clear to an Akandan child, even the switch that would turn the power within into deadly force. Seneca wondered when his captor would realize she had left her weapon behind.

The people of Akando might not have developed such tools, but they'd have better sense than to leave them lying around—especially within reach of an enemy. Good sense didn't seem part of Nisa's inherent makeup.

A wild temper, concealing the possibility of unrestrained emotion, seemed a more apt description of his captor. Seneca set the rifle aside, then foraged around his new quarters for his pack. He found the pack untouched—an item of little interest to his single-minded abductors.

Seneca opened the pack and found dried meat and carad-sticks. He had tired of such consumption on his trial, but it was a welcome meal after Nisa's flavorless gruel. Seneca took special pleasure delivering the food to his mouth with his fingers.

When finished, he returned to his pack and withdrew the sapling he had borne from the Zaltana Mountains. The opaque leaves remained crisp, unaffected by the change in environment. Even here. The soil would keep the small tree alive for many cycles.

"We journey afar, you and I. But one day we will both return where we belong."

Seneca carefully concealed the sapling and returned to his pallet. Did he not carry the wisdom of Akando with him everywhere? Even here? He had used the art of TiKay to subdue Nisa, though never had it offered such pleasure as when her soft body struggled beneath his.

Seneca hadn't expected the memory to stir his senses again, but he hardened immediately. This night should have been spent in his nuptial bed, with his new mate. A woman who disturbed nothing of the ordered patterns in his mind. A sacred act.

The act might be sacred with Elan, but with Nisa it would be the equivalent of battle. This image didn't lessen his desire. But this desire could destroy him.

With TiKay he would master this world. He would endure and conquer here, as he had conquered the Akandan trial of manhood. And then, when he conquered these forces that threatened to destroy him, when he conquered Nisa, he would return where he belonged. To Akando.

The door burst open and Nisa stormed into his room. Seneca folded his arms behind his head and watched her. She bit her lip.

"I . . . forgot something." Nisa looked wildly around the darkening room.

41

"On the table." Seneca restrained his pleasure when her face went white.

Nisa seized the rifle in both hands. "It's nothing," she said in a high voice. "Nothing you need to be concerned about."

Seneca rose from his bedding. His eyes held hers as he closed the distance between them. Seneca towered over her, his shadow cast from the fading wall lights, over her small body.

"Nothing?" Seneca kept his voice low, deliberately dangerous. "Was it 'nothing' you aimed at my heart, was it 'nothing' you launched from your hands to consume me?"

Nisa shrank away from him. Seneca caught her shoulders and held her fast. "I weary of your pretense, maiden. You've used your powers to bring me here, you've delivered your language into my thoughts. I assume your reason is pressing, and it involves this leader to whom I bear resemblance."

Nisa's lips parted in astonishment, but Seneca didn't let her speak. She didn't try, for once.

"What do you want from me? What is so vital that you should steal a man's life without asking?"

"Asking?" Nisa appeared stunned.

"You never considered it? I thought not. For beings as logical as you claim to be, it seems a simple matter. If you need help, you ask. But perhaps your people are more given to taking than to requesting."

"Asking?" Nisa repeated herself. Her gaze wandered across his face, as if seeing him for the first time. Seneca watched as she scrutinized his appearance.

"Asking! How could I ask? 'Pardon me, warrior, would you like to see other worlds? We need you to impersonate a demon. . . . ' You would have been terrified to learn of other worlds that way."

"This was so much simpler," concluded Seneca, his voice rich with sarcasm. "But your revelation surprises me very little. You exist, your vessel exists, so

42

that there are other worlds seems obvious."

"We had no way of knowing your reaction would be so . . . calm. Had we known—"

"What? You would have asked? And if I had said no, that I have no wish to see your world? What then, maiden? Would you have let me go?" He leaned closer. "Would you now?"

Nisa's eyes widened into blue pools, shading currents of fiery emotion. "I can't do that! I've already sent word to Helmar about your capture." She bit her lip at the revealing comment. "About your presence here," she corrected, "and about the success of my mission. I can't send you back!"

"Then I will find another way."

"Why should you desire to return there? It's cold and then hot, barren. Stars know what you live on. The life I offer is much better."

"Easier, perhaps. But not better. Unless you consider war better than a life at peace, a life where the rhythms of the ground and air and water are respected."

Nisa rolled her eyes. "We use those things to our advantage. That's respect."

"You don't use them to their own advantage. You use them to their destruction." Seneca paused. "Perhaps you use people to those same ends. Perhaps you use me to my destruction, also."

Nisa moved back from him, bumping into the wall. "You won't be destroyed. You just need to settle the Dakotans back where they belong. Maybe then we'll find a new leader, you can abdicate your authority, and we'll return you to your world. Would you agree to that?"

"No. I want nothing to do with your schemes, maiden."

Nisa stepped forward, her face plaintive. She touched Seneca's arm. He tensed, but didn't flinch from her touch. Despite himself, he welcomed it.

"You don't understand," she said in a small voice. "If the Dakotans seize power, we'll lose everything. If they travel to Candor, they'll advance far beyond us; they won't need us. If they find out what happened to Motega . . ."

"He died," guessed Seneca.

All blood drained from Nisa's face. She closed her eyes. "Yes."

"You would have me aid a murderer."

Nisa looked up at him, her eyes glistening with tears. "It was an accident."

"An accident?"

Seneca watched as Nisa struggled with a lie. She sighed. "He was assassinated in prison."

"By you."

"No! Not by me! We think his guard was responsible. But if I hadn't. . . ." Nisa's voice drifted. "It was strange, you see. The guard seemed devoted to Motega. But he was our only suspect."

"You interrogated this guard, I presume."

"No. He disappeared after the assassination. We tried, but we never found him. A shuttle was reported missing soon after."

"So you suspect this guard of murdering your prisoner? Why not explain this theory to the Dakotans?"

"They wouldn't believe us. We have no proof. You don't understand—they worshiped Motega. They would blame us for not keeping him safe."

"As I see it, your enemy's death was convenient." Seneca paused as he studied her expression. "His death must have pleased you."

Nisa's face drained of blood. "No. It didn't please me." Her voice lowered, haunted. "I found him, you see. He had been burned by a Nebulon torch." Nisa's eyes glazed, luminous with unshed tears. "I had taunted him, before. But when he died . . ."

"You grieved at his death?"

Nisa turned away. "I grieved." Seneca watched as

she steeled herself against her memories. Her shoulders straightened; her chin lifted. She turned back to him, her expression straight and devoid of emotion.

"You will be forced to do as we wish. There is no other way. If you don't, Helmar will have no choice but to order an assault against Dakota. War would devastate both our planets."

"So you will mold me into the image of their leader, is that it? And what is to prevent me from betraying your intentions to your enemy in exchange, perhaps, for my freedom?"

Her blue eyes grew colder, frost over a swift stream. "You recall the mind probe we used to teach you our language?"

"I do."

"The probe's strength can be intensified. We can control you, if necessary. But the effect would be lasting. Your capacity for independent thought could be . . . damaged."

Her expression softened. Seneca saw her shame at her own intentions. "I don't want to do that. You must believe me. If we have your agreement, it won't be necessary. But you must prove your intentions to cooperate."

Seneca gave no answer. He studied her face, assessing her sincerity. "If I agree, and adopt this man's ways, I will be returned to Akando? Is that so?"

"Yes." Nisa hesitated. "I'll have to get Helmar's permission, of course. But my uncle is a reasonable man. There's no reason to keep you once your purpose is served. Why do you want to return? Did you have a family there?"

"Am I to assume family bonds have no meaning on your world?"

"Of course they have meaning! My family—"

"I have a family. I have a father and a brother." Seneca paused. "And on the day you abducted me, I was to take a wife."

Nisa's eyes widened. Seneca wondered why she cared. "A wife? But our researchers said you weren't mated."

"Akandans mate for life. It is a ritual of honor, sacred. I doubt anything on your world compares."

"We mate for life, too." Nisa faltered. "At least, that is the intention when unions are formed. They don't always work."

"I'm not surprised."

"Your envy is that of the weak for the strong. I understand completely."

Seneca subdued an impulse to prove their relative strength and forced himself to ignore her superior attitude. "And you, maiden, have you taken a mate?" He scrutinized her body slowly while she squirmed in embarrassment. "You appear an apt prospect . . . at least physically."

"I have chosen to pursue a leadership role. I will follow in my uncle's footsteps."

"Ah. He isn't mated, either."

"No. Helmar considers all Thorwalians his family."

"How noble! Yet he gives no thought to another man's family."

"If you had children to care for, I swear we would have found another, even though your resemblance to Motega is nearly perfect."

"Nearly?"

Nisa studied him thoughtfully. "Well, you're darker than Motega was. You're also too strong." Her gaze wafted across his body and she sighed faintly. He smiled, and her cheeks flushed. "Motega didn't spend his life in hardship, as you have. He wasn't so . . . his musculature wasn't as formidable."

"Can I assume you find me formidable, maiden?"

"Not at all." Nisa cleared her throat. "But your size presents something of a problem to my scheme. Motega was Dakotan. Dakotans aren't known for powerful physiques. True, he was well built as a young man. . . ."

Seneca smiled and Nisa bit her lip. "But it's been seven years. By now he would be quite round." Nisa stopped and sighed. "A shame, really. Also, your hair is different. Motega's had a slight wave, brushed back from his face, around his ear, to the nape of the neck. Yours is somewhat lighter . . . he didn't share the auburn lights I see in yours."

Nisa's blush deepened. Her words betrayed her intimacy with the Dakotan leader, and too much scrutiny of Seneca. Her scrutiny pleased him almost as much as her memories troubled his heart.

"Your hair is straight, and much too long for a civilized being." She examined the long, narrow braid amid his hair, forgetting her critical intent.

"What are these?" She lifted her hand slowly, hesitating before touching him. Her fingers caught the bead-studded braid in his hair.

Her soft, wistful mood softened Seneca's resistance. When her shield lowered, the temptress emerged, even if she didn't realize it herself. "Shells from the Tremoring Sea. Our craftsmen form them into symbols."

"They're pretty. What do they mean?"

"They mean I like this shade of blue." Seneca touched Nisa's soft cheek. "But here."—he ran his finger gently around Nisa's left eye—"and here . . ." He outlined the other, bending closer to her. "Here is blue so fair, so perfect, that no child of the Tremoring Sea compares."

His lips brushed hers, but Nisa didn't move. She leaned against him; her arms found his waist. She started to pull away, then faltered. Instead she pressed closer.

Seneca felt the tips of her round breasts harden against his chest. His own body hardened to match, ready for her, ready to take her.

She resisted, but Seneca's lips gently persuaded, urged. His tongue flicked out to taste her, outlining the bow of her upper lip, then the lower. Nisa stirred against him, her lips parted, allowing him closer. She returned his kiss, and Seneca felt the wild power of her longing.

Seneca pressed a sensual kiss at the corner of her mouth. "Am I your prisoner . . . or are you mine?"

Nisa snapped out of his arms, her lips still parted, flushed and puffy from his kiss. Her breasts rose and fell with her short gasps.

"What are you doing to me?" she sputtered. She didn't let him answer. "I know perfectly well what you're doing! You think you can seduce me to gain your ends, maybe convince me to return you to your wretched mate. Well, I'll tell you something, wortpig, better men than you have tried! The last one ended up dead!"

Seneca nodded thoughtfully. "The last one . . . the man I'm to replace?" He enjoyed Nisa's shock at his shrewd guess. "Yes, I thought so. You desired him."

"I did not!" Her lie was so obvious that her already pink cheeks flamed to brilliant red.

"It is in your eyes when you look at me. In my world the emotion is known as lust. It can be a weakening force. . . ." Seneca paused. "Though pleasurable."

Nisa's chin quivered. For a moment Seneca thought she might cry. His mood gentled, and he touched her arm. She jerked away.

"You will not touch me again."

"I think I will." Nisa opened her mouth to speak, but Seneca silenced her with a finger laid against her lips—her lips still moist from his kiss. "Between us there is a desire to join. Had I not felt that at our first meeting . . ."

Seneca fell silent. If he alerted Nisa to his shielding ability, he might endanger his capacity to effect a return to Akando. Nisa blinked away tears, but Seneca saw and pity filled his heart.

"You're certainly perceptive." Nisa swallowed to hide her tears. "I'll grant you that."

Nisa lifted her proud, stubborn chin and looked him square in the eye. "Yes, I had feelings for Motega. He was a charming man. And yes, your resemblance to him makes that fact difficult to forget."

"Then perhaps I have found your weakness, maiden." Seneca fell silent, gauging the depth of her emotion. Emotion for both Motega . . . and himself.

"But then, we all have our weaknesses." Seneca allowed his gaze to wander from Nisa's indignant face to the swell of her breasts. With one finger, he touched the base of her throat. She froze, then smacked his hand away.

"Yes, I'm weak! I've been a fool. All of this—" Nisa's arms waved, gesturing around the room. "It's all my fault. Had I not trusted Motega, he wouldn't have learned about the Candor Moon. And had I not betrayed him to my uncle, he would still be alive!"

Sudden tears glittered in Nisa's eyes. Without another word, she spun away and darted from the room.

Nisa leaned against the wall outside Seneca's cell. The nightmare wasn't over—it just kept coming, tormenting her through every waking hour. She had known Seneca resembled Motega—she never imagined he would hold the same sensual power over her.

Nisa hurried to her private quarters and sat on the edge of her bed. Her whole body felt tight. Logic. Her mind needed logic, logic to drive away her treacherous emotions, the wild currents of primitive need in her body.

Nisa's back straightened. She considered what she'd learned from Seneca. Perhaps his sensual resemblance to Motega would be beneficial. Not to her, but for her purpose. Yes. The researchers had underestimated the Akandans, no question.

Seneca was intelligent. Far more than anyone had imagined for his primitive race. Not only had he understood the underlying nuances of her language, but he understood the concepts. He guessed easily what she wanted of him.

"I've been given another chance." Nisa spoke aloud. A weight of anxiety fell from her shoulders. "I can set right all I made wrong by my own weakness. This time I'll be stronger. I won't be swayed by a man's appeal."

Nisa adjusted the climate control in her room for cooler air. Thorwalian air. She lay back and stared at her ceiling, waiting for sleep. How would she control her physical responses? What if he touched her again?

"I won't let him. That's all. I won't allow it again."

Nisa's confidence trickled back. It was easy to explain. Seneca took her off guard by his advanced thought processes. He used his strong, well-proportioned body to confuse her. He fixed his smoldering, dark gaze on her to rattle her.

"Well, it won't work again, wortpig," she said to the empty room. "You may be handsome, your body may show to advantage in those tight skins you wear . . ." Every sinew showed in that lean body, every muscle that controlled his easy movement. Nisa wet her lips, then turned over on her side. "It's those cursed twinkling eyes . . . that's what's wrong with him."

Nisa saw Seneca's face in her mind. She tried to imagine the geometric structures of her beloved Thorwal. Nothing out of place, even precision. Instead she saw the perfection of Seneca's face.

"He's handsomer than Motega." Nisa rolled onto her back again, her fingers laced together over her chest. Motega had had a boyish quality Seneca lacked. Seneca was a man, a man with surprising perception. Her fingers folded and unfolded. Maybe if she had his hair trimmed . . .

"When the new cycle begins, I'll be ready." Nisa's vow solidified her intentions. She forced her eyes shut, and by the full power of her will, cleared her mind for sleep.

Nisa stood outside Seneca's door, fingering his new uniform. The first thing to be done was to cover his body. He looked too raw, too male dressed in soft leather. Her back straightened. She was in control.

Nisa opened the door and walked in. Seneca wasn't there. Nisa whirled around, but he entered the room with Tranor close behind, a stun rifle clasped in the navigator's shaking hands.

Seneca paid no heed to Tranor's quivering weapon. His dark hair fell loose and damp around his face. He wore a shipboard robe rather than his Akandan garb. The white cloth set off his dark skin, though the robe seemed too small for a man of his size.

"Tranor! What is the meaning of this?"

Tranor eased back toward the door. "Fedor ordered me to have him washed." Tranor's voice sounded high and nervous.

"Did he?"

"I think he was hoping your prisoner would make a break for it. He had us set the rifles on full force."

Nisa's lips pursed angrily. "You will, from this point onward, disregard Fedor's 'requests,' and adhere to my instructions. Do you understand?"

"I do, but the guards don't. They listen to Fedor."

"That will change." Nisa paused. Fedor had too much power. Helmar's tendency toward indecision gave his second-in-command leeway to alter policy. Well, not here. Not on her mission. Fedor never dared defy her directly. He preferred sneaking behind her back, confusing Helmar, subtly manipulating every situation.

"Why wasn't I consulted? This is my mission, Tranor. You know that, even if the guards don't."

"I called you earlier," Tranor told her hurriedly. "But you didn't answer."

Nisa hesitated. She vaguely remembered the call signal; she remembered ignoring it in favor of sleep. "You could have called again."

"Fedor ordered me not to bother you. He seemed put out that I'd called you at all. But your warrior gave us no trouble. Guess he's in awe of our weapons."

Nisa noticed Seneca's brow angle. She felt a wave of embarrassment, though she wasn't certain why. "I'm sure he understands we mean no harm."

Tranor looked at the bigger man doubtfully. "Don't imagine he understands much of anything. Didn't say a word."

"Didn't he?" Nisa realized that Seneca had only spoken to her. In the crew's presence, he remained stoic and expressionless, saying nothing. A wave of suspicion passed through her. If he refused to speak, how would she prove her plan was workable?

"The probes imparted our concepts as well as language. I'm sure he is cognizant of the situation."

"It's probably just a blur to him. His species isn't as evolved as ours."

"That may be true," agreed Nisa. "But if we speak clearly and simply, he may attain a grasp of our reason, subspecies or not."

She said this to prod Seneca into revealing his intelligence, but he remained silent. She suspected her attempt amused him.

"Hate to see him angry." Tranor eased away from the Akandan. "A primitive like that is capable of anything."

Seneca moved, taking a step toward Tranor, who gulped dramatically. Tranor froze, but Seneca walked calmly past him, picked up his pack, and withdrew a food stick. His eyes on Tranor's, Seneca took a bite.

Tranor seemed to find the act threatening. He backed into the doorway. "If there's nothing else . . ."

Nisa sighed. Seneca had gained the upper hand again. "You may leave."

She forced a cool, impersonal smile as she turned back to Seneca. "You will cease your attempts to intimidate my crewmen. Is that understood?"

Seneca's dark eyes widened with feigned surprise. Again Nisa noticed his full, dark lashes. He had beautiful eyes, soft and warm. A deep, rich brown. She licked her lips, and his eyes grew darker still.

Nisa felt an undercurrent of desire stir between them. She turned away. "I'm pleased that you made good use of the cleansing unit. You look much better." She hoped he understood that she had found his appearance before barely tolerable. "I suppose it's been a while, if ever, since you bathed."

Seneca ran his hands along the open fold of his robe. Nisa suspected he was teasing her again.

"I bathed the morning you chose to abduct me."

Nisa endured an image of Seneca bathing in the wilds of his hostile planet. She forced the thought away and thrust his new uniform into his hands.

"You will wear this until we can supply you with Motega's gear. You'll find it more comfortable than what you've worn before."

Seneca examined the new weave. "It won't endure much wear, but it's soft." A slow smile grew on his lips as he passed it back to her. "Not unlike yourself."

Nisa felt stung. "I have a very high level of endurance."

Seneca's brow rose as he assessed her body. "You're soft. True, you're soft in the right places, but durable? I think not."

"Get dressed!"

Seneca tore open his robe and dropped it to the floor. Nisa shook her head, but no words came. She couldn't force her eyes shut. She just stared.

Her vision seized a will of its own, traveling slowly across the plains of his wide, strong chest. Every muscle defined, part of a greater whole, perfect unison. Down across his taut stomach, lower.

Nisa's lips parted. It had been seven years since she had seen an unclothed man. The memory taunted her as she stared at Seneca's bold, masculine form. Motega never let her study him. He studied her. But Seneca just stood, as if he knew how his male body affected her senses.

Broad shoulders, firm muscles supporting his powerful, dense bone structure . . . Nisa tried to remain analytical. As she had been when studying his image on the reflector screen in Thorwal's lab.

She failed altogether. His large male organ stood poised from his body, full and engorged.

Seneca caught her fixed gaze and grinned. "If you weren't so blatantly interested in my anatomy, maiden, I might not be in this condition."

Nisa felt her cheeks flaming. She opened her mouth to speak, to insult him in some way, but the words wouldn't come. She closed her mouth, but Seneca laughed.

"Never have I met a more guileless woman than you, Nisa Calydon."

"Get dressed!" Nisa flung the uniform toward Seneca's head. He caught it in one swift, agile motion, still chuckling to himself.

"Are you sure?" His grin revealed slight dimples in his flawless, smooth cheeks.

"I'm sure."

"If you're done with your perusal . . ." Seneca lifted the garment, in no hurry to cover his naked body.

Nisa wanted to dart from the room, but leaving would concede to him the victory in their battle of wills. She gazed off at nothing while he dressed. She drew a quick, short breath to clear her senses.

"I take it an ungarbed male isn't within your usual realm of experience." Seneca was fully clothed now. Nisa relaxed.

"That's none of your concern."

"It is if I'm to become this Motega. I take it the two of you were . . . mated."

"We were not!"

"Do your people know that?"

Nisa hesitated. Her dalliance with the Dakotan leader was widely known, and often discussed in her absence. Her parents suffered the embarrassment of it; her female peers suffered the jealousy of it. Nisa wished it need never be mentioned again.

"Motega seemed an honorable man when I met him. I was wrong."

"You chose him as a lover. But not a mate?"

"I considered that possibility," she admitted, her expression as proud and unaffected as she could muster. "Unions between Dakotans and Thorwalians are rare, but they're not forbidden. Especially when—"

"When the union might benefit both your people?" Seneca tugged his uniform on without trouble. Nisa wondered how he learned so easily the snaps and fastenings of Thorwalian gear.

"It might have benefited both worlds. Had Motega been a man of greater honor." She paused. "Had I not been blind."

"Blind, were you?" Seneca spoke quietly, almost to himself. "So blind you betrayed him?"

Seneca's accusation shocked Nisa. Her throat constricted. "I didn't want him to die." She meant to shout. But only a whisper sounded. Seneca's dark eyes seemed to penetrate into her core.

"You told me his death was your responsibility."

Nisa felt shaken, forced to remember something she longed to forget. "I meant it was my fault. . . ." Her voice faded. "When I learned he had betrayed me, used me, I revealed his intentions to the High Council. They imprisoned him. I never dreamed someone would kill him."

"But you never alerted the Dakotans to this 'accident.'"

"How could we tell them? They'd never believe Motega died accidentally. I told you they idolized him. You have no idea how charming that man was when it suited his purposes."

"No more charming than yourself, I think."

"I'm not charming. And I didn't kill him."

Seneca studied her face silently, as if gauging the truth of her claim. "His intentions . . . what were they?"

"That is something you need not know. Now or ever."

"So you would have me do your bidding, knowing nothing of the reason. Knowing nothing of whether it suits my own code."

"The maneuvering and politics of Thorwal is far beyond your capacity of reason." Even as she spoke, Nisa felt foolish. Seneca's capacity had proven itself surprisingly adept. She changed her tactic. "The less you know, the better."

Seneca turned away, but Nisa caught his bitter expression. "That," he said quietly, "is certainly a truth."

Nisa wondered at his strange alteration of mood. Until now, nothing seemed to reach him, nothing troubled him. She pondered the matter, but Seneca turned back to her. The change in his expression astounded her.

His soft brown eyes darkened; tight rage controlled his stoic features. "I want nothing to do with your schemes, maiden. I care nothing which of your two violent worlds reaches this treasured moon first. I have only one purpose: to return to Akando, and honor my duty to its people."

Nisa drew back, astounded at his wild assertion. "That's ridiculous. I can't return you now! You're our last hope."

Seneca leaned toward her. Tension quivered between them. "No, maiden. You have no hope at all."

Tears sparkled in Nisa's eyes, but she swallowed and

forbade herself from letting Seneca see her pain. "I don't need hope," she told him in a steady voice. "I lost that a very long time ago."

Nisa started for the door, then turned back, her face stoic and her emotions controlled. "We will enter orbit around Thorwal soon. You will be transferred into another shuttle, where I will accompany you. You will be considered an honored guest of the councillor."

Seneca's brow angled, but he made no comment.

"My uncle is a patient and wise man. But our situation is desperate. We need you. Behave wisely, and I feel certain your request to return to Akando will be granted."

"And if I don't behave wisely?"

Nisa didn't answer immediately. "Then you will never see Akando again."

When the *Gordonia* entered orbit around Thorwal, Nisa returned to Seneca's holding cell. She knew what she had to do—convince him that her ordered, well-managed world was worth saving.

"I take it we've arrived," Seneca commented when Nisa appeared at his door. He glanced behind her. "No guards? No weaponry?"

"I'm sure that's not necessary. You're not a prisoner," she reminded him. "You're our guest."

"And you know very well that I haven't the means to return to my world on my own. Not yet, anyway."

Seneca had discarded the Thorwalian uniform, and again wore his primitive Akandan skins. Nisa debated forcing him to change, then decided it made little difference now.

"You'll be sorry for what you're wearing. Thorwal is cold."

"I'm not surprised." Seneca made no move to change.

Nisa bit back an argument and shrugged with an

attempt at carelessness. "If you're ready, our shuttle is waiting."

Seneca retrieved his pack while Nisa watched suspiciously. "You don't have to bring that. We can supply anything you need on Thorwal."

"Thorwal has nothing of such value." Seneca's icy tone stung Nisa, though she wasn't sure why.

"What's in it?"

Seneca looked down at her. "The future of Akando."

Nisa refused to tolerate his evasive comments. She seized the bag, tugged at the rough-stitched ties, and looked inside. Her face revealed puzzlement. "A tree? What's so special about a tree?"

"If you look more closely at the leaves . . ."

"They're white. And shiny." She paused, considering the significance. "What of it?"

"The climate of Akando can be brutal. In the barren season, only the Lasting Trees survive. But they do not propagate in the warm climes where my people live. Only far to the north, in the mountains, do they sprout. For this reason, each year a man is sent to retrieve another."

"The mountains?" Nisa tried to recall Akando's geography. "But that's . . . it would take . . ."

"It took one hundred and twelve days. Many who have tried . . . failed. The journey is not without risks."

Nisa's brow furrowed. "Before we landed, we were warned about dangerous animals and violent weather changes. I do not see how one man could do that alone. You must have been well armed."

"My only weapon is myself."

"Yourself?" Nisa felt uneasy. She remembered detailed reports of Akando's dangers. No one understood how the tribe survived as a group. How one man, unarmed, could venture into the deadly wilderness . . .

"The less you know about my abilities, the better." Seneca echoed Nisa's own evasive comments. Her jaw clenched.

"Very well. I'm sure your abilities will be of little use on Thorwal. Follow me."

Nisa led Seneca down the corridor toward the shuttle bay, refusing to glance his way or speak to him further. The man grated on her nerves. As they passed silently down the halls, Nisa noticed that several technicians made wide berths around Seneca. Nisa shook her head in dismay.

"Lilt-mice," she muttered.

"Despite the vast achievements of your civilization, it seems personal strength and power haven't evolved far."

Nisa glared at the tall man beside her, then quickened her pace. "Our personal strength and power created this vessel."

"And within, you cower in fear."

Nisa smacked her code into the door grid. The passage slid open, and she led Seneca into the shuttle bay. Fedor was waiting, his expression ripe with disapproval.

"I advised you to bring guards," Fedor said to Nisa, ignoring Seneca.

"And as you can see, guards aren't necessary. We'll be taking Shuttle Two, Fedor. You may report directly to Helmar."

"Where are you taking him?"

"Before I present Seneca to Helmar, I will introduce him to Thorwal." Nisa's tone brooked no argument, but Fedor wasn't pleased.

"I will have to inform your uncle of this delay."

"Please do." Nisa turned her back to Fedor and directed Seneca toward a smaller shuttlecraft. "This way."

Seneca crouched low as he entered the vessel. He seated himself within, then shook his head. "Comfort seems no higher valued than taste to your people."

Nisa settled herself at the controls and fiddled with

several dials. "Fedor's shuttle is more spacious. But this is mine."

Seneca glanced around as she secured the hatch. His eyes widened, the first trace of nervousness Nisa had seen since she captured him. "Who is flying this?"

"I am, naturally." Nisa paused, guessing Seneca required further convincing of her abilities. "I'm a very good pilot. True, I only learned last year. . . ."

Seneca closed his eyes. Nisa suspected he was trying to calm himself. She maneuvered the shuttle from the bay, but Seneca's tense condition unnerved her, and she scraped the side of the dock. Seneca groaned.

"If you'd relax, this would be easier," she snapped. "You're making me nervous."

"Just watch what you're doing. I'd like to live to see your icebound world, after all."

Nisa's lip curled in annoyance. "And you will."

The shuttle departed the larger transport vessel and lowered toward the surface of Thorwal. "The transport vessel remains in orbit," she informed Seneca. "It never lands, and was constructed out here, beyond our atmosphere. We travel back and forth from the planet in shuttles. On Thorwal, we travel equally fast in hovercraft."

"There's no need to hurry. Speed is overvalued."

Nisa's gaze wandered from his face to his legs. His Akandan leggings seemed molded to his hard muscles. Despite her insistence that he wear a Thorwalian uniform, Nisa had to admit that his own garb suited him better. His raw power couldn't be contained by civilized means.

"You seemed to appreciate speed. We saw you running across the plains."

"But I had reason to run then, maiden. I was home."

Again Nisa felt stung. Seneca had no reason to welcome this journey—she couldn't expect him to enjoy it. But she still felt disappointed by his obvious desire to return to his barren planet.

"Well, Thorwal is my home. That's where we're going, and you might as well accept it, because you'll be here a while."

"That," said Seneca, "remains to be seen."

Nisa fell silent. Why did she care if he hated her, hated her world? Why did it hurt to know he longed for another woman? A sweet, simple woman . . . As far from Nisa herself as could be imagined. She didn't want to attract him, but now that he showed no interest, she was disappointed.

Feelings don't matter. Just do what you have to do, and keep your feelings to yourself. Don't let him know you care.

Nisa didn't want to care about Seneca. She tried to convince herself that his likeness to Motega provoked her. She glanced covertly at him. He looked tense, staring out the viewport as if she might direct the shuttle into a mountainside.

The quiet, controlled strength remained. Motega had stirred her senses—everything around him revolved in a heightened state of activity. Seneca's power was similar, but within. Motega reached out toward the universe—Seneca carried it within him.

"You're honest. I appreciate that." Nisa spoke suddenly, and Seneca looked at her in surprise.

"What makes you think that?"

Nisa shrugged. "You've admitted your intention to return to Akando any way you can. I understand your reasons." She paused, her face softening as she studied his face. "You can't know what it means to me to be able to trust your honesty, at least."

Seneca's face revealed an emotion Nisa couldn't read. It almost seemed like regret. He looked back out the viewport. "You have no reason to trust me, maiden. We are at cross purposes. Never forget."

"I know."

They fell silent as the shuttle lowered beneath the high, thin cloud coverage.

61

"There, to your left, is Mount Thorwal." Nisa gestured at a distant pinnacle.

Seneca fixed his gaze ahead. "Watch where you're going."

"And just beyond is the Thorwalian Sea. It's frozen. The Plains of Thorwal are in the distance; River Thorwal cuts through there."

"Imaginative naming," noted Seneca with a grin. "But orderly. Since it all appears white and frozen . . ."

"We aren't near enough for you to see the complexities."

Seneca looked away from the viewport, to Nisa. "All the complexities I need to see, I see in you."

"I'm not complex."

"No? From another world, you stole me from my land. You may be a murderess with the face of an angel. If nothing else, you, maiden, are indeed complex."

Nisa ignored him as the smooth terrain surrounding Thorwal's most populated region came into view. "There, to our right, is the main city of Thorwal. That's where I'm taking you. It's my home."

Seneca gazed out at the small homes, the geometric precision of the city, as the shuttle drew closer to Nisa's destination. Everything appeared white. All the buildings were constructed to the same specifications. Perfect order.

"No wonder you needed the Dakotans. A society this lacking in imagination couldn't invent their way out of a box."

Nisa's back straightened. "We don't invent. We build."

A light flashed on the panel in front of Nisa. She didn't notice. "Is that important?"

Nisa noticed the light and bit her lip. "It's nothing." She quickly entered another code into her panel and the shuttle dropped violently. Nisa forced a smile.

"Just a little adjustment," she told him in a calm,

soothing voice. "I do this all the time."

"That's very reassuring." Seneca paused. "Something tells me a large number of staid Thorwalians are down there ducking."

"I am highly respected down there."

"As a pilot?"

Nisa's lip curled in irritation. "You must be quiet now. I need to concentrate to land properly."

"I won't breathe." Seneca gripped his seat, strapping himself in for Nisa's landing. The shuttle lurched in several quick adjustments, then settled down toward a flat but narrow surface. The shuttle bumped once, then coasted to an even stop very close to a large, low building.

Once securely on land again, Seneca looked over at his self-assured captor. His heart expanded with affection when she drew a concealed breath of relief. Nothing on Akando had prepared him for this feeling. On Akando he had been certain of his fate. But then, he had been sure of so many things that seemed uncertain now.

Chapter Three

"We have arrived." Nisa felt a surge of pride. What a landing! Never had her skills proven so . . . uneventful.

Seneca studied the scene outside the viewport. "That wall couldn't get much closer."

Nisa cleared her throat. Her fingers still gripped the braking lever. A quick glance told her that her knuckles were white. She released the mechanism quickly and brushed an irritating wisp of hair from her cheek.

Why had she kept her hair long, anyway? Because Motega had liked it. He had said she looked like an ancient Thorwalian goddess with her hair loose, from a time when Thorwalians still believed in fate. It was her one concession to her past, one thing she couldn't let go.

Technicians bustled outside the craft, but the door didn't open. Nisa seized a communicator. "What's taking so long? My landing was secure. Let us out."

No reply. She smacked the microphone into its handle just as the hull slid open. Several armed guards stood pointing stun rifles into the shuttle. Nisa rolled her eyes.

"What are you doing? I requested no guards."

"Fedor's orders, Lieutenant." The guard's voice quavered, and his hands shook. "Thought you'd need an escort."

Nisa rose from the helm and positioned herself in the doorway, hands on her hips. "I don't. What I need is my hovercraft."

The guards exchanged glances between themselves. "If you're sure . . ."

"I am always sure."

A chuckle from Seneca snapped Nisa's attention from the guards. She glared at him; he smiled. Nisa turned her back to him, trusting he understood her superiority. "Please report to the High Councillor that I will escort our guest through a tour of the city, then introduce him at the even meal. Ask him, please, to prepare a suitable feast for the occasion."

"Don't have much for feasting," noted the guard. "We're down to barlit-meal for every sitting now."

A faint groan from Seneca echoed Nisa's own feelings on the subject. Her shoulders slumped. "Very well. But see that the settings are proper for an honored guest."

The guards eyed Seneca, then scurried away. "It's a wonder they can lift those rifles," Seneca noted as the slender Thorwalian guards disappeared into the hangar port.

"Strength isn't important to logical beings. Of course, you wouldn't understand that. I'm sure it's important on your world. But you'll find little use for your primitive skills, such as they are, on Thorwal."

"I don't know. My skills may have more value than you suspect." Though Nisa eyed him suspiciously, Seneca said no more on the subject. "Shall we go, maiden? You mentioned a tour."

* * *

Seneca followed Nisa into the large port. He stopped at the entry and sighed. There was no adornment, only the white-clad technicians busy with their machinery. No smells, other than of fuel and metal. "A stirring environment."

Nisa frowned. "You can't expect a hangar port to be attractive. It's functional. All Thorwal is practical. But practicality has beauty, as you'll soon see."

"You have beauty," Seneca acknowledged with a veiled grin. "But then, your inherent practicality is in question."

Nisa's jaw tightened, but she waved Seneca in the direction of the hangar exit. "This way."

They started across the port, their footsteps echoing across the metallic surface. "I am eminently practical. I can't imagine how you'd question that facet of my character."

"Your lips speak divergent tales, maiden. Your words praise logic, but your kiss . . ."

Nisa stopped. "You will not speak of that here. It's unnecessary."

"But pleasurable." Seneca started off ahead of her, toward the open light. Nisa skittered along to keep up with him. She was breathless by the time they left the port.

"Must you walk so fast?"

Seneca studied her flushed appearance, then shook his head. "As I said, you are soft in the flesh. A brisk walk tires you, leaves your cheeks pink and your chest heaving." His gaze whisked across her front. "That aspect, I will admit, has its appeal."

"I don't like walking. It's not—"

"Necessary," cut in Seneca. "Much that is inherent to your Thorwalian physiques has been ignored and deemed unnecessary, it seems. To your own detriment, perhaps."

"Not so! No Thorwalian carries excess weight. You

66

should see the Dakotans, if you think we're soft."

"I didn't say you were fat. Just soft. Your men have no muscle development whatsoever. They are frail. Strange, since their bone structure could carry much mass. I would guess your ancestors were both tall and strong."

"As are all primitive people," said Nisa in disgust. "Your kind would value that, but we have evolved well beyond such basic needs."

"All the way to war."

"Your perspective is more warped than I imagined. Primitive, primitive." Nisa fiddled in her side pack and found her hovercraft controls. "Watch this, Akandan. You will be amazed."

Seneca dutifully watched as Nisa summoned her hovercraft from its slot. She punched in her code, then waited. A faint smile touched her lips as a small, round craft appeared from the storage unit. It buzzed up to her, hovering just off the ground, sensors flashing, speed controls waiting.

"This is mine," she announced proudly, patting the shiny white surface of the craft.

"I guessed that from the dents."

Nisa glared. "What are you talking about? Most of those were patched!"

" 'Most of those,' maiden? Just how many dents has this craft endured?"

"A few. None of them were my fault. And they weren't major."

"Is this your first vehicle?"

Nisa hesitated. "My fourteenth, I believe." She paused, her brow furrowed. "Fifteenth. But this one is much better than the others."

"Why do I think my life is in danger?"

"Not at all." Nisa snapped open the glass shell and gestured for Seneca to enter. After a long, drawn-out sigh, he did.

"Where to, maiden? Wherever it is, I trust we'll go

there at a reasonable speed."

"Of course."

Nisa's eyes changed as she settled at the helm of her small craft. They glowed. Her lips curved with satisfaction as she caressed the guidance controls. Her fingers twitched with suppressed aggression and delight as she fiddled with the speed dials.

Seneca closed his eyes. The shuttle leaped ahead, whisking toward buildings without caution.

"Why are your eyes closed? You're missing the outer city!"

"At this speed I'd just see a streak of light anyway."

The hovercraft slowed, a certain reluctance seeming to come from both Nisa and the vehicle itself. "I'm taking you toward the High Council Chambers. It's a magnificent building. Designed many generations ago, actually. It's the oldest building in Thorwal. Most consider it beautiful."

Seneca looked around at his surroundings. He saw rows of metallic white buildings, crafted in box shapes, all symmetrically aligned, unadorned. But all clean, well tended.

Snow covered the ground, though the sky was blue and bright. Trees were dark green, sparse, but placed by the buildings with well-considered precision.

"Did anything grow on its own, or was the location selected by Thorwalian minds?" Nisa glanced at Seneca doubtfully. "Never mind. I don't need to ask."

Nisa's hovercraft moved in any direction, side to side, back and forth. It did so with frightening abandon as she whisked the round vehicle from one building to another, barely avoiding the approach of a much larger craft.

The other craft dodged Nisa's, and she shook her fist wildly. Seneca wondered if she intended to chase the other craft down and do it damage. By the looks of her dented craft, she had chosen this solution before.

"You mentioned the Chambers," he suggested. Nisa glared over her shoulder at the fleeing craft.

"Occasionally I wish these crafts were armed," she muttered.

"There wouldn't be a Thorwalian left alive."

Nisa guided the hovercraft through the even streets, edging toward a snow-covered hill overlooking the city. She stopped the craft without warning, then pointed. "There! Isn't it magnificent?"

At the top of a steep cliff, Seneca saw a white building. Just as she said, despite its color, the building evoked another time and era, when Thorwalians depended less on rigid structure, and more on dreams. Giant white columns lined an open court surrounding the Chambers, and each gleaming surface seemed designed to catch light and reflect it.

"What do you think? There's nothing like that on Akando, I'd wager!"

Seneca didn't answer. It was beautiful. Cold and bright and offering a secret promise he'd forgotten. Like a crown on a staid head, the Chambers glowed with power, with ambition, with certainty. He expected to feel loathing. But a tremor of admiration still moved his heart.

"No, maiden. Akando has no such testimonials to ambition and greed. We build nothing stronger than ourselves. For that reason, we need nothing more."

Nisa's face fell. "Don't you think it's beautiful?"

Seneca hesitated. "Yes, it's beautiful." He turned his gaze from the Chambers to Nisa. "But then, so are you. Beauty isn't necessarily something a man desires to his best end. I learned that long ago. It is a lesson I will never forget."

"You're just being stubborn." Seneca started to extract himself from the hovercraft, but Nisa seized his arm. "Don't get out yet, Akandan. If man-made wonders don't move you, maybe natural wonders will. I've got another place to show you."

69

Seneca sank back into his seat, resigned as Nisa's craft jerked forward and spun around. "My knees are probably shaking too much to stand, anyway."

"You wouldn't understand the operation of such an advanced vehicle. But I assure you, others admire my skill."

Seneca tried to resist the temptation to remind her otherwise. He failed. "Am I the first to mistake your 'skills'?"

Nisa's small, square jaw hardened. She didn't answer at once. Seneca knew she struggled with memory. "Not exactly. You're not the first. But just because another man was mistaken about my abilities doesn't make you right."

"Another man . . . Motega?"

"His judgment was flawed."

"That much is certain." Seneca caught her quick glance. "If you escorted him in this craft, it's a wonder he lived to suffer his execution."

Nisa refused to respond and Seneca regretted his comment. Anger increased her grip on the speed lever. She sped around the Chambers, drawing close to point out the stone columns. "My uncle lives there. It's where I work, too."

The hovercraft tilted as Nisa turned from the Chambers. "I have a house nearby, down there." Nisa gestured toward neat, even rows of homes beneath the Chambers.

Seneca looked back. "How can you tell which one is yours? They all look the same."

"They're numbered, naturally. I am twenty-first from the right, as you face the Chambers."

Seneca shook his head and turned toward Nisa's destination. "Where are we going?"

Nisa smiled with veiled pride. "You'll see." She edged the hovercraft toward the summit of the hill, beyond the Chambers, where the trees grew in greater abundance.

Seneca watched her face as it changed from happiness to a strange expression of regret. The hovercraft slowed, then stopped at the entrance to a narrow path.

"Well? Is this it?" Seneca looked around. "It's good to see a few trees that have some say in their own placement, I admit. But I trust you have something more engaging to reveal."

Nisa didn't answer at once. "Thorwalians visit this place constantly. Even now there may be people there, viewing the majesty."

"And you, maiden, do you come here often?"

She didn't look at him. She just stared up the path. "Not in seven years." Nisa glanced at Seneca. He saw her pain and her doubt. "It's late. Perhaps you'd prefer to rest, to have dinner."

"The same gruel you fed me on your ship?" She nodded reluctantly. "I'm in no hurry. Show me your sight, maiden."

"It's not that special. You won't like it."

Seneca studied her face for a while, considering. "It would please me."

"You don't even know what it is."

"I know it bothers you. You don't want to go. I would know why."

Nisa rolled her eyes and puffed an impatient breath. "How do you know these things?"

"I see it in your eyes."

"My eyes are just the way they were before."

"Not so, maiden. A moment ago your eyes gleamed with a strange and somewhat frightening light. I believe the control of this vehicle produces this effect. But now you are facing something else. Something you don't want to face."

"Not at all!" Nisa's lips tightened. She seized the speed controls and the hovercraft jerked forward. "I have no objection to bringing you here. I was simply thinking of your needs."

Seneca gripped the front panel as Nisa sped along the narrow, wooded path. "How do you know that another vehicle isn't coming toward—"

Another hovercraft came into view around the corner. Nisa angled dramatically to the side, barely avoiding a thick evergreen. "I see," sighed Seneca. "You don't."

The near miss didn't slow her. Her eyes fixed on the trail ahead, Nisa aimed at her destination with grim determination. They reached the edge of the woods, and Nisa stopped her craft. She swallowed hard, then flipped open the shell.

"We're here."

Seneca swung himself out of the craft. "I'm grateful to be alive."

Nisa ignored him. "If you'll follow me . . ." She started off, her white boots crunching into the hard-packed snow. Firm footfalls, determined. Seneca watched her a moment, then followed.

Nisa didn't speak as she led Seneca to the edge of a sharp cliff. Neither spoke. A cold wind blew, tossing Seneca's dark brown hair behind his head, tugging at the confines of Nisa's until wisps flew at random around her face.

"You astound me, maiden. Truly, I have never seen anything more stirring."

Far below the high cliff, a red river flowed, hardened by a dark crust. The wind swept down from the cliffside, stirring the snow, which sizzled over the molten flow.

"I told you of our lava flows. Here is the point where the molten rock emerges and meets the surface. Just beyond, it hardens, and digs back into the earth. Our technicians long ago found and developed subterranean mines, where we construct building material, as well as our flight ships."

"Would this be the home of the subterranean wortpig?" asked Seneca with a grin.

"They live in the caverns, yes." Nisa eyed Seneca and smiled. "They are a particularly unattractive and pushy species."

Seneca watched the lava's endless cycle. "Yours is an ordered world, maiden, yet beneath the surface there is passion."

"We're not at all passionate." Nisa paused. "Maybe that term could apply to our ancestors, true. But we long ago gained control over such impulses, and make logical decisions on every matter."

Seneca appeared unconvinced. "In what way?"

Nisa considered this. If she came up with a good example, maybe Seneca would forget the small indications to the contrary. "Childbearing, for instance, is carefully controlled."

"I'm not surprised."

"Our ancestors threatened to overpopulate Thorwal with their wanton breeding. But today each family desiring children gains approval from the council, and is allotted two births, one of each sex. In this way, an equal number of males and females is produced, and the population remains controlled."

"Is mating equally flavorless on Dakota?"

"It's not necessary there. Many Dakotans don't mate at all. Family bonds are not strong among Dakotans. Motega's parents were killed on a research expedition beneath their sea, but he never mentioned their loss."

"Loss suffered isn't easily discussed. As I'm sure you've learned yourself."

Nisa suspected Seneca referred to her loss of Motega, so she refused to pursue his comment. Her obstinate silence brought a smile to his lips.

"And you, maiden, what of your family?"

"My family is very supportive of my efforts." Nisa nearly choked on the lie.

"Shall I have the honor of meeting them?" Seneca sounded suspiciously knowing, and Nisa checked his expression for guile.

"My parents live on the far side of Thorwal." She paused, searching for an easy explanation for the distance. In truth, they had moved as far away from the scandal of her love affair with Motega as they could get. "With age, they sought warmer climes."

"I didn't realize there were warmer climes on this frosty world."

"In some places near our equator, the snow gives way to patches of green. In a few spots." Nisa didn't like the way their conversation proceeded. She decided to alter it before it went any further.

"Ages ago, Thorwal was warm and temperate and harbored a thriving, albeit violent, civilization. Only last year, Dakotan researchers found conclusive evidence that a comet came through our solar system and disrupted the orbits of all the inner planets, yours included."

Nisa's tale interested Seneca more than she expected. "A comet . . ."

"It would appear as a shooting star across the sky. It's actually similar to an asteroid, on an extended orbit."

Seneca didn't seem to need a detailed explanation. "Akandan legends speak of comets. In particular, one great comet that seared the sky and threatened all life. My world, too, once thrived. Ancient ruins are found in all corners of Akando, indicating a much larger population."

Nisa wasn't sure what this signified. "They must have died off after the orbit changed."

"Perhaps. But Akandan legend speaks of several smaller comets that followed the first."

"Not likely. Comets don't come in packs, and that one has never returned. We found evidence that it burned up in the sun."

"Your tale interests me, maiden. Your world, moved farther from the sun's heat. Mine, altered perhaps by the pull of yours. And Dakota . . ."

"Dakota had been too hot for habitation, other than for birds and fish, but when it was pulled farther from the sun, humans evolved . . . at an extraordinary rate that has never been explained, although first evidence of human presence follows within an age of the comet's arrival."

Seneca nodded, as if Nisa's description clarified something he had long pondered, but never known. "For the three worlds, life changed. For Akando, near annihilation forced strict adherence to natural laws. For Dakota, an unexplained beginning. And for Thorwal, the need to control."

Nisa wasn't sure Seneca's description reflected well on her people. "The hardships of a colder climate demanded logic to survive."

"Strange that a world so vibrant, born of such passion, could have grown so detached from its beginnings."

"What do you mean?"

"You build upon your frozen soil, yet I see no connection between your people and their world. I see no sense of its rhythms, its mystery."

"My people have solved all the mysteries!" Nisa glanced toward the lava flows. The fiery rock bubbled to the surface, then burst into towering spurts of flame, sizzling the frozen snow. "There's nothing mysterious about magma."

A slight smile formed on Seneca's lips. He touched her cheek, then let his hand fall. "One mystery has eluded you, maiden. The mystery of yourself."

"I'm not at all mysterious." Nisa's heart took a strange, unfamiliar leap. She forced her attention from Seneca to the boiling lava. Another time, a time she struggled to forget, returned to haunt her.

Seven years past, she had stood in this same spot, her heart beating too fast as she gazed up at another man. A tall man whose eyes gleamed with fire to match the flows. A man whose every glance was desire. Motega had loved this spot. He chose it to begin his first seduction of Helmar's untouched niece.

Seneca studied Nisa's expression, then turned his gaze back to the lava flow. Neither spoke as they watched the unending push of the river as it met the surface, boiled to life, then disappeared.

"This, then, is the heart of Thorwal," murmured Seneca, speaking to himself. "I believe I understand what eluded me. . . ."

His voice faded and he turned to Nisa. She recognized the change in his expression. His eyes looked darker, the faint curve of his lips suggesting his mood had turned into something far more dangerous.

"This place . . . is you, Nisa Calydon."

"What are you talking about?" Her voice sounded shrill; she backed away, but Seneca caught her hand and lifted it. With one finger he traced the inside of her bare wrist.

"So cool." His finger ran along the soft flesh, beneath her sleeve, then stopped at her pulse. Nisa stood frozen, unable to yank her hand away, to stop him. She was trembling, but she couldn't speak. Seneca's gaze fixed on hers, his smile deepening.

"Yet there is fire beneath."

Nisa swallowed. He made the image seem sexual, passionate.

"Like your land, Nisa."

Nisa wanted to argue, to put him in his place. Words wouldn't form. His finger moved on her skin, sending fire along her nerves, just as he described.

"Do you know why the wind sweeps from these hills, maiden?"

He leaned closer to her, his head lowered as if to kiss her. But their lips didn't touch. Nisa tried to form an image to blot out his control; she tried to remember the technical reasons for the wind's motion. Nothing came.

"It sweeps, heedless of its fate, downward into the

fire, knowing it will be consumed. Do you know why?"

Nisa shook her head. Her heart slammed against her breast; she couldn't draw a breath.

"To touch," he whispered, his lips inches from hers. "For one touch of that fire beneath the ice, to bring the fire to life, to melt the ice and set the fire to flame."

"It's just rock." Her voice shook. "Heated by the pressure below."

Seneca's mouth brushed hers, barely. "I am the wind, Nisa. And when I touch you, you are fire."

Her knees went weak; she leaned toward him. He caught her and drew her close as his lips pressed against hers. Nisa closed her eyes, unable to resist, to think. She felt the distant lava as it flowed to the surface, hungry for the wind, bursting to flame. . . .

Seneca's lips played against hers; he tasted her with a soft touch of his tongue against hers. His body encased hers; his arms felt like bands of steel around her. Nisa felt his arousal, his deep passion. She yearned to draw him inside, to revel in the fire he created within her.

The cold air swirled around them, tossing her hair from its last bindings. Nisa felt Seneca's fingers in the tangled mass as he cupped her head, bending her back as he deepened the kiss. He drove her from reason, into the same uncontrolled madness Motega had once lured her.

Nisa pulled away. She stared at him, wide eyed, her breath coming in shallow gasps. She shook her head, then ran back toward the hovercraft.

Seneca didn't move. He turned back toward the distant river, feeling the cold wind. "What kind of fool walks down the same path twice, knowing his fate will be the same?"

Seneca watched the bursts of flame from the river; he heard the hiss and pop of the lava below. "The wind has no choice," he said quietly. "After a thousand years, it will seek the fire. And be consumed."

Seneca sighed. He saw Nisa in the hovercraft as she tied her hair back into a tight knot. Her chin rose as he approached; she seemed determined to ignore their passion. For tonight he would leave her to her defiance. But a time would come when nothing would be denied.

Nisa didn't speak as she whisked her craft back toward the Chambers. Seneca noticed that her mood hadn't affected her driving. Several evergreens had narrow escapes as she spun around corners, once revolving the hovercraft entirely as she fought to regain the path.

The cold, distant sun faded on the horizon, glinting sorrowfully off the sheer walls of the Chambers as Nisa glided toward the entrance. She smacked open the shell, got out, and waited for Seneca without a word.

"I assume the tour is complete."

"We're done." Her lips curved downward, she appeared defeated.

"The final majesty was the greatest," offered Seneca. Nisa gave him a stoic nod, but she didn't look at him. She punched a code into her hovercraft remote, and it departed toward a storage unit below the Chambers.

Another craft buzzed up the hill, oblivious to Nisa's programmed vehicle. Nisa's eyes widened. "No! Watch out!"

The craft slammed to one side, scraped its side on the frozen ground, then righted itself. Just in time to bump against Nisa's. Her craft sputtered, then sank powerless to the ground. Nisa clasped her hand over her eyes and groaned. "Not again."

Seneca watched the other craft progress gingerly toward them. If possible, it was even more dented and bruised than Nisa's. It stopped, but no one emerged.

Nisa's hands went to her hips, and one small booted foot tapped as she waited.

Very slowly the shell rose. Seneca watched as a blond head emerged. A black screen covered the young man's eyes; it wrapped around his head, over his nose. Protection against the glare. But apparently not helpful for navigation.

"This has to be . . ."

"My brother."

Seneca nodded. "I should have known."

The young man leaped out of his craft, glanced at Nisa's broken vehicle, then shrugged. He was taller than the Thorwalians Seneca had seen, thin, but broad shouldered. He tugged off the black cover, revealing a face as innocent and eager as Nisa's. His expression told Seneca this wasn't the boy's first collision. Nor likely to be his last.

"Dane . . ." Nisa's tone was more imperious than ever.

"You must have been his teacher."

Nisa glanced at Seneca reproachfully. "He's just learning." She eyed her crushed hovercraft and winced. "At least it didn't explode this time."

"That is a comfort," said Seneca, and Dane nodded enthusiastically.

Seneca waited for the boy to speak, but Dane was staring at him, wide eyed, mouth agape.

"This is the last time . . . I am never getting in another craft with you as long as I live." The voice didn't come from Dane's mouth, but from within his jacket. Seneca glanced at Nisa for explanation.

"What was that?"

A small furry head poked out of Dane's front pocket. Seneca stared in amazement. Two pointed ears twitched; a small, wrinkled nose sniffed the air and shuddered. The creature's expression immediately suggested disdain and superiority.

The creature's round eyes narrowed when he noticed Seneca. His disdainful expression intensified. "By the stars and saints, what possessed you to dig him out of the grave?"

"It can't be. . . ." Seneca turned to Nisa. "Not the rodent?"

" 'Rodent' is a fairly derogatory term," noted the little creature.

"Seneca, this is Carob. Carob is a lingbat. And despite his objections, he is a flightless, winged rodent. Normally they don't talk, but we used the same mind probes on him as we used on you. They worked surprisingly well."

"I see that," said Seneca.

"Don't recognize me, do you? Not surprised. Never did have much feeling. It was you and your Dakotan fiends that caught me, if you'll be so good as to remember the incident. Didn't mean much to you, I'm sure, but then you weren't nabbed from your place of residence and brought to a piddling world. . . ."

"Carob, this isn't Motega. This is Seneca."

"Seneca?" Dane helped Carob to his shoulder. "Is this the Akandan?"

"Yes," said Nisa.

Carob adjusted frail, leathery wings. One tip caught in Dane's hair. Carob tugged frantically while Dane waited, a grim expression on his youthful face. "I wish he wouldn't do that."

"Trim your hair, boy! It's inconveniencing me."

"No."

"Girls like it that way, I suppose," mocked Carob. "Why don't you take a mate and stop this flouncing around? In my land we take a mate as soon as we're able. You've been old enough, obviously, for quite a while. At your age I had produced several prime litters."

"Dane is too young for mating, Carob," said Nisa, though Dane's eyes shifted to one side with faint guilt.

"Tell that to the blue-eyed wench down at the Snow Port!"

Dane coughed to silence the lingbat. "Thank you, Carob. I am not yet interested in mating."

"That's not what you told—"

"Shouldn't we explain to Nisa's guest why you have such a gift for speech?" Dane cut in, his fair skin flushed.

Nisa eyed her brother suspiciously, but Seneca smiled. "The lingbat, maiden . . ."

"Carob was discovered when the Dakotans sent an unmanned probe to the Candor Moon. I found him in a test lab, when we . . . confiscated a Dakotan vessel. He seemed to prefer Thorwal—"

"Who wouldn't?" broke in Carob. "Would you prefer living in a metal box?"

Seneca glanced toward the rows of Thorwalian houses. "I don't see much difference from this angle."

"No, you wouldn't," said Carob, sarcasm ripe in his voice. "If you're Akandan, which I doubt, you're used to grass huts and dirt."

Seneca caught Nisa's arm. "Can those probes be reversed?"

"Why would you want to give up speech?" questioned Carob.

"I wasn't thinking of myself."

Nisa frowned. "No, they cannot. Not for either of you." She turned to Dane. "Are you alone? What about . . ."

Dane appeared uncomfortable. "Our parents were . . . delayed. They asked me to relay to you their regrets."

Seneca saw Nisa's disappointment and her subsequent attempt to hide it from her brother. But Dane touched her shoulder. "I'm here."

Nisa took her brother's hand. "As always. Thank you, Dane. Would you mind alerting Helmar and Fedor to our arrival?"

"Fedor?" Dane's voice was a near groan. "Doesn't he have something better to do . . . stir up a military insurrection or two?"

"I'm sure he does that in private." Seneca watched as Nisa and her brother exchanged a knowing glance. Here was someone Nisa truly loved.

The softness in Nisa's expression touched something in Seneca, something he had avoided until now. This was a woman capable of tenderness, however much she tried to hide those impulses. A woman capable of love.

"Before you go in, there's something you should know, Nisa." Dane's voice sounded heavy. Carob folded his wings across his chest.

"He's done it."

Dane eyed Carob irritably for spoiling his news. "Fedor put out the call for the military as soon as he got back. I just came back from reporting in."

Nisa's breath caught. Seneca saw tears sparkle in her eyes. "That can't be," she whispered. "Helmar swore he would wait for my return."

"Apparently Fedor set him against the idea." Dane hesitated, glancing at Seneca. "He seemed to feel Motega's replacement is . . . inadequate." Dane's bright gaze intensified. "I'm not sure why. He fooled Carob."

"Which isn't easy," cut in the rodent. No one commented. "He doesn't seem as dim-witted as Fedor implied, either. Maybe he lacks the pure, throbbing evil of Motega."

Dane frowned and adjusted his shoulder, deliberately dislodging the small rodent. Carob slipped, then dug his clawed feet into Dane's shoulder. "Watch it, boy! You try balancing on something as bony as you!"

"Motega wasn't evil," said Dane, ignoring the lingbat's slight to his physique. "He was Dakotan, and put their interests before all others." He looked quickly at Nisa, but she remained impassive. "I liked him."

"He was Dakotan," repeated Carob. "Which means evil."

"I see no evidence—"

"*You* weren't confined to a metal box and tested, were you?" Dane had no reply, so Carob nodded vigorously. "No. Don't speak before you've been there, boy. Your time will come!"

Dane's blue eyes fixed on Nisa's. "Every day I bless your decision to free this little treasure. And especially for your generosity in leaving him in my care."

Carob's head lifted, his lips smacked. "I'm cold, boy. And hungry. It's about time for some crunch bugs, wouldn't you say?"

Dane appeared defeated and forlorn, but he nodded miserably. A final, tragic glance cast Nisa's way confirmed that the lingbat's company was a trial beyond endurance. "You have no idea how disgusting this creature's eating habits have become. Crunch bugs!"

"Crispy on the outside, soft and chewy middles!" Carob smacked his lips again for emphasis. "Enjoy your barlit-meal pudding, humans! Until you're ready for something better, the crunch bugs are mine!"

Dane headed into the Chambers, Carob chatting on his shoulder. An occasional groan from the boy told Seneca the conversation hadn't shifted.

Seneca watched them go, then shook his head. "Can I assume from this development that my abduction was wasted?"

Nisa didn't answer at once. Her jaw was set in grim determination. "My efforts aren't wasted yet. Fedor hungers for conquest, but my uncle is a reasonable man. If you will show yourself to best advantage, we may yet convince him."

"And how would that serve my interest?"

Nisa closed her eyes, restraining her anger. "It will keep my brother out of war. Fedor will send him out as a pilot."

"I see your point."

Nisa whirled, her eyes sparkling with fury. "You mock us! Do you think because our world is unlike yours that our lives mean less? Do you think I love my brother less than you love yours?"

"No. But I think you've gotten yourself into this, and there are other ways besides deceit to regain your peace."

"We've tried other ways! The Dakotans want Motega. They want him now. They have fighting craft, and they will come for him. They can destroy the city. All that stops them now is thinking Motega is imprisoned in the Chambers. If they learn—"

"If you told them the truth, from the beginning . . ."

"We'd all be dead!"

"Would you?" Seneca's calm voice contrasted with Nisa's shrill fear. "Yet it took time for them to steal and amass your vessels, did it not? Negotiation tends toward peace, maiden."

Nisa rolled her eyes. "What would you know?"

"There are several tribes, far-flung, on Akando. The need for land, for food, has brought them to hostility many times. A method was learned for easing the tensions, but no doubt it's too primitive for your advanced society."

Nisa frowned at Seneca's sarcastic tone. "And what might that be?"

"My words have value?"

"That remains to be seen."

"You called me stubborn, didn't you?"

"I did." Seneca waited for her to recognize the discrepancy in her character, but Nisa glared defiantly.

"Unions between the tribes have produced greater understanding, and emotional connection."

"Unions? You mean marriage?"

"A prized female from one tribe is sent to the son of another."

" 'Prized female,' indeed! I've never heard such foolishness."

84

"The interests of both are served. And much is learned in the exchange." He paused, watching her face. "I was to join in such a union, for the betterment of both. Unfortunately you delayed our efforts."

"Well, we don't have a prize female. The Dakotans want nothing from us. And they don't have a sacred son anymore, either. I doubt marriage would benefit anyone now."

"But it might have . . . had you been a more honorable mate."

"Had I chosen a more honorable lover." Nisa stopped, her expression determined. "The past is gone. All I have now is you. And if you want to see your miserable mate again, you'll cooperate. Is that clear?"

"Your intentions are clear, maiden. I trust mine are likewise." For a long moment he held her gaze. Nisa didn't look away, though her chin quivered. Whether in an attempt to move his heart to pity or in genuine anguish, Seneca couldn't guess.

A light snow began from the graying sky. The cold wind stilled, but ice seemed to form the air itself. Nisa paid no attention to the cold, but Seneca felt its bite to his bones.

"In one way, at least, the Thorwalian constitution proves rugged. You have no sense of the cold. Inside, I assume the climate is more pleasant."

"Snow falls here at least once a day. Dakota, as you will find, is warm, and the temperature never varies between bright sun and soft rain. No doubt it will be to your liking."

"Two worlds, unyielding weather, unchanging. The people, I think, are the same. Yet on Akando we know such extremes as your world could scarce imagine. What you have seen for a lifetime, maiden, I have seen in the space of a day. Until you see the other side, you will remain forever cold. And untouched by your own frost."

"I've seen the other side. If I'm forever cold, Akandan, that is why."

Nisa broke Seneca's gaze and marched toward the Chambers' entrance. "Follow me."

Seneca glanced up at the falling snow. He shrugged, then followed Nisa into the ancient Thorwalian building. He had seen few people, none on the streets, few in hovercrafts. For a land as populated as Nisa claimed Thorwal to be, it seemed empty.

"Where are your people?" he asked when he caught up with her.

"These are sparse times." She paused before a giant door, hesitating before she entered her code into the panel. "Our people remain in their homes, waiting for news of war. Today is grim for us. The certainty of conflict darkens us."

"Nothing is certain, Nisa."

Nisa finished her code and the doors swung inward. "You will be treated well tonight, Akandan. Perhaps my uncle will convince you where I have failed."

"I doubt his charms surpass your own, maiden, so it seems unlikely."

Nisa's chin tightened. "Maybe not, but his power exceeds mine. He can do you greater damage."

"That, too, remains to be seen."

Thorwalian guards, clad in the same white uniforms Nisa wore, stood by the entrance. The guards watched Seneca covertly, but none spoke. When the door swung open, then closed behind them, Nisa discerned their stilted whispers, but she forced herself to ignore them.

The central hall spread wide before them. Thick, fluted columns lined the passage, and arched doors led into the different offices.

Unlike the low, practical homes built by modern Thorwalians, the Chambers was a testimonial to power. The ceilings reached the height of two houses, and were decorated with fine geometric shapes.

Rather than the light replacers, the interior of the Chambers' hall was lit by sparkling crystal droplets that cast shattered light everywhere.

Intricate tapestries woven by ancient fingers hung on the walls. Long-dead kings lived in the weave, regal and grand, leading bearded, blond soldiers into battles that once defined Thorwal.

Nisa checked Seneca's expression to see if the Chambers' majesty moved him. It moved her still. But Seneca appeared unaffected.

"This is the Hall of Ancients. Here we remember the past, the conflict and struggle from which logic freed us."

"Are you free, maiden? I wonder. . . . Once your people allowed their impulses to control them. Now you control those impulses, even deny them. There is no balance."

Seneca stopped by one of the tapestries. "Yours was a violent race. And greedy."

"My ancestors weren't greedy."

Seneca's brow rose and he cast a deliberate glance at the elaborate ceiling. "They weren't sparse, either."

"No. Why should they be? They made this frozen world a temple; they used the power beneath our earth to dominate and to reform a life comfortable and pleasant for all. No one goes hungry; illness is a thing of the past. The Chambers is a testimonial to our pride, Akandan, something you know little about, I'm sure."

"To honor one's forebears, that is wisdom. To rest in their shadow, folly."

Nisa drew a strained breath, but Seneca cut her off before she could argue.

"You honor the builders, maiden, but what of your distant past?" Seneca gestured at a tapestry that depicted a violent clash of men. "Those who conquered this world weren't so tame."

"No, they weren't. They were barbarians, violent

and cruel. Only when they learned to subdue their impulses did they begin founding our real culture."

"Yet those 'barbarians' live in your soul, maiden. Anyone who has seen you and your brother at the helms of your crafts knows that."

Nisa closed her eyes and fought the desire to strike her prisoner. "It is natural," she began, her voice thin through its constricted passage, "that you would admire a barbaric origin. You are in the throes of it now, so you can't see beyond. I assure you, however, that we are vastly superior."

"War."

Nisa fought against fury, lest his point seem accurate. "That is the cause of the Dakotans and their ridiculous affection for a—"

"Vile and greedy man," finished Seneca. "A man you desired and betrayed."

"One might think you have sympathies for Motega, too. You didn't know him, Akandan, but trust me, you wouldn't find him admirable. You think we have no connection to our world? Motega was worse, I promise you. He moved too fast to see anything, he talked fast . . . and he loathed natural habitats."

Seneca's expression remained unreadable, but his eyes seemed to darken. "I would say . . . a blind man. A man who saw only what surrounded him, and nothing inside."

"On this we agree. A man who caused nothing but trouble."

Seneca touched Nisa's cheek, his fingers stroking the softness, but she pushed his hand away. "It seems to me he caused something more, at least in you."

"He had gifts with women." Nisa stepped away from Seneca. "And he used them without restraint. But I was younger then, Akandan. Today it is obvious when a man seeks to control me by such forces. I have learned to be unaffected by such primitive skills."

Seneca nodded, his face serious and thoughtful. "I

have seen that." Nisa checked his eyes for deceit. The dark depths sparkled with amusement, and a smile flickered on his lips.

"You, of course, would not understand my nature. No doubt you have misunderstood my shock at your overtures."

"I misunderstood your kiss and the fire in your blood, the way your pulse raced."

Nisa seized his arm and yanked him down the corridor. "You will maintain silence." She checked over her shoulder for onlookers. "I've endured enough gossip over Motega."

Nisa stopped in front of the last door. Her fingers pinched into Seneca's arm. "Behind this door is the council dining hall. Should you attempt to eat with your fingers, I will draw out my stun pistol and blast you from your seat."

A deep laugh rumbled in Seneca's chest. "I wouldn't think of it."

Seneca watched as Nisa cleared her expression, a forced smile on her face. She nodded to a guard, who silently pulled open the heavy door. A long table stretched from one end of the room to another, covered with silver and crystal bowls, decanters of pale liquid, and decorated with dried branches.

The bowls appeared suspiciously empty, but the guests standing by their seats were stoic and proud. Despite the size of the table, only four Thorwalians were present.

A woman stood close beside Dane. She seemed more intent on the boy than on Nisa's arrival. Carob perched on the back of Dane's seat, far more imperious than the humans.

Dane smiled at Seneca, but at a quick glance from Nisa, his face returned to the grave Thorwalian disposition. Seneca recognized Fedor from the transport vessel, a pale, slender man, but Fedor made no acknowledgment of his presence.

Nisa led Seneca to the man at the head of the table. Only a band of gold around his collar indicated his importance. "Uncle. This is the Akandan I promised you. I trust Fedor has told you of my mission's success." She didn't look at Fedor, but kept her bright eyes on her uncle.

"Fedor has told me you captured a warrior." Helmar turned to Seneca. Seneca didn't move, though he knew every muscle in Nisa's body was held tense, fearful of his reaction.

Seneca held the man's gaze steadily. Despite his aversion to the situation, he sensed no deceit or cruelty in the Thorwalian leader. Instead he sensed indecision, fear. This was a man who would react, but take no decisive action. No wonder he depended on Nisa, and was easily swayed by the hungry Fedor.

Helmar seemed uncomfortable beneath Seneca's piercing gaze. He turned to Nisa and shrugged. "His resemblance to Motega is passable. Though those . . . skins will have to go." Helmar eyed Seneca's Akandan wardrobe with distaste.

"Indeed," added Carob. "I feel like I've known some of those creatures he's wearing."

"I intend to dress him in Motega's old clothes. We gauged his size from the reflector images. I had the Dakotan material altered before I left on my mission."

"You can dress him like Motega," cut in Fedor, "but only a fool could expect this subspecies humanoid to pass for our enemy."

Nisa glared at Fedor. "I've seen no evidence that warrants calling the Akandans a subspecies, Fedor." Seneca's brow rose slightly. He felt fairly certain he'd heard her call him just that.

Helmar studied Seneca's appearance with the dispassion of a technician analyzing a fighter craft. "He's darker than Motega, and he's certainly larger. How will you explain this to the Dakotans?"

"We've fed him well!" piped in Dane.

Carob made a whistling noise. "On what? A lilt-mouse wouldn't gain weight on this mush."

The Thorwalians ignored the lingbat, but Seneca grinned. Helmar seated himself, and the others followed. Seneca sat beside Nisa, facing her brother. Helmar poured a goblet full to the brim, then held it aloft.

"We greet our guest, and welcome you to Thorwal."

The others lifted their cups, though Seneca noted that Fedor took no drink. Carob hopped onto the table and pushed his head into a cup. The woman beside Dane grimaced in disgust.

"Introduce your . . . guest, Nisa." Fedor's tone sounded mocking, and Seneca felt a wave of irritation.

Nisa pushed back her chair and rose as she faced Helmar. "This is the Akandan we located, Uncle. He is called Seneca. It is my intention to offer him to the Dakotans as Motega. He will convince them to cease their hostility, and restore to our worlds the balance that made our union great."

Carob's head popped out of the cup. "It can't get much worse."

Nisa turned to Seneca. "You have met my brother and Fedor." She glanced at the woman beside Dane. "This is Garta, head of development. She oversees the production of our fleet, and the output of our mining operations."

Garta cast her eyes across Seneca's body. She smiled, but Seneca felt as if he'd been raked by claws. He met her bold stare, and her confidence dwindled. She looked away, and returned her attention to the boy at her side.

Dane's pained expression intensified when her hand brushed his thigh. Apparently his appetite for women ended here. Though the woman was handsomely built, Seneca understood the boy's reluctance. Garta seemed more interested in devouring a man than in pleasing him.

"Please eat." Helmar cast a fond glance Garta's way,

but she didn't notice as she brushed Dane's soft hair from his furrowed brow.

Seneca leaned toward Nisa, speaking low into her ear. "There is a certain . . . comedy to your people. I will grant you that."

Nisa frowned reproachfully, but she sighed when a guard deposited a crystal bowl of barlit-meal in front of her. The Thorwalians endured a pained silence as the guard circled the table, but Helmar cleared his throat and turned the attention elsewhere.

"I understand you lost another hovercraft, Nisa. We'll have it replaced at once."

Dane set his spoon aside. "I could use a few patches also."

Carob hopped back onto Dane's shoulder. "You could use a ground-hugging tank."

"I hope you weren't injured," Garta said breathily. Her voice didn't match her angular body. But Seneca guessed it spoke more clearly of her intent.

"I can barely move without pain," Dane replied meaningfully, and Seneca chuckled.

Without enthusiasm, the Thorwalians dined on the gruel, but Seneca noticed they all drank amply from the crystal decanter. A small sip told him why. Despite its benign appearance, the liquid burned his throat like fire.

"Do you like it?" asked Nisa as she set her goblet aside. "It's Ungan wine, from the underground caverns south of the Thorwalian Sea."

"It's certainly a distraction from the meal," Seneca replied.

"I find it relaxing," added Garta, her eyes on Dane, who didn't comment.

Fedor pushed his bowl aside. "We have more pressing matters to attend, do we not, High Councillor? Nisa has brought this . . . warrior to our table for a reason, and it's not to sample our wine. Perhaps she can explain her proposal. As I have said, her logic escapes me."

Nisa's mouth twitched with irritation. "It would be my pleasure to explain again, Fedor. The logic is simple. I intend to avert an unnecessary war and Seneca can help me. Uncle, this man has astounded me. His capacity for reason is much greater than our researchers believe. His command of our language is perfect."

Helmar glanced at Fedor, whose mocking expression defied Nisa's claim. Seneca saw his opportunity to destroy Nisa's plans. He looked down into her face. He saw her eyes wide with desperate hope, saw her white teeth biting into her full lower lip. Across the table he knew Dane waited expectantly, his own life threatened by the battle Fedor desired.

There was another way, and Seneca knew it. He wanted Akando, but Akando had trained him to deal with anything. Even this. He would do his part, then return and leave this confused and fragmented world behind.

Nisa closed her eyes, and Seneca endured a moment of doubt. He could leave Thorwal, but could he leave her now, when so much remained unsure between them?

"Your niece is generous in her assessment," Seneca began quietly. "Your probes instilled a meager understanding of your civilization, which I have used to good advantage during my . . . visit."

Helmar's mouth dropped, then formed into a hopeful smile. "By all the stars, Nisa . . . You've done well."

Nisa beamed. Despite himself, Seneca took pleasure in her happiness. He would soon destroy it, but joy experienced wasn't destroyed by its ending.

"I told you, Uncle, Seneca can remake Motega! The Dakotans won't question his identity, they'll be so pleased to have him back. And Seneca is much more reasonable than Motega."

Fedor moved around the table to study the Akandan. "Since Motega was devoid of reason, that isn't difficult." Fedor turned his back to Seneca and Nisa, facing Helmar alone. "The High Councillor may see hope only because he desires hope," he continued in a smooth voice. "Nisa may have programmed this primitive man into impressive speech, but this plan was flawed from the beginning."

Helmar hesitated, looking between Nisa and Fedor, trying to select between two strong-willed minds the proper course. "Uncle, how many will die if we don't try? Do you want that?"

Helmar glanced at Dane, who waited bright eyed for his own fate. Seneca studied the boy. He saw no fear, just curiosity. A slow chill of admiration touched his heart.

In the thin boy's face, he saw a shadow of another time, when young warriors raced heedless into battle, then sang songs of conquest, thrilling to life at every turn. That was the Thorwalian soul. But it wasn't staid and reasonable. The true soul of Thorwal was founded in courage.

Seneca turned his gaze to Nisa. She faced her uncle with as much determination as a Thorwalian shield maiden, ready to fight, to forge the future she wanted. Her good sense and foresight might be lacking, but her innate courage wasn't.

For a fleeting moment Seneca longed to aid her in her quest, to set right her world by lending it victory. He could mimic Motega, convince the Dakotans to yield to Thorwal's dominance. But by doing so, he would lose his own soul.

"Your debate is well considered." The others looked to him, waiting expectantly. "There is one thing you have failed to consider."

"What's that?" asked Nisa, a flicker of fear in her eyes.

"I will not do as you ask."

Nisa groaned, then drew an angry breath. "Curse you!"

A thin smile formed on Fedor's crooked mouth. "His defiance may indeed prove our undoing."

"His defiance can be . . . tempered." Helmar's jaw set with unusual resolve. "The mind probe—"

"No! That's not necessary, Uncle. I'm sure if Seneca has time to reconsider . . ."

"There is no time, Nisa. The Dakotans have massed their fighting craft outside their own orbit. They are moving this way now. For this reason Fedor has mobilized our own forces."

Nisa grabbed Seneca's arm. "Please." It was unlike her to beg, and her plaintive face touched his heart. He touched her hand gently.

"I cannot."

"Ready him," said Helmar. "Take him to the holding cell and assemble the probe equipment." He turned to Seneca and, this time, met his gaze without flinching.

"This is not my desire, Akandan. You seem a worthy being, one who, in another time, would live a full life. Our need is greater. That is all I will say."

"That is all you need say." Seneca felt no anger, no bitterness. His own reaction surprised him.

"Your mind will be emptied," Helmar continued, his face impassive. "After that I will implant the suggestions myself, so no tampering will occur. You will not believe that you are Motega, as that could work against our purposes. You will know that you work for our ends."

"I understand your purposes," said Seneca. "My own have not changed."

Dane rose from his seat. "Our victory will be tainted by this deed, Helmar."

Helmar smiled, but his eyes were sad. "You are young. Not all decisions have easy answers."

"But often answers lie hidden in unexpected places," said Dane. "Isn't that saying engraved on every coin? Surely this refers to more than the secrets of science and technology?"

"We have no time. Take him."

Nisa touched his arm, tears glittering in her desperate, wide eyes. "Seneca, you'll lose everything. You won't remember Akando, your family. If you'll change your mind and agree, this won't be necessary."

"I cannot."

Dane came to stand beside her. "War might be preferable to such a dishonorable solution."

"One man's life," Helmar said with a sigh, "against a whole country. Two countries. This is necessary. I have accepted your solution, Nisa. Let it be done. I will say no more of it."

Fedor's mocking expression had darkened into something unfathomable. He desired war. Why? Seneca couldn't guess, but uneasiness flooded his soul. More was at stake than the Thorwalians revealed. Fedor wanted more than victory over a defiant neighbor. That much seemed certain.

Helmar motioned to the guards. "Put the Akandan in the holding cell. It will take a few hours to assemble the equipment," he added to Seneca. "I suggest you use the time to reconsider."

Seneca said nothing as Helmar left the dining hall. The guards positioned themselves on either side of him, but both appeared nervous. They held stun pistols and glanced uncertainly toward Fedor.

"Do as the councillor commanded," said Fedor. Seneca wondered why Fedor's permission was needed after Helmar's instructions. But apparently the Thorwalian guards responded to Helmar's second-in-command before their leader.

He looked to where Nisa stood, her face white, her blue eyes wide. She had abducted him, brought him to this, yet he felt no anger. She thought she had no choice. A slow understanding grew in Seneca's heart. Maybe she had believed that all along.

The guards surrounded Seneca, and Nisa fought tears. He didn't fight as Motega fought, seven years before. He didn't curse her, nor vow revenge, as Motega had done. He seemed calm, peaceful as always.

Nisa didn't know what more to say, when Seneca appeared immovable. Dane took her hand as the guards gestured for Seneca to leave.

"This isn't what I wanted, Seneca."

He stopped and looked into her eyes. "I know that, maiden. But this is what you created for your efforts. Your risk was taken, and lost. If you didn't realize the cost when you set out to capture me, know now. It is better to know truth than to deny it, even when it causes pain."

Seneca turned and left with the guards. Nisa stood frozen beside her brother, tears streaming down her cheeks. Dane squeezed her hand. "He may change his mind. There's still time."

"He will never change his mind. It's not in his nature."

Dane didn't argue. "He may recover, then, after a time. We haven't studied the effects of the probe over long periods. At least it may be possible to relearn something of what he was."

"He isn't what I expected."

"No," agreed Dane. "I didn't have much hope our plan would work, but he could have done it. Your Seneca is the man Motega should have been."

Nisa looked at her brother. He was right. Her attraction to Seneca wasn't to the past, but to what might have been. To what still might be, if he weren't so stubborn, so determined to return to his primitive world.

"You always liked Motega. I've never asked you why."

Dane smiled. "It wasn't the easiest subject to bring up in your company."

"His memory is painful."

"I know. And I know he hurt you, Nisa. I suppose my memory is flawed. I was only a boy when he died. But I remember him fondly. He let me ride in his shuttle, if you remember." Dane sighed. "He was an amazing pilot."

"He distracted you from your studies. That is what I remember." Nisa couldn't help smiling. "Motega had no sense of responsibility."

"That's why I liked him," said Dane. "Sometimes I think we have too much."

"Sometimes I think so, too."

Chapter Four

Nisa returned alone to her small house. Dane had gone to visit friends at the Snow Port Tavern, Carob in reluctant tow. Nisa suspected her brother used the lingbat to lure women.

She stood in the central room, beneath fading light replacers, gazing out her glass wall toward the Chambers. There Seneca sat alone in a holding cell, waiting to have his mind ripped from him. Because of her.

She closed her eyes, seeing his face when she had first captured him. Surprise, even astonishment, but no fear. He faced everything that way, with the reason she claimed to possess herself.

Here, in the darkness of her small, unadorned room, Nisa knew she wasn't reasonable. She was desperate. She loved her stoic people; she loved her brother. She couldn't imagine the order of her world being torn asunder by war. So Seneca was the sacrifice, by no choice of his own.

Nisa turned from the window. A globe, a miniature

of her solar system, moved endlessly on a stand. Nisa watched it. Perfect unison, even to the small version of Akando that moved in and out toward the Day Sun.

There, farthest from a gaseous giant, moved the Candor Moon. The Dawn Star to the Akandans. Tiny, seemingly without power or value. Yet the cause of it all. Traces of vast riches, signs of a small but advanced civilization . . . these things tempted greedy men like Fedor. Despite all she thought she knew of him, they had tempted Motega, too.

Seneca wouldn't value riches. She had failed him. Why was he so stubborn? She had promised to return him to Akando. Perhaps he didn't believe her. Nisa considered the matter. What more could she say?

"I'll think of it when I get there." Before she realized what she intended, Nisa had seized her uniform jacket and headed for the door. She picked up her hovercraft controls, then remembered Dane's collision. With a reluctant sigh, she opened the door and headed toward the Chambers on foot.

When Nisa reached the Chambers' entrance, she realized she hadn't walked even this short distance since she was a child. Perhaps Seneca had a point. She was panting and her legs ached from the exertion. Before entering her code, she took several deep breaths and fanned her cheeks, despite the cold night air.

All around, the city of Thorwal was silent, watchful. Tense. By tomorrow every young pilot and technician might be loaded onto transport shuttles and given battlecraft. Men and women who knew more about building the vessels than flying them would risk their lives in an attempt to stop the Dakotans' advance.

"No. It will not happen. This is my world, and it won't happen."

Nisa marched into the Great Hall, passed several guards without acknowledgment, and made her way to the holding cell. Three Thorwalians stood guard at Seneca's door.

"Open the door," she commanded. The guards fidgeted.

"Fedor has given us strict instructions."

"When has Fedor's word superseded my own?" Nisa's voice trembled with warning. "This man is my prisoner, and I will see him. Now."

The guards exchanged doubtful looks, but one shrugged and opened the door. "Thank you," she said in an icy voice. "I trust this . . . misunderstanding won't happen again. You will take your leave, and leave the door unguarded until I call for you. Is that understood?"

Without waiting for a reply Nisa entered the dark room. Seneca lay on his back, his eyes closed, his features immobile. In this room Motega had been held captive. In this room she had taunted him, then found him dead.

Part of her had died then, too. But as she watched Seneca, his serene beauty pierced her heart. She felt life and desire awaken. She didn't welcome the change, but it was beyond her power to control. She couldn't lose him, too.

Seneca turned his head and looked at her. A slow smile grew on his face as he sat up. He looked powerful, broad shouldered and strong, his dark hair falling loose around his face, his eyes glinting in the darkness.

"I hoped I would see you again." His voice sounded lower than normal, seductive. Nisa gulped.

"You misunderstand my presence. I came to try again to convince you. You don't know what the probes can do."

"Don't I? I thought your uncle gave a very detailed description of the effect."

Tears formed in her eyes. Nisa willed them away. "You won't be the same."

"Why does it matter to you? I will do your bidding, thus weakened, maiden."

"There's no need!" Nisa caught her emotion and fought against it. She stepped toward him. "All you need do is convince the Dakotans that you're Motega, that he's all right. Settle them down. They're a very high-strung people, but they don't want war."

"They want a dead man. A man who is gone forever."

"We'll send you back to Akando afterward, I swear." Nisa stopped. She didn't want him to go back to Akando. "If that's what you want."

"What I want . . . what a man wants isn't always in his best interest." Seneca paused. "There is one thing I ask of you."

"What?"

"My pack. The contents within have great value to me, and to Akando."

"It will go with you, even if you forget." Nisa's voice cracked, her head bowed. "I won't forget."

"I know."

"I don't want to hurt you, Seneca." Her voice was a whispered plea. "Helmar doesn't want that, either. But we're desperate."

"Do you know what you ask of me?"

"I'm asking you to save yourself, to save a world."

"And if I do?"

"We'll all return to the way we were."

Seneca shook his head. "You ask me to betray my soul. I prefer to undergo your probes than to do that. Do you understand, Nisa? My honor means more to me than my life. For a life without honor has no value."

He wouldn't yield. Nisa knew that now. His primitive code of honor would be his destruction, but it was her fault. She had abducted him and forced him into a decision between life and honor.

Nisa's grief sank her to her knees in front of him.

She touched his legs, looking up at him, her face wet with tears. "I'm sorry. It seemed the only way. But I never meant to hurt you."

"I know." Seneca touched her hair. "Do I misunderstand your presence, maiden? I wonder. . . ." Nisa wanted to stop him, but she couldn't move or speak. "Could it be that you desire to be near me, while I'm still a man of my own free will, just once?"

"What vanity!" She struggled from her knees and stood, her hands on her hips.

Seneca smiled as he, too, rose from his bedding. "If these are my last hours as a man, I would spend them wisely. I can think of nothing more pleasurable than spending them with you."

"You might better consider your fate than waste time flattering me."

"We waste time in speech, you and I."

Nisa's temper flared. "It is your choice, wortpig! If you want to become brain-dead, I can't stop you." She swung around, aiming for the door, but Seneca caught her arm and drew her back.

The motion of his body was clean and Nisa wasn't sure how she ended up in his arms, pressed against him. "What do you think you're—"

Seneca's mouth came down on hers, warm and demanding. Nisa's thoughts fled as his tongue swept to taste her lips. Her mouth parted beneath his, allowing him sensual entrance. Seneca broke the kiss and ran his thumb across her cheek.

"Do you know how beautiful you are, Nisa? I wonder if you ever see yourself."

With strong, purposeful hands, Seneca turned Nisa in his arms. He faced her toward a tall mirror, standing close behind her. "Look."

Nisa saw her reflected image, but embarrassment coursed through her. "I look the same as always."

"Look deeper." Seneca's deft fingers slid through her hair, releasing the soft, pale length from its restrictive

103

binding. Its thick mass fell around her shoulders, reaching the swell of her breast like a coiled river.

"Here," he whispered as his fingers ran along the golden strand. His touch left her hair to run across her breast. Nisa stared, spellbound, as he unfastened her jacket, easing it back from her shoulders and dropping it to the floor behind them.

His hands cupped her shoulders, then slid down her arms, returning to the snaps of her bodice. Nisa couldn't breathe as the snaps opened, as his fingers grazed her bare skin. She trembled when he slid back the cool fabric to reveal the cleft of her breasts.

Nisa closed her eyes as Seneca bent to kiss her neck. Her head tilted to the side as his lips played against her soft flesh. "Watch," he commanded, his voice low and soft and irresistible.

Nisa saw her reflection; she watched as if it happened to another woman, a woman unable to restrain her passion. Seneca slid her bodice back, freeing her breasts to his touch.

"Do you see?" he murmured as his hands cupped their fullness. "Dark upon light."

Nisa couldn't answer. The fire consumed her. As he cupped her breasts, Seneca's thumbs grazed her tender nipples, bringing them into hard peaks against his touch. She heard the low groan in his throat; she felt his restraint as he teased her flesh.

"My flesh and yours, maiden. The wind upon the snow. Do you feel the fire beneath?"

His lips brushed against her neck, and she turned her head to receive his kiss. His tongue played at the corner of her lips, and Nisa's body turned to liquid fire. She felt his male length, hard and engorged against her bottom. She pressed back against him to increase the sweet torment.

Seneca slid his hand from her bare breast up her throat to cup her chin. His kiss intensified as his other hand slid between the sensitized tips, arousing one, then the other. Nisa squirmed against him. Nothing, no one, not even Motega, had ever made her feel this way.

Nothing else mattered. Sweet delirium overwhelmed her, left her powerless. She would surrender, give him one night of passion. What came after meant nothing.

Nisa tried to turn in his arms, but Seneca held her back to him. "Watch."

She was shaking, but she did as he asked. While her eyes fixed on her own image, Seneca pushed her bodice down to her waist. He circled her breast with one finger, a light touch that left her pulse racing.

"Here is majesty," he told her as his hand slid across her soft stomach. "Here is the sweetest power. Do you see, maiden? Where I touch you, you are fire."

Nisa watched as his hand slid to her waistband, unfastened her belt, then slid beneath the fabric, lower. She leaned back against him as his fingers found the soft curls between her legs, as he delved beneath and found the moist result of her desire.

Nisa felt Seneca's body quiver as his finger moved and teased. She felt his desire as it penetrated her and fanned her to a brighter flame. His hands shook as he dropped her uniform to her feet.

Her pale skin gleamed in the dim light. Seneca's hands slid up her thighs, over the flare of her bottom, cupping her waist. She knew when he freed himself behind her. She remembered his powerful, naked body as she had seen him on the *Gordonia*.

Desire throbbed in her veins. "Watch," he breathed in her ear.

Nisa felt him bend behind her; she felt his hard, slick male organ probing between her thighs. She ached for the forgotten sensation of a man's entrance. Primitive yearning took command of her, and she heard herself moan as he slid back and forth against her.

Nisa shuddered with fiery pleasure. She reached down and touched the tip of him, cupping him against her as her breath caught in fierce desire. Seneca groaned at her touch; he grasped her waist and lifted her to her toes as he sought access to her inner depths.

As her hand circled him in a demanding caress, her other arm stretched back to his neck. She caught his hair in her fingers as she turned her face to kiss him.

She felt his erection poised against her, swollen and hard, caressed by her own liquid warmth. She felt the pressure of his entrance, the hot, thick promise of satisfaction, just beyond her control.

The image of their entwined bodies flickered at the corner of her vision, a wild scene imprinted forever in her mind. Her pulse throbbed in her ears, mingled with the sound of his deep, full breaths and her swift gasps. Soft, primal noises escaped her lips; low guttural moans of urging rumbled in his throat.

They would fly. . . . A sharp, toneless buzz sounded outside Seneca's door. Nisa jerked away from Seneca, her eyes wide with shock and passion. Seneca calmly adjusted his Akandan tunic and leggings while Nisa struggled with her fallen uniform.

The door slid open as her shaking fingers did the snaps of her bodice. "We're ready for you . . . Akandan." Helmar's words faded when he saw Nisa. Helmar's brow furrowed doubtfully, and Nisa cringed.

"I didn't expect you here, Nisa."

"Your niece attempted to influence my decision," Seneca broke in. "She failed." Seneca paused, a veiled smile on his lips. "But it was a good attempt."

Nisa's lips twitched in irritation and embarrassment. "If my prisoner has no better sense than to surrender his brain, I cannot be held responsible." A good attempt, indeed! Seneca made light of their passion. Fine. So be it. It would be easier to let him go knowing his emotion for her had no weight.

Seneca touched her shoulder. "If your probes can

leave me with one memory . . ."

He was grinning. Careless, still teasing. Nisa shoved his hand away. "The probe isn't selective. You will be a shell, filled only with Thorwalian suggestion. But it's your choice."

"The night wanes," said Helmar. "When the morning breaks, I would have a shuttle on its way to Dakota. The Dakotan fleet has amassed on the far side of their planet. We will alert them to 'Motega's' return. When they have abandoned their vessels, we will send his replacement to their main city."

Helmar faced Seneca. "I offer you one last chance, Akandan. Join our effort, and I will spare you the mind probe."

"I will not make a promise to you I must later break. The mind probe is preferable."

"So be it." Helmar turned to the assembled guards. "Take him."

Nisa didn't understand Seneca's comment. It implied something, something she couldn't comprehend. It was almost as if his honor extended to the Thorwalians who intended to destroy his mind.

"Seneca . . ."

Seneca laid his finger to her lips and she closed her eyes. "Fate unfolds beyond our control, maiden. You still fight the currents that carry you. I fought once, too. But I learned that there is much we can't know until it happens. It takes courage to accept the unknown and allow it to unfold as it will. Courage, Nisa, is one thing you have in abundance."

Nisa looked up at him. Again she saw no fear. Nisa hated the unknown. It betrayed her at every turn. But when Seneca turned and left with the guards, she knew all her attempts to control the situation had failed.

Nisa sat alone outside the Chambers' lab, her head bowed, her loose hair around her face. A low pain throbbed behind her eyes.

"What's taking so long? I thought your barbarian would be speed-talking and twitching like Motega by now."

Nisa startled at Carob's chirping voice. Dane clasped his hand over the lingbat's mouth, then glanced sympathetically at Nisa. Dane sat beside her, and Carob settled on the back of the bench.

"He didn't change his mind," guessed Dane.

"No." Nisa leaned her head against her brother's shoulder, and Dane wrapped his arm around her. Nisa sniffed. "Did you have a good time at the Snow Port?" She didn't want to think about Seneca. It was too late. It was done by now.

Dane appeared uncomfortable. "It was a quiet evening, a few drinks, conversation. . . ."

Carob cleared his throat loudly. "Meaning he used his imminent demise to garner a lot more than conversation. I spent the whole night hanging from a light replacer."

Nisa's eyes narrowed while Dane blushed. "It might be my last night."

"Dane!"

"Humans never choose the easy route," noted Carob. "Why can't you just tell the female you want to mate? Why all the tricks and twists? And another thing, if you want offspring that badly, why do you use those—"

Dane grasped Carob by the neck and stuffed him in his pocket, then smiled weakly. "At least I'm responsible."

"If that's what you call it," added a muffled voice from inside his jacket.

Nisa considered lecturing her brother, but her heart wasn't in the reproach, so she fell silent instead. Dane sat quietly, too, grateful for the reprieve.

Long moments dragged by while they waited. The lab door slid open and the guards walked out, heading back to their tasks. Nisa's breath was held. Even Carob said nothing.

Helmar appeared, stone faced and resigned. Fedor accompanied him with Seneca at his side. A quick, pained glance told her that Seneca wore Motega's altered clothing. Dark green loosely fitting fabric. His hair fell to his shoulders, the Akandan shells still in place in the dark braid. An oversight, but one she had no heart to correct.

Nisa couldn't make herself look at him further. He was alive, but empty. Destroyed by her own hand.

Helmar removed his lab coat and tossed it on the bench beside Nisa. "It is done."

Dane hesitated, waiting for Nisa to speak. She didn't. "How did it go? Is he . . . all right?"

Helmar glanced at Seneca. "The whole process was slow. I'm not sure why. The machination must have been sluggish, but it seems to have been effective. My suggestions implanted perfectly. His responses are correct."

Nisa endured a wave of guilt so strong that she thought she might vomit. How could she look at him now, knowing his condition was her fault? How could she not? Seneca would expect her to face the results of her actions.

Her head felt like a weight on her neck, but she forced her gaze to Seneca. He didn't look at her. He stared blankly ahead at nothing. No light twinkled in his eyes. But Nisa saw something deeper. An unconquered soul. He had left this shell, but his true being remained untarnished.

She rose wearily from her seat and went to him, touching his arm. "Seneca . . . I am sorry."

He didn't respond, though his eyes moved to her, revealing no emotion, no thought. Like a machine. "Do we leave now?" he asked. He sounded robotic. Nisa's stomach clenched and she turned away.

"The shuttle is prepared," said Fedor. "It is time to

send a message to the Dakotans. I have our radar set to monitor their progress and reaction. I would also suggest proceeding with our fighter-craft launching, in case this plan falters."

Helmar nodded. "Keep them in a close orbit, Fedor. I want no misunderstandings from the Dakotans. As soon as they withdraw, I want our craft returned to port."

"Does that mean we still report in?" asked Dane. He sounded eager, despite the danger.

"You're on the lead transport, Commander." Nisa heard Fedor's mocking tone, and her anger churned. He meant to destroy her brother. Why, she wasn't sure, but she knew it was true. How a boy as young as Dane could threaten Fedor wasn't certain.

Nisa kissed her brother's face. "Take care."

"Where will you be, Nisa?" he asked.

"Nisa will stay with me," said Helmar. "As my adviser."

Nisa shook her head. "No, Helmar. My duty is elsewhere. I will go to Dakota with Seneca."

Fedor unexpectedly supported her. "That seems wise to me, also. We need someone to oversee the Akandan's progress. He was thoroughly programmed, I know, but he may need . . . prodding."

Helmar hesitated. "I don't like to leave you at the mercy of the Dakotans, not at this early stage. Your sense of order will be missed."

Nisa met her uncle's eyes steadily. "I will see peace restored. And when Dakota is once again our ally, I will return this man to his world."

"He won't survive on Akando now, not in this condition," Helmar warned.

"That was his wish. I will honor it."

Helmar didn't argue. Nisa wouldn't accept argument, anyway. "As you wish, Nisa. Your plan may have saved Thorwal from bitter chaos. For now, that is all that matters."

*   *   *

Nisa sat in the shuttle beside Seneca. As she promised, she carefully placed his Akandan pack in his lap. He let it slip to the floor, and her heart twisted. Nisa picked up the pack and tied it around her own waist.

Tranor again took the helm, but no one else accompanied them on the short journey to Dakota. Tranor set the coordinates for Dakota, then contacted the Thorwalian command.

"We're set to go," he told Nisa. "The Dakotans have withdrawn."

Nisa sighed. She knew they would. The slightest hope of Motega's return would be enough. Tranor guided the shuttle from the spaceport, then spun in his seat to observe Seneca.

"What about his hair? It's too long."

"We'll say he grew it long in defiance. They expect eccentricity from their leader. They won't care about his hair."

"He's not so intimidating now, is he?" noted Tranor. He seemed pleased, but Nisa looked at the navigator in disgust.

"I don't recall any intimidation. You were the one holding the stun rifle."

"There's no telling what a primitive creature like that will do when cornered." Tranor turned back moodily to his controls.

Nisa laughed, a short laugh without humor. "After what we've done to him, I'd think he could say the same about us."

Nisa stared through the viewport as Dakota's green shape came into view. Thorwal gleamed white and blue, farther beyond the smaller planet. The two planets were juxtaposed together against the black, endless space. Far beyond, Nisa's sharp eyes caught another light. A small speck just at the range of her vision.

The Dawn Star, the Candor Moon. Nisa saw in the moon something she'd lost. Beyond the strife of her planet, beyond Akando, there lay other worlds, mysterious. Possibly dangerous, but beyond. Beyond the known lay the unknown. And that was filled with endless possibility.

A peculiar contentment wrapped itself around Nisa's heart and she settled back into her seat.

"Entering orbit," announced Tranor. Nisa didn't respond. Tranor made contact with the Dakotan frequency and transmitted a code announcing their arrival.

"Set for landing," he told Nisa. She said nothing. "Don't expect any problems now. Do you suppose they'll have a celebration on his arrival?"

Nisa eyed Tranor doubtfully. "I don't think the Dakotans know how to celebrate. They'll probably tell him all their latest advances, take him into the research facilities, and fill him in on their new developments."

Tranor shrugged. "No wonder Motega preferred Thorwal."

Nisa couldn't argue. "The Dakotans are terribly nervous, but they don't do much for fun. I think that's why they eat so much."

Tranor chuckled. "Well, maybe we'll get a meal out of it, anyway."

A dark green haze filled the viewport as Tranor lowered the shuttle toward the Dakotan surface. Unlike Thorwal, thick, full trees grew in abundance on Dakota, and the Dakotans had done little to develop their world other than to construct research facilities.

Thorwalian wisdom taught that their Dakotan neighbors had no need for construction or tampering with their environment. Dakota was temperate and pleasant, so they needed little shelter. Thorwalians considered them soft, and they were, but their brains were agile and sharp.

112

No one, even the Dakotans, understood how they evolved on a planet that had almost no animal life. Though plants grew in rapid abundance, animals were limited to fish and birds and minor reptiles and amphibians. Humanoid existence here was the oldest mystery in Dakotan culture.

Tranor navigated low over the Dakotan landscape. Small dwellings dotted the land. Unlike Thorwalians, Dakotans lived evenly dispersed across their fertile land. There were no uninhabited areas, no cities. The main inhabited area was called Macanoc, its importance arising solely because of its large and secretive research lab.

Dakotan leaders lived sprawled across the land, reaching Macanoc easily in swift land-shuttles, but no major habitation had grown up because of the location. Nisa had traveled to Dakota only once, as Motega's guest.

She remembered her visit as a passionate blur. They barely left his home. Her only clear memory was of his large bed, and the displeasure of the Dakotan women over Motega's attention.

Nisa's gaze wandered reluctantly to Seneca. His eyes fixed dully on the viewport, he didn't see her, nor care that she sat beside him. *I have loved two men, and destroyed them both.*

No, she couldn't love Seneca. He stirred her soul, he restored her passion, but that was over now. Her pulse moved slowly again; her heart beat without power.

The best she could do would be to honor her word and send him, one day, back to Akando. For now, to honor her promise to her people was all that kept her going.

"What the—" Tranor's sharp voice was cut off when a violent thrust jerked the shuttle upward, then back. Nisa started to rise from her seat, but the blast came again, and she stumbled back.

"What's that?"

"Those treacherous devils are firing." Tranor struggled with the controls, fighting to steady the shuttle.

"Land! Quickly, Tranor. This craft isn't designed to withstand battle!"

Tranor's pale flesh drained of all color. "I know."

Nisa moved to steady Seneca, but he seemed oblivious to the attack. For a moment her eyes fixed on his vacant face, still beautiful, but devoid of the inner passion that drove him before the mind probe.

Nisa saw an orange flash as another blast struck the viewport. The outer shell cracked and shattered; a fire burst from an enclosed engine. Another blast followed close behind, penetrating the inner hull. Tranor's scream was cut off. Nisa saw him fall forward, then slump lifeless to the floor.

She should panic; she should be terrified. Instead Nisa felt numb. As if she had died when she had allowed Seneca to be destroyed. Nisa sat back in her seat, then reached for Seneca's hand. It felt cold in hers, as if his pulse nearly stopped. He seemed to be asleep, though his eyes remained open.

She saw him, dark with passion in the holding cell, forcing her to witness her own desire, her own primitive beauty. She remembered the taut energy in his body as he brought her to fire.

"I'm sorry I didn't make love with you," she whispered. "I have been such a fool."

A blast rocked the plummeting shuttle, but Nisa steeled herself against death. She heard the wall crunching in, but she didn't move as it crumbled around her. Something struck her; her thoughts scrambled, then fled. Her last awareness was Seneca's hand pulled from her own.

Popping noises permeated Nisa's brain. *I'm not dead.* How could that be? She felt dazed, unable to open her eyes or to move. She couldn't have survived that crash. Her last memory was of small trees a great distance away as the shuttle dove downward, no one manning its shattered helm.

She smelled smoke, burning metal. She felt strong hands on her shoulder, slipping beneath her. Lifting her. Nisa's eyes opened. She saw Seneca's face, his dark hair behind his head, crowned by the green canopy of Dakota's rich forest.

Nisa stared at him in disbelief as he bounded from the crash site. She felt his power as he ran from the burning shuttle.

"Put me down!"

Seneca dropped to the earth, holding her close, covering her with his body. A tremendous explosion rocked the earth. Debris flew and crashed around them. Several smaller explosions followed, then stillness as the smoke and dust cleared.

"Get this blood-ox off me!" Carob squirmed from beneath Seneca's chest, then huffed indignantly.

Seneca released Nisa, rising to his feet in his familiar, clean motion. Nisa propped herself up and stared at him suspiciously. This wasn't the vacant, emptied man on the shuttle.

"I've told myself again and again, never fly with a Thorwalian at the helm."

The lingbat's complaints distracted Nisa from Seneca's confusing behavior. "Carob! What are you doing here?"

Carob hopped from between them and flapped his frail wings. "I had a choice," he said between gasps. "Either join your brother while he tries to pilot a battleship, or come along and see you make fools of the Dakotans. Well, which would you choose?"

"Right now, Dane's flying seems safer," said Nisa. "So you came with Seneca?"

Carob shrugged a small shoulder. "Figured he wouldn't notice, being mindless and all." He hopped around Nisa to study the crash site. "Tranor didn't make it, eh?"

115

The lingbat's chirping voice betrayed regret, even sorrow. Nisa realized that his feelings were softer than his words. "No, Carob. He died in the first blasts." Nisa helped Carob to her shoulder, patting his round head gently. Carob seemed embarrassed by her sympathy.

"So how'd we land?" he asked in a gruff voice. "Your Akandan moved so fast, I couldn't tell what was going on in that shuttle."

Nisa glanced at Seneca. "He moved?" She made herself sit up and shook her head to clear her battered senses.

Seneca glanced back at her, but he seemed intent on the dark forest, watching it as if beasts might emerge. "Are you hurt? Is anything broken?" He spoke casually, as if he knew she was fine.

"I'm very sore." Nisa struggled to her feet. She swayed, and Seneca caught her arm to steady her. His attention was still fixed on the forest beyond the crashed shuttle.

"How did we land?" Nisa paused. "And why are you . . ."

"Uh-oh," muttered Carob. His claws dug into Nisa's shoulder.

Green-clad figures moved in the forest, like shadows, from tree to tree. Nisa's heart jumped to her throat, snapping her suspicions from her thoughts. "Who are—"

"Down!" Seneca moved so fast Nisa barely saw him. She found herself on her side, crumpled beside him. "Don't move! Whatever happens, stay here, don't move. They're not looking for you."

Seneca moved from her, but Nisa seized his arm. "Where are you going?" she hissed as panic began to overtake her ravaged senses.

"Stay here."

"Good idea." Carob's voice sounded even higher than ever.

Seneca disappeared into the forest behind her, moving in the shadows with astonishing stealth. Nisa couldn't see him; she had no idea what he was doing. Despite his instructions, she peeked through the brambles to sight the Dakotan warriors.

There, picking through the shuttle rubble, she saw several well-armed men. They wore the traditional Dakotan green outfit: a short-sleeved top, belted around the middle, loose trousers. Something seemed wrong.

These were thin, slight men. Not the round, clumsy figures she remembered from nearly every Dakotan she'd seen.

One of the men shook his head, then looked beyond the crash site. Looking for Seneca. And for her. One man turned her way, then called to the others.

Nisa ducked, but her heart slammed against the moist, fragrant earth.

"Wonderful," groaned Carob. "I'll be in the dissecting cart for sure."

"There!" shouted a Dakotan. Nisa couldn't help herself. She looked up in time to see Seneca bounding over the crash, toward his enemies. Nisa's mouth opened. Those men bore rifles set to kill; one carried a heavy Nebulon torch.

The rifles fired, whisking close to Seneca, but his motion seemed fluid. He seemed to dodge before they fired, drawing closer. His body worked in perfect precision as his limbs moved, slicing back to knock a rifle from one Dakotan, then swinging under to dislodge another.

In the space of a second, two men lay stunned on the ground. The Nebulon torch fired not three steps from Seneca, a great streak of burning plasma that roared with evil life. The same vile weapon that had destroyed Motega in his cell. Nisa couldn't make herself look.

A surprised grunt and subsequent thud told her the torch's aim went wild. Nisa opened her eyes. Seneca knocked the torch-wielding Dakotan to the ground.

Nisa had no idea how he moved that way, how his limbs worked in fluid unison. But even the advanced weaponry seemed unmatched to his power.

You aren't a warrior, she thought. You are an artist. His dark hair flew as his strong body dodged and pivoted, as he swung backward to disarm another attacker. For a brief flash Nisa thought he might succeed. But her hope died when another Dakotan patrol appeared at the edge of the crash site.

"He's done for, now," muttered Carob.

Nisa couldn't stand it. She had to do something.

"What do you think you're doing?" squeaked Carob as Nisa leaped to her feet and ran toward Seneca. "Put me down!"

Nisa ignored the bat as he clung to her shoulder. She couldn't leave Seneca to die alone. "Seneca!" she cried. "Look out! Behind you, more!"

Seneca whirled, then paused as he assessed the latecomers. Then, to Nisa's surprise, he turned his back to them, poised to defend himself against the remaining onslaught of the first patrol.

To Nisa's astonishment, the second patrol just gaped at Seneca. They seemed shocked. When he leaped through the air, both feet striking his opponent, an enthusiastic cheer rang from the Dakotan onlookers. "Deiaquande! Motega!"

Nisa's blood stirred. They recognized their leader, or thought they did. Her tension eased. Surely the first patrol would realize their error and lay down their weapons. But the wild cry seemed to stir Seneca's enemies into a greater fury.

The rifles fired in rapid precision, met by a hasty and ill-aimed counterassault from the defenders. Seneca leaped from the cross fire, watched his allies for a moment, then glanced toward the sky. Nisa felt sure he sighed in dismay.

"Now *those*," said Carob, "are Dakotans."

The defenders seemed to have no idea how to operate their weapons. Some even fumbled with the dials. One fiddled madly with his rifle, pointed, and fired a stun blast into the man beside him.

Nisa groaned. These were Dakotans. All overweight, excitable, and totally without sense.

Nisa darted around behind them, seized a rifle, and aimed at Seneca's attackers. "She's Thorwalian!" shouted the man who had stunned the other. Before Nisa could fire, the chubby man knocked her rifle away and grabbed her wrist.

"Let me go, you idiot! He needs help."

Nisa squirmed and tried to free herself, but the Dakotan held her fast. "Set him up again, didn't you? Well, we've got you now!"

It took two Dakotans to hold her back. Seneca had disarmed all but one of the attackers. The last dropped his rifle, and Nisa breathed a sigh of relief.

"Looks like we've got prisoners!" announced her captor.

"As if you'd know what to do with them," Nisa retorted fiercely.

"I don't think so." Carob made a whistling noise. "Better get your primate out of there."

Nisa's eyes widened in horror. The last attacker drew out a self-timed bomb, then pulled the release valve. Seneca wouldn't know his danger. . . . The blast would send everything around the bomb to tiny fragments. The bodies, the attacker . . . and Seneca.

The Dakotans recognized their enemy's intent. "Deiaquande! Get out of there!"

"Seneca!" Nisa's shrill voice reached him, but Seneca was already running and bounding from the battle site. He threw himself to the ground just as the bomb exploded.

The Dakotans ducked while debris flew through the air, but Nisa strained to see through the dust. Seneca moved like the wind, but the blast was widespread.

The cloud cleared; the dust settled. The enemy

patrol, defeated by Seneca, lay murdered by their own comrade. Little trace remained. A shallow hole gaped where the grenade had exploded, a self-made burial.

Seneca appeared beyond the blast site, tall and strong and unharmed. Nisa's relief sank her to her knees. The Dakotans tossed their rifles into the air in excitement, but most failed to catch them as the weapons fell back. One man was struck on the head for his efforts.

"Don't know how they ever caught me," commented Carob.

Nisa laughed. The relief of tension left her trembling, her emotions raw and bursting. Seneca walked toward them, picking his way through the rubble. He stopped to look at his fallen enemies, then turned away as if their deaths caused him pain.

"Sen—" In a cool, sick flash, Nisa remembered her purpose on Dakota. The drama of her arrival had driven reality from her mind, but this man wasn't Seneca. He was programmed for a task, a task to save her world. Her heart sank.

"Motega!" The Dakotans forgot about her as they gathered around their beloved leader.

Carob dusted himself off. "Looks like it worked. Although it doesn't take much to fool a Dakotan."

Nisa didn't respond. She made herself join them, to back up Seneca's story if need be. The leader of the patrol flung his arms around Seneca, then dropped to his knees, weeping.

"You're alive. It seems impossible."

"Your leader is gone."

The Dakotans quieted, round faces puckered doubtfully. Nisa's mouth dropped open. "No . . ."

The chubby leader rose to his feet and clasped Seneca's shoulder. "Motega . . ."

"I am not Motega."

"What have they done to you, that you should deny

your name? You know me; I am Manipi, head of bio-technical development."

"Motega was the target of assassination during his imprisonment on Thorwal, seven years ago. As the High Councillor's niece can verify."

Nisa boiled with anger. He had betrayed her! Somehow he had resisted the mind probes, all the while planning to betray her. She remembered his clever seduction, all done knowing . . .

"You . . ." She stepped toward him with violent intent.

"Ask her."

Manipi looked doubtfully at Nisa. "What say you, woman?"

Nisa glared at Seneca, but she lifted her chin in defiance. "I say imprison me, too, for I will say nothing."

Manipi seized her arm. "Very well . . . And we will see the High Councillor's niece gets the same treatment as did Motega." Manipi tied a gag around Nisa's mouth, then tied her hands behind her back. Carob hid himself in her jacket.

"It is my belief the assassination wasn't desired by the Thorwalian command." Seneca spoke calmly, as always. Nisa wasn't sure why they listened, but the Dakotans paused to hear his words.

"Who are you, if not Motega?"

"I am called Seneca. I am Akandan. My race resembles yours." Seneca's eyes narrowed at Manipi's stretched green suit. "Somewhat."

"What do you know of Thorwal's purpose?"

"Very little. But I have learned facets of Thorwalian purpose since my abduction."

"They abducted you?"

Seneca nodded at Nisa. "They considered me a likely replacement for your leader. But Thorwalians are not in the habit of asking."

Nisa's teeth clenched around the gag. Angry tears

formed in her eyes. She hurt inside. She meant nothing to him.

Manipi considered Seneca's words. "If Motega is dead, we have nothing."

"Your leader was a rash man."

Nisa marveled that Seneca dared speak against Motega in these uncertain circumstances. Even more, she wondered why Manipi listened.

"He was brave; he was a great man, a great pilot, a brilliant mind."

"He was selfish," added Seneca. "And he failed you."

Manipi bristled. "He was our hope, our future! The Thorwalians dominated us, and he broke us freè."

"You seek balance from forces outside yourselves," countered Seneca. "You sought balance with Thorwal for generations. You use one part, and leave the other to them. They do the same."

"What do you mean? We've done very well, until Thorwal started—"

"The Thorwalians build based on your designs, your learning, do they not? They build what you use here." Seneca nodded to the discarded rifles. "Yet the flight ships they build, they pilot with limited skill." Seneca glanced at Nisa. A reluctant smile crossed his face. Hcr eyes narrowed, and she hoped he understood the depth of her fury.

"It's true, we Dakotans make better pilots," said Manipi. "No one could angle a fighter craft like Motega. . . ." Manipi's clipped voice slowed, then quieted. He studied Seneca for a long while, his expression contemplative.

Nisa wondered what he was thinking. The Dakotan mind was veiled to her. Soft, wavy brown hair crowned Manipi's round head; his dark eyes seemed inscrutable. Nothing about the Dakotans seemed logical to a Thorwalian.

"Despite what you say, Motega was a great leader. The finest man our race produced in generations.

Maybe ever. Without him we have been lost. He turned defeat into victory. Today we watched you do the same. If you join us, the Thorwalians' evil plan may be turned against them."

"I have no more interest in aiding your people than I do theirs." Nisa felt a tug of relief at Seneca's words. "But I have terms to offer."

"What terms?" asked the Dakotan.

Nisa's relief changed to suspicion.

"I will aid your efforts on the condition that upon a successful conclusion, you will return me to Akando."

Seneca's request surprised Manipi, but Nisa turned away. He was certainly consistent.

"If that's what you want . . ." Manipi's voice faded and he looked between Seneca and Nisa. "But I warn you, should a conclusion be reached, you may find it harder to leave than you imagine. Your own desires may thwart your intent."

"That is my request. If you agree to honor it, my service begins."

"Agreed!" Manipi seized Seneca's hand and shook vigorously. "You will become Deiaquande of our people." Manipi paused. "What do we do now?"

"Seek balance," said Seneca.

"Balance? We can't do that, not with Thorwal—"

Seneca held the man's gaze. "Seek balance within."

Nisa waited, unsure what Seneca was suggesting, and where Thorwal's interests lay in his plans.

Manipi shifted his weight from foot to foot. "How?"

"I believe Helmar to be a man such as yourself," said Seneca. "He desires life without conflict, accord with your people. He would remain dependent and unchanging. But you both fail to see a truth: All life is dependent on change. You have used each other to deny your own natures. You have grown on the outside, and stagnated within."

Seneca paused, eyeing the sorry condition of Manipi's overweight body. "Some might even say atrophied. The Thorwalians are the same."

Nisa's eyes burned angrily. She wanted to argue. The slender, staid Thorwalians had nothing in common with the rotund, nervous Dakotan race. Carob popped his head out of her jacket and coughed.

"I'd say the Dakotans took more than their share of the foodstuff!"

Nisa nodded.

"Balance in diet as well," agreed Seneca. "The Thorwalians live on nourishment pills and gruel. It seems obvious that you spend your nervous natures in a diet far too rich for your limited activity."

At the word *diet*, several Dakotans groaned. "If Helmar wants peace, why this subterfuge?"

"He seeks balance, but his method is flawed. Helmar rules Thorwal, but his power is weak. Another, one with greater ambition, may seek to overthrow him. That is the one you should fear. That is the one you must prepare against."

"Who?"

"Helmar's lieutenant, Fedor, has gained power with the Thorwalian guard."

Nisa shook her head vigorously. Manipi noticed, then chewed on his lip. "What about her? What do we do with her?"

"For now she makes an excellent hostage," decided Seneca. Nisa's eyes flamed. "Let them think her plan succeeded, that you follow me as Motega. That will stall them long enough to assess this hidden leader's intent. But our hostage might be better pleased if allowed to speak."

Manipi untied Nisa's gag. She sputtered furiously, unable to form words. Without warning she attacked Seneca, swinging wildly at his lean, perfect jaw. Seneca ducked, moved to one side, and pinned her in front of him.

"It may take her a while to settle down. The crash and attack unnerved her."

"Wortpig! I trusted you—"

"And I told you not to."

Nisa tried to jam her elbow into Seneca's stomach. He prevented her and went on talking. "If you intend to form a resistance against invasion, I suggest you begin within yourselves."

Nisa struggled in Seneca's arms. "We aren't going to invade your wretched planet! It's Dakota that threatens balance. You stole our craft."

"You stole our leader!" Manipi looked Nisa up and down. "He trusted you. If not for your betrayal . . ."

"My betrayal! Motega ingratiated himself with my uncle; he used me, then tricked me into revealing . . . certain things."

"Motega was too smitten with you to recognize your true purpose," countered Manipi, though Nisa rolled her eyes. "He doted on you. He gave up several very promising relationships because of his obsession with you. I remember when he told me about you, about your 'flawless skin, golden hair, winsome voice. . . .' "

"We know he liked the woman," cut in Seneca. He sounded irritated by Manipi's reminiscence, and Nisa wondered why. Maybe he was jealous. That didn't sound like Seneca, somehow, but he obviously didn't want to hear more.

"Liked?" chimed in Carob as he made his way to Nisa's shoulder. "As I remember, he fawned over her. Never have I seen a species as eager to mate."

Seneca's jaw tensed. "Don't you have another litter to sire, bat?"

Carob chuckled. "Then again, I'd forgotten about yourself. Seemed fairly intent on this female yourself!"

"What is this creature?" Manipi poked Carob in the stomach, then fingered his wings. "This looks like one of the Candor specimens. But they didn't talk."

"Carob isn't a specimen," said Nisa. "He's a lingbat."

"Lingbat? Who calls him that?"

"We call ourselves that, roughly translated,"

announced Carob. "Had you bothered to ask."

"Lingbat!" Manipi whistled. "Imagine that."

"We found him on one of your research vessels. And freed him."

Manipi's eyes glowed as he studied the little creature. "Imagine having a talking rodent at our disposal. Think of the opportunities for discovery!"

Nisa felt Carob's claws digging into her shoulder; she felt the small animal's fear. "You'll do no such thing." She tried to think of a threat to save Carob.

"The bat shall be treated as a guest." Seneca sounded less than enthusiastic, but a small breath of relief escaped Carob's mouth and Nisa felt him relax.

"What about me?" asked Nisa.

"You are a prisoner," cut in Manipi. "And you'll be treated as such. We don't want you making pudding of another hapless man."

"Balance, Manipi," Seneca reminded him. "The man who is made pudding has himself to blame for his own weak will. Nisa will be a guest also. But one watched at all times," he added with a glance her way.

Manipi sighed. "I see it's started again. There's no keeping the two of you apart. Never was. Never will be. Well, I warned you the first time. . . ."

"You warned Motega, Manipi," said Nisa. "Not Seneca."

"Ah, yes." Manipi sighed. "I keep forgetting." He gestured toward the crash site. "What do we do about this? The Thorwalians will find out what happened here, and blame us."

"Well, we *were* shot down," said Nisa. "Who else would we blame?"

Seneca shook his head. "The group that attacked us wasn't Dakotan. They were Thorwalians."

"That's ridiculous! My people were called back from Dakota when Motega was imprisoned. There's been no interplanetary travel since."

"She's right," added Manipi. "We've got no Thorwalians here."

"You had some," said Seneca. "For one thing, their aim was better than yours. They had some training. Thorwal has maintained a military and a trained guard. You, clearly, have not."

Manipi fidgeted. "Well, we're a little out of practice, it's true. I'm not sure it's fair to say our aim—"

Nisa stepped in front of him and pointed at the still-stunned Dakotan. Manipi appeared pained and fell silent.

"We'll have to carry Langundo, sir," said another Dakotan. Nisa noted that the Dakotans already addressed Seneca rather than Manipi as their leader. She wasn't sure why they accepted him so easily, now that they knew he wasn't Motega.

"If not Helmar, who do you think put them up to it?" Manipi's silence didn't last long. Nisa guessed he had too much energy to be long restrained. "This Fedor?"

"It can't be Fedor," said Nisa. "I'll admit he's a bit . . . aggressive, but my brother and I have kept a close eye on his activities. Dane assures me—"

"Dane?" Manipi's brow furrowed. "We interrupted a transmission from a 'Dane.' He offered a trade, research data in exchange for our leader. The message hinted at a change in power."

"That's absurd! Dane has no interest in Helmar's seat. In fact, I am in line to the leadership, not my brother. He's more interested in exploration and adventure. He's still a boy."

"He's more interested in females," added Carob. "I've seen enough of him to know he doesn't spend his spare time issuing secret transmissions."

"Nonetheless, it is suspicious," decided Manipi. "The councillor's nephew has reason to see his uncle disposed, and his sister dead. More interest than a minor commander such as Fedor."

Nisa glanced at Seneca impatiently. "Tell them my brother wouldn't do such a thing."

"It seems unlikely. But you base your judgment on trust. Trust is just a wish, maiden. It is a desire to control the future, and that we cannot do."

"I hate it when he talks like that," muttered Carob.

"He has a point," said Nisa, her voice cold. "I made the mistake of trusting him, didn't I?"

"Even after I told you not to," agreed Seneca with a grin. "Your desire to control is far out of balance to reality."

Nisa didn't like the way their conversations turned against her. She turned her back to Seneca, determined to ignore his new status. "Where are your hovercraft, Dakotan? I am tired and bruised, and I need to plan my escape."

Manipi gestured beyond the crash site. "We left them hidden just a short walk away." He hesitated, with an apologetic glance at Seneca. "They're not in the best repair. Of course, our repairmen and technicians were all Thorwalian. I wouldn't say the craft are in prime working order."

"Perhaps our *guest* might assist you in fixing the vessels," suggested Seneca.

"I will not! Let them all fall into disrepair. I am not in the habit of assisting my enemies."

"Then you'll be walking soon," said Manipi. "As will we all."

Seneca considered the matter. "A state which might benefit you both. Come, to avert further disruption, let us send a message to Thorwal assuring them all progresses as they planned."

"Dane will expect to hear from me," said Nisa. "He'll know something is wrong if I don't contact him."

"Then you will contact him." Seneca seemed unconcerned with Nisa's threats.

"Helmar won't put up with your defiance any more

than Motega's. It won't take long for them to realize the mind probes failed."

"It will take long enough," said Seneca. "If we work quickly your uncle will face a rejuvenated race, and a much stronger defense."

Manipi hadn't exaggerated the sorry state of Dakota's hovercraft fleet. Nisa nearly succumbed to the desire to tinker with the craft before entering it.

"Make her fix it!" urged Manipi. "She knows how."

"Do you?" asked Seneca. Nisa drew herself up proudly.

"As it happens, I'm one of the finest technicians on Thorwal. I kept my own hovercraft in the finest form."

"It was the piloting that wanted skill."

Nisa absorbed this slight, determined to ignore Seneca's prodding comments. "Thorwalians have naturally deft fingers. Dane and I are particularly adept."

"That's what I heard at the Snow Port," injected Carob.

"My brother and I could have your entire fleet working to perfection. Of course, since you've chosen to defy every Thorwalian suggestion . . ."

"You mean order!" Manipi's face was still flushed from the short walk through the trees to the hidden craft. "We tired of your suggestions, woman!"

"Her manner is dictatorial," agreed Seneca. "I assume she has been taught no better manner."

Nisa seated herself in the hovercraft, ignoring their remarks. "If your holding cells are in this much disrepair, escape should be simple."

"You won't get far in our shuttles," said Manipi. "We're left with only one, and that's busy transporting our pilots back from the fighter fleet."

This satisfied Seneca. "I suggest you remain and learn patience, maiden."

"I will not."

"You're too soft with her." Manipi struggled into the

hovercraft, though it was a small step. "She'd be better kept in shackles. This woman is poison."

The engine of the hovercraft sputtered painfully as the small fleet made its way from the crash site. Though the Dakotans guided them slowly and with light hands, the hovercraft all jerked and fought against their condition.

"It's a wonder they're still running at all." As Nisa spoke, one of the crafts sank to the ground.

Manipi shook his head. "Leave it there," he called. "Climb onto Langundo's." The stunned Langundo lay in a round clump, strapped to the shell of another craft. Nisa watched as a Dakotan climbed into an already overloaded vessel.

"That's probably a mistake."

The overloaded craft choked and collapsed. Several Dakotans piled on top of each other, shoving as accusations flew. "I'm enjoying this," noted Carob from Nisa's jacket. "It was worth the crash."

Seneca watched the spectacle, a grim, weary expression on his face. "Do the remote controls still work?"

"Front and back work," said Manipi. "Side to side, well, that's a little iffy."

"Then I suggest we walk, and guide the remaining craft along ahead."

The Dakotans groaned. "There must be another way."

Seneca jumped down from the hovercraft. "Unless you want to end up carrying your stunned friend, I suggest you act now."

Nisa saw the Dakotans' reluctance. She felt it, too, but she considered herself far more fit. She hopped out and stood with Seneca. Carob positioned himself on her shoulder, seeming pleased with the spectacle of the already sweating Dakotans.

Seneca noticed his Akandan pack tied around Nisa's

waist. "Let me take that," he offered. "You don't need to carry anything extra."

Nisa relinquished the pack, though she endured a wave of fierce irritation that Seneca had had his way in everything so far. "It was clever of you to manipulate me into bringing your shrub."

"I made a request. It was your choice to honor it." Seneca checked the contents, satisfied with the sapling's condition, then fixed the pack to his shoulder while the Dakotans reluctantly abandoned their vessels.

Manipi was last to leave his hovercraft. He coded in a remote pattern, and sighed as the craft disappeared through the trees. "It will be nearly dark before we reach Macanoc."

"At least it will be cooler," said Nisa. Dakota's mild climate felt hot to her. "I'd almost welcome rain."

"Rain will fall soon enough," Manipi told her. "Almost every night we get a good wash. At least, I considered it good until now. Don't relish the thought of walking in the rain."

Seneca started off after the hovercraft. A path had been cut through the trees, but apparently had never been traveled on foot. The higher branches were trimmed, but the footing was uneven and littered with fallen limbs.

The woodland debris gave Seneca no trouble, but the others floundered. Manipi attempted to step over a rotting branch, tripped, and fell backward, his feet up in the air. Carob cackled and gestured, and Nisa repressed a smile. How the Dakotans threatened her people seemed inconceivable.

Seneca offered the round scientist a hand up, then continued down the path. "What's his hurry?" grumbled Manipi. "Motega never walked this fast."

"Motega never walked." Nisa felt breathless, too, but she forced herself to keep stride with Seneca.

"You've made a dangerous mistake, wortpig. If

you'd trusted me I would have sent you back to your wretched world. But even if the Dakotans want to send you to Akando, they don't have the flight ships to do it."

"They will."

Nisa caught a hurried breath and jumped over a bramble. Seneca grabbed her arm as she tripped, but she refused to acknowledge his assistance.

"You are a changeable creature, maiden. It is part of your charm, perhaps."

"What do you mean? I am perfectly consistent. Unlike yourself."

Seneca laughed at her assessment. "I recall your words on the shuttle, maiden. But I assure you, your grief at our interrupted passion doesn't exceed my own."

Nisa stopped in her tracks. Seneca stopped, too, waiting for the straggling Dakotans.

"Of course, you were faking the results of the probe. It was all a ploy to gain me as a hostage for your vile scheme. My words on the shuttle meant nothing. I thought I was going to die."

"So you spoke your true heart."

"Not at all!" Nisa's cheeks flamed to bright pink. "I suppose you think you did very well for yourself back there. Well, let me tell you something, Akandan. Your primitive skills surprised a more advanced race, that's all. You're just lucky they didn't blast you into unrecognizable bits."

Seneca didn't argue. He seemed pleased with her anger. "Surprise is generally an advantage, maiden." He paused, watching her stomp on ahead. "You should know that better than anyone."

Nisa ignored Seneca's comment as she forced her aching legs to continue. A swift stream bisected the path ahead. She pushed a damp strand of hair back into its binding. "Do we have to cross this? Aren't there bridges?"

"Hovercraft don't require bridges." Seneca started across the stream, offering his hand to Nisa. She refused and chose a solid rock to step on instead.

"It's not so hard." Nisa found another rock. A slight jump and she landed. Seneca leaped to the far bank and watched her progress.

"Try the left," he suggested. "It might take longer, but—"

"I'm perfectly capable." Nisa chose the longer jump. Her foot slipped, and she smacked down into the water. It wasn't deep, but it was cold. *How humiliating!*

"Ack! Would you be more careful? I'm getting wet!" Carob scrambled to Nisa's shoulder and shook himself dramatically, spraying droplets everywhere.

Nisa glared at the bat. "Why don't you fly?"

"If you remember, I am a flightless species. True, we can flap around enough to locate suitable perches, but that's a throwback to our forebearers."

Nisa struggled to her feet as Carob clung to her shoulder. His precarious position didn't slow his speech. "We lingbats evolved from savannas, where flight was necessary, to a tunnel-dwelling existence that found wings useless. Insects abounded in the dark caverns . . . generally worm-based, tender, filling. True, when I observe some of the hard-shelled flying species, I regret the absence of a more developed flight musculature."

"Never mind." Nisa picked her way across the stream. She held her head high as she reached the bank where Seneca waited. She saw him from the corner of her eye, his arms folded over his chest, laughter in his eyes.

Nisa pulled off her wet jacket and tied it around her waist. Seneca's eyes darkened as his gaze shifted to her breasts. Her damp bodice turned semitransparent when wet. It clung to her flesh.

"Only a crude, primitive species has such a fixation with female breasts."

"I suppose your brother is interested in conversation when he frequents the Snow Port establishment?"

Nisa wanted to argue, but Dane was a poor choice for comparison. Carob chuckled, and she knew there was no use. She snapped her bodice from her skin, hoping to diminish the effect. The dwindling sun turned the air cool, a relief against the exertion.

The Dakotans fumbled over the stream, arguing and shoving each other. "Each man to his own progress," called Seneca. Nisa scoffed, but to her surprise the Dakotans obeyed Seneca's instructions and toiled individually across the stream.

"They might listen to you for a while," said Nisa as Manipi reached the near side and collapsed onto his back to rest. "But it won't take long for them to realize how little your simple methods will avail a people as advanced as the Dakotans. They are scientists. Concepts mean more to them than physical reality."

"Concepts are nothing but the mind's interpretation of reality. For life to have value, reality itself must be respected. Even honored."

Nisa tried to dismiss Seneca's reasoning, but his words seemed true to her. There was no need to tell him that, however. "Are you going to let them rest?" She hoped he didn't notice how much she, too, desired a break.

"For a brief while. I trust you all have water. If not, drink sparingly from the stream."

Nisa sank to the ground. Her legs hurt; her feet hurt. Her chest burned from the exertion. Seneca stood beside her, unaffected by the walk. Nisa gazed up at him, remembering the image of him racing through the dry Akandan forest, his hair streaming in the wind.

No wonder the Dakotans were so willing to follow him. In a confused and fluctuating world, Seneca remained calm. Nisa's eyes narrowed. He might be a formidable enemy. Maybe even more dangerous than Motega.

Nisa forced herself to her feet. "I will be watching you, wortpig. In service to Thorwal, I will monitor every move you make."

"Then it appears you and I will be spending a great deal of time together. It may be that your final wish on the shuttle will be granted after all."

Chapter Five

By the time Manipi's party reached Macanoc, several Dakotans demanded hospitalization. Only the promise of the evening meal kept them from stretchers.

Nisa's whole body ached. Her lungs burned. But nothing would make her admit her weakness in front of Seneca. Seneca remained unaffected by the arduous walk, but Nisa was determined not to credit his abilities.

Macanoc was just as she remembered it, except more dilapidated. Long, low buildings tucked amongst the trees contrasted with narrow, high structures that reached nearly to the treetops. All were painted green or brown, and blended with the dark shades of the forest.

Seneca stood at the town center, surveying the Dakotan village with a strange expression on his face. Nisa joined him.

"What do you think of your new domicile, Akandan? It's not as glorious as Thorwal, is it?"

Seneca didn't answer at once. He seemed moved, deeply, though Nisa couldn't understand why. Dakotan villages were nondescript to her eye. The structures blended with the forest, made with handcrafted wood rather than Thorwalian forged metal.

The Dakotans spent much more time in artistry than did the Thorwalians, who considered design a wasted effort. Practical functions motivated Thorwalian architects, but comfort and beauty were most important in Dakotan design.

Nisa shook her head. "It's all so . . . impractical."

"The Dakotans tamper less with their habitat," commented Seneca. "Your people could learn much from them. But neither race, it seems, has learned anything from the other."

"You know very little. Who do you think built these buildings? We did."

"Maybe so, but you've learned nothing in the process. You live in metal boxes, but functional boxes. Here the homes fall into disrepair, yet they have beauty."

Manipi put out a call, alerting the Dakotans to Seneca's arrival. People raced from the buildings, cheering as they gathered around the village square. Nisa watched dispassionately. No Thorwalian would make such a fuss, even if they felt the emotion.

"So undignified!" she muttered. Carob folded his wings in front of his small, round stomach.

"They know how to make fools of themselves, don't they?"

Manipi stood beside Seneca. "We have been without our leader for seven years. For seven years, we have kept the seat of the Deiaquande vacant, in hopes of his return."

Cheers rang out at this, and Manipi waited for relative silence before continuing. "Today we welcome a new beginning." More cheers, but Manipi wasn't finished. "The man we knew as Motega is gone." A stunned silence followed.

"In their treachery, the Thorwalians subjected him to an assassination plot." No Dakotan commented, though their expressions hardened.

"In Motega's place, this man has come. He calls himself Seneca, who has lived on the planet Akando. The Thorwalians chose him as a replacement for our leader."

Manipi paused, and several Dakotans laughed. Nisa wasn't sure why. Manipi gestured at Nisa. "This female, the High Councillor's niece—many of you may remember her as Motega's concubine."

Nisa's temper flared. "I was nothing of the sort!" More laughter as her face colored.

"As I was saying . . . It was Motega's mistress who chose this Akandan to replace him. She abducted him, brought him to Thorwal, and subjected him to the Thorwalians' most devious weapon, the mind probe."

The Dakotan audience gasped and grumbled in outrage. Nisa felt a wave of guilt, but she kept her expression clear and defiant.

"Apparently the device isn't infallible, because he remains untarnished for their efforts. In exchange for his eventual return to Akando, this man called Seneca has agreed to assume the seat of the Deiaquande. Do we accept him as our leader? The choice is yours: yea or nay?"

In unison, the Dakotans cried, "Yea!" Nisa wondered why. How could they expect Seneca to lead them in an interplanetary conflict?

Manipi turned to Seneca. "From the time of our most distant ancestors, our people chose their leader, the Deiaquande. In him we place our trust and our hope. Do you accept this high office?"

Seneca hesitated. "For the time I live on your world, I will serve you as leader. When my task is complete,

I will hold you to your promise, and return to Akando."

"If that is what you wish, it will be done."

"Then I accept."

More cheers rang out as the Dakotans closed in around Senecca. Nisa noticed that many of them touched him, as if drawing power from his strength. Maybe it was just his resemblance to Motega that inspired them. Maybe they couldn't completely forgo the memory of their beloved leader.

Young Dakotan women gazed lovingly at Seneca. Nisa remembered their admiration of Motega. While new to womanhood, Dakotan women were exceptionally lovely: soft features, dark hair, delicate feet and hands. With age they lost their slender shapes, but the delicacy remained.

Nisa never felt delicate. She felt large and bold and conspicuous. She saw pretty girls cast shy glances at their new leader, and her lack of delicacy soared. Had they no sense? But maybe he would find Dakotan women more like his Akandan mate.

Nisa turned away, refusing to watch the spectacle any further. If Seneca preferred these young, silly females, it simply proved his own vanity.

"We will reopen Motega's dwelling, untouched these seven years." Manipi's words sent a cool chill through Nisa's veins. Motega's home loomed across the square, the largest in Macanoc. High, flowering vines covered the walls, surrounding the upper-story windows.

Nisa remembered Motega reaching through his bedroom window to pick her a flower. She had rewarded him too well for his efforts. Nisa noticed that Seneca's attention had drifted from Manipi and was now fixed on her. Her eyes shifted to her feet.

Carob whistled. "Seven years! It's probably loaded with bugs." The lingbat hopped over to Seneca, peering up at him in a friendly fashion. "You might welcome a little help straightening up the place."

Manipi eyed the lingbat. "Maybe you'd prefer a nice, comfortable cage, little fellow. We'll give you all the insects you want there."

"The bat will stay with me," said Seneca. "And forage for insects to his heart's content. His first stay in Dakota lacked welcome. His needs will be met with sensitivity, and your research will continue without live creatures."

Manipi looked doubtful. "That will set us back."

"Respect life. When you take life for consumption, honor it. Respect its gift."

"What do you mean, 'for consumption'? You don't expect us to hunt, do you? We don't have animals on Dakota."

"You have fish," Nisa reminded them. "This should prove interesting."

"From now on you will only consume what you grow or retrieve with your own hands." Seneca waited for the shocked gasps and groans to subside before continuing. "The power cells you use for the food-processing units can be applied to your hovercraft. Isn't that so, maiden?"

"It is," admitted Nisa. "But how do you know—"

"I learned more from your language implant than you realized."

"Truly?" asked Carob. "I had to learn all that on my own. Of course, lingbats have incredibly swift neuro-transmitters."

"You expect us to eat fish?" Manipi sounded doubtful. "I've never actually seen a fish. How do we catch them?"

"With nets, with bait attached to hooks, suspended from lines. This is the manner of Akandans in the warm season of my world. Many consider the practice enjoyable."

"It sounds tedious," said Nisa.

"I suggest that a committee be banded to undertake

this task," said Manipi, clearly intending no part in the procedure.

"A good suggestion," said Seneca. "You will head it. Another group will research the planting of seeds for direct consumption."

"We grow fields of barlit-meal and sweet cane on the far side of the planet," argued Manipi. "Fed all of Dakota as well as Thorwal on that produce. Of course, much of the harvesting machinery has conked out on us."

"Thorwal will learn to feed itself," said Seneca. "Each section of Dakota will be expected to fend for itself, taking nothing not used immediately. There is no need for storage with a climate as benign as this."

The Dakotans grumbled and objected, but Seneca remained unyielding. "I told you it wouldn't last," remarked Nisa with subdued pleasure. "You're taking away their food. Even Motega wasn't worth that!"

"When they taste freshly roasted fish, their arguments will subside. It might prove a welcome change to your gruel, too, maiden."

"I prefer to go hungry."

"As you wish. But I won't hold you to those words."

Manipi shook his head. "With all this foraging and hunting fish, we won't have time for our research projects."

"Balance, Manipi. Your research will receive its due."

"What about the woman? I say we put her to work in the fields."

"Nisa is a prisoner, not a slave," said Seneca, to Nisa's relief. "She will do nothing she doesn't offer to do."

Nisa exhaled, realizing she had held her breath in fear of what tedious task he would assign to her.

Seneca's promise didn't please Manipi. "Nothing? As I said, you're too soft."

"I trust she will learn which tasks benefit her, and which don't."

Nisa sensed Seneca's veiled meaning, and she frowned. "I will do nothing to aid your progress, I assure you."

"How will changing our diet guard against the Thorwalians, should they decide to invade?" asked Manipi, echoing Nisa's own unspoken thoughts.

"These changes begin the process you must undergo," replied Seneca. "You do not change what exists by working on the outside, but on the underlying structure. You ignore that structure to rework the surface. I propose that you change the structure, and the rest will follow."

"I find that unlikely," said Nisa.

"As you change your consumption, you will strengthen your bodies."

At this comment, the Dakotans exchanged doubtful glances. "What do you mean?" Manipi asked suspiciously. "You're not suggesting . . ."

"It sounds like exercise to me!" chimed in Carob, relishing the Dakotans' pained reaction.

"On my world, no one consumes more than their body needs. We respect the gift of our bodies, and the gift of motion."

"Is that how you managed to defeat the Thorwalian ambushers?" asked Manipi.

"It is. All warriors learn this art on Akando. It is called TiKay, and with its use anyone can protect themselves from attack. As well, the body's motion becomes clean; no energy is wasted. Much can be accomplished in little time."

The mention of speed intrigued the Dakotans. "How do we learn?"

"I will teach you. At the first light of dawn, you will join me here in the village center. I will begin your instruction. When you have learned, you will become the teachers, and spread TiKay across your world."

"The first light of dawn? Now, we're not normally early risers."

"You will be."

Nisa repressed a groan. "I hope this doesn't apply to prisoners."

"You may sleep as late as you wish, maiden."

"Doesn't sound entirely fair," muttered Manipi.

"Only those who choose to undergo learning will profit. Nothing is accomplished without choice."

"Good," said Nisa. "Then I choose to sleep and eat as I please."

"Where will we put her?" asked Manipi.

"As my guest, Nisa will stay with me."

"I will not!"

Manipi thumped his fist into his palm. "You'd be wiser to send this woman to the other side of the planet! Stay as far away from her as you can get."

Seneca ignored Manipi's protests. "She will stay near me, where her capacity for mischief is limited."

"I prefer the holding cell."

"As I told you before, this planet itself is your holding cell."

Seneca assessed Nisa's rigid posture. "Can it be that you fear the idle gossip of others? Do the opinions and whims of the Dakotan people have so much hold over you?"

Nisa suspected he was leading her into something, but she couldn't resist. "It matters very little where I pass the night, since I will have effected my escape by tomorrow."

"We'll discuss tomorrow's itinerary tomorrow. For tonight, I suggest you rest."

Manipi sighed and shook his head. "What about the evening meal? The Deiaquande's return calls for a celebration."

Nisa rolled her eyes. "What would a Dakotan know about celebration?"

Manipi's brow furrowed. "Well, we could take him through the lab, show him what we've come up with in the last seven years!"

"While that would prove interesting, it might better be left for tomorrow," suggested Seneca.

"I could show you the graphs on the agricultural output. . . ."

"Another time."

Seneca sounded weary. Probably remembering Akando. Nisa's heart sank, though she wasn't sure why. "I suppose the Akandans practice revelry."

"We do. There are dances of ritual, sacred feasts, the hour of dusk when the storytellers speak of our forebearers."

"We'll have a banquet!" Manipi clapped his pudgy hands together.

Nisa eyed him doubtfully. "A banquet? I hope you've got more to offer than barlit-meal."

"We're down to the bare essentials, thanks to your siege. Can't keep the machinery going, so our foodstuffs are severely limited. But we can do better than barlit-meal." Manipi smacked his lips. "I will alert the cooks! We'll have to eat in the lab cafeteria. It's the only place big enough for a feast."

Manipi didn't wait for permission. Nisa suspected he feared a denial of the elaborate meal. Manipi bowed twice, then hurried off across the village square.

"What about me?" asked Nisa.

Seneca bowed. "What do you desire of me?"

"My uniform is dirty and torn from our jaunt through the forest. I would like something else to wear."

A smile flickered on his lips as he glanced at her bottom. Nisa wondered why. "I will see a new garment provided. Anything else?"

"I'm hungry."

"You will sit at my left hand at the banquet."

"Isn't that the position of the Deiaquande's consort?"

"How would I know that?"

"The consort sits to his left, until the bond is made permanent, when she moves to his right. When the Deiaquande has been female, the settings are reversed."

"Your knowledge of Dakotan custom is impressive, maiden. But then, you've been here before."

"That's none of your concern." Nisa's jaw tightened, but she remained stoic. "I would like to wash."

"You may make yourself comfortable in my predecessor's dwelling." Seneca paused. "I assume you know where that is."

Nisa's cheeks warmed. "I do."

Seneca stood in silence as Nisa whirled away, then stomped across the village square. When anger mixed with determination, Nisa marched like a guard on duty. A wave of affection soaked his heart.

Three Dakotan women watched her, then whispered behind their hands as she passed. Nisa paid no attention, but Seneca knew she felt every veiled comment, every knowing glance. Her pride touched him, but that shield might become impenetrable over time.

Nisa seized the door and yanked it open. She entered, then slammed the door behind her. Seneca longed to follow, to shut himself away with her, alone, beyond the watchful eyes of the Dakotans.

Not yet. She needed time to confront her memories. She needed time to confront him.

The door closed behind her, but Nisa couldn't move. Everything in the long room was just as Motega had left it. High, narrow windows overlooked the village square; a curving stairwell led to the second level and Motega's sleeping chambers. At the far end of the room, Nisa saw his eating area, still decorated, as if they had just finished their morning meal.

Nisa closed her eyes. She felt him here. She heard his teasing voice echoing in her brain. Maybe that was

Seneca's voice. Though Seneca's voice was lower, softer, the teasing quality was similar. Equally annoying, but compelling, too.

It felt like being dragged into the past. For seven years she had moved forward. Until she captured a lone Akandan warrior and remade him in Motega's image. Until she allowed his touch, his kiss. . . . It had to stop here.

Nisa opened her eyes. She would control her emotions and her reactions to Seneca. She tried to move, but her limbs felt heavy. A sharp but low rapping on the door broke the spell of memory.

Nisa opened the door, looked down, and saw Carob waiting. He seemed impatient. His small foot even tapped. Nisa wondered how he mimicked humans so well, but the effect was strong. The lingbat's presence relieved her tension and she laughed.

"Haven't you forgotten something? Someone?"

"I'm sorry, Carob." Nisa stepped back and Carob hopped inside. He looked around, assessing the potential for feeding.

"I don't see much. . . ." began Nisa, but Carob's eyes widened dramatically, then narrowed to slits.

"Quiet! Don't move!" With impressive stealth, Carob crept across the floor, easing his way past a large seat, then freezing his motion. He quivered.

Without warning Carob pounced. His wings flapped violently for a moment. Then silence. Nisa heard a loud crunch, and she cringed. No wonder Dane complained about the rodent's eating habits.

"I think I'll bathe now."

"Very good." Smacking sounds followed, and more crunching. "Prime, ripe . . ."

Nisa didn't wait to hear more. She hurried up the stairs to the cleansing unit.

She stood outside the enclosed chamber, trying not to remember its sensual promise. Its design was more elaborate than the Thorwalians' practical unit, designed for pleasure and relaxation as well as bathing.

Nisa set the dials to soak first, then cleanse. From downstairs she heard another violent flutter of wings. Something squawked, then crashed against a window as if a battle ensued.

"Got him!" came the victory cry. Nisa added another soak cycle before the final rinse. With luck, Carob would be full by the time she finished.

Nisa stripped away her uniform. A large, embarrassing dirt spot covered the seat of her white trousers. She remembered Seneca's smile and she clenched her teeth. Nisa shoved the whole uniform into the disposal and listened as it was ground to oblivion. This was one memory that wouldn't return to haunt her.

She entered the cleansing unit and closed her eyes. A fine, warm spray misted from every angle, down upon her head, against her sides, up beneath her feet. She didn't seat herself; she just stood as the water turned to a powerful jet and soothed her tired muscles.

The cleansing spray followed, and the water swirled around her like a cyclone. The rinsing cycle washed over her, and she finally sank onto the seat. It was padded and comfortable. Nothing on Dakota was sparse. Motega's tastes least of all. His cleansing unit was designed for pleasure, not function. Large enough for two, or more . . .

Nisa frowned. Motega's prowess was legendary on Dakota, and rumored on Thorwal with equal fervor. Even Fedor made mention of Motega's "seduction chamber." This very unit, where Motega had lured her as if thinking of the idea for the first time.

Nisa remembered her hurt when she realized it was nothing more than an amusement to him. A well-practiced amusement. She didn't wait for the final rinse. She abandoned the unit, leaving it to complete its cycle alone.

She stood dripping, wondering where Motega kept his towels. When she visited him, he had done everything. Fed her, brought her drinks, wrapped her in barlit-fiber towels . . .

No wonder Manipi and the other Dakotans thought he fawned over her. To outward appearances he did. At least Seneca didn't pretend. Nisa checked a shelf and found nothing. She stood on tiptoe to search through a high cabinet.

A warm towel wrapped around her shoulders, covering her. Nisa jumped, then froze. Her pulse thundered. Strong hands steadied her, then pinned the towel at her throat. Trembling, Nisa looked over her shoulder, half expecting Motega behind her.

"Seneca! What are you doing in here?"

Despite his dark, seductive gaze, Seneca moved away from her, leaning back against a basin. "The bat informed me that if you needed a new garment, I could bring it to you myself."

"I see." Nisa tightened the towel and tried to calm her racing pulse. "Where is it?"

Seneca held up a dark blue Dakotan suit. "I thought blue would suit you better than green. And the fabric is light."

"How fortunate." Nisa seized the garment. "If you will leave, I will dress now."

Seneca seemed in no hurry. "I had requested something more appropriate for a banquet, but the suggestion mystified the Dakotan supplier."

"I'm not surprised. On Thorwal we have suitable garments for such occasions. I have a gown, in fact." Nisa paused. "Of course, I haven't worn it for a while."

"Seven years, perhaps?"

Nisa glared. "The last occasion was for Motega's welcome, yes."

"Is that when you met?"

Nisa turned away. "I need to dress."

Seneca fell silent, watching her. Then he sighed and

left without a word. Nisa's heart thudded. Yes, it had been the day she met Motega. She still remembered his dark gaze across Helmar's long table, his penetrating smile that told her no one else in the room interested him. Only her.

Nisa forced the thought away. Curse Seneca for reminding her! She dried herself and pulled on the Dakotan clothing. The shirt was fastened with two hidden ties, bound on the outside with a cloth belt. The trousers were loose also, and too large at the middle. She pulled the waist string tight, then marched downstairs.

Seneca stood by the window, watching the final shafts of sunlight through the trees. Nisa noticed that his Akandan sapling had been placed by the window, tended with care. The sight bothered her, though she wasn't sure why.

Carob sat on the heavy chair, his wings folded over his stomach, his eyes closed. Nisa stared at the lingbat in amazement. Seneca noticed her and chuckled.

"He's been snoring," he told her in a low voice, careful not to wake the sleeping rodent. "I suggest you and I enjoy the banquet, such as it is, without our small guest."

Nisa couldn't help smiling when a rumbly snore emanated from Carob's open mouth. "This is too disgusting for words."

Seneca held out his hand for her. Nisa hesitated, but he smiled. Like a friend. Nisa wanted to take his hand, to walk at his side. To accept. But she remembered his betrayal, the way he had tricked her, and she clasped her arms tight around her waist.

Seneca dropped his hand and his smile faded. "This shield you carry, maiden . . . It may prove a heavy weight."

He opened the door and waited for her. Nisa swallowed. "You deceived me. If you expect me to forget that . . ."

Seneca caught her chin in his hand and tilted her face to his. "There is much I haven't told you, Nisa. Much I never will. But I haven't lied to you. What a man keeps to himself is his right. That is not deception."

"A trick of words." Nisa twisted her head away from his touch. "You led me to believe certain things."

"What things?"

Nisa's gaze fixed in accusation on his. "That I mattered to you!" She spat the words, then instantly regretted them.

"I care."

Nisa fought tears as she looked away. "Well, I don't."

Seneca touched her face. "Your actions, and your eyes, defy that claim, maiden. I think you do."

"I don't want to." She didn't look up, and her voice came small and without force.

"I know." Seneca laid his hand on her shoulder, then bent to kiss her forehead. "It's better to face your feelings. But not always easy. I know that, too."

Nisa peeked up at him. "What feelings do you have to face? Missing your family?"

"For my family, yes. My father, my brother. They must imagine me dead. It grieves me to think of their pain. But those feelings exist, and I acknowledge them. It is the more dangerous feelings that prove the challenge."

"What are they?"

"You know."

Nisa hesitated, fearing to say the words lest he humiliate her again. "For me?"

Seneca made no effort at denial. "For you. Has it occurred to you, my beguiling maiden, that I have no more desire to care for you than you do for me?"

"Why not?"

"You complicate my life. And my heart."

Nisa wasn't sure what he meant. Perhaps he referred to his Akandan mate. The woman he still intended to wed. "I have no wish to complicate you in any way."

"Which is why you abducted me from a reasonable world and deposited me here, among people who imagine revelry to include computerized graphs and a tour through a research facility."

Nisa couldn't deny the inconsistency of her comment. A small smile spread across her face, and a short laugh erupted despite her intention not to enjoy his company.

"When you put it that way . . . it appears I have complicated things for you somewhat."

Seneca laughed and took her hand, whether she desired his company or not. "You have, maiden. You have indeed."

The lab cafeteria was crowded with Dakotans. There seemed to be more Dakotans than seats to accommodate them.

"Maybe we should eat outside," Nisa suggested, striving to be heard above the din. Seneca didn't seem opposed to her suggestion, but Manipi seized his arm and led him to the table's head.

"We have kept the Deiaquande's seat empty. You do us honor by filling it tonight."

The Dakotans rose to their feet and cheered at Seneca's entrance, but he seemed more interested in the Deiaquande's chair. Nisa peeked over his shoulder to see why.

Though the other seats were squat and solid, Motega's chair was carved with ancient symbols, hewn from dark wood and fashioned with elaborate detail. Seneca studied the symbols, a strange expression on his face.

"Those are Dakotan runes, from a time before we adopted the Thorwalian language," said Manipi. "Don't know what they mean precisely, though we've done some studying on the subject. They seem to refer to animals, weather, even planetary motion. Not really a language."

"They resemble Akandan runes." Seneca fingered the carvings. "Too closely to be coincidental in origin."

Manipi nodded, his enthusiasm raised by scientific discussion. "True enough. These runes fascinated Motega. That's why we carved them into his chair. He felt certain our people descended from similar origins. Don't know how, though. Before our contact with Thorwal, we had no thought of space travel."

Seneca's smooth brow furrowed as he pondered the connection. "The Akandan legacy is ancient, deep into the past of their world. The legends of my people speak of a time when many more inhabited our world. At that point, the stories diverge into fantasy, into myths. Or so I thought. . . ."

Nisa couldn't restrain her interest as she examined the runes. "What kind of stories?"

"They spoke of gods borne on comets across the sky. Gods who made their home on . . ." Seneca paused, but his dark eyes flashed. "On the Dawn Star."

"Candor? But the star your people worship is the gas planet, not the moon."

"From a distance, they would be the same," put in Manipi. "Interesting! But our probes revealed no runes." He paused. "Unless that's something else you Thorwalians hid from us."

Nisa frowned at the reminder of their common goal. "No runes."

"Not now . . ." Seneca's voice trailed off, but he said no more. He seated himself, and the Dakotans sat, too.

Nisa hesitated before accepting the seat beside him. Since no other was available, and her stomach churned at the sight of food, she sat, but she eased her chair a good distance from Seneca's.

Manipi sat to Seneca's right, waiting with his spoon held aloft as the Dakotans passed plates and large bowls around the table. They exhibited no formality as they loaded their plates with puddings and sauces.

The elaborate concoctions smelled both inviting and filling to Nisa, after nothing but barlit-meal. She waited hungrily for her portion.

"I hope they leave some for us."

Seneca took a small portion of the offerings to his own plate. Nisa resisted the impulse to load her plate to its highest capacity, but it wasn't easy.

"The evening meal is best kept light." No one heard Seneca's suggestion and he sighed. "After tonight, we will limit your intake of pudding."

No Dakotan responded, but several heaped extra portions of the gelatin onto their plates.

"The barlit-meal is overprocessed. It is better ground into a cake, and eaten in its natural state."

"Dipped in pudding?" asked Manipi hopefully.

"No."

Nisa ate sparingly until Manipi diverted Seneca's attention. She slipped a crusty roll into her pocket, then quickly placed her hands back on the table. She peeked up at Seneca, checking to see if he noticed her theft.

Seneca's face appeared sincere, so she relaxed. The Dakotans knew how to prepare food. No denying that. The crusty rolls crumbled, then dissolved pleasantly in her mouth. One wasn't enough.

Nisa waited for Seneca's attention to shift back to Manipi, then seized another roll. Her eyes widened guilelessly as she dabbled in the rich pudding. A faint tilt of his lips told her he repressed humor.

She attempted to distract him. "Perhaps you would like to inform your new subjects of your intent toward my people."

"That depends on the intent *of* your people."

Nisa frowned at the evasive reply. "You are wily. No doubt a characteristic useful on your primitive world. I'm sure it helped you avoid countless ferocious beasts."

Nisa turned back to her pudding, but the Dakotans fell into a relative hush. "Were there fearsome beasts, Deiaquande?"

It was Langundo who spoke, the Dakotan Manipi had stunned. Nisa noticed that he took a second helping even before the others had finished their first.

Seneca leaned back in his seat. "Fearsome? I don't know. There are creatures who live on the flesh of others. Their urge to survive conflicted with my own." Laughter from the Dakotans. Nisa maintained an imperious frown.

"Then you have battled such creatures?" asked Langundo, his eyes blazing with admiration.

"I have dissuaded them from their purpose, and taught them to seek other prey."

The Dakotans nodded and murmured appreciatively, but Nisa repressed a groan. "His ability to battle large feline predators should serve in any number of ways on Dakota."

Manipi eyed her without affection. "His ability served well enough against your traitorous Thorwalians today. It seems your people have trouble maintaining faith even amongst yourselves!"

Nisa's fist clenched. With one punch, well aimed, she could bring Manipi's meal to an early end. "As is typical of your people, you overlook the obvious. Why should my people sabotage our own mission? We were trying to replace Motega. Which would have worked if this Akandan hadn't somehow disarmed the probes."

"The Deiaquande's abilities are beyond a Thorwalian's imagination."

"Ha! Our probe equipment was obviously faulty."

Both Nisa and Manipi waited for Seneca's explanation. He hesitated before giving one. "Part of TiKay involves shielding ability."

"Does it?" asked Manipi.

"That seems unlikely. Vague superstition and no

more. You were lucky, wortpig."

Manipi's broad brow furrowed. "You will not refer to the Deiaquande as wortpig again, wench!"

Nisa's head tilted, her lips curved in a defiant smile. "Since the primal drive to survival seems similar, it seems an apt term. I shall use it as I please."

Manipi leaned across Seneca. "You will not!"

Nisa seized her spoon and aimed it at Manipi's head. Seneca leaned forward, separating them. He took Nisa's hand in his firm grasp, holding it despite her efforts to free herself.

"Terms of respect mean little to a defiant heart. But this term has an endearing quality." Seneca paused as if reflecting. "I believe she has an affection for the beasts."

"Certainly not!"

Seneca ignored Nisa's outburst and turned her hand in his. His dark eyes met hers as he pressed his lips to her palm. Nisa shuddered, her face flushed. She heard the Dakotans' chuckles and murmurs, but she couldn't take her eyes off Seneca's seductive face.

How dare he! He attempted to humiliate her by using her own weak nerves against her. Nisa snatched her hand from his, then wiped her palm with the dining towel in her lap.

Seneca laughed, then returned to his meal.

Nisa glared at him. "You did that on purpose."

Seneca's expression altered. He set aside his meal and looked at her. "I did. I'm sorry."

Seneca didn't resume eating. He fell silent as the Dakotans chattered around him. Nisa wondered what he was thinking.

"You will need to select a new Deiaquande."

Seneca's announcement stunned the Dakotans. They dropped spoons, splattered pudding. Manipi stared, mouth agape. Nisa didn't move, but her heart labored.

"But you accepted." Manipi's eyes shifted in

accusation to Nisa. "We can send her away."

"Nisa is not the reason. I have given you my word to settle your dispute with Thorwal. I will not fail in that promise. But it is necessary that you also remember your vow, and have an eye toward your future. A future that will not include me."

Nisa's appetite waned. She set aside her spoon. He really intended to leave. He seemed so comfortable on Dakota, as if he belonged here more than Motega ever did. But he was leaving.

"We have no one to take your place," Manipi argued.

"Not yet. But you will. One among you will earn the seat you bestowed upon me, just as young Akandan warriors earn the title of chief on my world. On my world, when a new leader is chosen, the chief surrenders life as he seeks out the world beyond. Instead, I will return to the world I left behind."

Nisa kept her eyes focused on her half-finished plate. Why did she care what Seneca planned? And if he really meant to return to Akando, why did he force his attentions on her? Men, she decided, were unreliable from any world. Intimacy meant nothing to them, just a base, physical appetite that, when satisfied, was forgotten.

"What about this woman? You can't haul her to Akando. She wouldn't last a half-cycle on a planet that harsh." Despite his objections to her presence, Manipi seemed desperate enough to use Nisa as a lure. Nisa cringed.

"When the dispute between our worlds is settled, Nisa will return to her planet. As she desires."

"It can't happen soon enough." Nisa struggled to sound unaffected. She rose from her seat. "If this *celebration* is finished, I would like to rest. I assume you have no musicians or dancers to entertain us?"

Her comment puzzled Manipi. He shook his head. "No dancers."

"Good." Nisa turned to Seneca. "With your permission . . . ?"

"You may leave. I will join you shortly."

"It matters little to me what you do, Akandan. But see that your return is quiet. I will be asleep."

Nisa lifted her head and made her way through the thronging Dakotans toward the door. She stepped out into the warm night, and her rigid expression softened. The noises of nighttime creatures filled the air, chirps and squeaks that she remembered from her visit seven years before.

Thorwalian nights were cold and silent, with bright stars that glittered like eternal campfires. The stars in the Dakotan sky seemed softer, muted by the moist air. The air was soft and warm, smelling of sweet flowers and lush trees.

Tonight the starlight shattered like crystals. Her own tears distorted their image.

Why do I care? What is wrong with me that I should care this way? Nisa forced control on her emotions. Stars forbid that a passing Dakotan should see her cry. Nisa hurried across the village square to Motega's door. She reached for the antiquated knob, but it opened on its own.

Carob started, jumped back, then hopped out again. "Your kind isn't in the habit of knocking, I see." Again the lingbat's presence disarmed Nisa's emotion.

"I am staying here, too, Carob."

"True, true." Carob gazed out at the night, sniffed, then sighed. "Fine night, isn't it?" He sniffed again, then twitched his ears. "Lots of activity, I'd say. Insects . . ."

"You'll never want for a meal on Dakota." Nisa tried to sound light and cheerful, but her voice betrayed her sorrow.

To her surprise, Carob noticed her downcast mood. He hopped to her foot, fluttered madly, then lodged himself on her shoulder. Nisa noticed that while he dug his claws into Dane's shoulder, he remained gentle and careful with her.

"Did they give you a difficult time of it in there?" Carob didn't wait for an answer. "You should have brought me along to put them in their place."

Nisa swallowed hard to contain her wayward emotion. "They don't like me much, and they keep calling me Seneca's mistress . . . but I'm not imprisoned."

"Thanks to Seneca."

Nisa eyed the lingbat. "I got the impression you didn't like him much."

Carob shrugged, leaning himself against her head. Nisa hoped her hair was braided tightly enough to keep him from entangling himself. "I didn't, at first. Guess I was comparing him to Motega. But your Akandan seems a sensible sort. I particularly liked the way he handled the matter of research."

"That was noble."

"Told me while you were bathing that he and I would see about freeing the other specimens tomorrow. Getting them situated and all. Seems to feel my ability with language will serve in some sort of translation." Carob considered this, a faintly condescending expression on his small, scrunched face.

"Don't know if I'll get far. I'm the only Candor specimen, you know. The others, they're just Dakotan fowl and a few creatures from Thorwal. Your Akandan mentioned learning what the wortpig has to say for itself."

Nisa coughed to conceal a giggle. Her eyes twinkled, which Carob noticed. He had meant to cheer her, and Nisa touched the bat's head fondly. "Thank you, Carob. You're a kind little fellow, whether you mean to be or not."

Carob seemed embarrassed by the praise. "It's not that I'm interested. . . . I thought I'd spend the night on the hunt. It's been a while since I've had such a lush feeding ground."

"You're not staying here?" Nisa's relaxed mood turned to panic. She had intended to keep the lingbat with her, sleeping on her pillow, if necessary. She needed a buffer between herself and Seneca. "Aren't you tired?"

Carob hopped from her shoulder, eyeing the nearest vine as if assessing its possibilities. "No, no. Not tired. Lingbats require only light rest, when properly fed. Of course, we are generally nocturnal creatures, though I got off schedule being clamped in a cage."

"Are you sure?"

Carob wasn't listening. His ears twitched; he trembled. With a sudden flapping of his wings, Carob sprang onto the vine and disappeared among the leaves. A winged insect darted out and fluttered away. Nisa heard a sharp, disgusted utterance from within the vine.

Carob poked his head out from the leaves. "I'm a little out of practice. Ah, what a night! The thrill of the chase, the crunchy reward. Farewell, human! May your own pleasures await!"

Nisa saw Carob scramble from vine to vine, to the nearest tree. The Dakotans emerged across the square, heading to their beds for the night. She didn't want Seneca to think she was waiting for him, so she hurried inside and secured herself in Motega's bedroom.

The light replacer had faded, sending soft, sensual shadows across the wide bed. Nisa just stared. How many more reminders must she endure? *I can't stay here.* Nisa left the bedroom and stood outside the door, considering how to spare herself these bitter memories.

She heard Seneca downstairs. He was Deiaquande. Maybe he should live like one, too. Nisa marched down the stairs and saw him lying on his back on the floor.

"You're not going to sleep there, are you?"

Seneca opened his eyes. "Have you another

159

suggestion?" He sat up. Nisa's stomach fluttered. His dark hair hung around his face, below his shoulders. The Dakotan humidity had encouraged a slight wave to his hair, giving him an even more sensual appearance.

Nisa tried to speak, but her voice caught. Of course he would misunderstand her question. Nothing between them happened as she intended.

"From your behavior at the banquet, I sensed my company wouldn't be welcome in your bed tonight."

"It wouldn't. That's not what I . . ." Nisa paused, regaining command of herself. "I only thought that as Deiaquande, you might prefer Motega's sleeping quarters. His bed is quite large."

Seneca studied her face. "Are you inviting me to join you, maiden, or not? From your words, I cannot tell."

"Certainly not!" Nisa puffed an impatient breath. "I'm merely suggesting that you take the bedroom, and I'll sleep down here."

"On the floor?"

Nisa hesitated, but then nodded. "Yes. On the floor." She looked around the room to the chair where Carob had napped earlier. "Or perhaps on that chair."

Seneca lay back. "It's not necessary, maiden. I prefer a firm surface. You may keep the bed."

Nisa chewed her lip. How would she get him to take Motega's room without confessing the real reason? "Manipi resents me enough. If you're stiff and tired from sleeping on the floor, he'll blame me."

Seneca glanced over at her. "I am used to such surfaces. Akandans don't have fluffy mattresses."

Curse you! Nisa drew a quick breath. "Are you afraid I'll try to escape if you leave me down here? Because, if you are, I'm much too tired. . . ."

"If you escape you'll get lost, but I have faith you'll find your way back." Seneca sounded tired; he didn't open his eyes.

Nisa couldn't think of another persuasive argument. "Are you sure?"

Seneca opened his eyes and looked at her suspiciously. "Is there some reason you don't want to sleep up there?"

Nisa's chin firmed. He was prying. Deliberately. "Not at all. I was only thinking of you." Her eyes fixed on his, daring him to question her further.

Seneca shrugged. "As you wish, maiden. I am comfortable here. Sleep well."

Nisa watched his chest rise and fall with slow breaths. She glanced toward the second floor. No choice. Unless she humiliated herself by an explanation, she would have to face the past through a long night.

Nisa tried to sleep. The nightshirt she wore was lightweight, but she still felt hot and uncomfortable. She lay staring at the light replacer on Motega's high ceiling. It had faded to black, but the light from Thorwal gleamed like a moon.

For many ages the Dakotans had thought Thorwal was a moon. Maybe life on both worlds would have been better if that illusion had remained.

Nisa rolled over in bed. She felt small and alone. When she closed her eyes she remembered Motega's body curled around hers, his arm over her, protecting her as he slept. Waking her when his passion flared, shifting her hair over her shoulder to kiss her neck . . .

Nisa sat up. She drew a strained, deep breath to clear her battered senses. He said he loved her, that he wanted her as his mate, that they would rule Dakota and Thorwal as one world. Nisa would have lived with him in the Thorwalian mines if he had asked her.

Her eyes felt heavy with weariness. Her limbs ached from her walk through the forest. She felt bruises all over from the shuttle crash. But she couldn't sleep.

"It's your fault, wortpig," she said to the night. "You've brought these memories back. Curse you!" Nisa got up and paced around the room. Maybe

Seneca didn't mean to remind her of Motega. It was possible.

She sat on the edge of the bed, her head in her hands. He had kissed her palm. Just as he had done when she showed him Thorwal's lava flow. True, this time he meant to embarrass her. But she reacted with the same oblivious desire. Curse him!

Nisa flopped back in bed. Everything Seneca did reminded her of Motega's sensual power. When Motega was held prisoner on Thorwal, she meant to stay away, never to see him again. Instead she visited his cell daily, with the intention of tormenting him for his betrayal.

On her last visit, she made the mistake of getting too close. Motega had grabbed her, forced her into his arms, and kissed her. She shuddered at the memory of his violent hunger, his kiss without love, but of raw passion and a man's need.

Worse still was the memory of her own response. She had hit him and summoned the guard, who reluctantly shackled him to the wall. But her body had seethed with desire.

Nisa's pulse quickened. She hadn't slept that night, either. When she returned the next morning, it was with the intention of enticing him again. And perhaps surrendering . . .

That morning she found his guard missing. Nisa squeezed her eyes shut, blotting out the hideous memory of Motega's death.

"Please," she whispered. "Don't make me think of you again."

He haunted her. Somehow Motega's spirit had enlisted Seneca, and returned to torture her. Maybe she deserved it. Hot tears burned beneath Nisa's closed lids, swelling past her lashes and dripping to her cheeks, onto her pillow.

The door opened and she froze. One quick look told her that Seneca stood in the doorway, his tall body a silhouette against the hall lights. Nisa held her breath. She heard him move across the room and knew he stood by the bed, watching her. Her lungs hurt from lack of air.

The bed sank as Seneca sat beside her. Nisa drew a small, silent gasp of warm air, then bit her lip until she tasted blood. He couldn't see her pain. No matter what, she would hide her weakness.

Seneca touched her hair, softening the wisps of hair at her brow. He released the tight braid, and her hair fell across her face. He stroked her hair gently, saying nothing. Nisa wondered if he thought she slept.

Seneca bent and kissed the side of her forehead. "Are you going to tell me what troubles you, maiden, or shall I guess the cause on my own?"

He knew she wasn't sleeping. Nisa drew a long breath, then exhaled in irritation. "I should have known you couldn't last the whole night without pestering me."

Seneca's fingers played in her loose hair, relaxing her despite her anger. "Your efforts at sleep seem futile. You've been pacing this floor like a guard on duty."

Nisa peeked up at him. "You imagined that."

From the light of distant Thorwal, Nisa saw Seneca's face as he smiled. "You lay in bed, probably on your back. Then you rolled over. You sat up and found occasion to insult me, aloud. Then you rose to pace the floor. Then you fell back on the bed, and gave in to whatever grief possesses you tonight."

"One might think you were spying on me."

"It wasn't necessary. Your movements aren't particularly stealthy."

Seneca sifted her hair through his fingers. Nisa shoved his hand away. "What do you want?"

"I don't think you'd welcome my most honest response, so I will keep it to myself."

Nisa glared. "Please do."

Despite her hostile response, Seneca lay down beside her, ignoring her gasp and attempt to squirm away. He slid his arm over her and held her gently in place. "I won't hurt you, Nisa. But I find I can't sleep knowing you suffer. So I will lie with you and guard you from your demons."

"You are my demon!"

"Tonight let me be your avenger. We'll both sleep better."

Nisa lay taut and unyielding, but she felt her rapid pulse, the sudden heat of her body against his.

Apparently Seneca felt it, too. "Sleep, maiden. I won't harm you."

Nisa trembled. His warm, masculine scent softened her resistance; his powerful body drove away the memory of Motega. She had no power over the past. But Seneca was alive and strong, and the future remained uncertain.

He promised not to hurt her. She believed him. Nisa relaxed. Seneca's fingers returned to her hair, and she closed her eyes. She adjusted her legs for more comfort, curled up next to his body. Her calf muscle spasmed, and she winced.

Seneca noticed her twinge. "Are you in pain?"

"Not at all. A bit. I may have twisted something when I fell."

"You're not in the habit of walking. Your muscles will adjust. They are well formed, even if underused."

Seneca's teasing manner relaxed her further. "They'll get no further use. Not if you uphold your promise."

"You may find activity more pleasurable than you imagine, maiden."

"Impossible." Nisa rested her cheek against his arm. His skin felt smooth and warm. Even hot. She moved to look into his face. "Are you ill?"

"No."

"You look . . . flushed."

164

A slow smile told Nisa the cause of Seneca's warmth. She blushed and looked away. Seneca slid his arm around her, settling her head on his shoulder.

"TiKay teaches restraint, maiden. Rarely has it been tested as it is this night. But you have nothing to fear from me."

Nisa wasn't sure it was fear she felt. But better Seneca think so than learn the truth. She felt warm and damp in her secret depths, reminded of the feminine desire she had repressed until Seneca entered her life.

Nisa swallowed and tried to slow her breathing. She closed her eyes, but she remembered his powerful body, stripped of clothing, aroused. . . . She fidgeted. She remembered his masterful seduction in Helmar's holding cell. How he felt between her thighs, probing.

A quick gasp escaped her lips. She coughed to disguise her emotion. A low groan emanated from deep in Seneca's throat. "You're not making restraint easy tonight."

Nisa looked at him, suspicion ripe in her eyes. "How do you know what I'm thinking?" Realizing how revealing her comment was, she bit her lip and hid her face.

Seneca chuckled. "Something tells me we're both thinking the same thing. But that shouldn't surprise you, maiden. Our encounter in your holding cell is rarely far from my thoughts."

Nisa cringed. He knew. "Nothing could be further from the truth." Her whole body raged at her denial. A faint moan rippled through her. Her lips found his shoulder, and she tasted his flesh in mindless oblivion.

"You test me, maiden." Seneca sounded hoarse; his muscles quivered. His effort at resistance destroyed what remained of her control.

Her tongue swept out to tease his skin; her breath came in rapid, fierce gasps. *I must know you.* She slithered up his body, caught his hair in her fingers, then kissed his lips. Nisa's open mouth played against

165

Seneca's; she nipped at his lower lip, slid her tongue between his lips.

Seneca's arms closed around her like a passionate vise. His tongue sought hers, a wild burning to join surging through his veins. "I have never been able to resist you."

He broke the kiss and looked into Nisa's face. "You seem young tonight, maiden. But battered. As if your heart can stand no more weight without bursting."

She couldn't argue. "That is how I feel." Combined with the weight of her unwilling desire, her pain overwhelmed her. "I am drowning, I think."

"I will never let you drown, maiden. Never."

Seneca eased her onto her back, kissing her face, her throat. She felt the last remnants of control slip away, and she knew what she was becoming. Knew it, and could do nothing to alter its course. The wild passion of her Thorwalian ancestors raged inside her body, her soul—the Ravagers, who lived for conquest, for lust, for gratification.

She clutched Seneca's shoulders, kissing his throat. Seneca had been right about her. Her ice gone, she became fire. Seneca was the wind across the snow, seeking the fire. Fanning her to an irresistible flame.

It was madness. The same madness that possessed the Ravagers when they pillaged their world. She had no control, no restraint. Her logic fled, leaving her at the mercy of her savage impulses.

She touched the tip of her tongue against the base of his throat. She arched beneath him, trying to reach the source of her pleasure. She moved against him, creating erotic friction between them.

She was tired, tormented by a past she couldn't change. She was drawn by a man she didn't know, couldn't begin to understand. Yet the currents between them seemed irresistible. But Seneca seemed to resist, denying her what she so desperately needed.

Nisa's hand slid down his side, under his open robe.

Before Seneca realized her intention, she cupped his manhood, squeezing and kneading him toward the same mindless oblivion that consumed her. His hips rocked with her greedy skill, and her teeth nipped at his shoulder as she felt his surrender.

She teased the engorged tip of his erection with a light, delicate touch. A low, raspy moan shuddered in her throat as he moved against her hand. Her back arched beneath him, a primitive invitation to mating, raw and unencumbered by reason.

Seneca's hands worked feverishly at her collar. He stripped open the front of her nightshirt, then freed her breasts to his kiss. The tips pebbled against his mouth, and she moaned and writhed as he teased her. Beneath him she squirmed and urged, soft murmurs and pleas deep in her throat. Her fingers squeezed around his length, stroking, urging.

Seneca took her hand and drew it to his lips. "Don't move."

"Seneca . . ." Her voice came desperate, toneless, yet filled with need. "I want you."

"You want relief." His own voice quavered. "From desire, maiden, from lust. I will give you relief."

Nisa's mind was a blur. No thought formed, just need amid sensation. Seneca's lips pressed against hers, tasting her, savoring her. She felt his fingertips circling her breast, then felt his lips and tongue as he teased her, drawing on one peak, then the other.

He unfastened her nightshirt, then peeled it from her skin, leaving her flesh bare as he dropped the shirt to the floor. His hand slid down over her stomach, avoiding her woman's mound as he stroked the inner flesh of her thigh. Over and around, but never touching, he brought every nerve alive, throbbing, desperate.

When his fingers grazed her damp, inner flesh, Nisa cried out, her head twisting from side to side. He moved as if in a dream, slowly, deliberately. His finger found the small peak crowning her entrance, barely touching, sliding into her voluptuous warmth, back again.

She reached for him, desperate, but Seneca stopped her. "Don't move."

"I must. . . ."

The touch of his hand intensified, and her words caught. He pressed his palm against her sensitized flesh, not moving, releasing his touch when she squirmed to increase the friction.

"I told you once you must learn what serves you, maiden. . . . Don't move."

Nisa groaned at his husky command. The pressure of his touch increased, moving slowly, circling the tiny peak. His whole hand moved against her until she shuddered and cried out with every breath.

Her legs quivered; her pulse raged. Her hips writhed of their own accord. The pressure stopped, and she screamed. Seneca chuckled, then laid his hand against her. Her head tipped back and he kissed her throat, nipping gently.

With a slow, light touch, he traced small circles around her aching flesh. He dipped his finger into her fiery, moist depths, groaning when she arched and squeezed around the shallow probe.

"Don't move." His voice came so hoarsely she barely heard him. But she lay still as his finger dipped in and out, then returned to the sweet torment.

"This is what you want, what you need." A sweet, mesmerizing rhythm echoed with Seneca's words. His touch intensified, stroking and sliding over her delicate flesh. From deep inside her, spiraling currents of fire rose toward the surface.

The currents destroyed all resistance. All she had so long denied rose up before her. She saw Motega's image in her mind, blending with Seneca, reducing her to mindless, blind lust. She saw Motega as she had once believed him to be, passionate and sweet, in love.

Her heart fought, her mind struggled, but Seneca's fingers kept up the torturous teasing, his lips pressed against her face and her neck.

Motega first had showed her this passion. She buried it deep, but Seneca unearthed it again. *Please, no* . . . Her hips writhed, twisted. She fought to block Motega's memory. She opened her eyes and looked at Seneca. The likeness between the two men damned her. She saw Motega.

In rippling waves, sensation sparkled through Nisa's body, turning to fire. She couldn't stop it. All the fire in her soul rose to meet him, then turned to flame. He met her like the wind, and the fire burst to the surface.

A wild cry shuddered from Nisa's parted lips as wave after wave of hidden desire burst and fragmented around her. The fiery pleasure coursed through her, reaching a fierce climax, then subsided to a still, shocked relief.

She lay beside him, her eyes wide and stunned, gasping, her nerves twitching in the aftermath of cataclysmic joy. Seneca settled beside her, holding her close, his own strong heart pounding.

Nisa's senses returned; her thoughts re-formed. She felt weak, shocked. Now, in the aftermath, she found the strength to repress Motega's image. For a horrible second, he and Seneca had been the same.

They weren't the same. Motega never denied himself anything, but Seneca hadn't taken her. She begged him, but he hadn't satisfied himself with her. She tilted her gaze upward. His face was drawn and strained, his lips tight. All his effort was centered on restraint.

"Why?" Her voice came tiny, shaken.

Seneca looked at her, his eyes black with desire. He wanted her, she saw that. But he hadn't surrendered to the madness that consumed her.

"Sleep, my little Ravager." He kissed her forehead.

"I promised not to hurt you, and I won't."

"I wanted you."

"I know."

"Don't you want me?"

"I want you. But not when you're weak, Nisa. I want you when you're in control of all that emotion and all that force. I want you when you're strong."

Nisa wasn't sure what this meant, but the day's weariness stole over her, and her limbs went leaden. Tonight it was enough. She didn't need to know his intentions, or the fate of her world. He cradled her head against his shoulder, again stroking her damp hair from her cheek.

"Sleep."

Nisa closed her eyes and yawned. She tucked herself close beside him, and abandoned her doubts and questions. She abandoned everything, and sank into the blissful freedom of sleep.

Nisa's breaths came even and deep as she slept. Satisfied. Seneca fought to deepen his own breaths, to relax his taut body. Nothing worked. He tried to empty his mind, to feel the rhythms of the night. All he felt was Nisa's soft, warm skin touching his.

"There is a price," he muttered aloud. *It was easier when I lived without restraint, without forethought.* Blood pounded in his veins. But he had protected her from herself, from the secret hold he possessed over her. If she understood that hold, she would never forgive him, never understand the strange path his life had taken. But he protected her. Tonight that was all that mattered.

Chapter Six

Soft, golden light filtered through the vines outside Motega's bedroom window. Nisa felt the light before she saw it. Her limbs ached from the previous day's strain, but her insides felt good. Tingly, satisfied.

Her eyes snapped open. She looked around. Seneca wasn't there. She clasped her hand to her forehead and groaned. "What have I done?" The memories of her night flooded back. "What has *he* done?"

He yielded to her pleas and her relentless provocation, that was what he had done. Nisa respected truth enough to admit that. If only to herself. *How will I face him now?* She contemplated remaining in bed and simulating a debilitating fever. Maybe he'd think the fever inspired her. . . .

No, Seneca wasn't the kind of man a woman could fool. He would just smile that knowing smile and see exactly what motivated her sudden illness. *The only thing to do is to face him as if it never happened.* Nisa started to get out of bed. She was naked. Her

171

nightshirt lay in a crumpled pile beside the bed.

No, she couldn't pretend it never happened, either. She would have to face him honestly, knowing what she had done. If only Thorwal's legions would attack, and spare her the humiliation!

Nisa rose with painful reluctance. Beyond her embarrassment, her legs were so stiff she could barely stand. Her only consolation was knowing Manipi's scouting party must be in far worse shape this morning.

She dressed in her blue suit, then fished around in her pack for lighter shoes. Thorwalian snow boots wouldn't do at all on Dakota. She went to the basin and splashed her face and polished her teeth. She examined herself in the mirror. Her complexion looked too pink.

She splashed cold water, then eyed the cleansing unit. Maybe if she soaked her whole body at the lowest temperature . . . A damp towel hung over a warming bar. Seneca had bathed. Her nerves tensed at the image.

The unit's control setting caught her eye. All dials set to "cold." A slow, satisfied smile formed on Nisa's lips. Apparently he hadn't been unaffected by their nighttime passion, either.

Nisa abandoned the idea of bathing. She fixed her hair in a neat braid, then headed out to begin her scrutiny of the Dakotans' new leader. She would learn his intentions, in service to Thorwal, in order to report to Helmar at the earliest opportunity.

She stood by the front door, gathering her courage to face the Dakotans' prying eyes, to face Seneca. Maybe her plan to regain peace would work, after all. Nisa tried to restrain her hope. It was founded on nothing.

Nothing but her knowledge of a man who kept to his word despite the persuasive temptation of a woman mad with desire.

Carob met Nisa at the door. "You don't want to miss this." He hopped aside and gestured toward the village square. Every Dakotan in Macanoc, young and old, formed rows, lining up as Seneca addressed them. A reflector screen was set up, broadcasting the session to every village on Dakota.

Nisa's heart quickened when she saw him. His dark hair was tied back behind his head; he wore Motega's dark green Dakotan attire, but his feet were bare. No Dakotan wore shoes, either.

"This," spouted Carob, "could make my abduction worthwhile." He hopped to the vine and positioned himself high for the best view. Nisa seated herself cross-legged to watch, cooled by the shade of the trees while the Dakotans suffered in the morning sun.

"I have explained the premise of TiKay, but its real mastery is in the doing." Seneca assumed a well-balanced posture, his knees slightly bent, his arms to the side.

The Dakotans exchanged doubtful glances, then tried to emulate their leader. Their efforts brought loud chortles from Carob. Nisa restrained her amusement, if only to keep Seneca's attention off her.

"We seek balance. We develop it by testing."

Seneca proceeded to demonstrate various motions while the Dakotans and Nisa watched. His motion was fluid, precise. Every muscle supported him in perfect grace. Nisa felt a too-familiar tingle in her stomach. She tried to focus on his actions, and not on the man.

As Seneca moved his body through different positions of balance, Nisa recognized the same defensive movements he had used against the disguised Thorwalians at the crash site. All part of a fluid whole.

Seneca stopped. "When you have learned the stances of balance, they become part of your memory, your soul. With TiKay, you follow the natural path, the path of least resistance."

The Dakotans appeared confused, but listened

attentively. Nisa's mind wandered. It was impossible to focus on actions. Now she knew why. The actions were part of the man. They couldn't be separated.

"Assume the first position."

Since the Dakotans all placed themselves in similar stances, Nisa assumed she had missed much of Seneca's early morning instruction. The Dakotans splayed their feet well apart, knees bent, arms curved at the elbows.

"It was worth the crash." Carob chirped in the vine, distracting several Dakotans, who weaved from their balanced stance.

"Balance is in the soul first, in the mind second, and in the body last."

This wasn't evident in the Dakotans' posture as they tried to follow Seneca's example by balancing on one leg. Manipi tripped and knocked Langundo from his position.

"Why always me?" grumbled Langundo as he tried to regain his balance.

Carob cackled and pointed. Seneca noticed the lingbat. "Rest." He approached the vine. "Carob . . ." Nisa wondered if he intended to put the bat back in his specimen cage. "Yesterday we discussed freeing the research specimens. If you could check on their condition now, it would speed the process."

"Might take a while to establish communication, sir."

Sir. Nisa shook her head.

"Yes," agreed Seneca. "But I'm sure you'll be successful. Your suggestions as to freeing or rehousing the creatures are vital to their survival."

Carob didn't seem to recognize Seneca's flattery. Instead, he puffed himself up in obvious pride. "I'll see what I can do."

Carob hopped off the vine and bounced across the village square, intent on his new vocation. Nisa felt more conspicuous without the bat.

Seneca didn't meet her eyes as he returned to his instruction. She wondered what he felt this morning. He had a way of keeping passion separate from reason. Maybe it meant nothing to him, just the primal mating desire between two healthy specimens.

"The first stance is the most simple, but also the most vital. Here is the basis of balance, the foundation. Through all moves I will teach you, this is the starting point, and the end. Balance."

"This is all very interesting, Deiaquande." Manipi paused, already out of breath. "But kicks and punches won't stand up to Thorwalian riflery, not in an all-out assault. As you said yourself, our aim could be better. You aren't suggesting we abandon the weapons, are you?"

"No. I'm suggesting you learn the power in yourselves first. When you learn TiKay, when you learn true balance, any weapon you select will become part of that power."

The Dakotans appeared skeptical. Nisa watched as Seneca retrieved a stun rifle. "At what range would you consider yourselves accurate?"

Manipi looked around the square. "I'd say, if I could knock one of those nuts from the Alben tree, I'd be a fair shot."

Seneca aimed the weapon. Just as he said, it seemed an extension of himself rather than a tool he applied. He fired. The nut fell from the tree amid gasps from the Dakotans.

Seneca set the rifle aside. Nisa remembered his quick examination of her weapon on board the *Gordonia*. Apparently he learned with unmatched speed.

His shot convinced the Dakotans. "Balance begins within. You'll find it nowhere else, if not inside yourselves."

Nisa yawned. The morning sun felt warm, and she wasn't used to heat. Thorwal's cool breezes kept her sharp and quick, but the balm of Dakota's weather slowed her thoughts and eased her tension.

A round, furry insect buzzed by, seeking flowers for nectar. It settled on a red blossom. No wonder Thorwalians had visited Dakota for relaxation. During her visit with Motega, Nisa had experienced very little of their climate. But it seemed more a part of his sensual appeal than a contrast.

"From this position, the right leg swings back, arched." Nisa watched Seneca move from a forward motion to face the other way. He turned back. "Forward, back, follow . . ."

The Dakotans tried. The children accomplished the motion with little trouble, but for the older Dakotans, Seneca's move wreaked havoc. Manipi ended up on his back, feet up again. Langundo crashed into a Dakotan woman, who fell, then thrust herself up to punch him.

Nisa laughed. Seneca turned to her and smiled.

"Perhaps you, maiden, would care to join the lesson?"

"I would not."

Manipi struggled to his feet. "Make her!"

"She must learn what serves her." Seneca's words echoed his husky whisper in the erotic haze of the night. Nisa's cheeks flamed. She rose hurriedly to her feet despite her aching muscles.

"As a matter of fact, I find your instruction tedious." She lifted her chin. "If you don't mind, I will take a walk now and ponder my escape."

Seneca nodded without concern, then turned back to his class. "Try again. . . ."

Nisa wandered along the stream as it flowed through Macanoc. She knew a small pond formed just north of the village. Motega had brought her there in his hovercraft when they first arrived from Thorwal.

Small woodland flowers grew along the river; amphibians hopped from mossy rocks into the water, making small splashes and louder croaks. Red birds sang in the overhanging branches as Nisa walked along.

She didn't think about escape. She thought about Seneca's teasing smile, about his strong, masculine body as he controlled his powerful limbs in fluid grace. Nisa found the pond and seated herself on a flat rock. She picked up a small stone and hurled it into the smooth water, pleased with its wide splash.

She felt restless. The bank leading to the pond was wide and grassy. She glanced over her shoulder toward the village. Only a few green and brown rooftops showed. No one would see her. . . .

Nisa slipped off her shoes and found an open space on the grass. She positioned her feet wide apart, knees bent, her arms curved, fists tight. "It's not so hard." She lifted one leg under her, balancing on the other.

"Only a Dakotan could bungle this." Nisa's balance wavered and she tripped, catching herself. She tried again. Her brow furrowed as she concentrated. She lost her balance and sighed in exasperation. "Of course, my legs are sore from yesterday."

She forced herself back into Seneca's position. This time she held the position for several seconds before leaning too far to the right. "Better." Nisa decided to move to the next position.

One leg forward, then swing back. She tried. She spun full circle and almost fell into the pond. Nisa looked around in embarrassment, thankful no one could see her. She tried again. Too much effort. Her legs tangled, and she fell on her bottom.

"You seem intent on staining that portion of your anatomy. It is, I will admit, a very appealing angle."

Nisa wanted the ground to open and swallow her whole. It took all her effort to rise and turn toward the soft, teasing voice. Seneca stood leaning against a tree, arms folded, watching her. She closed her eyes as humiliation scorched through her.

Seneca ambled down the bank and studied her strained expression. He said nothing. Nisa forced herself to look at him, a light, casual smile glued to her lips.

"Shouldn't you be instructing your new subjects?"

"The prospect of instructing you intrigues me more."

"I do not desire instruction."

"No? You seemed fairly intent on practicing a moment ago."

Nisa cringed. "They'll be brawling if you don't get back there."

"I allowed them a break for the morning meal. They considered it a severe trial to begin the day with activity rather than food, so I'm allowing them dry portions of barlit-meal. That should limit their intake."

Nisa couldn't resist a smile. "You have a cruel streak, Akandan. As I said, your desire to separate them from their food will see you soon deposed."

"If that is their wish . . . Now, maiden, shall I advise you, or will you continue to flounder on your own?"

"I wasn't floundering."

Seneca smiled and Nisa's insides fluttered. It might be better to have him instruct her than to remain alone with him, images of his lovemaking fresh in her memory.

"Very well. But I won't tolerate you making a fool of me."

"That isn't my intention." Seneca positioned himself behind her. Just as they had been in the holding cell. Nisa hopped away.

"What are you doing?"

"Adjusting your position. Turn around."

Nisa turned, but she held her body tense, ready to spring away if his intentions proved more erotic than instructive.

"Take the first position. I assume you learned what that is from watching."

Tentatively Nisa spread her legs, bent her knees, and positioned her arms. Seneca adjusted her elbows closer to her sides. "Keep your feet pointed forward. They're pointing out now."

Nisa moved her toes as he directed.

"Very good. You have natural balance."

Nisa felt an irrational surge of pride. Yes, she was balanced. As a child she ran faster and jumped higher than the other children. As an adult, she relinquished dignity enough to teach her young brother sliding games that involved balancing on the ice and snow.

Nisa's attention wavered and her stance faded. "Concentrate."

"I was concentrating."

"In the teaching of TiKay, the pupil does not argue with the master."

Nisa huffed. "Master, indeed."

"Shift to one leg."

Nisa hesitated, then obeyed. She held her breath to maintain the pose.

"Breathe, always. Even and deep."

Nisa breathed, then lost her balance. She whirled around, her face knitted and angry. "If you hadn't made me breathe . . ."

"You would have fainted." Seneca seized her shoulders and turned her to face the pond. "Again."

Nisa tried again. She breathed as deeply as she could. She looked at her feet to be sure they pointed forward, then stumbled.

"Keep your eyes ahead. Across the pond."

" 'Breathe, look here, look there.' What torment!" Before Seneca could comment on her disobedience, Nisa assumed the position and held it. Seconds passed, and she remained immobile.

"Return."

Nisa collapsed, but Seneca tapped her shoulder. "Into first position." She assumed the first stance.

"Well done. Again." Nisa repeated the two positions with equal success.

"You learn quickly, maiden." Nisa beamed.

"We're not finished. Now, you will learn to combine balance with motion. . . ."

Nisa spent the whole morning under Seneca's tutelage. He was gentle, yet relentless, easing her forward. Before she knew what he wanted, she had learned a new motion, a new way to transform her body into power.

The sun was high overhead when he finally allowed her to rest. "I have driven you too hard, maiden. But rarely does a master have such an apt pupil."

He wasn't teasing her. He meant it. Nisa bit her lip to restrain a foolish smile. "If we don't go back, the Dakotans will have eaten all the barlit-meal from this sector."

Seneca laughed. "That seems all too likely. And Carob may have staged an insurrection of his own backed by the freed lab specimens. Come, maiden, let us go."

Seneca held out his hand and Nisa took it. She smiled up at him, and Seneca kissed her forehead. "You are beautiful today, Nisa Calydon."

He used her family name, a throwback to the age of the Ravager clans. He made it sound magical. Seneca seemed to appreciate that side of her nature. The side she tried so desperately to subdue.

"On Thorwal we have spent generations separating ourselves from our Ravager ancestors. Yet here I've spent the whole morning with you teaching me to fight."

"Not to fight, but to protect yourself from the aggression of others. The Ravager blood is strong in your people. Maybe stronger than you realize. The more it is subdued, the more it appears in unexpected—and dangerous—places. Tempered, it may prove a powerful force."

"I want to be a powerful force. At times, though, I feel . . . less."

"Think before you react, maiden. Then, no matter what situation you find yourself in, the outcome will be your choice, a result of what you want."

Nisa studied Seneca's face. His deep calm penetrated into her soul. She wanted that, too. "Have you always been this way? I suppose you were a calm child, too."

Seneca didn't answer at once. The light in his dark eyes turned distant, and a little sad. "No, I haven't always been this way. There was a time I fought life at every turn."

"Truly?" Nisa's head tilted to one side. "I can't imagine that."

"Can't you? Some things, perhaps, are too obvious to see."

"What changed you?"

"My father."

"Your father?" Nisa endured a wave of remorse. The father she had separated him from in her abduction. "Were you very close?"

"He was the best man I have ever known. He saw truth where I was blind. He brought me to face my own reckless nature, then showed me the strength in myself."

"How?"

"With TiKay."

Nisa wasn't sure she understood. Until this moment she had considered Seneca unflappable, innately strong. It hadn't occurred to her that his journey included obstacles.

"From him, I learned I was more than a result of the circumstances of my life. I learned to determine my own fate."

A frown curled Nisa's lips. "Until I abducted you . . ."

"No, maiden. You are part of my fate, for good or for ill. What I do with that fate remains undecided."

Nisa considered this. Since Motega's betrayal, she had felt at the mercy of circumstance, powerless. Today Seneca had taught her Akandan techniques, but beneath the learning, he taught her the power in herself.

Her perspective altered. Circumstances were arbitrary, good and bad. It was she who chose her own direction. "I might be powerful."

Seneca drew her hand to his lips. "You might, indeed. When you decide what you want, nothing in this world or beyond will stop you."

Nisa didn't respond. What if she wanted him? Nisa wanted to ask his intentions. But he had never wavered, never hinted that he might prefer to stay with her. He never said her kisses erased the memory of his Akandan mate.

"Shall we go, maiden? I have much to accomplish in a short time if peace is to be secured for your worlds."

Nisa's eyes widened, hope flashing through her. "Peace? But I thought . . ."

"I didn't say peace on Thorwal's terms. But peace is preferable to discord, for both people, is it not?"

"Yes. That's what I tried to tell you."

"It is a beginning, not an end. But this is what I promised the Dakotans, and this I will strive to achieve."

"They want more than peace! They want the power and technology to plunder the Candor Moon!"

"Have you seen evidence of such a desire?"

Nisa hesitated. "No."

"Then you assume to know another's mind."

"They wouldn't share their new developments—plans for a new power cell that could send a flight ship to Candor and beyond. Why, if they have no interest?"

"From what I've seen, plans aren't enough. They would have to construct or renovate a craft. For a people unable to keep hovercraft in working condition, that seems unlikely."

Nisa couldn't argue with that. The Dakotans were hardly likely to plunder anything in their sorry condition.

"Maiden, it seems more likely to me that your people desire those plans for their own use."

"Ridiculous!" Nisa's lips tightened into an angry ball. "That's what Motega suggested, too."

"For one as logical as you claim to be, the concept often eludes you. The Dakotans might be unable to build such a powerful craft, but for your Thorwalian technicians . . ."

"You accuse us!" Nisa snatched her hand from Seneca's and poked his chest fiercely. "Well, I'll tell you something, wortpig! Had we desired to ravage Candor, we would have done it long ago!"

"Without sufficient power? Your Thorwalians may be dexterous, but they're not particularly creative. One thing is missing to aid such a quest—the Dakotan design."

"Ha! We sent the probe to investigate that moon, and we're the ones who discovered its riches. If I hadn't confessed our discovery to Motega, none of this would have happened."

"Perhaps he saw a danger."

"Perhaps he saw an opportunity for untold power! It was then that he began openly defying Thorwalian . . . suggestions, and issued his first demands for equal Dakotan representation at council."

"That doesn't seem unfair."

"It's blatantly unfair! We far outnumber the Dakotans."

"Yet you share equal power. They have much to lose by serving your ends."

Nisa's temper boiled. "I had forgotten how tiresome you can be. I've had enough of your instruction, wortpig."

" 'Wortpig.' That reminds me, my task is incomplete. It is time for us to return."

"Past time."

Nisa stomped away, fists clenched at her sides as she stormed along the stream. She didn't wait for Seneca. It was bad enough that he resembled Motega. To speak his words was unforgivable.

"It can't be done!" Manipi's shrill voice sounded above the rest as Seneca reached the village square. A crowd of Dakotans circled around Manipi, all angry, shaking fists and arguing.

Seneca saw no sign of Nisa, or he would have assumed she started the heated debate.

"Deiaquande! Over here." Manipi's face appeared flushed and red; fury snapped in his dark eyes.

"What troubles you, Manipi?"

"This . . . this rodent was caught trying to free our specimens. Now, I know you told him to investigate the possibility, but he can't just release them. Some of them are aggressive. The wortpigs in particular are unsuitable for village life."

Seneca spotted Carob in front of Manipi, wings splayed dramatically. "Just following orders, sir. I did what I could about communicating with them. True, I didn't get far. Just a general malaise from their incarceration."

Carob hopped over to Seneca. "I couldn't stand it, sir. To see creatures so apathetic that they wouldn't leave an opened cage without prodding."

"He should know," injected Manipi. "The little monster loosed several before we nabbed him. Found a wortpig heading toward our kitchen."

Seneca considered the dilemma. "Dakota's habitat could be ruined by the introduction of such animals."

"They'd do just fine here, sir," argued Carob.

"They might, but what of the native creatures? Balance, Carob . . . in all things."

"You can't keep them locked away."

Manipi shook his fist at the lingbat. "I see no reason why not. We'd all be better off if you'd been shut in a box and forgotten."

"And I was." Carob's round eyes narrowed, and he positioned himself for attack. Seneca reached down and picked up the lingbat.

"When relations with Thorwal are restored, we will return the creatures to their native habitats. Until then we will build enclosures to keep them comfortable."

"You can't mean to treat those swine as guests." Manipi groaned. "Food, maybe. But not guests."

"Wortpigs weren't what I had in mind for your meals. Let the Thorwalians harvest the creatures, as they did in the past. For you, fish is the natural selection."

"Fish?" Manipi shrank back.

"Yes, fish. This afternoon's lesson will be on obtaining fish. I happened upon a suitable pond this morning. We will assemble there as soon as the matter of the wortpigs has been settled. Bring nets, line, and hooks."

Manipi nodded, though he looked dejected at the prospect. "As you say, Deiaquande." With a deep sigh, he turned away and went to fulfill Seneca's request.

"What about the wortpigs, sir?" asked Carob. "They were just getting used to puttering about on their own when those portly devils stuffed them into a storage unit."

"I know little about the species." Seneca looked around for Nisa. "But our Thorwalian guest may know more. Have you seen her?"

"She came thundering through here just before you showed up. Didn't even speak to me when I greeted her. Last I saw, before Manipi and his villains closed in on me, she was headed for your new quarters."

Seneca glanced toward Motega's dwelling. He considered retrieving Nisa himself, but her mood wasn't one easily persuaded. "If you would fetch her, Carob, we will make a decision concerning the creatures."

"Don't think she'll take orders from you, eh? From the way she marched through here, I'd say you're right. It may take some tact, a little persuasion, but I'll have her meet you in the lab, sir."

"Very good." Seneca didn't ask what kind of "persuasion" Carob intended to use. But the lingbat's capacity for tact seemed questionable.

"You can't eat our pigs!" Nisa crashed through the lab door, banging it against the wall. When it bumped back against her, she slammed her fist into it and it banged again.

Nisa jumped out of the way when the door slammed back. "Why do you keep these ridiculous antiquated doorways?"

Manipi's brow rose. "We've never had trouble with them before. Of course, we're a much more docile race."

"Ha! So docile you're after a harmless, pleasant species like—"

"Wortpigs?" Seneca's jaw dropped. " 'Harmless, pleasant?' That's not what you told me."

"Never mind what I told you. Only a true barbarian would consider eating a wortpig."

"I gathered from your ancient tapestries that the wortpig was once a common source of food."

"Maybe so, but my ancestors were truly vile. They spent equal time killing each other as they fought over land."

Seneca stared at her in astonishment. "What affection do you bear these creatures?"

"That's none of your business."

"It is if I'm to keep them from the Dakotan larder."

The Dawn Star

Nisa hesitated. She didn't meet his eyes. "I learned much of their nature as a child." She paused, shifting her weight from foot to foot. "I kept them as pets."

"As *pets?*" Seneca's voice rang with irony. *"Pets?"* It was too much. He couldn't resist pursuing the matter. "Are we talking about the same 'unattractive and pushy species' to which you've constantly compared me?"

Nisa blushed, and Seneca's laugh shook the room. He contained his amusement, but it wasn't easy.

"They are pushy." Nisa didn't look at him. Her eyes fixed on her feet. "And most consider them unattractive."

"But not you. You are fond, even devoted, to these beasts. Well, well."

Manipi appeared disgusted and bewildered by Nisa's reaction. "Only a Thorwalian would befriend food."

Nisa made a tight fist, ready to strike. "Wortpigs aren't food! Of course, to a Dakotan, anything may be assessed for consumption."

"You see, Deiaquande. This woman is peculiar. Unreliable."

Seneca wasn't listening. "Devoted to wortpigs . . ."

Nisa suffered his amusement. "Where are they? You haven't done them any harm yet, have you?"

"We've done them no harm. In fact, that was never my intention." Seneca eyed Carob, who perched on Nisa's shoulder with a guileless expression on his scrunched face. "Although the suggestion certainly got you here in good speed."

"It did, at that," added Carob, pleased with himself.

Nisa looked between the lingbat and Seneca. "Do you mean . . . you never considered eating the wortpigs?" She breathed a sigh of relief.

"I hadn't decided what to do with them, although they seemed a good food source for your own people."

"Never!"

"What do you suggest we do with the creatures? Keeping them caged serves no purpose if the researchers choose other methods. Letting them run wild on Dakota seems equally unwise."

"They make good pets. Dakotan children don't keep pets as we do. Thorwalian children learn much of responsibility by caring for our creatures."

"She's got a point," said Carob. "Her brother took good care of me. Even brushed my coat a bit, when he had nothing else to do."

Manipi shuddered. "Your dwellings must stink. I'm not surprised you'd keep these filthy things in your homes. We are *not* keeping them as pets."

"Wortpigs are very clean. But they wouldn't like running wild in your forests, either. They prefer dark spaces, such as their subterranean tunnels. They like rooting around in the soil, digging up mushrooms and such."

"Mushrooms?" Manipi's face revealed sudden interest. "Edible ones?"

"A wortpig can tell the difference between a poisonous mushroom and the finer varieties with ease," Nisa stated proudly.

Manipi rubbed his chin, pondering the matter anew. "Might be useful, if we could use them for harvest. In place of the machines! Wonder how they'd be in the barlit-fields?"

"You'd have to dig them tunnels for comfort."

"That's a possibility. . . ."

Seneca enjoyed the discussion as it progressed. Wortpigs replacing intricate machinery.

Manipi seemed to like the idea. "As a matter of fact, we've had trouble with mushrooms invading some of our barlit-fields."

"Then it's settled." Seneca stood between Nisa and Manipi and took their hands. "We will keep the wortpigs, but contained for service. They will not be raised for consumption. Is that agreed?"

Manipi hesitated. "They might be flavorful."

"They are not!"

"Oh, very well. Agreed."

"On Akando, such agreements are made binding by the clasping of the right hand."

Nisa and Manipi clasped hands, eyes fixed in challenge.

"The bond is sealed."

Nisa and Manipi released their grasp, both suspicious, but tentatively in agreement. Nisa turned to Seneca. "Where are they?"

"Who?" Seneca grinned. "Ah, your harmless, pleasant species . . . Manipi, where did you put the creatures?"

"We herded them into an empty storage unit," said Manipi.

Nisa made a fist. "Without water? It's hot! Wortpigs dislike intense heat."

"The mines aren't cold," Manipi reminded her.

"They'll be thirsty. Let me see them!"

Seneca relished the image of Nisa and her pets. "Show us the wortpigs, Manipi."

Manipi led the way to the storage units and opened the door. Three stout, black creatures emerged. Their skin was loose and wrinkled, and their tails were short points. They issued snorting noises as they explored the outer lab.

Nisa's face softened when she saw the wortpigs. Seneca watched as she knelt and held out her hand to the smallest. The wortpig made grunting noises, then touched her hand with his large, flat nose.

"They know a friend, it seems."

"They know when someone means to eat them, that much is certain." She scratched behind the wortpig's ear, and it leaned into her hand. She smiled with affection.

Carob hopped to the floor and made his way from one side of the wortpig to the other, examining its structure like a scientist. "They don't communicate much. Just a general pleasure for living, digging, that sort of thing."

"As I said, they're very agreeable," added Nisa.

Manipi's nose wrinkled. "They stink."

Nisa glared. "Only because you've kept them in small crates, and never allowed them to bathe."

"Bathe? Where would a wortpig bathe in the wild?"

"They take dirt baths in their tunnels. You will provide suitable arrangements to keep them happy as they toil."

Nisa looked to Seneca for authorization. He shrugged. "If the creatures desire dirt baths, it will be arranged. We have plenty of dirt."

This satisfied Nisa and she returned her attention to the wortpig. "I think they would appreciate pens in the shade rather than in here, so they can dig during their leisure hours."

Manipi rolled his eyes. "Let's not go too far."

"They'll have to be housed somewhere," said Seneca. "This might prove an enjoyable task for the children."

"It would," said Nisa, her enthusiasm mounting. "Wortpigs make excellent companions."

"When we return from fishing, I will set the children to the task."

"Fishing?"

"I am leading a fishing party to the same pond where I found you . . . relaxing. Would you care to join us, maiden?"

Nisa considered the matter. "Can the wortpigs accompany us?"

"If you wish . . . and if they'll follow."

"They are herd animals. They follow with great obedience, and are easily trained. Stump and Spike performed tricks at my command."

Seneca pressed his lips together to keep from smiling. Nisa sounded so proud. "Stump and Spike?"

The smallest wortpig scratched its head against Nisa's leg. She patted his head. "Those were my favorites. Maybe I'll name this little fellow after Stump. And that one, the thin one, will be Spike."

"What about the third?"

Nisa's lips curved in a devious smile. "Seneca seems appropriate."

Seneca laughed. "Summon your wortpigs, maiden. They can bathe in dirt to their hearts' content while the Dakotans fish. For you, I have another lesson involving water."

Nisa's eyes narrowed suspiciously. "What lesson?"

Seneca seized her arm. "That, you will learn when we reach the pond."

"Very well. I'll go with you. To watch."

Carob didn't like the suggestion of water. He cleared his throat and eased toward Motega's quarters. "Think I'll stay put where I am. Maybe rest up for tonight's hunt . . ."

Without waiting for approval, the lingbat darted across the square and eased through an open window. Nisa shook her head. "I suppose he wouldn't be much use at fishing." Nisa considered this. "Then again, I doubt we'll see much of the creatures."

Seneca headed toward the village center. "That remains to be seen. You, at least, will profit from our adventure."

"I can't imagine how."

Nisa followed Seneca to the center of Macanoc. Small children waited in the square, a striking contrast to the adult Dakotans. Unlike their overweight but high-strung parents, Dakotan children were light limbed and strangely passive. Nisa wondered why. It took years of careful training to teach the Thorwalian youth discipline and good manners.

Dane, in particular, had been a rambunctious child. He hovered now between the wildness of youth and the dour, staid composure of adulthood. In many ways Nisa was sorry to know his wild manner would soon fade into the stoic dignity of a Thorwalian adult.

"They should learn to play." Nisa didn't realize she had spoken aloud until Manipi huffed.

"Play! A waste of time for the intellectually superior. Their time is best spent with their lessons and in study."

"No wonder they're so pale and thin," said Nisa.

Seneca watched the children. "Nisa is right. Your children suppress their delight in the pleasures of youth. No wonder your people seek comfort in food. You've allowed yourself no other pleasure."

Manipi grumbled incoherently, but a wily grin spread across his face when he looked at Nisa. "You may have a point. Motega found other avenues besides a good meal to pleasure himself. Women . . ."

Nisa frowned, but said nothing.

"One in particular," continued Manipi. "Of course, if he'd kept her in her proper place . . . But no, he fell blindly in love with the woman, allowed her to drag him around at will."

Manipi's conversation didn't please Seneca. Again Nisa suspected he was jealous. "There are many forms of pleasure, Manipi. As you'll soon find. If you would retrieve a net and lines, and some form of hook, we will head to the pond."

Manipi chuckled. "Langundo, fetch what the Deiaquande requires at once."

Langundo headed off for Seneca's supplies, but Manipi seemed unusually pleased with himself. Nisa wondered why he revered Seneca, yet delighted in taunting him with Motega's memory. A discrepancy arose, but she didn't understand its meaning.

A small Dakotan girl approached Seneca. She seemed shy, biting her lip before tapping his leg for attention. Manipi noticed her and gave the child a forbidding look, but Seneca smiled, kneeling beside her.

"What is your name, little one?"

A wave of emotion swept through Nisa as she watched him with the little girl. Motega had paid little attention to children, though Dane followed him around Thorwal faithfully. In contrast, Seneca was gentle and approachable.

"I am called Wicasa." The little girl studied his face intently. "Your skin is dark. And you have rocks in your hair."

"Shells," said Seneca. "Do you like them?"

"They are pretty. I would like shells in my hair, too."

"Perhaps we will find some by the pond. Have you been to the pond, Wicasa?"

"Only to collect specimens for my mother. She works in the lab."

"Today you will collect shells and learn to fish."

Wicasa's large brown eyes widened. "Are we really going on a fish hunt, Deiaquande?"

"We are."

"Can my brother come? He is Hinto, over there." Wicasa pointed at a smaller boy who waited expectantly with the others.

"All the children can come."

Manipi grumbled again at this. "It will be loud. If you put large amounts of children together . . ."

"They play." Seneca stood, then took Wicasa's hand. "That is what children do best, Manipi. Play."

Nisa nodded, but her heart was too filled with emotion to comment. Wicasa's brother ran across the courtyard and grabbed Seneca's other hand.

"Are they coming, too?" he asked excitedly.

To Nisa's great pleasure, Hinto gestured toward the three wortpigs who waited patiently by her feet.

"Our Thorwalian guest has requested their presence."

The little boy shook his head in dismay. "They're ugly, aren't they?"

Nisa stepped forward. "Not at all! Come here and

193

see for yourself. They are friendly, and beauty depends on the beholder."

Seneca's brow angled. "You mean another wortpig may see in Spike what I see in you?"

Nisa felt her cheeks warm. "Something like that, yes."

With obvious misgivings, Hinto approached the wortpigs. They rumbled and sniffed, but they didn't appear threatening to the child.

"See," said Nisa. "They like you. If you scratch behind their ears, they will be your friend forever. Wortpigs have long memories."

Hinto tried scratching Spike's ear. The wortpig's eyes closed, long lashes shading the wrinkled face. "Good pig. I like animals. I tried to play with the lingbat, but he talks too much."

"That much is certain," said Manipi.

Langundo joined the others, his chubby arms filled with various fishing supplies. Seneca relieved Langundo of the heaviest gear and shouldered his pack. "We're ready."

Manipi sighed heavily, then slung a tangled web of line over his shoulder. "If we're really going to do this, let's get it over with. But something tells me it's barlit-meal for supper . . . again."

Wortpigs in tow, Seneca led his fishing party along the stream toward the pond. Nisa distracted herself by telling the children how to care for wortpigs, while Seneca explained the rudimentary theory of fishing to the adults.

They gathered at the pond and Seneca positioned the adult Dakotans around the farthest edge. "The water appears deeper at that end. There you will cast your nets as I have described. Manipi, you and Langundo will attach hooks to lines and utilize the earthen-grubs as bait."

Nisa grimaced. "How revolting!"

Seneca watched the wortpigs as they scratched and puttered in the dirt. "You might use the wortpigs to rifle through the dirt and dislodge the grubs."

Nisa's reaction altered. "They would serve admirably in that task."

Seneca lined up the children, who waited expectantly for their duties. He stood in front of them, his expression grave and thoughtful.

"The trouble with fishing is that our prey may remain in this end of the pond, and never reach the nets. We must find some way to drive them toward Manipi's corner."

"That sounds sensible, Deiaquande," agreed Hinto. "What do we do?"

"I will show you." Without another word, Seneca stripped off his shirt and tossed it on the ground, then dove into the water. He disappeared, then emerged halfway across the pond.

With leisurely, long strokes, he guided himself back toward the bank. Nisa imagined she watched a legendary figure, bold and without fear. He was magnificent. Her thoughts flashed to his sultry passion during the night.

This man had held her, touched her, and brought her to fire. She had touched him, too. Nisa felt suddenly warm. The afternoon sun glinted on the auburn lights in his dark hair, lending gold to his burnished skin. Such a beautiful man . . .

Nisa sighed. More than beauty, she admired his easy command of every situation.

Seneca let the air dry him as he called to the children. "The first fish have been driven. But one man is not enough to frighten them."

Nisa guessed his intention, and her heart filled with affection. She liked him. He was a good man, a man with the capacity to love many. A true leader.

"Can we do what you did, Deiaquande?" Wicasa watched their leader in amazement, but she sounded uncertain of her own abilities.

Seneca's dark eyes glinted as he glanced Nisa's way. "If our Thorwalian guest will assist me, I will teach you to swim."

Nisa chewed her lip in agitation. The children watched with thinly veiled excitement, so she nodded. "I will." She paused. "What do you want me to do?"

"Swim."

Nisa stared, mouth agape. "Swim? Do you mean you want me to go in that water, too?"

"That is swimming, maiden, yes."

"You can't be serious."

His eyes fixed on hers. "I will respect your modesty enough to let you swim clothed, but swim you will."

"I will not. I've never heard of such foolishness."

Seneca didn't take his eyes off her as he approached. Nisa backed away. "Stay away, Akandan. I have no wish to swim."

With one quick, fluid motion, Seneca caught her, lifted her, and carried her to the water. "You wouldn't dare!"

Before the words were completed, Nisa splashed into the warm pool and submerged completely. She popped to the surface, sputtering and coughing, her face flushed with fury. Seneca stood knee deep in the water, waiting.

"You tried to drown me, you—"

"Harmless and pleasant creature . . . Maiden, if you try your footing, you will learn you are no deeper than I."

Nisa touched the bottom, finding it solid and sandy rather than squishy as she expected. She stood, shivering as her damp suit clung to her flesh. "You will regret this, Akandan."

Solemn applause startled her. The children watched with admiration. "She is very brave, Deiaquande. Can we try, too?"

"Certainly. One at a time. Nisa will stay put so you

can swim to her and back."

Bolstered by the children's praise, Nisa sank into the water and waited for the first child. Wicasa flung herself into the water, emulating Nisa's unwilling attempt. She splashed and bobbed, but reached Nisa with a broad smile.

Nisa caught the child and looked up at Seneca. He was smiling, too, his dark hair wet against his head, his powerful body glistening with droplets. Nisa stared, unable to look away or to speak.

She was having fun. She was playing with children; she was swimming. She was in love.

"Swim back, Wicasa," he called. The sound of his voice sent tremors of shock through Nisa. She loved him. More than she had loved Motega, because Motega never gave her a choice.

But here, in the water, Nisa chose to love Seneca. It didn't matter what followed between them, or if she lost him to Akando. She loved him.

Seneca caught her wistful look. "Nisa?"

"What?" *I love you.*

"Are you ready for the next?"

"I'm ready." Nisa held out her arms, and the little boy splashed eagerly toward her. She caught him and clapped her hands in praise. Hinto beamed. The other children, encouraged by the mood, clapped, too.

As the swimming lesson intensified, Manipi shouted wildly, then held up his first catch. A very small fish struggled in a net, glinting in the sunlight.

Seneca waved. "Well done!" The Dakotans needed no further encouragement as they returned to their task.

By the time the sun lowered beneath the treetops, the Dakotan nets overflowed with fish. The children chased each other around the pond, diving and splashing while Manipi issued futile orders for quiet.

Seneca oversaw the fishing activity, helping and

advising when the Dakotan lines tangled with the nets. Before Langundo and Manipi came to blows, he positioned them on opposite corners of the pond.

When he called them to return to Macanoc, they seemed surprised and reluctant to leave. "These fish must be brought to the cooks. I trust they'll need no instruction to prepare the food."

The mention of food was all it took. The Dakotans gathered their catch and hurried back toward Macanoc. The children enlisted the wortpigs and followed. Nisa stood alone by the pond, a blank, stunned expression on her face.

Seneca stood beside her, saying nothing. The day had proven far more successful than he had imagined. Nisa delivered him to a senseless world from Akando's primal order. But here, where two senseless cultures clashed, he found unexpected charm and beauty.

Something hovered just beyond the reach of his understanding. Something he felt, but didn't know. On Akando he had chosen another way of life. He accepted the woman chosen for him, in accordance with their customs.

Nisa looked up at him, her face tinged with color, her hair glistening in the fading gold sunlight. She looked so surprised, beyond words. Her soft gaze sent urgent pulses through his body, reminding him over and over of their night together, of his own desire.

"You appear . . . bemused, maiden. Tell me, what are you thinking? Was the swimming too much for you?"

"No . . ." Her voice trailed off, but her lips remained parted.

Seneca took her hand. Her fingers closed around his. They walked together, hand in hand, along the river toward the Dakotan village. Neither spoke. Small, orange-breasted birds chirped in the trees, positioning themselves for sleep.

"Dakota is so much sweeter than I knew."

Seneca glanced at her. She gazed upward through the branches. He had never seen her so peaceful, so content.

"Water agrees with you, it seems."

A soft smile formed on her face. "Yes . . ."

Seneca stopped and drew her hand to his lips, kissing each fingertip. Nisa laughed, a low, husky laugh. A woman's laugh. Seneca's pulse erupted like fire.

"Maiden, you tempt me."

Her eyelids drifted seductively over her dark blue eyes. Her smile deepened, a knowing smile that sent shivers along his spine, deep into his limbs. Cold mist from the cleansing unit wouldn't be enough. Diving into the cool pond hadn't been enough. Nothing tempered his desire.

Seneca bent and kissed her, her hand still held in his, close to his heart. She returned his kiss with languid, sensual desire.

Seneca drew back to look into her face. "You have changed, maiden. Why?"

A flash of doubt showed in her eyes. She bit the corner of her lip, hesitating as her gaze shifted from his. "I don't know."

She was lying. Seneca caught her face in his hand and forced her to look at him. "You know."

"I'm afraid." For an instant, Seneca saw into Nisa's soul. He saw her fear. He felt it like his own.

"What frightens you?"

"Today I imagined a perfect life." Nisa stopped. There was something veiled in her words, something she wasn't ready to say. Seneca knew it involved him. "I saw how things could be, if only . . ."

"If only these worlds knew peace once more?"

Nisa hesitated, then nodded. That was part of it, but not all. "I would like my people to feel the way the Dakotans felt today."

"I told you there would be other ways to reach your

199

peace. Do you think your uncle might be willing to hear them now?"

"It's possible. Yes."

"Then it may be time to arrange a truce."

Nisa's head tilted to one side. "How?"

"I will communicate with your uncle and invite him to Dakota, that he may see what you have seen. We will make an arrangement concerning the moon you both covet, one that will accommodate both sides."

"That seems wise." Nisa sounded sad. Seneca touched her face.

"Isn't this what you wanted?"

"Yes. For a long while, it was all I wanted. But now . . ."

Nisa moved from Seneca and continued along the river toward Macanoc, her eyes fixed on the ground ahead of her. Seneca caught up with her, tempering his long stride to her pace. "You hide part of yourself, maiden. It is unlike you."

"This part of myself . . . I thought it long dead, Seneca."

The sound of his name on her tongue pierced his heart, but Seneca wasn't sure why. She knew so little of him, of his world, of his past. Yet she accepted him. Without question or suspicion.

Seneca stopped, but Nisa kept walking. If she knew the truth . . . Nisa kept alive every portion of her being, even her bitterest memories. A cool wave of admiration flooded through him. He had long ago abandoned his past.

This bliss couldn't last. He knew it, but as Seneca watched Nisa picking her way along the stream, he couldn't bring himself to hasten the outcome. If he told her the truth, if he tried to explain, the peace she hoped for might be threatened beyond recall.

But could he return to Akando now, never knowing what might have been between them? Nisa stopped and looked back at him, her head tilted to one side.

The bulk of her hair had escaped its binding during her swim, and it fell like a pale gold river down her back and around her face.

"Aren't you coming?" Nisa started back toward him, her eyes tilted with a mischievous light. "Or perhaps my endurance rivals your own more than you realized."

When Nisa unleashed her femininity, Seneca's resolve faltered. His pulse quickened. She had power, power to reach inside him and dissolve his resistance.

She stopped, her face soft, her posture inviting. Seneca came to her, bound by an unseen cord to her bidding. "Do you know what you're doing? Have you any idea?"

Nisa's lips curved in a tantalizing smile. "If I do half what you do to me . . ." Her voice trailed and she drew closer to him. Seneca's heart raced, sending unmerciful shocks to his groin, ravaging his senses. "This night will never end."

Her hand rested on his chest for a brief moment, then slid away. She turned, cast a beckoning and deliberate glance over her shoulder, then headed off along the river.

Seneca couldn't force his limbs into motion. He had wanted her strong. Today, as the sun faded, he had never seen her so strong. His whole body ached from her veiled suggestion. He fought his need when she seemed weak, but tonight, if she looked at him that way . . .

Seneca followed her, his mind filled with images of loving her, of sweet, forbidden fulfillment. He intended to set right the two worlds, to earn her understanding and trust. Only then could her memories find balance with her current reality.

Balance hadn't been attained, not yet. The future consisted of possibilities. Nothing more. The past was strong; it dominated both Dakota and Thorwal. It dominated Nisa, too.

If he could find balance, the past would seek its rightful place, casting shadows that darkened nothing. If not, those shadows would destroy whatever chance they had at happiness.

A growing bonfire filled the village square. Seneca and Nisa exchanged doubtful glances, but the Dakotans hurried back and forth from the kitchen with heavy pots and cooking utensils, intent on their new task.

"Did you put them up to this?"

"They've gone beyond my instruction this time." Manipi circled the fire, poking at the bracken and logs with a long stick. He noticed Seneca and waved excitedly.

"Deiaquande! In honor of your Akandans, we have instigated this burning. It seemed the proper fashion in which to roast our fish."

"Well done."

Nisa eyed the fire. "If it gets any bigger you're going to ignite the trees and all your homes."

Manipi scowled. "I am in complete control."

"Cooking requires only a low fire," Seneca advised. "It should die down before any cooking is attempted."

"We've learned that." Manipi sighed. "I'm afraid, in our eagerness to test the results of our expedition, we stuck a few fish in the fire. They're a bit too black now for consumption. The wortpigs like them, though." —

Nisa looked around for the wortpigs. "Have you fashioned them pens yet?"

"The children are on that task now," said Manipi. "That rodent is giving them directions."

Manipi gave Nisa a hard stare, then turned to Seneca. "There's another matter I need to bring to your attention. Don't know if I should mention it in front of her."

Nisa drew an irritated breath. "Why not?"

"What is it, Manipi? Nisa is no threat in these circumstances."

Manipi hesitated, then shrugged. "We received communications from a Thorwalian transport craft. They've assumed an extended orbit around Dakota, and want contact with you personally." Manipi chuckled. "Helmar himself is in command. Checking up on his puppet, I suppose."

"That is likely." Seneca paused to consider the matter. "I hoped for a few more days' preparation before dealing with Thorwal."

Nisa chewed her lip. Helmar wasn't a rash man, but if Fedor was with him, suspicions would soon be aroused and compounded when they learned the mind probe had failed.

"Shall I speak with my uncle?"

Seneca looked at her in surprise. "What would you say?"

"I could reassure him."

Manipi groaned. "You can't trust her, Deiaquande. She'll squeal like one of her wortpigs, and we'll be in for a bombardment for sure."

"I will not! And wortpigs don't squeal. They issue small grunts."

Seneca sighed. "I hoped for more time, but since an opportunity presents itself, I see no reason to delay. Manipi, contact the Thorwalian transport and invite their High Councillor to join us here."

Nisa touched his arm. "He'll know as soon as he sees you that the probes didn't work."

"I have no intentions of deceiving him, maiden. But as the Dakotan leader, I will offer him terms for peace. Terms which will benefit both sides, and insure security for all."

"What terms?"

"Those, you will learn when your uncle arrives."

Nisa didn't question Seneca further. Peace seemed imminent. Yet her heart felt heavy. If Seneca's duty was fulfilled tonight, she had only tonight to convince him to stay.

Manipi also appeared hesitant about Seneca's plan. "What about the fish?"

"The fish?"

"Are you thinking we'll have the Thorwalians join us for the evening meal?"

"Your group caught enough to feed double our numbers. Yes, Helmar's party will attend the banquet. If you phrase the communication carefully, he may bring the Thorwalian wine as an offering."

The suggestion of wine pleased Manipi. His doubt faded. "Thorwalians don't eat much, as I've seen with this one." Manipi gestured at Nisa. "Not much flesh on her, is there? I always wondered what Motega saw in a scrawny thing like her. A woman should be full bodied, healthy, but delicate. Like my Aponi . . ."

Nisa remembered Aponi as the woman who punched Langundo during the TiKay lesson. She repressed a groan. Seneca slid his arm over Nisa's shoulder and patted her.

"Nisa will eat well tonight. Contact the Thorwalians, Manipi. We will test Helmar's desire for peace tonight."

"What do you mean, 'test'? Of course my uncle wants peace! Why should you think otherwise?"

"I don't think otherwise, maiden. I simply offer him the chance to make his intentions known to the Dakotans."

This satisfied Nisa. "And he will." She looked around the village square. The sun disappeared, and the fire sent dancing light over the homes, the lab, through the trees. "Do you suppose the Dakotans lived this way once, long ago?"

"It seems likely."

Nisa looked up at Seneca. The light flickered across the strong lines of his face, glinting on his dark hair. "This must be common to you."

"Rarely have we cause on Akando to build such a fire. Wood is scarce, and used sparingly. Fish is common, for we live within a half day's journey of the Tremoring Sea."

"You miss it still." Nisa sighed, then realized her expression betrayed her sorrow. "Is there nothing here that you prefer to Akando?" She wished she hadn't asked. She hadn't meant to ask.

Seneca didn't answer at once. Nisa felt his eyes on her, but she didn't look at him. "Surprise. I knew what to expect on Akando. Until I looked up and saw you, I knew the path my life would follow."

Nisa frowned. "That doesn't sound like a preference."

"There is an element contained in surprise that I find hard to resist."

"What element?"

A slow grin spread across Seneca's face. "It has the effect of fanning desire, maiden. As you well know, for you are adept at the unpredictable."

"I am completely predictable." Nisa stopped. Until now. If Seneca valued surprise, she would use that to her advantage. If that was his weakness, she would use it in her favor. But how?

I'll discover that when the time is right. Nisa banished her doubts. She had faith in Seneca's ability to secure peace. She knew Helmar longed for stability, and would accept whatever reasonable terms he offered. So tonight she would offer Seneca something he desired beyond anything. She would offer him surprise.

Chapter Seven

Under Seneca's supervision, the Dakotans arranged tables outside, with places of honor provided for Helmar and his aides. Manipi allowed Nisa to contact her uncle's shuttle, though he remained to monitor her conversation.

Manipi seemed suspicious of her last request. "What do you want with Thorwalian flutes?"

"Never mind. Music is an unknown concept among your people, but many Thorwalians enjoy it. Helmar in particular is well skilled with the instrument."

Manipi huffed. "I suppose he has to do something to occupy his time, when he's not dominating us."

Nisa ignored Manipi's provocative comment and went outside to await Helmar's arrival. Her plans were formed; she felt her own power, controlled, ready. Tonight she would see peace for both her world and herself.

The Thorwalian shuttle hovered above the trees, then lowered to the landing strip built on the lab roof.

Nisa waited at Seneca's side, her heart pounding as Manipi led Helmar to the transport tube.

"Maybe I should have spoken to him alone." Nisa bit her lip as Helmar emerged from the lab.

Seneca stepped forward and bowed after the manner of the Dakotans. "You honor us with your presence."

Nisa was right. Helmar knew the moment Seneca spoke. He turned to her, his pale eyes wide with shock. "The mind probes . . ."

Nisa opened her mouth to speak, to explain, but Seneca answered for her. "They were unnecessary. You will find the Dakotans willing and eager to treat with you. Perhaps you will not find our demands unreasonable."

" 'Our?' " Helmar seemed to shrink.

Nisa went to her uncle's side and patted his thin shoulder. "The Dakotans asked Seneca to lead them, for the time being. He accepted. It was a shock to me at first, too. But if you'll listen, I hope his terms will be agreeable."

Helmar seemed to draw strength from Nisa. "Do you trust him, Nisa?"

Nisa hesitated, and her gaze flicked to Seneca. He stood tall and powerful, a man beyond her dreams. "I do." Excitement and hope filled her heart. "Dane trusted him, too." She looked around. "Where is my brother?"

Helmar hesitated and shifted his weight. "Dane was . . . detained. He remains on Thorwal."

Nisa's declaration of faith seemed to disturb Seneca. "It isn't a matter of trust, Councillor. I offer terms that will benefit both worlds."

Helmar studied Seneca's face, then nodded. "Then I will hear them."

Nisa relaxed. Helmar wasn't strong, but he was reasonable. Emotion never tainted his decisions. "The Dakotans have prepared a feast, Uncle."

Helmar's brow angled. "Not barlit-meal?"

Manipi puffed with pride, and a trace of condescension. "Fish!"

Helmar remained uncertain. "Where did they obtain fish, and for what purpose?"

Manipi rolled his eyes. "We obtained them from the treetops! Where do you think?"

Seneca gave Manipi a stern, forbidding look, and Manipi forced a weak smile. "Just a little humor . . . The Deiaquande has taught us the benefit of catching our own food, since your faulty machinery has proven less than reliable."

"The best machinery needs careful and accurate tending, Dakotan."

Nisa seized her uncle's arm before the conversation deteriorated further. "Come, Uncle. We will sample the Dakotans' new fare, and perhaps offer some of our own. Did you bring the wine?"

Helmar seemed reluctant, but he nodded. "It's with my aides. Ungan wine is not commonly shared with Dakotans. They can't handle it, you know."

Manipi glared. "We'll just see about that!" He snatched the bottle from Helmar's aide and held it up to the light. "Looks weak. This won't serve more than three, at most."

"It will serve twenty," Nisa corrected. "Ungan wine is best taken in small doses."

Helmar nodded. "We brought several bottles, but it is best taken sparingly."

Seneca relieved Manipi of the bottle. "Advice we will take. Tonight we will need our senses intact." Nisa wondered why. Helmar would accept almost any terms Seneca offered. He had no choice.

Seneca led the group toward the square, but Nisa held her uncle back. "Did you bring your flute, Uncle?"

"I did." A small smile formed on Helmar's thin lips. "Haven't played it in a while, though."

"After we feast you might demonstrate your skill to

the Dakotans. It will impress them."

Helmar eyed her knowingly. "It will impress their leader. And give my niece an opportunity to dance."

Helmar wasn't usually so perceptive, and Nisa's cheeks colored in embarrassment. Generally their conversations remained on council matters. Though he never condemned her, they never spoke of her relationship with Motega.

"If the occasion should arise . . ."

"In truth, I am relieved to find your Akandan unaffected by the probes. It pleases me to see your eyes shining this way."

Nisa didn't deny her affection for Seneca. She couldn't. Helmar knew her better than she realized.

"I know Motega hurt you, Nisa. But your instincts were wise in selecting him, despite what your parents say. I have long believed our only hope is to unite with the Dakotans, and to produce heirs among us."

"Truly?" Nisa looked at her uncle in surprise. This was the first he had spoken of any such inclination.

"It is important that you take a mate, Nisa. I want the blood of Calydon to pass to later generations, one way or another."

"If I fail, Dane will surely leave heirs." Nisa sighed and shook her head. "If he hasn't already."

"Our people have succumbed to . . . lesser impulses. We need Dakotan blood mingled with our own. Such unions will promote stability."

Helmar spoke in veiled terms. Nisa sensed he was hiding something. "Is something wrong, Uncle?"

Helmar hesitated, confirming Nisa's suspicions. "We won't speak of this now. Tonight we will make a new peace with Dakota. Then I will be free to handle matters on Thorwal with a firmer hand."

"What matters? Is it Fedor?"

The mention of Fedor surprised Helmar. "Fedor? No. Why do you ask? It was Fedor who encouraged my acceptance of your Akandan's offer, in fact."

"Then what troubles you?" An unfamiliar pang of worry tightened around Nisa's heart. Helmar seemed reluctant to divulge more.

"We have uncovered several suspicious communications involving sabotage."

"Sabotage? Then you know of the attempt to shoot down my shuttle?"

Helmar nodded, his face weary and grave. "Fedor reported it at once. The culprit has been incarcerated. For now, that is all you need know."

He was protecting her from something. Nisa knew that, but Helmar seemed unusually resilient to her prodding. "Uncle . . . I am in line to your council seat. Dane follows me. If there are matters involving sabotage, we both must be kept informed."

Helmar's narrow jaw tightened. "Dane knows. But tonight, let us rejoice in the promise of peace. Nothing will darken this moment for you, Nisa. Your courage and inspiration have brought it to pass."

Helmar paused, looking deep into Nisa's eyes. With a wave of affection, she knew her uncle loved her. She kissed his cheek and hugged him. Helmar appeared surprised by her impulsive action. He patted her awkwardly.

"You stood by me after the . . . unpleasantness with Motega, Uncle, and I will never forget that. My parents have barely spoken to me since. It would have been easy to disinherit me and promote Dane in my place."

Helmar's expression darkened. "I could have done that, yes. I resisted encouragement to replace you with your brother. In time the correctness of my action will be proven to all."

Helmar's words confused Nisa. Perhaps because Dane had no interest in council matters, Helmar knew he would be a poor choice.

"You have handled yourself admirably, Nisa. My pride in you is great. I trust you will handle the future with the same wisdom and patience you have used with the Akandan. Only a sensible, calm woman like yourself could have guided him this way."

Nisa forced a weak, pained smile at her uncle's definition of her character. "Seneca can be . . . surprising, Uncle." Nisa felt a tingle of anticipation. "But tonight he will see that I can be surprising, too."

Rather than light replacers, the Dakotans fashioned torches from hewn branches and positioned them around the banquet table. The square danced with ancient light as Seneca led Helmar's party to the table's head.

"Here, beneath the stars, we will welcome a new era of peace. Here, in the shadow of the ancients, Dakota and Thorwal will renew an old friendship, and renew the bond that made both great."

Both the Dakotans and the Thorwalians appreciated Seneca's words. The Dakotans cheered loudly, and the Thorwalians exchanged doubtful glances. The Dakotans weren't renowned for revelry.

Seneca motioned to Nisa. After a moment's hesitation she came to stand beside him. "Guided by the High Councillor's niece, I have learned much of Thorwal's desire."

Nisa cringed at his choice of words, which she suspected he used intentionally, but she offered no objections.

"There are times when a stranger sees what those involved have missed. The rift between your people is not insurmountable, but is based on a common fear. The fate of the Candor Moon, known to my people as the Dawn Star."

Manipi glared at Helmar in accusation, and Helmar cast a cold glance in return.

"Without the threat of untold power, your people have no quarrel. Dakotan researchers have devised a method of power to reach this moon, but lack the means to craft such a vessel. Such means are easily available to Thorwal."

Helmar shook his head. "What you say is true, and poses a great threat to my people. What assurance can you give that such a conquest isn't planned already?"

"Time, and reason. We hold the plans, you hold the power to construct them. Let us, together, learn more of this moon from afar, then make a joint effort when communication with that world is well established. A treaty will be signed to this effect."

"The moon is a threat to all. We on Thorwal desire nothing from it, riches or no."

Manipi shook his fist. "We only wanted to study the moon, not conquer it! Conquering is in your history, not ours."

Helmar scowled. "Since little is known of your history, that information seems unreliable in the extreme."

Seneca held up his hand to silence them. "The future, not history, is of value to us now. Will you agree to enter this truce? If so, negotiations will follow."

After a pause, Manipi nodded. "If they'll stick to an agreement, I'm for it."

"The Council of Thorwal has never failed in its word. It was Motega who reached beyond the reasonable in his demands."

Helmar's slight to Motega aroused angry mutters, and Nisa held her breath. "Let Motega's failure lead to a new peace." Nisa cringed at Seneca's words, but to her surprise, the Dakotans' angry murmurs subsided to silence.

"In the morning we will meet for negotiations. I will preside until good relations have been established."

Nisa waited. And then what? Would he leave? If he meant to leave he would have said so. No, Seneca remained undecided. Tonight she would give him reason to stay.

"If that's settled, perhaps we can eat." She didn't

want to hear his plans now.

Manipi seated himself before the others. "Good idea. We'll worry about hammering out the details tomorrow."

Helmar seemed confused by the lack of formality. He nodded to his aides, who seated themselves and waited for a formal invitation to feast. In the meantime, Dakotans heaped their plates with food and poured the Ungan wine liberally.

Helmar reached across the table and seized Manipi's cup. "Go easy on that, Dakotan! It's not water."

Manipi retrieved his cup and drank. "Just about as weak, I'd say."

Helmar took a suspicious drink of his own wine, smiled, then drank again. "The Dakotan appreciation of taste is clearly undeveloped."

Nisa watched as her uncle drained his cup and poured another. In contrast, the Dakotans took little of the wine, preferring their rich, creamy beverages. Dakotan women appeared, carrying plates of fish.

It wasn't like them to perform service tasks, and none looked pleased. Manipi spotted his mate and laughed. "Aponi, you are well suited to serving!" Aponi glared.

Manipi recognized his mate's limit, and he rose to take the serving dish. "I assumed primitive people used their women as servants. Might have gone too far."

Aponi's dark eyes flashed. "You might, at that."

Nisa looked at Seneca. "Is that true? Do your women perform servants' tasks?"

Seneca seemed uncomfortable. "Akandans keep no servants. But the roles of male and female are separate on Akando."

Nisa suspected he was hedging. "In what way?"

"Akandan women perform such tasks as they are best suited to perform."

"What a pathetic, evasive answer!"

213

"The respect given them is great."

Nisa's lips curved to one side and she shook her head. "I think you evade much, Akandan. But I don't want to hear any more."

Seneca touched Nisa's hand. "Rest assured that you are best placed on Thorwal, maiden. The labor demanded of Akandan women wouldn't suit you at all."

Nisa didn't respond. He considered her weak. Maybe he preferred women who did his bidding without question. But such a woman wouldn't be particularly stimulating.

Nisa tried a portion of fish, but her appetite waned as her stomach fluttered. Helmar took his third cup of Ungan wine, and began humming to himself. Nisa peeked up at Seneca to see if the wine affected his senses, but he appeared the same. She took a large gulp, then rose to her feet.

Now or never. "Your flute, Uncle. It is time."

Helmar appeared bleary from the intake of wine, but he drew out a wooden flute and tried the sound. "I'm out of practice, I'm afraid."

"If you'll excuse me for a moment . . ." Nisa didn't explain her intentions as she darted toward Motega's house. She knew Seneca watched her go, but she didn't look back. She found Carob in the soft chair, sleeping. She touched the bat, and he jumped.

"Are they here? Is it war? Did your brother come along for the ride?"

Nisa puffed an impatient breath. "Yes, Helmar is here. No, there will be no war. And no, Dane didn't accompany him." Nisa paused at this. A vague sense of unease returned, but her attention snapped back to the matter at hand.

"Did you do as I asked? Do you have my dress?"

Carob squirmed upright, then gestured across the room. "I had the children tear up some sheets and knot them together, if that's what you mean. As for it being a dress . . ."

Nisa examined the cloth. It appeared simple, but the cut was good. "It will have to do." Nisa eyed the bat. "Turn around, if you please."

Carob flopped back onto the chair. "Humans!"

Nisa tore off her uniform and pulled the gown over her head. It felt strange, loose and billowy, but when bound by a belt, it hugged her waist in a satisfactory fashion. She adjusted the front to reveal the cleft between her breasts, then yanked the binding from her hair, fluffing it around her face and shoulders.

"What do you think?"

Carob opened his eyes and studied her. "No difference."

"What?" Nisa frowned. "Of course there's a difference! You are a rodent. I suppose I can't expect a rodent to recognize humanoid subtleties."

An expression of disgust contorted Carob's face. "You're as bad as your brother. I thought only the male of the species went to such ridiculous lengths to secure a mate, but I see I was wrong."

"Never mind about that." Nisa tightened her belt and headed for the door. Another concern struck her and she turned back. "Are you spending the entire evening here?"

"Thought I might enjoy a midnight hunt. Those torches should draw the shyest denizens of the insect domain."

"Good. See that you don't return before morning. Late morning." Nisa didn't wait for Carob's reply. She took a deep breath, then returned to the banquet.

As the Dakotans finished their meal, they, too, had turned to wine. Helmar was practicing with his flute. Though faulty, the melody undulated and seemed easy to follow. His aides tapped the table in accompaniment, while the Dakotans swayed and hummed in relative tune.

Nisa closed her eyes and gathered her courage. *Surprise.*

*   *   *

Seneca saw Nisa coming toward him, and his heart leaped. She wore a long, flowing white garment, tucked at her waist, open at the front to reveal the swell of her breasts. One look at her face told him her intention. His blood erupted like fire blown across a dried field.

She moved across the square with fluid grace, her motion slow but purposeful. Her eyes never left him as she drew near. She stood beside his chair, then bowed.

"You wish us to remember our ancestors. Tonight I will show you that Thorwal's past isn't entirely forgotten."

Helmar accepted the cue, and his music turned purposeful, low and haunting. Seneca couldn't tear his gaze from Nisa.

Her hips swayed in subtle rhythm, her eyelids lowered seductively, her lips parted. Her body moved with the undulating pulse of the music, giving him brief glimpses of her shapely legs as she bent and turned.

In this way, Thorwalian women had driven their ancient lords to battle, to madness, Seneca had no doubt. He couldn't move—he would do whatever she wanted, no matter the cost to himself, or to her.

"Nisa . . ." His lips moved, but no sound came. Beside him, Helmar pursued the music with mindless oblivion, the other Thorwalians chanting in their low, sonorous voices. Nisa's dance didn't shock them; it resonated in their ancient souls.

Seneca heard Manipi's groan of defeat. "I knew it. He's lost." But Seneca couldn't look away.

Her lips curved in a soft, knowing smile as she moved and swayed. The intensity of the music deepened, and her hips moved forward and back. Seneca saw himself buried within her, the wind consumed by fire.

She read his thoughts. Her hips circled as if encasing his length within her woman's fold. He knew, in the portion of his brain that still functioned, that no other man interpreted her dance as he did. It was meant for him alone.

Her eyes drifted shut as she twirled, her head tipped back, revealing the smooth, white column of her throat. An offering to his kiss. Dimly Seneca was aware that the Dakotan women mimicked Nisa's seductive dance. He knew Manipi seized Aponi and spun her around, laughing.

The soft fabric of Nisa's dress swirled around her bare feet. Her arms slowly echoed the motion of TiKay that he had taught her. One soft, shapely leg arched and pointed with unmatched grace.

Nisa's subtle interpretation of the Akandan art drove him beyond control. Seneca rose to his feet and joined her, catching her small waist in his hands.

She gasped and her eyes widened briefly, then softened when she knew she had won. She moved close to him, her swaying hips bare inches from his. Her hands went to his shoulders as they moved in perfect, seductive rhythm.

He guided her beyond the torchlight, and they danced alone. Her head tilted back, and he touched his lips to her neck, feeling the wild pulse that raged beneath the cool surface of her skin. She trembled, her fingers gripped his shoulders, but Nisa still moved, a graceful sway just beyond his touch.

Her hips grazed his, inflaming his desire and his soul. He groaned. "I can't resist you."

Her blue eyes blazed. "Then show me."

Seneca's nerves vibrated with restrained lust. "If you ask it, I will take you on stone."

Helmar's music filled the air, unceasing. They moved together in a slow and sensual rhythm. A rhythm that anticipated the passion to follow.

Nisa glanced purposefully toward Motega's dwelling. "Softer than stone . . ."

Seneca lifted her from her feet. He held her in his arms and carried her from the banquet. He glanced toward Motega's dwelling. *No, not to the past, but to the future instead.*

He changed his course and carried her along the stream path. Nisa eyed him doubtfully, a trace of impatience curving her lips. Seneca smiled. "Where are we going?"

"Where no shadow of the past can touch us."

They reached the pond, and Seneca set Nisa on her feet. Soft mists rose from the pond; the stars glimmered with fragmented light above shadowy tree limbs. Above his shoulder, one star outshone the rest. The Dawn Star.

Though passion burned in his dark eyes, Seneca stood motionless, a sultry temptation to Nisa's restraint. He wanted her strong. She would be strong.

Nisa dampened her lips with a small flick of her tongue. His eyes narrowed with desire, but he didn't move or speak. She reached to touch his face, running her finger along his wide, high cheekbone, down the flat plane of his face to his jaw.

She touched his lips, firm and well defined. Everything about him emanated strength. She dipped her finger between his lips, and he tasted the tip. She closed her eyes and swallowed. She wouldn't falter tonight; she wouldn't fall helpless, leaving him to lead her through pleasure. She would lead him.

Her hand drifted to his chest. She felt his strong heart throbbing beneath her touch. She moved closer, then kissed the base of his neck. She kissed beneath his jaw, then trailed her lips softly to the corner of his mouth.

Seneca's breath came deep and hoarse, ragged. His eyes closed as Nisa ran the tip of her tongue around his lips. He answered her kiss, but she drew away, her bright eyes glinting.

She kissed his shoulder beneath the light fabric, then ran her hands along the muscle of his arm. She caught his wrist and lifted his hand to her lips. She caressed each strong finger, her eyes on his as she traced the tips with erotic intent.

Seneca stood like stone, but beneath the surface, she felt his intensity quiver. Her lips curved seductively and she pressed her lips to each finger. Her tongue swept out to taste him, to circle and to tease.

When she took his finger deep in the softness of her mouth, he groaned and his head tipped back. A soft laugh rumbled in Nisa's throat at her success. She traced a line with her tongue from the tip of his finger to his palm.

"Maiden, you torment my restraint." His voice was husky and ragged, torn with desire. Nisa pressed his palm to her heart, over her breast.

"As you torment mine . . ."

Her fingers worked at the ties of his shirt, loosening them to fall back, baring his wide chest to her touch. His skin felt smooth and warm as she slid her hand across the line of his muscle.

She felt her own breaths, warm and swift, as she pressed her lips to his chest, as she tasted his flesh with small darts of her tongue. Her senses swam, exploring with abandon every sweet offering of his body.

He smelled warm and musky and perfectly male. She wanted to be part of him, to dissolve herself around him, to make him part of her. She pushed his shirt from his shoulders, exposing his warm, dark skin, taut with muscle and with restrained power.

She grazed his flesh with her soft mouth, licking and nipping gently. She pulled the shirt away and let it fall. "You are beautiful, my sweet Akandan."

He reached for her, but she slid away and moved behind him. From behind, she slid her hands around his waist, playing over his taut stomach, teasing as she untied his waistband. She slid the fabric down over his hips, then ran her hands down his thighs, kissing his back, standing on her toes to kiss his neck.

Seneca turned his face, and she kissed his cheek. Her fingers grazed him then circled his length with a light, tormenting touch. Her tongue flicked across his skin as her caress tightened. With long, smooth strokes, she massaged him until his every breath was a low moan.

"You did this to me," she whispered. "And I thought I would die of pleasure." Her fingers teased his swollen tip as she spoke; she kissed the back of his neck.

He opened his mouth to speak, but she touched his chin, turning his face to hers as she slid around to kiss him. "Whatever you want, I will do."

"I want what I've dreamed of since I met you. I want what I've never been able to forget."

Seneca's words throbbed with husky passion, with something just beyond Nisa's understanding. As she fought him, he had fought her. His denial sparked her primal desire for conquest. His hands shook as he tore her dress from her shoulders, exposing her breasts, her stomach. He pulled off her belt, and the dress slithered to her feet, leaving her bare skin shining in the night.

"You will never forget me, Akandan. No matter what comes between us, no matter where you go. I will never let you forget me."

Her vow inflamed him. She saw the effect with a thrill of victory. As he haunted her, she would haunt him, too.

His engorged member stood hard from his body, a rampant demand he couldn't begin to deny. Nisa slid her hand across his chest, weaving a light trail across his taut stomach until her fingers met the tip of his erection.

She ran one finger along his shaft, then closed her hand around him, caressing and kneading as her eyes fixed on his. His power surrounded her, quivering and glowing around him like a magical force.

Nisa kissed his chest; she ran her tongue across his flat, male nipples. Her fingers tightened, and her strokes grew more rapid as she imagined him inside her.

As if he knew her thoughts, a low moan rumbled deep in Seneca's throat. "Maiden, I can endure no more."

He clasped her shoulders and sank to his knees, drawing Nisa with him. He kissed her face, the corners of her closed eyelids, her temple. He found her mouth, and his tongue slid between her parted lips. His hands cupped her bottom and he drew her onto his lap, her moist flesh close to his own need.

Nisa feverishly kissed his neck and his shoulder as he cupped her breasts in his hands, lightly grazing the sensitive peaks with his thumbs.

Violent shudders erupted along her nerves. Nisa leaned back as he bent to kiss her breast. He laved his tongue over the hard bud, drawing gently as she moaned her pleasure.

His hand slid down between them, delving beneath her parted thighs, seeking her entrance. She arched toward his touch as his fingers played just above her desire. He grazed the small peak, dipping his finger into her moisture, circling until she thought she would go mad with wanting.

"Seneca," she breathed. "I can bear no more." Her lips arched and twisted, seeking his hard flesh. She moved against him, sinking her teeth into his shoulder.

Seneca let her play against him; he let her please herself with his size. Her breaths came hot and swift, sharp moans escaping her lips. "Please don't make me wait."

"Not for the world . . ."

Seneca's dark eyes blazed. He leaned back, bracing himself on his powerful arms as she positioned herself above him. She clasped his wide shoulders and lowered her body over his. She felt him, large and hot at her entrance.

Nisa hesitated before taking him inside her. She had forgotten this feeling, this acute ache that promised untold fulfillment. She had forgotten what it meant to join completely with a man.

He would be part of her. She would belong to him. Nisa met Seneca's eyes. She had given herself to only one man this way. She had loved him with all her being. But Motega had taken her, sent her into delirium, taught her every pleasure . . . all while withholding his own heart.

Nisa saw Seneca's heart in his soft, dark eyes. He said he cared for her, and she believed him. "All myself," she whispered. She sank slowly over him, taking him into her body as he penetrated her heart.

She watched his face, mesmerized by the erotic strain written there. With his tip just inside her, she stopped, half joined, waiting. She would savor this moment. Her toes curled as she balanced herself, hovering above him, touching, but not joined.

Seneca's jaw clenched. "Maiden . . ." Nisa laughed softly, then moved away, then sank down again, stopping before he entered.

"Do you want me, Akandan?"

Mimicking her Thorwalian dance, she circled him. A low, rumbling growl shuddered from Seneca's throat. He seized her waist in his firm grip, then thrust deep inside her. Nisa cried out, shocked with the sudden pleasure of his entry.

"Is that the answer you wanted, maiden? Yes, I want you." As he spoke, Seneca grasped her hips, moving her above him with impossible strength. She kissed him wildly, nipping his lower lip, catching his tongue between her lips as he mimicked the motion of their bodies.

Swift and clean, he eased her onto her back, his

masculine length still deep inside her. His thrusts came harder and faster as her legs wrapped around his. She clasped his shoulders as he moved inside her, her back arched to take him deeper still.

"I want you." His words echoed the force of his thrust, but he withdrew to enter again, to draw her higher into oblivion.

He slid his powerful arms under her shoulders, holding her close. They moved as one body, a fluid, rhythmic dance, primal and surging. She squeezed tight around him, increasing the friction between them.

He buried his face in her neck, but Nisa's eyes opened to the soft stars overhead. They swirled and spun, then opened all the heavens to her eyes. He was part of her. He had always been, and always would be, her soul.

He filled her, deep and strong, the most primal part of her being. He belonged here, inside her. She had known him always. Seneca. She closed her eyes, shutting out the distant stars, the luminous globe of Candor, and felt only his size, engorged within her, moving slowly, then deeply, carrying her.

She writhed beneath him; the vivid, sweet pleasure intensified and spiraled tighter and tighter. Deeply and slowly, he moved inside her. Her hips joined his in perfect rhythm.

Waves of pleasure spilled from him into her, returned in force as she murmured his name, lost in sweet delirium. Seneca's mouth found hers; his tongue entered her mouth in sweet mimicry of their bodies as they fused into one being.

"I've missed you so."

Nisa barely heard his hoarse whisper, but his words formed a warm blur in the depths of her heart. The past and the present became one. She had longed for this. She had missed this in the seven cold years after Motega's death. This perfect joining, this rapture.

As Seneca surged and thrust inside her, Motega's image flashed in her brain. Nisa fought the image, helpless as her wayward body responded. *Not again* . . . She saw him, desperate and passionate, his hair swept from his face, his eyes of reckless fire. She saw his wild longing; she felt the intensity of his sexual energy.

I've missed you.

She opened her eyes and saw Seneca, his dark hair falling to his broad shoulders, his beautiful head tipped back as passion consumed him. He was strong and sure, a man where Motega had been a boy.

Motega's image faded. Seneca had won. She trusted him. Nisa's body fragmented, shattering into shards of forbidden light, forbidden pleasure. She cried out his name, arching beneath him as the wild currents spun and shivered through her.

Seneca groaned, surging inside her as his own release shook his core. When the wild currents eased, he stilled his motion, but he remained inside her. Nisa's breath came in swift, shallow gasps. Gasps of pleasure. And shock. She was free.

The night air met her damp skin and she shivered, but not from cold. Seneca withdrew from her body and eased her into his arms. Nisa leaned her face against his shoulder, hearing the heavy beat of his strong heart.

Seneca brushed her hair from her face, then kissed her forehead. Nisa kissed his warm, moist flesh. "You set me free."

"I sensed no restraint in you tonight, maiden." He wrapped his arms tighter around her, protecting her.

Nisa moved to look down into his face. Her heart felt full, safe. "I thought I would never feel this way again. That he killed this part of me."

The pleasure in his eyes faded and he sighed. "Motega."

"I thought I would never be free of him. Last night,

when you . . . when you touched me, I saw his face."
Nisa bit her lip, embarrassed by her confession. "I
thought I would never love again. But I love you."

Seneca smiled, but Nisa saw sadness in his warm,
dark eyes. "The past has no meaning now, Nisa."

Nisa settled back on his shoulder. "Maybe not to
you. But it has haunted me more than you could
know."

"The past is a burden and a delight. It is harder to
escape than I ever imagined."

"That's true. You don't know how I loved him. I
thought the world began and ended where he was.
When I learned . . . when he betrayed me, part of me
died. I had been such a fool. But not now. The past
can't hurt me anymore." Nisa closed her eyes and
smiled. "I am happy."

Seneca sat up, drawing Nisa with him. A smile
curved his lips; his eyes glittered. Nisa's stomach fluttered. "Why are you looking at me that way?"

He didn't answer. He rose to his feet and held out
his hand for her. Nisa hesitated. If he asked, she would
fly. Nisa gave him her hand and he pulled her up.

"Seneca . . ." He shook his head, then led her toward
the water. When he didn't stop at the pond's edge, Nisa
pulled back.

"No! Not that again!"

"It's different at night, maiden. You may enjoy the
experience more than you think."

His soft words promised secret pleasure, and Nisa
couldn't resist. "You're not going to throw me in again,
are you?"

"Tonight my mood is otherwise."

"Good."

Seneca lifted her into his arms, bare flesh against
bare flesh. Nisa buried her face against his warm,
strong shoulder, inhaling his musky male scent. She
heard him enter the water; she felt it lap at her toes as
he went deeper still.

"Here, maiden." Seneca slid Nisa's body down along his, deliberately slowly. She felt his stiffened manhood against her and she forgot the water.

"I promised you pleasure. . . ." He pushed her hair over her shoulder and kissed her neck. His hands ran along her arms, to the small of her back, to her bottom as the evening water lapped against her thighs.

Holding her against him, Seneca moved deeper into the water until it reached Nisa's waist. Nisa shivered, but the water wasn't cold. She felt his heart slamming beneath his chest, felt his tensed muscles.

Rather than cooling her inflamed body, the water formed a sensual curtain, encasing them, alone, free. Seneca took her face in his hands and kissed her. Nisa leaned against him, lost in his arms.

"Do you know what we are, Nisa? Do you feel us, not flesh, not blood, but what we truly are?"

Nisa's senses flowed in a dizzying spiral. Seneca's words formed images, resonating deep within her, but she couldn't hold them.

"The wind flows in water, Nisa. But fire . . ."

She knew what he meant now. "Water extinguishes fire!"

"Does it?" He cupped his hand and filled it with water. "See . . ." He trickled the water across her breast. Tiny rivulets swirled around her round, taut breast.

"Have you seen water droplets on fire, maiden? Does the fire die, or does it writhe?"

Nisa's breath caught. His finger trailed the same path along her breast, dipped into the water, then moistened her lips with a slow, sensual touch.

Nisa trembled as Seneca's finger moved to the tip of her breast. The peak hardened as he circled and teased, her head tipped back, and he bent to kiss her throat.

He caught her waist in his hands and bent her backward. Nisa stiffened as the water surrounded her, but Seneca held her secure. Her breasts jutted upward,

226

and she knew his desire responded.

She closed her eyes and let herself float on her back. The ceaseless rhythm of the water hummed in her ears, the sweet smell of the woodland night reflecting on its surface and filling her senses.

Seneca watched her, spellbound. The light of Thorwal reflected on her creamy skin and pale hair like silver. Nisa's womanhood captivated him. Tonight she felt her power. She had never been stronger. He knew this, and he knew he was the reason.

Young and guileless, innocent and pure. He had seen her as a woman-child, surprised by desire. But not tonight. Tonight she was a goddess. A goddess he couldn't resist.

Seneca bent forward and touched his lips to her exposed breast, still supporting her back beneath the water. Nisa shuddered, but she didn't open her eyes. Seneca slid his hands from her back to her bottom, then eased her legs around his waist.

His hands freed, Seneca guided the water over her breasts, up her throat. Her long hair splayed and undulated on the water, around her shoulders and face like a soft cloud.

The soft, Dakotan water circled his length. He felt like the fiery metal forged in Thorwalian mines. He was aware tonight of his own size, his own maleness. Where Nisa was soft and yielding, he was hard and urgent. Made for her.

Seneca gripped his full length in his hand and positioned himself to enter her. A low, raspy sigh escaped her lips when he brushed himself against her, but Nisa didn't open her eyes.

He saw her white teeth chewing the soft pulp of her lower lip; he saw her pink tongue. For a moment, Seneca prolonged his sweet agony, delaying his entry as their bodies touched without pressure.

Nisa's legs tightened around his waist as she urged him closer. He gripped her hips and guided himself just inside her opening. Her breasts rose and fell with short gasps, but she waited, savoring.

"We are nothing, Nisa," he murmured as he slowly moved deeper inside her. "Just wind and fire and water. In a storm . . ."

The cool water flowed around them as he moved in her, cool on his skin as her tender woman's sheath squeezed his length. The shock of cool against her heat heightened his senses and his pleasure, and Seneca thrust with ever-increasing abandon.

His own head tipped back; his jaw clenched as he deepened his strokes, holding her as she floated, receiving him, soft cries and moans pleading him to carry her further still.

She clasped her legs tighter around Seneca's waist. Nothing existed beyond them. Her slender arms spread out in the water as she moved with his thrusts. Water lapped over her neck, splashing over her face.

He filled her, touching the places of her most secret longings. Seneca felt her wild, tiny spasms as they erupted around him. Her toes curled in an effort to prolong her pleasure. He moved, harder and faster, guiding her in an ever-intensifying rhythm.

Nisa called his name and he pulled her up against him, still deeply preferred embedded in her body.

"Seneca, I love you so."

She wrapped her arms around his neck and he eased her down until her toes touched the pond's sandy bottom. Nisa steadied herself on one foot, then wrapped her other leg around his.

Her teeth sank into his shoulder as he thrust upward inside her. He buried his face in her hair, murmuring her name, driving himself harder, lifting her from her footing with the power of his thrusts.

Her round breasts crushed against his chest. Her heart beat in wild rhythm with his. Nisa circled him again with her legs and they writhed together, one body, one motion as he carried her to a mindless pinnacle where nothing existed beyond them.

A low moan shuddered through Nisa as her pleasure crested. Seneca felt her spasms around him, squeezing him, until his own release erupted with shattering force. Over and over the tight waves crashed through him, pouring into her.

She collapsed against him, supported in his arms, her breaths warm and fast against his shoulder. Seneca set her to her feet, sliding from her body. Nisa sighed, but he released her and sank beneath the water.

Nisa stared. She shook her head to clear her senses. Seneca had disappeared beneath the black water. Electric pulses of joy gave way to shock. She felt around for him as her mind fought to regain control.

"Seneca! Where are you?"

Nisa panicked, looking wildly around. She saw no sign of him. "Seneca!"

Nisa struggled through the water, deeper, until the water reached her neck. Tears puddled in her eyes. How could he disappear? What if his heart gave way to some Akandan illness and he needed resuscitation?

Nisa's panic soared. If she could find him, she could save him. The Dakotans had the best doctors on either world. No illness couldn't be treated.

"Seneca!"

Nisa had to swim. She didn't know how. But if he wasn't on the surface, he had to be on the bottom. He couldn't have gotten far. Unless a fish of unusual size captured him . . .

Nisa's thoughts went to wild extremes. She would fight the fish. She took a deep breath, then plunged beneath the surface. The black water closed over her head, but it didn't pull her down. Instead she bobbed to the surface again.

Nisa took a smaller breath, then tried again. She kicked her feet as he had done earlier that day. Her close scrutiny of his movements had value, after all.

Her arms propelled her down and forward, but she didn't find him.

She came to the surface for another breath, then tried another spot. Nothing. She was crying. He couldn't disappear. She started down again, but something caught her feet. Something that wouldn't let go.

Nisa screamed and kicked. This must have captured Seneca, too. It wouldn't take her before she won vengeance.

Nisa gulped, then plunged beneath the surface, aiming to grab the creature. She caught something that felt like soft reeds. She yanked as hard as she could. The creature released her and rose to the surface, bringing her with him.

"You are the most violent woman that ever lived."

Seneca pried Nisa's fingers from his hair. He was laughing. Nisa's heart nearly stopped, then beat so fast that she felt faint.

"What . . . Where have you been?" She sounded violent. Seneca was still laughing. "You did this on purpose!"

Nisa grabbed his hair again and pulled him close to her, bending him down to her eye level. "Didn't you?"

Seneca tried to nod. She tugged again, and he winced. "I was impressed with your abilities, maiden."

"My what?"

"Swimming." Seneca eased his hair from her tense, Ravager fingers. "You were very graceful."

"You saw?" Her voice sounded very low and, she thought, very threatening.

"You didn't look far enough." Seneca pointed toward the middle of the pond. He had been watching her, and all the while, she thought the world had ended.

"I thought you were dead!"

"Very close, my sweet Ravager. Rarely has a man been so thoroughly spent as I this night."

"So spent you disappeared?" Nisa's hands went to

her hips. She forgot her nakedness.

"I just wanted to cool off." He was teasing her, and after she had endured such fear. . . . Nisa aimed for his hair again, but Seneca avoided her attack and swung her into his arms, carrying her dripping from the water.

"There's something about your Ravager blood that inspires me, maiden. But the light of Thorwal wanes. I'd prefer to see you beneath light replacers, after all."

Seneca set her on her feet and found their clothes. He slid her makeshift dress over her head and pulled his trousers on, leaving his shirt untied and hanging open. Nisa stood staring at him.

"I thought you were dead." Her voice came small and quavering. Seneca drew her into his arms.

"I'm sorry, Nisa. I didn't mean to frighten you. I assumed you recognized the game. It is often played on Akando."

"Game? That was a game?" Her voice turned shrill. "To make love, then disappear?"

Seneca smiled at this description. "Not exactly, no. This is the first time I've played it while making love. Although it made the sport far more enjoyable. . . ."

"Did it?" Nisa glowered. "How very fortunate for you!"

"Didn't you and Dane ever play hiding games?"

"Well, yes. When he was a small boy I played such games with him. But never underwater."

"A minor difference." Seneca took her hand and kissed her fingers. "Shall we return to Macanoc, maiden? If we're fortunate, your uncle and the Dakotans will have abandoned revelry for sleep, and we will pass unnoticed."

Nisa's emotion cooled. "I will forgive you, since it appears you didn't intend to frighten me." She closed her fingers around his hand. "The Ungan wine will have put them all to sleep. My uncle tends to imbibe more than his share."

"I noticed that. But he'll sleep well tonight. He and his aides are housed in the guest quarters above the lab."

"He didn't return to his shuttle? That is unlike Thorwalian policy during times of unrest."

"The unrest between your worlds is passing, maiden. Tonight your uncle accepted my offer of friendship, and sleeps as our guest. If I understand Thorwalian custom, such an acceptance indicates a desire for unity."

Nisa felt a soft wave of happiness and contentment. Her world returned to peace. Her plan succeeded, and the man she chose to replace Motega had healed her heart as well.

Nisa touched Seneca's face, and her heart felt swollen with love. "When I first saw your face, I didn't think I'd have the heart to meet you."

"Why is that, maiden?"

"Because you look so much like Motega." Nisa's head tilted as she studied Seneca's calm face. "More so in pictures than in person. Your nature is quite unlike his. We had taken images of many of your young men. All bore some resemblance, but none was close enough. Until you."

"When was this? I had been many days on a solitary journey. How did you find me?"

"Our first sighting of you was nearly a year ago." Nisa fingered Seneca's narrow braid. "After I found you I had to get approval. It wasn't easy to convince Helmar to attempt my plan, and Fedor was against it, naturally. But Dane helped me, and together we proved the mind probes could be used on humans."

"By your test on the lingbat?"

"Carob's result was astonishing. He convinced Helmar, actually."

"So I have him to thank." Seneca shook his head, but Nisa's heart wrenched. So he still resented his capture. If so, he must still intend to return to Akando.

She didn't have the courage to ask tonight. She didn't want to know.

"By the time I got council approval, you had disappeared. We feared you had been killed until one of our scans discovered you to the north of your tribe. They said you were followed by several unpleasant predatory species, so we hurried to you, thinking we might save you."

Nisa paused, her brow knitting. "Apparently that wasn't necessary."

"As I told you, the trial of manhood isn't without dangers."

"By the time we reached you, you were almost home. We didn't want to risk unnerving your people. . . . But it was close." Nisa didn't wait for him to speak. She didn't want him to speak. "I'm sorry for abducting you that way. I hope that you will forgive me."

Sorrow echoed in her soft voice. Seneca drew her into his arms and kissed her head. "After tonight, do you need to ask?"

Nisa swallowed hard to stop tears. "You once suggested I ask, didn't you?"

"I did." Seneca touched her chin and bent to kiss her lips. "And tonight, the answer is yes."

Chapter Eight

"We've got trouble." High, chirpy words yanked Seneca from the depths of satisfied sleep. He opened his heavy eyes to see Carob's scrunched face bare inches away. The lingbat perched on his chest.

The hope he was dreaming faded when the bat hopped from his chest to Nisa's shoulder and tugged at her tangled hair. "You'd better hear this, too."

Nisa started, gasped, and yanked the covers over her head, dislodging the bat. "Carob!"

Seneca rubbed his eyes, squinting at the early morning sun. "Come back when the sun passes the tree line, bat. We were late to our rest."

"Anyone with ears as well attuned as mine knows that."

A horrified moan came from beneath Nisa's covers. Seneca chuckled and patted her shoulder. "We're working on our first litter."

"No time for that now. As I said, there's trouble brewing."

Seneca sighed and sat up. "What trouble?"

"The door to Helmar's guest quarters is jammed. Someone burned out the locking panel, and we can't reach anyone inside."

Nisa sat up, heedless of her nudity. "What do you mean, you can't reach anyone? The walls aren't that thick. Shout!" She started out of bed, but Seneca met the bat's eyes and saw a look of warning.

"The Dakotans are shouting, believe me. There's no reply."

Nisa's face went white as she looked at Seneca. "How could that be? What happened?"

Seneca shook his head. "I don't know." He rose from the bed and dressed. Nisa was shaking as she pulled on the blue Dakotan suit he had given her.

"Let's go."

Nisa and Seneca found Manipi outside the guest quarters. Nisa fought panic. Everything would be all right. There was an explanation. She stood by the door.

"Uncle! Are you in there? Are you all right?"

No answer came, just deathly stillness. The Dakotans exchanged uncertain glances, waiting for Seneca's instruction. "We've called in," said Manipi. "Nothing. Thought we might cut through with a blow torch."

Seneca nodded. "Do it."

Time crept painfully slowly as the Dakotans cut away a section of the wall. Nisa's heart thundered. "Uncle." A dark premonition swarmed her brain, reminding her of Motega's death.

The section fell inward, and Manipi stood back. Nisa started forward, but Seneca grabbed her arm and went in first. An agonized moment passed.

"Keep her out there, Manipi."

Nisa heard everything in his voice. The Thorwalians were dead. She moaned in agony and sank to her knees. Carob positioned himself beside her, but said nothing.

Seneca emerged and knelt beside Nisa. In his hand, she saw Helmar's flute. She took the flute and held it against her heart. She saw Helmar, lost in his music, the Thorwalian aides chanting, Their low, sonorous voices echoing in the still air.

They had spent their last night in the shadows of their ancestors. Nisa's eyes filled with hot tears.

"My uncle . . ."

Seneca laid his strong hand on her shoulder. "He's dead, Nisa." Her sharp cry cut him off; she fell into his arms and wept as he stroked her hair.

"How?"

"I would say laser rifles at full force."

Manipi put his hand to his forehead. "All of them?"

Seneca nodded. "All."

"That Thorwalian commander, Fedor, has been demanding contact with Helmar. Says he'll send down a shuttle with or without our approval. What do we do?"

Seneca rose to his feet, but before he could answer, a Thorwalian shuttle lowered to the landing strip above the lab. "It seems our options are limited. Fedor is here."

Nisa grabbed Seneca's arm. "He'll blame you. Seneca . . ."

"It's all right, Nisa. I can handle Fedor."

Seneca and the others started across the square to the lab, but Fedor had already led a party of guards to the transport tube. They weren't carrying rifles, but Nisa knew they were armed with shorter-range pistols.

Seneca met Fedor at the transport entrance. Nisa held her breath as they faced each other. Tall and dark and impossibly strong, Seneca towered over the slender Thorwalian. Yet Fedor's expression remained scornful and betrayed no fear.

Nisa hurried to Seneca's side, but Fedor didn't address her. "We have been denied communication with our High Councillor. Is this the manner of the Dakotan treaty of peace?"

Seneca's eyes fixed on Fedor's, but Fedor didn't shrink away. "Helmar and his aides have been murdered, Fedor."

Fedor's pale eyes widened in shock. In a flash, it occurred to Nisa that his shock stemmed from Seneca's honesty, and not Helmar's murder.

"The circumstances of their deaths are unknown."

Fedor still didn't speak, but his expression hardened. "Much is unknown this day, it seems." He turned to Nisa. "I will assume, since you are of the house of Calydon, that you know nothing of this outrage."

"Of course not! Nor does Seneca. There are saboteurs, Fedor. Helmar warned me. . . ." Nisa's voice cracked. Helmar. Her uncle, closer than her own parents. Seneca touched her shoulder and she leaned against him.

Fedor's eyes darkened at the intimacy obvious between Seneca and Nisa. "There is no question who is responsible for your uncle's murder, Nisa."

Nisa looked at him. Her insides quaked as though knowing an impending doom. "You can't know who did this. There is no one here with reason."

"No one?" Fedor's gaze turned mockingly to Seneca.

"One man, Nisa." Fedor's voice trembled. "One man has had reason from the beginning. One man who could enlist even wayward Thorwalians to his bidding to aid his quest for supreme power. Even you, Nisa. Even you."

"Seneca? That is absurd. He, least of all, has reason to murder my uncle. He is Akandan and cares nothing for the politics of our world."

"Not Seneca . . ."

Nisa didn't want to hear. She felt dizzy. "Then what man could possibly . . ."

"Motega."

The air filled with heavy silence. No Dakotan spoke. Nisa heard her own heartbeat. "Motega is dead." Her voice shook.

"Is he? Haven't you wondered, Nisa? What happened to the guard? There was only one body. We assumed it was Motega shackled to the wall. But what if it wasn't? What if it was—"

"It was the guard."

Seneca spoke, and Nisa turned as if in a dream. She shook her head, her senses fighting to rally. "The guard stole a shuttle, because he killed Motega, or thought he'd be blamed. . . ."

Seneca's gaze held hers, unwavering. "It was the guard." Even the birds fell silent. Nothing moved; the wind stilled. "He was called Balduin."

Nisa stumbled back, her soul stricken with denial. "You can't know that."

Seneca moved toward her, but she backed away, her arms clutched around her sides, shaking her head to block the meaning of his words.

"I know."

"No."

Fedor trembled with suppressed excitement and victory. "He knows, Nisa. He knows because he is Motega. If you've been fool enough to doubt until this moment, know it now. Once again Motega has made a fool of you and used you, and again threatens us with his lust for ultimate power. And now he has murdered Helmar before your eyes, while you follow him like a blind, smitten wench."

Nisa squeezed her eyes tight, bending over as pain ripped through her. "No." *Seneca.* He would protect her. He had healed her. She was free. "Seneca . . ." She dared to look at him. "Tell him it's not true."

He didn't answer for a long moment while their eyes

held, hers stricken blue, his dark and warm and filled with hidden emotion. "It is better to face truth than to deny it, even when it causes pain."

Nisa swayed and turned away, shaking her head. "No."

"Nisa, I was going to tell you."

Nisa whirled around, backing farther from him. "Tell me?" She laughed, hysterically. "Tell me what?"

Seneca reached for her, but she recoiled, and his hand dropped to his side. "I am not the man I was. Akando changed me."

Every word drove home the madness amid her disbelief. The fool she had been, had always been.

"I didn't kill your uncle. Please listen. . . ."

Nisa shook her head wildly. "It can't be. . . . You can't be."

Seneca stepped toward her, but she moved behind Fedor, trembling.

"Balduin took my place when you shackled me to the wall. He allowed me to rest. While I slept, the assassin entered and . . ."

Fedor drew a stun pistol and aimed at Seneca. The Dakotans surrounded him, but Seneca held up his hand. "Wait." Though the Dakotans muttered angrily, they obeyed his command.

"Do you expect us to believe such a mockery of truth? It is obvious that you killed the guard, then escaped to Akando, where you hid like the coward you are, waiting. Your accomplice waited for the right time, then set this ridiculous impersonation scheme in motion."

"Nisa knew nothing of my escape."

Fedor's eyes narrowed to slits. "I don't speak of Nisa."

Nisa couldn't think; she couldn't question Fedor's insinuation. Fedor turned to her, disregarding the furious Dakotans. "The plans, Nisa. Where are they?"

She barely heard Fedor's voice. "What plans?"

Fedor leaned toward her. "For the cell, the power cell that will send him to Candor after he annihilates Thorwal. Where are they?"

She was drowning, dying.

Fedor grasped her arm. His hand trembled. "Will you let him make you an even greater fool? Will your blind infatuation for his demon's charm aid in your own people's destruction?"

Seneca didn't exist. Motega had made her love him again. And betrayed her. She didn't recognize her own voice. "He keeps them in his house, in the far cabinet by the white tree."

Fedor held the gun to Seneca's head, then nodded to a guard. "Get them. If anyone tries to stop us, Motega dies."

Seneca didn't move. His attention remained fixed on Nisa. "Nisa, don't do this. I don't want that cursed moon. I never did. Don't do this."

Rage filled her heart. Logic meant nothing. She was raw and elemental now; she was a Ravager daughter, and she had nothing but hatred and fire. Her blue eyes burned, and she shook with fury.

"No! I promised you that you'd never forget me. You destroy me again and again, but I'm not dead, and I will fight you to the last breath of my life. I will return, and I will destroy you!"

The guard raced from Motega's house carrying the small cabinet. Fedor backed toward the transport tube, still aiming his pistol at Seneca's head. Manipi placed himself in front of Seneca, but Seneca pushed him aside.

"If you shoot the Deiaquande, we will blast you from the sky, Thorwalian! Those plans won't avail you if you're splattered across the sky."

Fedor laughed. "Motega means nothing now, alive or dead. You arrogant fool . . . Did you think by getting between a woman's legs, you and your pathetic Dakotans could challenge Thorwalian supremacy?

You have failed, Motega, for the last time."

Seneca wanted to stop her, to take her away, alone. To explain. "Nisa, please wait. Don't leave this way."

He stepped toward her, but Fedor took her arm and pulled her into the tube. She didn't resist. Her long hair fell around her face, wild and as primitive as the Ravager queens who led their legions into bloody conquest.

Her eyes glowed with madness, with blue fury. The transport tube lifted, and she entered Fedor's shuttle. The Dakotans raced for their weapons, but Seneca stood like stone, watching as the shuttle lifted from the lab strip.

"Do we fire, Deiaquande? The defense system is still operative. We can knock them from the sky."

"No." The shuttle rose above the tree line, then swerved in a blast of energy toward the sky. In seconds it disappeared into the low clouds.

The Dakotans gathered around him, waiting. Manipi touched his shoulder. "They will destroy our fleet."

Seneca nodded. "I know."

"She may lead them. She is their main weapons expert."

"I know."

Seneca could still feel her on his skin, her soft scent lingering in his memory. He stared into the empty sky. Tears filled his eyes, blurring his vision. She was gone.

Nisa lay sedated in Fedor's shuttle. She hadn't fought the injection. She hadn't fought at all. She woke and had no sense of time. She lay on her back, alone.

The sedative slowed her thoughts, or was it shock? Nisa tried to sit up, but her limbs felt heavy. The dosage must have been unusually high.

The door hissed open, and Fedor entered. He sat on a stool by her bed. Nisa tried to focus on his face. He looked larger; he wore the mark of the High

241

Councillor. As Helmar's heir, her mark.

"Fedor . . ." Her words slurred. The sedative. "What is the meaning of this?"

A slow grin spread across Fedor's face. His once deferential gaze perused her boldly, lingering on the swell of her breasts beneath her covers. "We approach Thorwal, Nisa. There is much to discuss before we land."

"Such as what?"

"Much has . . . altered during your brief absence."

Nisa's brain labored, but a dark fear rose in her heart. Her madness eased under the weight of the sedative, but she needed her senses clear now.

"What has changed? Helmar mentioned a saboteur."

"Your uncle didn't want to disturb you with the details, but it is time you were made aware of the situation. Your brother, Dane, has been in constant communication with Dakota for several years. And they with Motega."

Icy fear clutched Nisa's heart. "That's not possible. Dane was a child when Motega—"

"His connection was with the Dakotans. Obviously he won their confidence, and began treating with Motega."

Nisa shook her head. She tried to gather her thoughts, to maintain control. The sedative fought against her logic. "Dane wouldn't . . . he has no reason."

"No reason?" Fedor's tone turned mocking and Nisa knew worse disaster had come. "With Helmar—and you—gone, Dane becomes commander. Or would have, had I not wisely secured allegiance among the Thorwalian guard."

Nisa knew now. "If anyone desires command, it's you, Fedor. Not Dane. And if that's true . . ."

Fedor's expression darkened, but he made no effort at denial. "Your uncle found it difficult to believe, too.

242

I offered him irrefutable proof, and the result has been the security of Thorwal."

Nisa's heart quailed for her young brother. "What have you done? Curse you, what have you done?"

"Nothing . . . yet. Dane is imprisoned in the holding cell in the Chambers." Fedor paused, and his lips curved in a treacherous smile. "The same cell where Motega escaped his assassination."

"You . . . it was you."

"Motega's escape set me back, without question. It took a while to reform my plans. Your brother proved an apt solution. He was old enough, barely, to accomplish much . . . shall we say, mischief? If he'd spent less time at the taverns, he might actually have formulated such an ambition himself. But his only ambition is to bed wenches and play fighter."

Nisa's blood ran cold. *Dane.* "He's a boy. What kind of evil could condemn a boy?"

"Your brother is dear to you. I think you would do anything to protect him from his fate."

"What do you want?"

"You have always been a problem, Nisa. But a beautiful problem." Fedor touched her hair, catching a thick strand between his fingers. Nisa froze; her skin crawled.

"The guard is thoroughly under my control, I assure you. But the population of Thorwal will expect . . . propriety. They want their 'rightful' heir. You. The solution is obvious. You will mate with me."

"I will not." Nisa's voice shook. "And you won't succeed in this, Fedor."

"I have already succeeded, my temptress. I have your brother shackled to the same wall where Motega's guard met his fiery end. Unless you want the same fate to consume Dane, you will do exactly as I ask."

Nisa swallowed, but her limbs went cold. She had no power. Her power had disappeared with Seneca.

"What a fascinating creature you are, Nisa! It

seemed obvious to me since you first entered the council that you and I should mate. But then Motega arrived with his demands and his seduction, and you played his whore. Motega, whose plans for Candor rivaled my own, had to be destroyed."

"But you failed."

Fedor shrugged. "It took a while for me to realize my error, even after I saw your Akandan. He bears little resemblance to a Dakotan now. It was the probe's failure that alerted me. When Helmar communicated that, I knew we had been fooled for the last time."

"You killed Helmar."

"That weak fool would have made peace with Motega, to save his own skin, to return to the way things had been. I want a brighter future. I want Candor."

"I will fight you."

"Once we reach Thorwal, you will be imprisoned like your brother. I will give you one cycle to accept my offer. If you fail, your brother will die. But either way, I will take you as my due."

Fedor's eyes wandered hungrily over Nisa's body, but he rose to his feet. "It's time you took a Thorwalian to your bed, Nisa. You might find the change . . . satisfying."

Nisa couldn't speak as Fedor left her room. She stared at the door as Fedor locked it from the outside. She was a prisoner.

Nisa wanted to die. Without Seneca she had no hope, no reason to live. She hated her life and her weakness; she hated the love that destroyed her. But Dane . . . his life had promise. His bright eyes, his young face . . .

She had been more his parent than their own aloof mother and father. Dane was her responsibility. She loved him when nothing else mattered. When she lost Motega, only Dane had given her joy.

"Well, what are we going to do? That boy may be a flouncer with females, but he's no saboteur."

244

Nisa's heart almost stopped. Carob popped from beneath her bed and flapped himself to her shoulder. She buried her face in her hands and sobbed.

Carob waited patiently while she cried, then began tapping on her head with the tip of his wing. Nisa pulled herself together. "I don't know what to do, Carob."

"Fedor will kill the boy whether you're his mate or not. Otherwise he'd be leaving a possible usurper on the loose."

Nisa nodded. "I know. But they'll imprison me, too, Carob. What can I do?"

"Not much."

Nisa frowned. "That's very comforting. How did you get here?"

"I figured you'd run off without thinking first. Thorwalians always do. So I tucked myself into the shuttle and hid out. When they drugged you, I slipped in here and waited until you snapped out of it."

"I couldn't stay on Dakota."

"Dane needs you, it's true. But you'd have done a lot better to think it out. You need Seneca to get you out of this."

Nisa's face paled. "Seneca . . . There is no Seneca, Carob. He is Motega."

Carob shrugged. "No difference. But it doesn't count for much now. You're on your own. Seneca can't get to you in time. From what I saw, Fedor blasted what remained of the Dakotans' fleet. He couldn't get here if he wanted to."

"I'm sure that's not his intention."

Fedor's shuttle lurched, then grated as it landed on Thorwal. Nisa's breath caught as the door panel lit. "Carob . . ."

The lingbat hid beneath the bed. "We're on our own."

"Find Dane."

The door slid open and Fedor appeared with his

245

guards. One held a syringe. "We've arrived. It's time you rested, Nisa. It's been a long, tiring journey."

"The Dakotan leader is no match for me, Uncle! I will show him around Thorwal, if he's not too fat to squeeze into my new hovercraft."

"Take care, Nisa. This Motega is rumored to have a way with women."

Nisa tossed her head at Helmar's warning. "Dakotan women would fawn over a wortpig. I have no interest in soft speech, Uncle."

"He will be our guest at the noon meal. After that you may show him the Chambers and our city. The lava river might interest him."

"If he's a typical Dakotan, he won't have the energy to waddle from my vessel to the viewsight."

"By all accounts, Motega isn't typical."

Nisa's dream faded. She tossed in her bed, fighting. The sedative claimed her, and she descended again into the bittersweet nightmare of her past.

The Chambers' dining hall was filled with guests. Nisa saw her parents sitting stiffly at the far end. Garta wore a red, revealing dress. Apparently, she, too, had heard rumors of the Dakotan leader's supposed prowess.

Dane darted through the room and stole a sip of Ungan wine. Nisa's father spotted the small boy's theft. "Dane! To your room!"

Nisa cast a sympathetic glance at her little brother. He grinned and shrugged, then raced from the dining hall. Nisa looked around for the Dakotan leader. He wasn't there yet, nor was Helmar. Their meeting stretched over its allotted time.

Nisa took her place beside Fedor. He eyed her dress with misgivings.

"Why do you honor this arrogant Dakotan with traditional garments?"

"Because my uncle requested it, Fedor. That's why."

The Chamber door opened and Helmar walked in with a tall, dark man at his side. The room hushed, but Nisa watched him dispassionately. He looked much younger than she imagined, little older than herself.

"Is that Motega?"

Fedor's pale eyes narrowed to slits. "Yes."

Motega was speaking with Helmar, so she couldn't see his face well, but his hair was dark and swept back from his forehead. It curled around his ear. Her insides fluttered, though she had no reason to be nervous.

He turned toward her and her world stopped. His eyes slanted slightly at the corners, soft and wide and brown with black lashes. Even across the room the intensity of his gaze pierced her young heart.

He nodded almost imperceptibly, but her senses reeled. He sat across from her, one seat down. Those beautiful eyes never left hers. She couldn't eat. She made conversation with Fedor, but she heard nothing he said.

The noon meal ended, and the Thorwalians surrounded Motega, speaking of nothing. Garta tried to engage his attention, but his gaze returned again and again to Nisa.

"Come, Nisa, and meet the Dakotan leader. He is known as the Deiaquande."

Nisa didn't feel her feet touching the ground as Helmar led her across the room. "Deiaquande, allow me to present Nisa Calydon, my niece and heir."

The Dakotan leader was taller than she had realized. She had to look up to meet his eyes, and she considered herself tall for a Thorwalian woman. She opened her mouth to speak, but he took her hand and kissed it. Vibrant energy flowed beneath his skin. It quivered between them.

"Nisa. It is a pleasing name, for an astonishingly pleasing woman." His voice caressed her. He spoke quickly, his motions fast and static, as if his rampant energy couldn't be contained.

Nisa forced a quick bow, as Helmar had instructed. "It is my honor to meet you . . . Deiaquande." He smiled at her mispronunciation of his title, but he didn't correct her.

"The pleasure is mine. Do I understand that you will show me your city? It is magnificent. It pleases me to spend the hours in company with a woman equally so."

They spent the day together. Nisa took Motega through the Chambers, through the city, and finally to the viewsight above the lava river. He teased her about her piloting, then seized her controls when she rolled her hovercraft.

They stood together, watching the sun set over the lava river. In the hours since their first meeting, Nisa had endured the greatest shock of her life. She had fallen in love.

"This place . . ." Motega's quick voice slowed. His dark brow furrowed as he fell into an unusually contemplative mood. Until now, his rapid speech and brilliant thoughts had filled every moment. "There is something I don't understand."

Nisa smiled, her heart light and wild, racing. "I can't imagine that."

"This place . . . I find it stimulating. Something is here, something I have never felt before."

"Lava beneath the snow. It's common in other parts of Thorwal, but this is one of the finest locations for viewing. Up close, the fumes are overwhelmingly hot and noxious."

Motega laughed and shook his dark head. "You can be painfully literal, Nisa. But perhaps that is part of your charm."

Nisa felt foolish, but Motega moved closer and drew her into his arms. Her limbs went weak; she felt dizzy as he bent to kiss her. His lips teased hers; his tongue slid sensually over hers. He broke the kiss, his dark eyes smoldering.

"I've wanted to do that since I saw you."

The Dawn Star

She didn't know what to say, but Motega didn't wait for her answer. As the sun lowered beyond the lava river, he kissed her again, long and deeply, and Nisa's heart was lost.

Nisa bolted upright in the narrow bed. The light replacer of the holding cell had dimmed, indicating night, but Nisa had lost all track of time. Tears streamed down her face.

Her dream throbbed in her brain, a relentless reminder of the past. That day, they had returned late for the even meal, incurring the anger of the council members when Motega missed his scheduled conference.

Her parents had taken her aside, coldly outraged that she had embarrassed them by her wanton behavior with the seductive Dakotan leader. They ordered her to leave, to stay away from him.

Young and torn, hurting with love, she went to the Hall of Ancients, leaning miserably against a giant pillar. If she stayed, she would humiliate her parents. But if she left, she would die.

She felt his hand on her shoulder, his lips against her ear.

Come with me.

She knew what he meant. He wanted her, this night. She fought the overwhelming passion that swarmed her senses and blurred her rational mind. *I cannot.*

Come with me.

Her knees went weak. She shook her head, but she couldn't speak.

Motega unbound her hair and let it fall around her shoulders. *You are beautiful thus freed, Nisa Calydon. Like a goddess on these tapestries.*

He slid her hair over her shoulder. He kissed her neck and she leaned back against him. She turned her face to him, and he kissed her mouth. His tongue teased her lips, tasting her. *Come with me.*

249

She couldn't deny him. Though all Thorwal witnessed her surrender in silent outrage, she couldn't deny him. She gave him her hand, and he led her from the hall and toward the guest chambers.

He led her past the dining hall, past her parents, past Helmar and Fedor. It didn't matter that her destination was obvious to all.

He asked, and she went.

Nisa brushed away the tears, but more followed. The memory replayed; she felt each wrenching emotion as if it happened all over again.

Ignoring gossip and her parents' shocked orders, she had gone with him to Dakota. When Helmar ordered her home, she returned with the promise of becoming his mate.

Nisa's throat hurt from crying. Tears stung her cheeks and fell to her clasped hands. She didn't want to remember. But she was raw and unprotected, and Seneca was gone.

She saw it all. Helmar and Fedor, standing on either side of her as she sat with her head bowed, cloaked in the illusion of Motega's love.

How much did you tell him, Nisa? Does he know about the Candor find?

Fedor's voice followed Helmar's, cold and impersonal, mocking. *Perhaps this will convince you . . .* He played a rough, scratchy recording . . . Motega's voice. The voice she adored.

I will seduce Helmar's gullible niece, and find out what they're hiding. . . . Laughter followed.

Nisa clutched her sides as the memory assaulted her. Sobs racked her chest; the old pain returned in its full force. He never loved her. She meant nothing to him. *He knows everything. I told him everything. . . .*

Her young life shattered. She did whatever they asked. They told her to contact Motega, and she did. They told her to lure him back to Thorwal, and she

250

did. She died slowly that day.

He arrived, and she saw his face when the Thorwalian guard surrounded him. She felt his fury when he realized she had betrayed him. Helmar imprisoned him while he searched for a solution to the young leader's influence.

Nisa couldn't stay away. She was driven to him; she taunted him. They fought bitterly. He dared to kiss her, taunting her with the desire she felt for him. In vengeance, she shackled him to the wall, despite Balduin's objections.

She had suffered through a long night of erotic misery. The next morning she went to his room to increase the sexual frenzy between them. There, in a room of dark blood and charred walls, she found the burned body.

Nisa couldn't blot out her memory. She moaned as misery overwhelmed her. "Motega . . . No."

Hot, burning tears flooded her vision. Nisa wept until there were no more tears, until her throat was hoarse and bloody and raw. Then she rose, calm and quiet, and went to the holding cell door, engaging the communication grid.

"Message received, Fedor on line."

Nisa's voice came low but clear, certain. "Fedor . . ."

A shocked pause followed as Nisa waited. "Nisa! I didn't expect to hear—"

"I have changed my mind. If you will release my brother and send him to Dakota, I will become your mate."

Seneca sat by the pond and stared at nothing. The Dakotan air hung hot and heavy. No wind lifted the oppressive heat.

"Thought I'd find you here."

Seneca didn't look up, but Manipi seated himself and tossed a pebble into the pond's still surface. "From the research I've done, I gather fish don't take to bait on days like this."

Seneca said nothing. The ripples on the pond spread to the side and disappeared. The rich scent of the forest seemed stagnant today.

"We've made quite a turnaround here. Never thought I'd find myself looking forward to a fish hunt."

"You knew."

Manipi fiddled with a blade of grass and nodded. "I knew."

A long silence followed. "You said nothing. Why?"

Manipi shrugged. "A man has a right to call himself whatever he wants."

"And under two names, I have failed you."

"Maybe we failed you."

Seneca looked over at Manipi. "I was your leader. I led you into disaster, by virtue of reckless pride and ambition."

"You were a boy. We placed all our hopes in you, because we'd never had another like you. We wanted change, so you tried to change things."

"I set in motion our destruction."

"Maybe. But you told me something a few days ago. You said we had to find balance within ourselves. It wasn't up to you to give us the life we wanted. But you're the one who showed us what we can be."

Seneca hurled a rock into the water. "For all the good it did."

"It seems to me we've got Helmar's adviser to blame for that."

Seneca's fists clenched in helpless frustration. "Fedor . . ." Seneca rose to his feet and paced along the pond's edge. "She's in danger, Manipi. I can't reach her."

"She'll come back. She always does."

Seneca stopped and looked down at Manipi. "And if she returns in a warship? What then?"

"You'll follow your heart, as you have always done.

We will follow you. Not because you're Motega. Because the man who calls himself Seneca gave us back our soul."

Nisa waited by the holding cell door, her face grim and determined. She heard footsteps. Armed guards, coming for her. At least two, coming to bring her to Fedor for the mating ceremony.

She heard them enter the code into the panel. The door slid open. The first guard entered the room. He noticed her strange, square stance, her bent knees. His brow furrowed doubtfully.

Nisa stepped back, then spun around, kicking behind her. The guard grunted in surprise when her small foot contacted with his groin. He doubled over, and she slammed her elbow into the top of his spine. Nisa leaped through the open door, surprising the second guard.

She crossed her arms in front of her chest, then blocked his rifle, knocking it from his hands. He expected a kick, but she swung her leg and caught his, snapping his knees out from under him. He fell forward into the cell.

Nisa jumped through the door and smacked the locking code into the panel.

"Well done! Magnificent!"

Carob appeared around the corner. He flailed his wings and flapped to her shoulder. Nisa drew a deep breath.

"You're shaking. Calm down. There may be more."

Nisa looked back at the holding cell. "I can't believe I did it."

"Surprise. Isn't that what Seneca said?"

"Yes." Her throat felt tight. "Where's Dane? Did you locate a rifle?"

"We won't get one till the way out, assuming you can get him out of there. Better hurry. I dismantled the connection panel, but as soon as Fedor realizes you're out, he'll send every guard in Thorwal after you."

Nisa sped down the hall, guided by Carob toward Dane's cell. At the far end of the Chambers' upper level, Carob directed her to the last door.

"That's not a cell; it's an old lab."

"Not anymore. From what I've gathered, Fedor didn't want anyone knowing where your brother was kept. Probably afraid some well-meaning female from the Snow Port would attempt to break him out."

Carob chuckled at this, but Nisa's pulse was racing too fast for humor.

"Fedor imprisoned Garta, too. Probably for the same reason."

Nisa hesitated. She wasn't fond of Garta, but the safety of all Thorwalians was her responsibility. "Maybe we should break her out, too."

Carob snorted. "Don't bother. She might prefer your young, energetic brother, if she could sink her fangs into him . . . which he's wisely avoided, you'll be glad to know. But when she realized who held the power, she turned her sights on Fedor. Kept him busy, too."

Nisa grimaced at the visual image of Fedor and Garta. "How foul!" The sound of footsteps shattered her concentration. "Someone's coming!"

"In there . . ."

Nisa darted into a storage unit and waited for the sound of footsteps to disappear. "All clear."

"How do you know, Carob?"

"My ears are much superior to humanoid ears."

Nisa swallowed hard, but she trusted the lingbat's senses. She slipped out of the unit and hurried down the hall to Dane's door. "Are you sure you got the right code?"

"Watched them enter it three times. Always the same."

Nisa tried Carob's code, holding her breath as the

panel lights glowed. The door opened, and her knees
weakened with relief.

There, in the darkness, she saw her brother, and her
heart quailed. His sweet face was blotched and swollen, stained with dried blood, bruised and blue from
beatings. Nisa fought a wave of sickness. His eyes
were swollen nearly shut.

"Dane . . ."

He looked up, trying to see through the slit of his
eyes. "Nisa?"

She ran to him, hugging him close as she cried.
"What have they done to you?"

Carob looked nervously out the door. "No time."

Dane groaned. "No, it can't be . . . not . . ."

"There's gratitude for you." Carob hopped to Dane's
shoulder. "Who do you think masterminded your
breakout, boy? I did."

"Carob. I never thought I'd miss you, but it's good
to hear your voice. For the time being. I trust you've
eaten already, and will spare me the details of your
feast."

Nisa sniffed, but she laughed through her tears. "I
guess you'll live."

Dane squeezed her hand. "I'm all right. What about
you? Where is Seneca? Is he still on Dakota?"

Nisa bit her lip hard. "Seneca is Motega."

Dane's mouth dropped, but Carob flapped his wings
impatiently. "This is no time for catching up. We've
got to get out of here. Now."

"Carob is right. Dane, can you walk?"

"Of course." Dane stood, swayed, and Nisa caught
him. "I can do anything."

By the power of his will and nothing else, Dane
straightened his back and forced himself to move. "I
can't see very well, though."

"No need," chimed in Carob. "I'll guide you."

Dane shook his head. "We should reach approximately the first storage unit before we're nabbed."

Nisa seized his hand. "We'll get farther than that." She listened at the door, then led her brother from the cell. "Carob says we can get a rifle when we get to the shuttle bay."

"If we get to the shuttle bay."

Carob dug his claws into Dane. "Optimism, boy. Now!"

Dane's condition prevented them from running. His ribs were broken, his breath came labored and short, but the boy still seemed cheerful, pleased to be part of any adventure. "Just out of curiosity, where are we going?"

Nisa stopped to listen around a corner. "Dakota."

"That sounds good."

Carob huffed. "If they don't shoot us down, we'll be in fine shape."

"That's very encouraging. Thank you, rodent."

Nisa glared at Dane. "Hush, both of you! Follow me."

"She always was bossy," Carob muttered, and Dane nodded.

Nisa reached the Chambers' lower entrance without being seen, but there she stopped. "What now, Carob? There are guards everywhere."

"I haven't heard the escape alert yet." Just as Dane spoke, a blaring alarm rang all through the Chambers. He sighed. "I stand corrected."

Nisa gulped. "There's nothing else to do. As soon as they turn in to find out what's going on, we make a run for the shuttle bay. Dane, can you do it?"

"I can do anything."

"He's stronger than he looks," added Carob.

They waited, motionless, breath held. The guards thronged in, confused. Nisa closed her eyes. She saw Seneca's face in her mind, calm and powerful, encouraging her while she practiced TiKay.

"Now!"

They ran out across the hard-packed snow, out into the open light. A loud cry sounded from the guards. "They're getting out the guns," squeaked Carob. "And Thorwalians have better aim than Dakotans."

"Quiet, rodent!"

The first blast streaked over their heads, but Nisa kept running. She heard Fedor's voice, shouting orders. "Cut them off! Ready the missiles!"

Her lungs burned. A quick glance told her that Dane kept up with her despite his pain. His long legs carried him with easy speed, but he matched his stride to hers, and her heart filled with love for her brother.

They reached the shuttle bay. "Where's the rifle, bat? They're coming."

Carob pointed to a stack of supplies. "One in there, but how are you going to see . . . ?"

Dane fumbled through the supplies. Carob groaned loudly when the boy selected a pipe rather than a rifle. "Can't you see anything?"

Dane tossed the pipe aside. "Same shape."

"There, to the left, just up   "

Dane seized the rifle and spun around just as a guard leaped toward them. "Aim straight, boy!"

Dane fired. The guard fell.

Nisa stared at her brother in astonishment. Another guard bounded into the hangar. Dane fired another well-aimed shot, but he couldn't hold them alone. Nisa felt Seneca like a part of her. She knew what he would do.

With all the courage of her Ravager blood, she ran toward the oncoming guards. She jumped and spun, her leg extended. Her aim was pure luck, but she knocked the guard aside.

Dane let out a whoop of shock and pride. Nisa gathered herself to take on the next. She remembered Seneca's blocking maneuvers, turn, foot back. She punched another guard in the chest, knocking the wind from his lungs.

Dane fired again, and Nisa reached the control panel on the hangar door. She jammed in a code to lock the system, then raced back toward her brother. "It won't hold them for long. Which way, Carob?"

"First dock on the left."

They ran past startled technicians, toward a medium-sized fighter craft. Nisa stopped. "A fighter? Carob, there must be something else. Isn't there a long-distance shuttle anywhere?"

"Not if you want to get through Fedor's missile defense."

"The rodent is right, Nisa. Shuttles don't have the speed."

"I can't pilot a fighter craft!"

"I can."

Dane bumped into the ramp and Nisa groaned. "You can't see!"

A thunderous crash boomed at the hangar door as the next wave of guards tried to break through. Carob squeaked. "They're coming. One of you had better start piloting something, or it won't matter."

They jumped onto the ramp and Dane sealed the door. "I'll tell you what to do."

"Might as well have gotten shot out there," muttered Carob as he settled himself in the viewport.

Nisa took the helm. Her hands shook so much she could barely grip the controls. "We've got one chance, and that's all."

Dane touched her shoulder, a quiet gesture of love amid terror. "Are you ready?"

Nisa nodded. The guards burst into the hangar just as she started the engine. With a choking roar, the fighter craft leaped to life and burst from the shuttle bay into the pale blue Thorwalian dawn. Missiles fired, but too late to reach Thorwal's fastest vessel.

The fighter craft shot through the sky and broke through the atmosphere. Nisa set the heading for Dakota, then exhaled a long, shuddering breath.

"We did it. We escaped."

Dane corrected Nisa's faulty heading, then leaned back in his seat. "You were amazing, Nisa. Leaping and punching and kicking. How did you learn that?"

Nisa hesitated. "Seneca taught me."

Dane leaned forward. "Ah, yes . . . You mentioned something about Motega. I can't wait to hear—" Dane's eyes spun around in their sockets, and he fell face forward onto the control panel.

"Dane!"

Carob hopped down beside Dane's unconscious body, then shook his head in dismay. "He's out."

Nisa gently eased her brother onto the floor. "The Dakotan doctors can help him."

"How are you going to land without him? Not that he's the pilot I'd choose, either, but . . ."

Nisa stared at Carob. Her face went white. "I have no idea."

Manipi met Seneca in the village square. "Fighter craft spotted on radar, Deiaquande. We've got the defenses set for your order."

Seneca stood immobile, staring into the sky. "How many?"

"Appears to be only one, for now."

Seneca's eyes narrowed. "One? That's hardly an all-out assault. What's its heading?"

"Right here. Macanoc."

Langundo charged across the square. "Here it comes, sir! Awaiting your orders."

The Thorwalian craft blazed across the sky, then spun around, turning back to try again. Seneca scratched his forehead. "That's not exactly attack formation. In fact . . ."

A slow smile grew on his face. "Disengage defenses, Langundo. Allow for landing. And keep your heads down."

Langundo's face fell. "Are you sure, sir? We have a good bead on it."

Manipi started to swat at Langundo, but stopped at Seneca's reproachful look. "Do as the Deiaquande says, and be quick about it."

"Manipi, greet the pilot on my behalf. I'll be in my quarters."

Manipi's brow furrowed. "Sir?" But Seneca had already started away.

Nisa closed her eyes as the fighter lowered toward the Dakotan landing strip. "Carob? Does this look right?"

"A little to the left."

Nisa made an adjustment and held her breath. "I've never been very good at braking."

"Well, you'd better start now."

Nisa braked. The fighter tilted to one side, then righted too far to the other. Carob's claws scraped the control panel as he leaned to look through the viewport.

"Steady!"

The craft came to a stop. Nisa went weak and leaned her head onto the control panel. Carob had already hopped to Dane's side. "Don't like the sound of his breathing."

Nisa was still shaking, but she lowered the ramp. "I'll get help."

Manipi was waiting. He sighed when he saw her. "I knew it. What took you so long?"

Nisa glared. "My brother is injured. We need a stretcher."

Manipi moved faster than his shape appeared to allow. He disappeared in the transport tube, then returned followed by several Dakotans. They carried Dane from the craft and Nisa followed them into the transport tube.

Manipi gasped when he saw the young man's battered face. "What happened to him?"

"He was beaten by Fedor's guards."

"Your brother, is he?" Manipi sounded unusually sympathetic. "We'll take care of him." His gentle tone shocked Nisa. "Take the boy to the hospital."

Carob positioned himself on the stretcher and nodded at Nisa. "I'll keep an eye on him while you straighten things out here."

Manipi sighed in dismay, but allowed the bat to accompany Dane to the hospital. Nisa felt a wave of relief. In Dakotan hands, Dane would recover. She looked around.

"Where is he?"

"Who?"

Nisa hesitated, refusing to say his name. "Your leader."

Manipi chuckled. "The Deiaquande is engaged in serious matters just now, but advises that you be directed to the guest quarters by the square."

Nisa stared hard at the Dakotan. "You knew who he was all along, didn't you?"

Manipi nodded, but he made no comment.

"It must have amused you to see me make such a fool of myself."

"No, it didn't amuse me. I watched you destroy him once before, and I didn't want to see it happen again."

"I destroyed him? Ha!"

"Motega was a great man, but he was young. We placed all our troubles on his shoulders, and he did what he could. When he returned, calling himself Seneca, I knew he had changed. He didn't want to be here. But he stayed because of honor, because we needed him."

"He doesn't want to be here . . . still."

"He speaks of returning to Akando. I hoped you would be enough to keep him here. I guessed you'd be trouble, but Seneca seemed as fascinated by you as Motega was."

"You speak of him as if he were two people."

Manipi's heavy brow rose. "Isn't he? I have known two men. One is gone, but he lives in our hearts. Seneca is our soul. We don't want to lose him."

"I don't care what you call him. I just need to speak with him."

She had to see Motega, and she had to see him now. She had to get it over with, before her nervousness overwhelmed her. "Please inform your leader I have returned and wish to speak with him."

"If you'll just make yourself comfortable in the lab sitting room, I'll take him the message." Manipi hesitated. "He's busy, though."

Nisa restrained her impatience, and Manipi hurried away. She waited for an inordinately long time, time enough for her nerves to jump and quiver when anyone entered the room. Manipi returned without Motega. He appeared uncomfortable, and her anger grew.

"Where is he?"

"The Deiaquande is pleased you have arrived safely, and has asked me to assure you our doctors will put their very best effort into caring for your brother."

Nisa closed her eyes in an effort at restraint. "I asked to speak with him."

Manipi hesitated, shifting his weight from foot to foot. He wouldn't meet her eyes. "As I mentioned, the Deiaquande is busy. He assures you that at his earliest convenience, he would be happy to meet with you."

"At his earliest convenience? And when would that be?"

Manipi shrugged in a noncommittal way. Nisa twitched. She couldn't stand it. She hopped to her feet and seized Manipi by the front of his shirt.

"Do you know what I've been through since I left here? I've been drugged and imprisoned, almost forced to become the mate of my uncle's murderer, and I've been shot at. I've piloted a fighter craft by a lingbat's guidance, and I'm not in the mood for this, Manipi!"

Manipi appeared pained, and he nodded. "I'll see what I can do."

Nisa released him and stepped back, forcing a quick smile in acknowledgment for his efforts. Manipi scurried away and she sat down to wait.

When he didn't return after a sufficient period of time, she began to pace. She looked out the window, then out the door. Dakotans passed to and fro, but she didn't see Manipi anywhere.

Nisa sat back down, fidgeted, then returned to the window. Her anger surged. "How dare he leave me waiting this way!" She paced around the room. "The Deiaquande assures me, indeed!"

Nisa stopped. She wasn't nervous now. She was furious. "So you've regained your position, have you, wortpig?" She seized the door and yanked it open. "We'll just see about that."

Ignoring the surprised Dakotans, Nisa stomped across the village square to Motega's house. Manipi spotted her. "Now hold on there, woman! You can't go bursting in on the Deiaquande without permission."

Nisa whirled, her eyes a fiery warning. "Can't I? I wouldn't try to stop me, if I were you!" She opened the door, stormed in, then slammed it with all her strength.

She locked the door, then looked around. He stood at the far end of his house, his back facing her. He seemed to be going over notes. He didn't look up. But he must have heard her enter.

She chewed the inside of her lip. As much as she expected Motega, it was Seneca she saw, his long dark hair falling to his shoulders, his powerful body appearing almost languid in his loose Dakotan clothing.

Her heart pounded. She cleared her throat and swallowed hard. "I understand you don't have time to see me." She assumed he heard the cold sarcasm in her tone.

He didn't turn around. "My adviser relayed the pertinent information." He sounded so calm. Serene. Nisa's whole body tensed in fury.

"You know Fedor destroyed what was left of your fleet."

"So I understand." He flipped a page of his notes.

Nisa quivered. "He has technicians working continually on your power cell. It should be complete in a few days."

He nodded, then turned another page. "That seems a reasonable assessment."

"He will implant the cell in one of our largest transport vessels and start for Candor."

"I assume that has always been his intention." He paused, glancing back, but not looking at her. "Your information is useful. I'm not sure what we can do to reward you at this time, but rest assured that we will do our best to rectify the situation. Is that all?"

"I require a report on Dane's injuries."

"Your brother's condition has stabilized, though he remains unconscious. If there's nothing else . . ."

Nisa fingered her belt, wishing she were armed. He was a stranger, this man who had made love to her under two names. He didn't even look at her. Over and over she had relived his supposed death, and he didn't even look at her.

Her escape from Thorwal flashed through her mind. She wasn't armed, but she wasn't without power. Nisa moved across the room, silent and light, her body tense with violent intent.

She poised herself behind him, grabbed his hair, and yanked his head back. He moved so fast and smoothly, Nisa didn't know what happened until she landed on her back.

She set her chin in fierce determination. In one swift movement she braced her arms, swung her legs around his, and flipped him backward.

Surprised by her success, Nisa pounced. She straddled his chest and clutched his hair in both hands. He laughed, but his face was wet. Tears ran from the corners of his brown eyes into his dark hair.

Nisa stared down into his face. He was crying. He had been crying all along.

In his face she saw the young man she had loved with the mindless, selfish passion of her youth. Her fingers loosed his hair, but she didn't move. Her chest caught on sharp breaths, her eyes welling with hot tears.

"You're alive."

Nisa buried her face in his neck and wept. His arms closed around her, protecting her.

He sat up, holding her tight against his chest. "Nisa."

He was alive. Nisa touched his face. "Motega."

He closed his eyes. "I was."

"Seneca." Her voice sank to a whisper.

"I am."

She loved him so much, she thought she would die. She had known him, but never knew him. She knew him now, but he was a stranger. "What happened?"

Seneca brushed her hair from her face. "I've always wanted to ask you that."

Tears glistened in her eyes, and her chin quivered. "I thought you loved me."

"Why would you think I didn't?"

Nisa looked down; she couldn't face him. "I thought nothing could separate us." She swallowed, fighting her emotion. "They, Helmar and Fedor, said you were using me to learn about the moon."

"How could anything they have said turn your heart from me? Nisa . . ."

She looked at him. The ache in her heart opened so wide that she couldn't stem the flow of tears. "It wasn't what they said. All the things they tried to make me believe, I wouldn't hear. They kept me in the council room for hours, and I wouldn't tell them what they wanted to know."

"Then why?"

Nisa didn't answer at once. Even when he had been imprisoned, she never said the words, never confronted him. She wasn't strong enough to hear his answer. "Fedor played a recording of your voice."

She stopped, but Seneca waited. Nisa's gaze drifted to her hands. "You were talking to another Dakotan. I think Fedor had placed a listening device in your quarters."

"I should have guessed."

"I heard you say you intended to seduce me . . . because of the moon." The words spoken, her heart clenched. "It could have been faked. I know that. . . . Fedor would do that."

"That was my intention."

"Oh." Nisa felt like the girl she had been when Motega formed her world, and when she learned it had been a lie. She looked away to hide her tears, but Seneca touched her chin and turned her face to his.

"Whatever you heard, Nisa, I said. I had heard you were young, and beautiful, and cold. I was angry then. I blamed Thorwal for Dakotan hardships. It pleased me to imagine seducing you for our ends."

Nisa tried to look away, but he wouldn't let her.

"Beyond that, there was something about Thorwalian women that attracted me. It's the coolness, I think."

Nisa winced, but Seneca didn't stop. He ran his thumb along her cheek to her lips.

"I hadn't met you, Nisa. When I saw you, I thought my plans might serve even better than I imagined. You were beautiful and sweet and untouched. I wanted you from the moment I saw you."

"That's very comforting."

Seneca touched her hair. "It never occurred to me

that I could fall in love with you. But the day we spent together . . . when you raced me around in that little deathtrap of yours . . ."

"You don't mean my hovercraft, do you?"

"It wasn't the craft, but the pilot that unnerved me." Nisa frowned. "You made me nervous."

"An effect that hasn't changed over time. If possible, I think you're worse than you were."

"I'm surprised you allowed me to pilot you this time."

"I took too much control over you, Nisa."

"You did. But my brother and I are both unlucky with our crafts. It has nothing to do with piloting skill."

An incredulous expression crossed Seneca's face. "If you and Dane weren't charmed by some ancient power, you'd both be long dead, taking half Thorwal with you."

"Not at all! What does this have to do with your deception?"

"That day spent in your company, I realized there was more to you than your cool surface. When you brought me to see the lava river, I felt it."

A cool thrill sped along Nisa's nerves. Her pulse quickened; she fought to breathe.

"I loved you, Nisa. I saw you, the most beautiful woman that ever was, standing before me, with your violent, cold world burning behind you. And I loved you."

Tears welled beneath her lashes and fell to her cheeks, but she couldn't look at him.

"Then it's true. . . . I really did betray you."

"So it seemed." Seneca slid his arm around her shoulders and drew her close to him, cradling her head on his chest. "You were young, and they hounded you. That was my fault."

"No. They were scared of you."

"I did nothing to alleviate their fear. I saw Helmar

as our enemy. I was blind. I liked their fear, Nisa. I wanted it. I was too proud, and I wanted to take you from them."

Nisa looked up at him. "We were both young. And we had nothing but what we wanted."

"Each other."

"When you were imprisoned, I tried to stay away. But I had to see you. It was better to fight with you than never to see you again."

Seneca smiled, though his dark eyes filled with unshed tears. "I must confess a certain warped enjoyment of our encounters, too."

"Especially the last."

"Until you shackled me to the wall, the night had its promise."

A sharp pang of misery gripped Nisa and she leaned against him. "I didn't want you dead . . . you must know that."

"I know it now."

"But you didn't then. You must have believed I tried to kill you."

"Yes."

"When I came back the next morning . . ." Her voice cracked and he held her, though he smiled through his tears.

"You must have had some agonizing torment planned."

Nisa nodded against his chest. "I did."

"Dare I ask? Did you intend to have me hung by my feet?"

"I was going to kiss you."

Seneca's brow arched. "I probably could have survived that."

Nisa peeked up at him. "Not on the lips." The admission embarrassed her, and she hid her face in his shoulder.

"Cursed assassin."

"Yes."

"Did you intend to keep me shackled?"

"That was my intention, yes."

"Both hands?"

Nisa looked up at him, wondering why his voice had turned husky and strained. "Yes, both hands . . . Well, I'd have to do that, so you couldn't stop me."

"As if I'd want to."

A small smile curved Nisa's lips. "I thought, after a while, I might let you go."

Seneca moaned deep in his throat. "And I would fall at your feet."

Nisa met his eyes. "That's not exactly where I wanted you."

His gaze smoldered, penetrating her with the memory of what they had been. "I would have ripped the shackles from the wall to have you."

A hot wave of emotion tore through her. "If Fedor hadn't tried to kill you, we would have been together again. Instead . . ."

"Instead, fate took its own turn, and we were torn asunder in the storms of our worlds."

Nisa leaned her head against his shoulder, her fingers gripping his strong arm. "Why did you flee to Akando? Why not Dakota, where you belong?"

"By the time I escaped Thorwal, the fleet had mobilized. I couldn't break through without raising suspicion. I went to Akando with the intention of waiting until the orbit neared Dakota, then returning to my own planet."

"Why didn't you? Did you crash?"

"No, I didn't crash. I was, if you remember, a very capable pilot."

"I remember." Nisa considered this, and another mystery became clear. "That's what happened when we were shot down on Dakota. You landed our shuttle, didn't you?"

"I did. And it wasn't easy to keep my shield around you while piloting a vessel. Never had I used two such

269

divergent facets of my learning."

"What are you talking about? What shield?"

"The teaching of TiKay involves shielding ability, as I told you."

"Is that why you seemed to disappear when I was abducting you?"

Seneca nodded. "Had I not sensed your presence, your efforts would have failed."

"Why did you stay on Akando, if you didn't crash?"

"It wasn't my intention when I landed, I assure you. I was consumed with anger. I wanted vengeance on Thorwal, on you. I had tried to find you before I left, with the intention of taking you prisoner."

Nisa sighed at the thwarted prospect. "I suppose I was already on my way to torment you again. By the time I reached the cell, you were gone."

"Our purposes have crossed too often. But when I reached Akando, I thought nothing could stop me from returning."

"But you didn't return. Why?"

"When I reached Akando, it was at its farthest point from Dakota. My shuttle couldn't have made the journey then. I had to wait."

"So you found help with the Akandans?"

"No. I avoided them. I thought they'd be more trouble than help. It wasn't long before I learned how ill equipped I was to survive in the Akandan wilderness."

"Didn't you have weapons?"

"The shuttle wasn't equipped with weaponry, other than a stun pistol. Without recharging, that was soon useless."

Nisa watched Seneca's calm, beautiful face, her heart swollen with admiration and love. "How did you survive?"

"I almost didn't. As you know, there are many aggressive creatures on Akando. The weather was brutal, so cold that Thorwal seemed balmy in comparison. I was nearly frozen, and I was starving, torn and bleeding from a run-in with an oren-cat."

Nisa's eyes were wide, her lips parted. "What did it do to you?"

Seneca laughed at her expression. "It decided I looked just feeble enough for an easy meal."

"You're not feeble!"

"I wasn't strong. Even to a yearling oren-cat, I seemed an easy target."

"I can't believe that." Nisa patted his arm. "But you defeated the beast."

"I used the last of my stun pistol's power to drive it away. When it returned the next morning, I had no way of defending myself."

"It came back?"

"It did. And if an Akandan hunting party hadn't come by, the cat would have enjoyed a fine breakfast."

"They saved you? How did you communicate with them?"

"Their language resembles Old Dakotan, from the time before our language changed to suit yours."

Nisa considered this. "Then you were right. There must be a connection between the two races."

"I believe that. But I never learned how the two came to live on different planets."

"Maybe Akando was once part of Dakota, and the comet split a larger planet in two."

"That's unlikely. In such a cataclysm, how could any species survive?"

"Good point. What happened when they found you? Did they see your shuttle?"

"I had left the shuttle hidden, and gone to search for food. The Akandans shared their dried meat and carad-sticks, and they brought me to their village."

"You must have admired them."

"I scorned them. They nursed me back to life, and all I thought about was finding my shuttle and leaving, hunting you down."

Nisa squirmed uncomfortably. "There seems to

have been a particular inclination toward vengeance on your part."

"The notion obsessed me."

"What a comforting thought!"

"But at that time, the orbit was still too far from Dakota to attempt escape. I passed the time by watching my new hosts, though I refused to help them in their tasks."

"What happened when the orbit reached Dakota? Did you try to leave?"

"During the warm season, violent storms flood the coast and rage across the inland wastes. The chief insisted we move to the high plateau, and he had the gall to insist I help."

"He sounds like a dreadful man."

"I thought so, too. I loathed him, though I had little feeling either way about the other Akandans."

"So this chief made you work?"

"He tried. I refused. But Nodin is a strong-willed man. I told him I had more important matters than the fate of his village."

Nisa couldn't help smiling. "You were very arrogant."

"I was. 'Arrogant' is a gentler term than what Nodin used, however. When I tried to leave, he challenged me to battle."

"Battle? How exciting! Did you fight him?"

"I believe I laughed and called him a crazy old man. At that point, I made the mistake of turning my back and attempting to leave."

"Did he attack you?"

"I suppose you could call it that. All I knew is that somehow I ended up on my back, with him standing over me."

"I know how it feels."

Seneca kissed her forehead. "I was gentler with you. Nodin followed the move with a rather unforgiving kick."

"He kicked you? What a horrid man!"

"He kept at me until I fought back. Everything I tried, he countered. I hit the ground more times that day than ever before, and I was bloodier than after my tangle with the oren-cat."

"He hurt you!" Nisa's chin rounded into a fierce ball. "I hope you injured him right back."

"Not a scratch. I never touched him."

"Oh. That's not terribly impressive, Seneca. Especially if he was an old man."

"He was older than Helmar by several cycles, but he could inflict more damage than your brother in a fully armed hovercraft."

"I'm not sure that's possible. I take it you didn't return to your shuttle in time to leave orbit."

"I didn't. And I found myself helping the Akandans move their village and, later, joining the hunting parties as they foraged for food."

"Did this Nodin make you?"

"I didn't argue with his requests after that."

Nisa's heart felt strange and heavy, yet it pounded with excitement. She saw him, Motega, young and reckless and brash. His heart filled with anger and pride, forced to exist among primitive warriors.

"Did they know who you were?"

"I never told them. But if I had, it would have meant nothing to them. They assumed I was an outcast from another tribe, and after my behavior, they could see why."

Nisa's brow furrowed as she pondered Seneca's story. "When we located you, the researchers said you were some sort of nobility. How did they get that wrong?"

Seneca hesitated, but his dark eyes sparkled. "My first year in Akando was less than glorious. By the second year I had come to value their world."

"So you decided to stay?"

"No. But the second year gave me another reason

not to leave. The hurricanes came early that year, before the villagers could be moved. Nodin's village was destroyed, and many were injured. I found I couldn't leave them in such misery. I used what medical knowledge I possessed to help them, and won favor."

"You were very noble."

"Nodin didn't think so. He was angered to learn I had such skill and didn't use it before."

"What a grumpy old demon he must have been!" Seneca smiled, but Nisa saw an expression on his face that she recognized. Love. "You cared for him, didn't you? Why?"

"Speaking as someone who cares for wortpigs, need you ask?"

"Wortpigs are charming and gentle creatures. This Nodin sounds dreadful in the extreme. And it doesn't sound as if he treated you very well."

"He managed to engage me in battle almost daily. At first I thought the old man was trying to kill me. But after a time I came to look forward to our encounters. And after the first year, I began to avoid his blows. By the end of the second, I had delivered some of my own."

"It took you two years to hit him back?" Nisa shook her head in dismay, but Seneca laughed.

"I was told that my progress was exceptional. No one connected with Nodin in battle."

Nisa remembered Seneca fighting the disguised Thorwalians. "Is this how you learned your TiKay?"

"It is. Although I didn't learn the true meaning and power of TiKay until my third year on Akando."

"What is the true meaning?"

"TiKay is the soul of Akando, the way they survived. It teaches balance and unity, between mind and body, between each other. And between ourselves and our world."

Nisa gazed into Seneca's face. He seemed wise, calm. As unlike Motega as night from day. Yet in his brown eyes, she saw the man he had been. The deep passion in Motega found balance in Seneca. She had fallen in love with him twice.

"If you were so dreadful, why did this Nodin teach you his sacred craft?"

"I've never known that. But when my third year began, he started taking me with him on solitary hunts, teaching me of his world."

"Did he still hit you?"

"Occasionally. I think he missed our earlier battles. But there came a time when neither of us was able to contact with the other. A standoff was reached, and he turned to other lessons. He taught me to use my own power to shield myself, and others."

"I don't understand that part of it."

"I'm not sure I do, either. But it's something inherent to Akandans. And apparently to Dakotans, though our ability has long been dormant from disuse."

Nisa watched Seneca's face as he spoke. She saw his inner peace, a peace she couldn't imagine. "Why did you call yourself Seneca?"

"I didn't. For my first three years, I was Motega. Then, as the third year came to a close, as the warm season approached and the sky was black with storm, Nodin took me to the high cliff that overhangs the village."

"The cliff where I saw you running?"

"It is a sacred place to the Akandans. It is called the Birth of the Wind, and many rituals are performed there."

Nisa remembered him standing there as she watched him on the viewing screen, his dark hair flying behind his head. Her heart had tightened, her eyes had puddled, but she hadn't known why the emotion came so strong.

"Nodin brought me to the cliff and he told me his people were born on that wind. He said I had spent my life couched in flame, but I was a creature of the wind, and it was time I accepted my own nature."

Nisa's heart stirred, but she couldn't speak. She longed to touch him, to hold him. But Seneca seemed beyond her now, stronger and wiser, eluding her . . . like the wind eludes fire.

Seneca took her hand. "What he saw in me, I saw in you."

Nisa pressed her lips together. She wanted to be like him. But she saw no place where he didn't tower above her.

"You, with your brave declarations of logic and control, were the wildest thing I'd ever seen, my little Ravager. It seemed so obvious, but until you captured me on Akando, I hadn't realized how wild you are."

Nisa's chin tensed and lifted. "I'm not wild."

Seneca's brow raised and he smiled, shaking his head. "Where to begin? Most recently, you attacked me from behind and flipped me onto my back. Before that, you seized my adviser by the throat and threatened him."

Nisa cringed. "Manipi told you that? The worm!"

Seneca kissed her hand. "He was terrified to return with my last message."

"He didn't. What was it?"

A grin spread across Seneca's face. "I instructed him to schedule a consultation with you in two days."

"He was wise to stay away. What were you thinking? Why didn't you want to see me?"

"I wanted to see you. If that hadn't provoked you, I intended to offer you steamed wortpig for dinner."

"What? Seneca!"

"Unnecessary. You responded admirably." Seneca touched his head where she had pulled his hair. "With good force."

Nisa stared. A slow dawning grew in her mind. "You did to me what that old man did to you! You pestered me until I attacked you."

"You, my sweet woman, are nearly as irritating as I was."

"I am not!"

" 'We call them Dakotans because they're from Dakota.' " Seneca's tone mocked her first instruction. Nisa flared with anger, but then giggled at the memory of her own imperious attitude.

"I suppose that was a bit much."

"I didn't realize at first what I was doing. I simply felt the need to provoke you, to prod you into revealing your true nature. I assume this is what Nodin felt for me. But later I knew."

Seneca fell silent, but his eyes burned. Nisa bit her lip, wondering what he had discovered about her character that she didn't know. "What?"

"I did it because I love you. Because when I look at you, I see inside you. And I know what you can be."

Her eyes stung with sudden, hot tears. Her throat tightened; she felt every pulse. Seneca touched her face gently. "I know, because Nodin taught me, without ever saying the words."

"He loved you, too."

A gentle, sad smile lingered on Seneca's face. "He did. And when he took me to the cliff he called me Seneca, for the son of the wind."

Nisa's tears fell, and she sniffed. "He meant you were his son, didn't he?"

"That day he adopted me into the Clan of the Wind, and he named me his son and heir." Seneca's eyes glittered with tears, and Nisa ached. "That day I journeyed alone to my shuttle. I set the stun pistol to explode, and destroyed my last connection to the man I had been, to Motega."

"And to me."

"No, not to you. By the third year, the TiKay had relieved me of my anger. My hatred faded, but I couldn't forget the love."

Warm tears streamed down her face, but Nisa didn't

push them away. Seneca cupped her face in his gentle hands and kissed her, but she knew he cried, too. "Seneca."

"I became Akandan in spirit and in mind. I forgot the name Motega, and became Seneca. One thing I couldn't forget, and that was you."

He rested his cheek against her head, rocking her against him. Nisa wrapped her arms around his waist. "I never forgot you, either."

"When you came to abduct me . . . I felt you before I saw you. That day I intended to banish your image from my memory forever. Instead I turned around and saw your face, and I knew I would never forget. You wouldn't let me."

Nisa wasn't sure what Seneca's words portended. Would he be happier without her? She wanted to ask, to know. She wanted to influence his decision. The young woman who loved Motega would have done anything to keep him, even shackle him to his prison walls.

She hurt him once. If not for a kindhearted guard, he would have died. Because of her. Nisa knew what she had to do. She knew, but her courage failed. She couldn't say the words.

"You said you have a brother."

"Carack. He was orphaned, ill, and very shy. Using what medical knowledge I had from Dakota, and with the herbal treatments of the Akandans, I was able to heal him. He reminded me of Dane, actually. He followed me everywhere."

"You are very good with children. Dane adored you."

"I paid no attention to Dane then. I had no interest in a child's world. I was a fool. But I taught Carack the TiKay; I taught him to hunt."

"And to swim?"

"And to swim. Unlike myself, he had no confidence in his abilities, he had no value in himself. He had been abandoned, and he had nothing."

"Did Nodin adopt him, too?"

"He did." Seneca paused. "But he didn't knock Carack around as he did me. His gentleness with the boy astounded me."

"I suppose Carack didn't require smacking around."

"That's true. And thank you for pointing it out."

Nisa kissed his face; she squeezed him as her heart expanded with painful love. She saw his life now; she saw his journey from reckless youth to the power and glory of manhood. One thing remained, and she gathered the courage to ask.

"You said . . . you were to take a mate that day." Her voice sounded small and uncertain. She wished she hadn't asked.

"I was."

Nisa swallowed hard to contain her emotion. "Did you love her?"

"Akandan matings are rarely decided by love. Love is expected to grow after respect and honor."

This sounded noble to Nisa, but she felt a tug of relief. Better that he married for honor than for passion. Then again, Nisa couldn't imagine Seneca in a passionless union.

"But you chose her."

"Carack chose her for me. As is the custom, he traveled to a neighboring tribe, a much smaller clan that occasionally ambushed our hunting parties. To arrange better relations, Carack treated with them for their chief's daughter, Elan."

"Elan. It is a pretty name." Nisa's frown tightened. She remembered the dark, lean Akandan women with shiny black hair. They were beautiful. "I suppose she wasn't irritating."

"Not at all." Seneca laughed and kissed her forehead. "Unfortunately for myself, I have a penchant for irritating women."

"Indeed. But you were going to mate with her."

"That was my intention. It was the final break from the past. From you. I thought passion had destroyed me. I never wanted it again." Seneca hesitated. "I sometimes wondered, with that attitude, what kind of mate I would be. The nuptial bed might have been less than rewarding with this mind-set."

Nisa brightened. "True. You would have been very disappointing as a lover."

"Again, thank you."

"Did she love you?"

"I believe she liked me. She told me once she would take whatever I had to give, and ask for no more. She said also that she knew I loved another, and that she would never expect to live in my heart, because you were living there already."

Nisa sniffed. "She sounds very noble."

"She was."

"She would have made you a good wife."

"She would."

"I took you away. You were happy, and I took you away from what you wanted."

"Akando is with me wherever I go, Nisa. If I can bring its wisdom here, to Dakota, then I will have fulfilled the promise Motega made as their leader."

One question remained, but Nisa had no heart to ask. *Do you want to go back?* She tried to form the words, but they wouldn't come. She closed her eyes. If he wanted to leave, how could she ask him to stay? If she loved him, she would honor his freedom. And she loved him with every fiber of her being.

Chapter Nine

The mists had cleared between them. Seneca held Nisa in his arms, but he felt a new distance rising. Here, where no secrets remained, she withdrew. When he had never been more sure of her heart, she fell silent.

"Nisa? What troubles you?"

Nisa chewed her lip, hesitating. "I am worried about Dane."

Seneca knew more existed behind her mood than Dane, but Nisa had endured shock, terror, and death. He couldn't push her further now.

"Come, then. We will visit your brother, and you will see for yourself."

Nisa breathed a small sigh of relief, then moved from his arms. She rose hurriedly, as if she couldn't wait to get away from him. Seneca sat on the floor, his brow furrowed as he wondered at the cause.

Nisa waited. Seneca didn't move. *You won't pull away this easily, maiden.* An expression of irritation started on her face, growing impatience.

"Well, what's keeping you? Are your legs numbed?"

"I need a hand."

"You need feet!"

Seneca smiled and waited. Nisa rolled her eyes, then gave him her hand. He rose without effort, but kept her hand in his.

"Motega, Seneca . . . It makes no difference. You are still irritating in the extreme."

Seneca kissed her cheek. "Which is why you are drawn to me, maiden. We are the same."

Nisa glanced up at him. "Ha! I see no similarity between us whatsoever."

"Lust, maiden."

Nisa's cheeks colored, but she made no effort at denial. "There is that."

"There has always been that. And, my sweet Ravager queen, there always will be."

Dane was surrounded by doctors. All female. Nisa shook her head and sighed. Carob was perched on a regulating device, giving instructions that the doctors ignored. Seneca surveyed the scene and laughed.

"Is his condition so poor? Never have I seen so many doctors assigned to one patient."

The doctors started at his voice. "Deiaquande!" A young, pretty doctor dropped a sponge meant for Dane's supposedly heated flesh. "We are apprentices, and since we rarely see a case so . . . so . . ."

"Interesting," offered Seneca. Nisa hit him.

"These women are tiring my brother. Maybe they should leave him to rest."

Dane glanced at Nisa and shook his head. "Their care has been more than adequate."

Carob whistled. "You can say that again! He's got the cleanest wounds anywhere . . . and a few clear places I didn't think were damaged at all."

"I want to speak to my brother. Alone!"

The women hesitated. Seneca grinned. "It would be a shame to confine his attendants to males."

That was enough. The women hurried away, though Nisa made a tight fist. "Dakotan women are shameless."

Carob coughed. "No worse than Thorwalian females, I'd say. It's the same scene from the Snow Port Tavern all over again. Although I'm not sure he got this much attention when healthy."

Dane lay in his bed, a smile on his face. His eyes were only partially opened; his face was still swollen, though his bruises were turning brown. Nisa sat down beside him.

"You look awful."

Dane sighed, his smile still wide and satisfied. "I know." Nisa glanced at Seneca, and he shrugged. "I don't think I've ever seen you so pleased with yourself."

Dane gazed at her through squinted, purple eyelids. "It's not my face."

"What are you talking about?" Nisa touched his forehead for fever. "You feel cool."

"It's not my good looks."

Nisa rolled her eyes as Dane's point came clearer.

"I thought women wanted me because I'm so handsome."

Both Nisa and Carob groaned. Seneca laughed and shook his head.

"But that's not it. . . ." Dane's voice trailed away, his expression pure, youthful bliss.

Nisa kissed her brother's forehead. "Of course it's not your looks. It's your sweet heart, the way your emotions show in your eyes."

Dane eyed her doubtfully. "What?"

"It's your soul that attracts women, Dane."

Dane appeared bewildered by Nisa's gentle sentiment. "No . . . it's my body!"

Nisa clapped her hand to her head; Seneca pressed

283

his lips together to keep from smiling and turned away to hide his laughter. Carob jumped down to Dane's chest.

"Your body? Are you insane?"

Dane's brow furrowed indignantly. He glanced at Seneca, and his confident expression wavered. "Perhaps I could use a little more mass."

"You could use a muscle implant. You've spent your whole life being carried on some sex-starved female's back."

Dane rolled over suddenly, dislodging the bat. "Shouldn't you be practicing your nonexistent flight skills, rodent?"

Carob hopped back to the boy's chest. "As a matter of fact, I have used TiKay to develop a very promising gliding maneuver. Mind and body, boy! Every time."

"TiKay? What's that?"

Nisa beamed with pride. "It's how I got past the guards."

Seneca looked at her in surprise. "What did you do?"

"I defended myself."

"Defended herself!" Dane struggled to sit up, winced, then lay back again, but his arms gestured with excitement. "You should have seen her! My once dormant sister, leaping here, leaping there. Kicking and punching the guards as they came at us. One would aim at her, and her foot slammed into his chest before he knew what hit him!"

Seneca's heart ached with love. When he'd found her practicing alone by the lake, he thought he had never been so moved. To see her now, beaming with pride, biting her lip to restrain herself from adding to Dane's praise—there was no limit to his feeling for her. "Your sister is nothing if not . . . surprising."

Dane looked over at Seneca. "I might say the same about you."

"My life hasn't been without its twists."

Dane's eyes glittered with youthful curiosity. "So

you've been on Akando all this time? You must have had your share of adventures."

"A few."

Nisa puffed an impatient breath. "An oren-cat almost devoured him, and the Akandan chief smacked him around until he made him heir."

Dane appeared unusually thoughtful. "I'm not sure about the 'smacking around' part, but I envy you."

Nisa brushed her brother's soft hair from his forehead as if he were a small boy and ill. "You could probably use smacking around yourself."

Seneca pondered the kind of transformation that would take Dane from enthusiastic boyhood to the maturity of a man. "Your brother needs defiance. He needs a woman more interested in fighting than in love."

Nisa clapped her hands together. "Maybe we should send him to Akando!"

Dane's head moved back and forth as Seneca and Nisa debated his fate. Seneca studied the boy's innocent face. Whatever they decided, Dane would do. He would put the full force of his cheerful heart into whatever task they assigned him, then emerge the same as always.

"Akando wouldn't suffice. He's too . . . agreeable. Before the first cycle, he'd be surrounded by admiring villagers, making up stories. It wouldn't work. He's too charming."

"Then he needs a world where women aren't so easily charmed. Obviously that's not Dakota or Thorwal."

Carob began to chuckle. "There are more worlds beyond yours. One in particular."

Nisa turned to the lingbat, her eyes narrowed suspiciously. "Candor?"

"Well, that may be, but I was thinking of one farther away than Candor. It is reached through a wormhole in space. Don't know what it's called, but it's the home of the Ellowan. And a fiercer, meaner people never existed."

Dane grimaced. "That doesn't sound very encouraging. It's the last place I'd go looking for adventure . . . or a woman."

"An Ellowan female would put you in your place soon enough, boy."

"What appeal have they?"

"Don't know. No man who went there ever came back."

"Then why would I desire to visit such a grim world?"

"Don't know. Just a feeling. And I didn't say it was grim. Just mean. Their females are reputed to be attractive."

Dane's expression changed. "How attractive?"

"Spellbinding. And dangerous."

"No woman is that attractive. I will avoid the Ellowan at all costs."

Seneca patted the boy's shoulder. "I wouldn't worry, Dane. That wormhole is beyond our technology to reach."

"But not beyond Candor's technology," guessed Nisa. "Is that right, Carob?"

Carob shrugged, but his round eyes glittered. "Now, how would I know that?"

"I expect you know very well."

Dane dislodged the bat again. "He knows a lot more than he lets on, but he's not talking. I guess we'll just have to find out for ourselves."

"That," said Carob with a satisfied chuckle, "should prove interesting."

Nisa looked up at Seneca. "If they're as advanced as Carob hints, what will happen if Fedor takes a vessel there with the intention of pillaging their world?"

"They will consider the inner planets hostile. And they might not wait to check further before destroying us."

Dane seized Carob by the neck. "Is that true, rodent? If it is, if they're capable of wiping us out, you'd better start talking."

Nisa pried her brother's fingers from the lingbat's neck. "Dane, Carob must make his own choices. Let him go."

Surprisingly Carob didn't seem bothered by Dane's temper. "They're capable of annihilating this and any other world. That's all I'm saying. They're not predators by nature, but they fear aggression. If they see a danger, they do what they can to stop it. And if Fedor isn't a danger, I don't know who is."

Nisa turned to Seneca. "What do we do? We can't let him reach Candor."

"We can't stop him, Nisa. There's only one thing to do: reach Candor before he does, and stop him there."

"Reach Candor? How?"

"If you and your brother will assist us, we will reconstruct your fighter craft into a long-range vessel. With your help, we'll construct the power cell and install it." Seneca saw Nisa's expression and he smiled. "So Motega will go to Candor, after all, as Thorwal always feared. And you, maiden, will help him do it."

Seneca and Nisa left Dane to rest, though Carob insisted on remaining with the boy. The lingbat's voice followed them down the hall.

"Now, the wood-boring species, those take a little more chewing effort. . . ."

Nisa laughed at Dane's subsequent defeated groan. Seneca held open the door and motioned her through. "Wherever your brother ends up, I have a suspicion Carob will be with him."

Nisa stepped out into the warm Dakotan sun and sighed. "Poor Dane."

Seneca stood beside her. Dakotans bowed and nodded when they passed. Nisa looked up at him and her heart ached. The golden sun shone on his face, in his

Stobie Piel

warm, unfathomable brown eyes.

Manipi passed by, arguing with Langundo. "What would a man who swims in pudding know about power cells? Obviously I'm the most fit to find a way to alter the power cell for installment." Manipi's raised voice indicated an ongoing, heated battle.

"What would a man who aims his stun rifle into the nearest warm body know about anything? The Deiaquande would be wise to tie you up and leave the power cell development to me."

Langundo seemed equally ready for a fight, and Seneca sighed heavily. He stepped between them and held up his hand.

"At the heart of TiKay is respect, Manipi. For yourself, for others."

Manipi groaned. "Even for him?"

"Treat everything you encounter as worthy of respect. Had we learned this earlier in our past, much ill might have been averted."

Neither Manipi nor Langundo seemed eager to put this facet of TiKay into practice, but they ceased their argument.

"What about the power cell, Deiaquande? You'll need a project leader if we're going to get it installed and ready."

"Manipi, you worked on the cell development. You are most logical to restructure it to a new craft. Langundo, your specialty is weaponry. We may need defensive capacity on the new craft. Please start on that now."

Seneca's assignments satisfied both. They headed off in opposite directions and Nisa came to Seneca's side.

"I suppose things like this didn't happen often on Akando."

"Never."

Nisa's heart labored. "You must feel surrounded by madness."

288

Seneca glanced back toward the hospital ward. "I never noticed it before I left." Seneca's face darkened, a slight frown curving his mouth. "I suppose Motega was part of the madness. Your brother argues with a freed lab specimen, and loses. Two overgrown scientists bicker and fight at the slightest provocation."

Nisa hesitated. "What about me? Do I seem peculiar to you?"

Seneca's eyes glinted. "The matter of the wortpigs surprised me, I have to admit. That is one facet of your character you didn't share with Motega."

Nisa noticed that Seneca referred to Motega as another person. She remembered his reaction to Manipi's veiled teasing. She considered him jealous, but a new explanation formed. Seneca didn't want to remember the passionate young man who adored her.

On Akando he had escaped his past, until she robbed him of the life he had come to love. But only Motega could have grown into Seneca. For all his faults, Motega had been a great leader. Maybe Seneca didn't realize how great.

"This Nodin, you respected him as a great man, didn't you?"

"I did."

"Do you think his growth to manhood was smooth and easy, without obstacles?"

"I know little of Nodin's youth."

"I think I do," she said in a soft voice. "I think he was just like you. Arrogant and proud and born to be a leader. I suspect someone, probably his own father, smacked him around just as he did to you."

"You may be right. I can't imagine Nodin ever being passive."

"You think Motega failed Dakota, don't you?"

Seneca didn't answer, but his expression told her all she needed to know. For all his strength, Seneca couldn't accept the young man he had been. He couldn't forgive himself for his reckless pride and ambition.

Nisa took his hand and held it against her cheek. "You never failed anyone, Seneca. And you never will."

"If I had allied sooner with Helmar, Fedor would never have gotten this far."

"You can't know that. He might have killed you both, and we'd have no one to protect us. Don't question the past, Seneca. Maybe we did the best we could. Maybe there was no other way."

Seneca didn't respond. If he couldn't accept the man he had been, she would lose him. She was part of Motega. If he left Motega, he left her, too.

She had no right to force him. Tears threatened beneath her lashes. She kissed his hand, then turned away.

"If we are to develop the power cell, I must discover what you have here that we can utilize for production. Dane should be well enough to help me soon. I will assist Manipi."

Nisa didn't look at him as she started toward the lab. Seneca was astounded by the change in her mood. "How did you become so wise?"

Nisa stopped, then looked back over her shoulder. She held up her hand, her palm facing him—the palm he kissed when he made her face her love. "Do you need to ask? I learned from you."

Nisa studied the plans for the power cell while Manipi looked on in agitation. "You're the first Thorwalian to see these designs." He didn't sound pleased.

Nisa skimmed the succeeding pages. "Not the first, Manipi. I'm sure Fedor has studied them thoroughly."

"Thanks to you."

Nisa set aside her work. "I was wrong. Does that please you? But do you think Fedor would have left without those plans? He would have killed Seneca if you hadn't surrendered them. He would have killed you all."

Manipi had no further argument. "I suppose you can't be blamed for your Thorwalian temper."

"Weakness can be turned to strength, if we have the courage to face ourselves."

Manipi chuckled. "He's gotten to you, too, hasn't he?"

"Sometimes I think the only one he hasn't reached is himself."

Manipi's expression changed. His adversarial posture softened. "I've noticed that. He's afraid of his own power. On Akando he had nothing to lose. As much as he thinks he belongs there, this is his home. We are his people. He knows it, Nisa. And he's terrified."

Nisa turned to Manipi. "I know."

Manipi patted her shoulder. "Don't give up on him. Motega was a boy, a boy with no fear, no doubt. Seneca, he knows what's at stake. He knows he could lose."

Nisa's eyes filled with tears. "I love him so."

"I know."

For a long while neither spoke. The tension between them disappeared as they acknowledged a common love.

"Need any help?" Dane's cheerful voice interrupted the tentative friendship.

"Dane! What are you doing out of bed?"

Dane shrugged as he looked over her shoulder at the power cell design. "I heal quickly. You can't do this alone."

Nisa studied her brother's appearance. He looked better. "Where is Carob?"

"The little fellow went out hunting. But not before sharing the details of previous conquests." Dane shuddered and Nisa laughed.

"I think you're fond of him."

Dane glanced around the room and lowered his

voice. "I have to admit, now that he's out of earshot, I missed the miserable creature."

Manipi looked between them and shook his head. "Thorwalians! If you two have a handle on the plans, I'll see how Langundo is progressing."

"Thank you, Manipi."

Manipi left, and Dane's quick eyes scanned the power cell design. "This is simpler than I thought. We should be able to come up with a way to use stun rifle components combined with hovercraft motivators to produce a replica of the power cell."

"I've considered that. But with these components, we'll never be able to match Fedor's speed. We'll be using a remade fighter craft, and he's got a long-range transport."

"But we've got something he doesn't. We've got the best pilot Dakota ever produced. We've got Motega."

Nisa nodded, but she didn't comment.

"Where is he? I thought you two were . . . together."

"We were."

"I envy you." Dane jotted down notes over the design, but his young face appeared unusually serious.

"I can't imagine why. You're never lonely, Dane."

Dane looked at Nisa. For an instant she saw him as an older man, his boyish sweetness filled out and strengthened. Her brother might become a surprisingly formidable man.

"I am lonely, Nisa. Do you think my . . . friendships, shall we say, are satisfying? They're not. I've never met a woman I haven't forgotten in the space of a minute. It's fun, and then its over. Nothing more."

"You're very young."

"You weren't much older when you met Motega."

"And look what happened to us!"

Dane smiled, and again Nisa was struck by the man inside the boy. "I see. . . . I see that you were separated for seven years, and couldn't forget each other. I see a man who could have as many women as he wants, and he wants no one but you."

"I hope you're right. But I'm afraid there's something he wants more than me. He wants the life he knew on Akando."

Night fell, but Dakota didn't sleep. Their progress astounded Seneca as he checked on the various assignments. Langundo and Manipi marshaled a vast collection of hovercraft components, all strewn across the village square.

"We should have enough to add on to the Thorwalian fighter. If that boy knows what he's talking about, anyway."

Seneca was impressed by their speed, but more, by their surprising ability to cooperate. "Dane is well versed in craft technology."

Seneca went to the lab. Nisa fiddled with a stun rifle while Dane picked through hovercraft motivators. They didn't notice Seneca's presence, and he didn't speak.

Nisa looked tired. Her pale hair fell down her back in a long braid, and her shoulders slumped. She rubbed her eyes, then forced a breath meant to keep her awake.

"Try this one." Nisa passed Dane a rifle clip, and he tried to fit it into the motivator.

"No good." Dane flung the clip against the wall, and Seneca ducked.

"I should have known this room would be dangerous."

Both Nisa and Dane started. Seneca noticed that she didn't look at him, but returned quickly to her task. Dane stood up and stretched.

"We've got a structure going here, just not the right part to go in it. Shouldn't be too long, though. Cursed Fedor has a lot more to work with."

"Maybe, but he'll be taking a much larger vessel, if I guess correctly. He intends more than travel; he intends to bring back a substantial quantity of valuables, and he'll be bringing firepower to assure his success."

"What are we going to do about weapons?"

Seneca thought a moment, considering the dangers. "If we go to Candor armed, we'll be as dangerous as Fedor. I would trust Carob's advice in this, and arrive with peaceful intent."

Dane sighed in disappointment. "I suppose you're right. I've been practicing with riflery all my life. No one has better aim. But if we go blasting each other, the Candorians, whoever they are, won't see a difference."

"Your skill won't be wasted, Dane. Make it a part of you, and use it as a shield. You can adapt to whatever you encounter. That will never fail you, whether you're armed or not."

Seneca's words pleased Dane. "I did all right during our escape."

Nisa patted his hand indulgently. "You were magnificent."

"I'm more impressive when I can actually see. But I wouldn't mind learning how you defended yourself. You already look stronger."

"Do I?" Nisa checked her arm for muscle and Seneca's heart warmed with affection.

"You are both well formed for strength. It shouldn't take long to condition yourselves. But Dane must heal first. You won't be any help to anyone if you collapse from your injuries."

Nisa nodded. "Seneca is right. You must stop now and rest."

"I'd prefer to stay and help you."

"I can work on the cell alone. Tomorrow we'll have to refit the fighter vessel. That's where I'll need you most."

Dane relented. "Very well." He rubbed his shoulders. "In fact, I am quite stiff." A small smile grew on his lips. "Perhaps I can engage a well-meaning doctor to rub my back . . . and whatever else interests her."

Nisa shook her head in dismay. "I thought you wanted a meaningful relationship."

"I do. But since true love eludes me for the moment, I'll make do with what's available."

Dane kissed Nisa's cheek, then slipped from the lab before she could continue her lecture. Nisa turned back to her work and Seneca watched her silently. She didn't look at him as she focused on the stun rifle. He seated himself beside her, and she still didn't look up.

"You might benefit from rest, too, maiden."

"I'm not tired. I want this done before tomorrow. Fedor won't sleep."

"Something tells me he's leaving this task to others."

"As Manipi pointed out, Fedor got the plans because of me. I must correct my own wrong."

Seneca felt the distance between them. Conversation felt stilted. "It is my wrong as well. I will help you."

Nisa bit her lip, her brow tightening. "That's not necessary."

Seneca pulled apart another rifle. "Try this."

"What would a Dakotan know about rifle components?"

"Try."

Nisa placed the wire into the hovercraft motivator. She closed her eyes and sighed. It fit.

"I told you, maiden. I am no longer Dakotan."

Nisa's patience crumbled. "I hadn't realized Akandans were so thoroughly versed in Thorwalian technology."

"Actually I thought the colors went well together. Green and blue."

A reluctant smile formed on Nisa's lips. "This cell requires testing, Akandan. You are not needed for that. In fact, you are something of a distraction."

"Where will you sleep?"

"I don't need sleep."

"As you told your brother, there is much to be done tomorrow. Without rest, you also will be useless for the task."

"If I grow weary I'll sleep here."

Seneca saw her tense expression, saw her wet her lips in nervous agitation. She knew as well as he did that, sharing the same bed, nothing would keep them from making love. She was trying to prevent that. She wanted him, but she wanted something else, too. She struggled for balance.

Seneca rose from his seat, looking down at her as he fought the desire to sway her decision. She needed time. If they couldn't reach each other in free will, nothing they formed together would last.

"As you wish, maiden. If you need me, I will be waiting."

Nisa couldn't remember when she fell asleep. She woke to find her head on her folded arms, rifle components scattered all around. The fully operative power cell lay on the floor beside her.

She lifted her head. Her neck felt stiff and her back ached. She had worked all night. She remembered birds singing at dawn, so her rest hadn't been long.

Nisa drew a long breath. She wondered if Seneca waited all night. In another day, there would be no need to avoid him. They would journey to Candor. He would need to bring crewmen. They wouldn't be alone again.

She knew Seneca would stop Fedor. He had never failed his people, and he never would. With the situation rectified, there would be final peace between Thorwal and Dakota. His promise would be fulfilled. And he would return to Akando, where he belonged.

Nisa fought a surge of painful emotion. How could she let him go without holding him again? She couldn't endure another night without him, and she couldn't avoid him much longer. She had to get the fighter craft readied today.

Nisa forced herself to stand. If she was going to work all day, she had to eat. "One more day."

Nisa left the lab. Outside, the Dakotans filled the village square. Barefoot. Nisa's heart labored at the sight of Seneca standing before them, teaching them TiKay. His dark hair was tied back again, his strong body supple and radiating power.

Dane was positioned among the Dakotans, his young face serious and determined as he followed Seneca's instructions. Nisa saw her old dream like a shadow of the future. Her people and Motega's together, finding strength in the union.

Her eyes welled with tears and she turned hurriedly away.

"Nisa . . ."

She couldn't look back at him. If she did he would see her heart, and her pain might influence him to stay. "I have the power cell."

"I see that."

"I need to install it."

"The craft isn't ready. Another day's work is necessary."

Nisa glanced back. "Surely it will be ready by tonight."

A faint, sorrowful smile crossed Seneca's face. "According to Langundo's calculations, the best time for us to leave orbit is tomorrow morning. We have time."

Another night. Nisa felt the weight of her own weakness. "I need to eat."

Several Dakotans groaned. "As do we all."

Nisa saw Manipi strike Langundo, and her insides constricted. She loved Dakota. For a timeless moment she watched them, seeing them as if from a distance. Seneca turned back to his instruction, but she didn't hear his words, just the low, beautiful sound of his voice.

The children obeyed his commands with quick precision, though Hinto skittered away to play with the freed wortpigs. Carob hopped up onto a vine and launched himself into the air, gliding with masterful ease into the center of the practice field.

Dane shook his head and laughed, then imitated Seneca's kick with surprising power.

Nisa hurt. All she wanted transpired before her eyes. The only man she ever loved had created the perfect world. If he left, that world would continue. But Nisa's heart would die.

Nisa spent the day working on the fighter craft. Dane proved himself adept at redesigning the vessel, and the Dakotans obeyed his instructions with little argument.

"There is a life to machinery," he informed them. "If you respect the intricacies, the performance improves."

Dakotans surrounded the vessel, over and under, as Dane circled them, correcting their errors and offering advice that echoed Seneca's wisdom. Manipi looked up from beneath the craft and met Nisa's eyes, issuing a long sigh.

Nisa shrugged. "It's almost operative. We have made good progress."

"He's dictatorial, like yourself, but he seems to know what he's talking about."

Nisa installed the cell in place of the old motivator. Dane tried the power, and all sensors responded. "We should try a liftoff, since we've got time. Work out any bugs in the system. Where's Motega?"

"Here."

Nisa started. Seneca stood watching them, and her heart leaped. She hadn't seen him since that morning, though she had anticipated his arrival all day. He stood casually, his hair loose to his shoulders. His eyes met hers briefly, and Nisa's insides tingled.

Dane waved his arms. "We've got it running. Thought you'd want to take it up, check it out on a trial run."

"You deserve that honor, Dane."

Dane's eyes widened, though he appeared doubtful. "Are you sure? I'm not always . . . successful."

"If you remember what you learned this morning, I have faith in your ability."

"Balance!" Dane didn't give anyone time to argue Seneca's decision. He jumped into the craft and positioned himself at the helm. "Where's Carob? He should enjoy this."

"Not a chance." Carob fluttered to Nisa's shoulder and folded his wings over his round stomach. "You're bad enough in a hovercraft."

"You'll be sorry, rodent!" Dane closed the ramp and the fighter roared to life.

Nisa closed her eyes as the vessel lifted above them. Manipi whistled. "Smooth! Never saw a Thorwalian take off without blasting the landing strip."

Nisa dared to look as Dane maneuvered the vessel above the trees and circled in the sky. Her mouth dropped and she turned to Seneca. "What did you teach him?"

"Balance."

"Looks fine," added Manipi as the vessel glided back to the landing, poised, then lowered with perfect accuracy.

Dane appeared as the ramp lowered. Nisa saw his effort to remain dignified after his success, but when the Dakotans applauded, his face lit in a bright smile.

"What do you think of that, rodent?"

Carob shrugged. "At least it didn't explode this time."

Dane glowered, but Nisa patted his shoulder. "I'm proud of you. How did it run?"

"No flaws, more power than I expected. It should carry ten of us, at least, without strain."

"Us? Dane, you must stay here. If we both go, and don't return, who will head the council?"

"Not me. You know I have no wish for council membership, Nisa. Don't deny me this. Adventure awaits!"

"What if death awaits?"

Her warning made no impact on Dane. "I want to go."

Manipi turned to Seneca. "Who will accompany you, Deiaquande? Let me be the first Dakotan volunteer!"

"I had thought to leave you in command here, Manipi."

"I belong at your side! Leave my Aponi in charge. She's got a way with command."

Aponi stepped forward, her hands tight fists. "I do, and I'm not wasting it here. You're not going anywhere without me, old man."

"Very well. Then Langundo will take command as Deiaquande in my absence. Your scouting party will join us. That will make ten, with Nisa and Dane. We won't take on Fedor in numbers, anyway."

Carob hopped from Nisa's shoulder to Dane's. "What about me? Candor is my home."

"Very well. Carob's knowledge of Candor should prove beneficial. Thank you."

Manipi sighed at the lingbat's invitation. "Well, if that's settled, I suggest we start loading the vessel with supplies."

"Leave that to Langundo," suggested Seneca. "Those who journey tomorrow must rest well tonight." His gaze fixed on Nisa as he spoke. Shivers ran along her spine to her toes. She had to think of something to get her through this night.

"I'm hungry." She wasn't. But Seneca accepted her excuse.

"The dining hall is on its second serving. Enjoy your even meal, maiden."

Seneca's dark eyes twinkled, but he turned and went

to his house without looking back. Nisa breathed a sigh of relief, but her heart fell. She had expected some persuasion, at least. But maybe he wanted things this way.

Nisa forced herself to eat, but she had no appetite. The Dakotans chattered with Dane as she fought to keep her thoughts from Seneca. Dane's agreeable nature endeared him to their former enemies. With Carob on his shoulder, he regaled the Thorwalians with stories of Fedor's insurrection, and his own imprisonment.

Nisa's attention wavered. She expected Seneca to enter the hall, but she didn't see him. She was tired, but still tense and restless. If she walked in the cool night air, she might calm her nerves.

Nisa left the hall and went out into the square. Instead of a cool breeze, a soft rain fell. It hung in the warm, heavy air, soaking her hair with a fine mist. Nisa felt as if the whole world were crying.

She saw Manipi and Aponi walking together, hand in hand toward the pond, oblivious to the rain. Nisa considered returning to the lab, pretending to work. She could sleep there.

Nisa stood alone by an Alben tree, miserable and uncertain. Its wide leaves sheltered her from the light rain, but Nisa's misery saturated her heart. Perhaps Seneca already slept, or maybe he worked on the course they would follow to Candor.

What do I do? She wanted to go to him; she ached for him, but her reason told her to stay away. How could she give herself to him, and not try to keep him from the world he loved? How could she do both?

Nisa closed her eyes, her arms clasped around her body. Sweet floral fragrances mingled in the rain, filling her senses. Evening creatures sang and chirped, all in primal rhythm as the eternal rain drummed on the leaves above her head.

"Come with me."

Nisa froze. He touched her shoulder. Her nerves erupted like fire, but she couldn't speak above a strained whisper. "I cannot."

He spoke close to her ear. "Come with me."

She swallowed, her heart throbbing. She shook her head, but her knees went weak. She felt his fingers in her hair, loosening her braid, and she began to tremble.

"You are beautiful thus freed, Nisa Calydon. Like a goddess . . ."

He slid her hair over her shoulder and kissed her neck. Nisa leaned back against him and turned her face to his.

Seneca kissed the corner of her mouth. "Come with me."

One night. She would give him all of herself, then return him to the world he loved. She loved him that much. Nisa caught his hair in her fingers and kissed him back.

She turned in his arms, her body full against his. There would be no promises between them this night. She would take what he offered, and give him all she had. She would hold him, and love him, and it would be enough.

Nisa looked up at him. He opened his mouth to speak, but she laid her finger against his lips, stopping his words. "No. Tonight I am yours. I will do whatever you ask. But we need no words between us now."

Without a word he took her hand and drew it to his lips. He led her across the square to his house, through the living quarters, up the stairs to his bed. He engaged the light replacers to a low, soft glow, then took both her hands in his.

"You and I have shared this bed before. I thought nothing could come between us then. But all the world stood against us, my own ambition most of all." Nisa started to shake her head, but he stopped her.

"Motega offered you the rule of two worlds. Tonight I have nothing but myself to give."

"I want nothing but you. That is all I ever wanted."

"You and I carry the weight of two worlds on our shoulders, maiden."

"If you asked it, I would leave everything." Nisa's bright eyes glowed with emotion, and Seneca touched her cheek.

"How could I ask such a thing? I see you, Nisa, and I see an ancient Ravager queen. You could no more abandon Thorwal than I can forget Akando."

"Akando is deeper in you than Dakota."

"Dakota is my responsibility now. But Akando taught me what I really am. When I have brought to Dakota what I found for myself, I will have fulfilled my promise."

Nisa's breath held. "And then?"

"And then I will be free."

Free to return to the world he loved. Nisa slid her arms around his waist. With all the courage she possessed, she met his eyes and smiled. "When I first loved you, I loved blindly. When I hated you, it was the same. Tonight I would love you for all that you are. What comes after means nothing."

"If Fedor reaches Candor before we do, this night may be all we have. We can't know the future, maiden. But tonight is ours." Seneca touched her damp suit. "I wondered if I would spend this night alone. How long did you stand in the rain?"

"A while. I don't know." Nisa feared he would ask why she had avoided him, but Seneca seemed to accept her strange behavior.

"You're cold." Seneca glanced toward his cleansing unit and a smile grew on his face. "I might find a way to warm you."

He moved toward the unit, but Nisa hesitated. "Not there."

Stobie Piel

"Why not? As I recall, you enjoyed our previous encounters."

"That was before I realized how well practiced you were."

Seneca eyed her doubtfully. "Well practiced? I never pretended to be . . . unlearned, shall we say. But you were the one whose taste for water inspired such a creative use of my bathing facility."

Nisa frowned. "That seems unlikely. It didn't get a reputation as your 'seduction chamber' for nothing."

Seneca laughed. "Where did you hear that?"

"Fedor."

Seneca rolled his eyes. "An unquestionable source, if ever there was one. Maiden, will you take my word or his?"

Nisa felt foolish. "I suppose he is not entirely trustworthy. Still . . ."

Seneca drew her into his arms. "You were the only woman I entertained here, Nisa. While I wasn't exactly dormant before you, there has never been another since."

Nisa's eyes brightened. "You haven't been with anyone else?"

"No." Seneca paused. "Have you?"

"Only a few guards, a technician here and there . . ."

Seneca's eyes widened, and Nisa laughed. She kissed his face and moved closer into his arms. "What do you think? If a man dared speak without using my title, I reported his insubordination. My bed was empty without you."

"Good."

"I am pleased by your abstinence also. What stopped you?"

"For one thing, Akandan women have much to lose by mating without bonding first. There is an unpleasant stigma attached to births without acknowledged parenthood. Also, the soul of Akando is respect. A man

304

doesn't ask of a woman what he isn't willing to give in return."

Nisa imagined Seneca entering a sacred bond with a woman who understood the Akandan way. For an instant she imagined going with him to Akando. But where she went, reminders of Motega went also. Nisa's neck muscle spasmed and she winced.

"Are you in pain?"

Nisa hesitated, then nodded. "I'm a little stiff. I slept in an awkward position last night."

Seneca laid his hands gently above her shoulders and massaged her stiff tendons. His touch felt warm, penetrating into her skin. His fingers eased the tight cords and she closed her eyes.

"The cleansing unit might suffice, after all. It has use for healing as well as . . . bliss." Seneca stripped away Nisa's clothes before she could offer any objection. He pulled off his own, then adjusted the spray.

Nisa's gaze fixed on his large, aroused member. Fierce currents of need swept through her, and her teeth sank into her lower lip. She peered up at the ceiling until he turned around.

Seneca opened the unit and ushered her inside. He followed, sealing them both inside. Nisa was shivering, more from desire than from chill. But Seneca ignored his condition as he began to rub her sore back.

Nisa endured a shade of disappointment. She expected his hands on her breasts; she expected his kiss. Instead his touch grew firmer, centering on tender spots. Nisa winced.

"Stop that! You're too rough."

"You have contorted yourself into a cramped position, and your body suffers, maiden. Hold still."

Nisa frowned, but she allowed him to continue his merciless ministrations. "I felt better before you started."

"Complaint is part of your nature." Seneca ran a

firm pressure along her spine. Nisa twisted, but he didn't relent.

"I suspect you enjoy causing me pain."

Seneca kissed the top of her head. It was a friendly gesture, an act of affection. Despite herself, Nisa wanted his desire.

"I am attempting to relieve pain, maiden. Here, in particular, you are very tense." With the side of his hand, Seneca massaged a spot beneath Nisa's shoulder blade. She winced and struggled, but he increased the pressure. Tenderness gave way to a numb warmth, then eased.

Seneca stopped and waited for her reaction. Nisa peeked around at him. "You are skilled, Akandan. I will grant you that. I am no longer stiff. You, on the other hand, appear still in a state of great . . . tension."

She cast her eyes down across his body, lingering on his arousal. She wet her lips deliberately. Seneca's eyes darkened to black as he read her intent.

"It is a shame the walls of your cleansing unit have no shackles." Nisa didn't wait for Seneca's response. She sank to her knees before him, looking up to see his face taut with passion. He watched her as if spellbound.

Her lips curved in a smile. With one hand poised on his hip, she clasped his length in her other hand and kissed the engorged tip.

She peered up at him to see his reaction. "Do you like this, Akandan? I would do nothing to cause you pain."

"Maiden, you defy my dreams."

Nisa shuddered at the sound of his voice, raw and husky, constricted with desire. "No matter what happens, no matter where you go or what comes between us, you will be in my heart always."

"We live in each other, maiden."

It was enough. If she had something of his heart she could endure anything. Seneca stood transfixed, watching her face as she took his length between her lips. Water misted her face; her damp hair fell over her shoulders, a veil over her breasts. Her eyes still held his, and his whole body quivered as she teased him.

Seneca sank to his knees and gripped her face in his hands. He kissed her with passionate demand as the water circled and sprayed against them. She felt like a wild creature in his arms, untamed and violent and pure. She tipped her head back and he kissed her throat.

Seneca lifted her in one motion and carried her from the cleansing unit. Nisa's eyes widened in surprise. "Where are we going?"

"This night won't end so quickly. Let the unit finish its cycle alone."

Nisa's pulse raced, but Seneca seemed in no hurry. He set her to her feet and wrapped a large towel over her shoulders. He dried her hair, though his hands shook with the effort.

Nisa seized another towel and proceeded to dry his body. Slowly. Seneca stood as she ran the towel over his back, kissing his shoulder as she moved around him. She knelt beside him and dried his powerful thighs, grazing, but not touching, his erection.

She rose, sliding herself up against him, her eyes glowing with satisfaction when he moaned. "There is no hurry, Akandan. The night is young."

Nisa stood back to survey Seneca's unclad body. "I should have noticed that your skin is lighter where you wore leggings. And your hair, I suppose the Akandan sun lightened that, too."

"Maybe you didn't see because you didn't want to see."

Nisa took his hand and kissed the palm. "If there had been no difference at all, Seneca . . . I would not have believed you were Motega. Not because I didn't

307

want to know, but because your death was so much a part of me."

"I'm sorry. At the time I never imagined it would cause you such pain."

"You imagined I had you murdered, so probably not." Nisa smiled, but her eyes filled with tears. "When I found your body, what I thought was your body . . . I wouldn't let go. Helmar had to pull me away. They sedated me and took you away."

"Not me."

"I know. But I didn't know then. I died that day. Nothing mattered anymore. Until Helmar took me to watch my brother play, and reminded me of my duties."

"So you concocted the mad scheme of replacing me."

"It would have worked!"

"I don't think so, maiden. You overestimate the capacity of your mind probes. While the probe indeed has the power to offer language, it doesn't alter the brain's function."

"But Carob . . ."

"Ah! That is an interesting quandary, isn't it? Our Candorian friend keeps much to himself."

Nisa's brow furrowed. "Dane says that, too. I wonder what he's hiding, and why?"

"He'll tell us when he's ready, or let us find out for ourselves. But I sense no ill will from Carob. I don't believe he means us any harm."

"I suppose it wouldn't do any good to ask. He'd just assume that smug expression and say nothing."

"We will learn Candor's secrets on our own, you and I. Carob's willingness to accompany us indicates the possibility of success. That is all we need."

Nisa's thoughts wandered. "Not all, Akandan. As you have said, the night is still young. I am unsatisfied from our encounter in your seduction chamber."

"Perhaps the term was chosen in reference to your

own arts, maiden. You made good use of the unit."

"I will make equally good use of your bed." Nisa seized Seneca's hand and led him into the bedroom. "You are too well practiced at restraint. A result of your TiKay, perhaps. It pleases me to learn your limit."

Nisa sat on the edge of the wide bed and guided Seneca in front of her. "There is no hurry." Nisa brushed her lips across his swollen member. He moaned, and she laughed softly.

She took him in her mouth, mimicking the motion of lovemaking. Seneca clasped his hands in her hair as she ran her tongue along his shaft, circling him. She suckled with sudden intensity, and his fingers clenched.

"Maiden, you have passed my limit."

Seneca sank to his knees beside the bed and pulled her legs around his shoulders. "Now, my sweet Ravager, we will test yours."

Nisa's eyes widened and she squirmed away, but he cupped her hips in his firm grip, holding her secure. "You can't do that!"

Seneca only chuckled and kissed the soft flesh of her inner thigh. Nisa stared at him in astonishment. *I give you all of myself.* His lips grazed her most sensitive spot, and her breath caught. When his tongue circled the small bud, Nisa fell back onto the bed. He could do whatever he wished. Such delirium couldn't be stilled by fear of the future.

Seneca teased and tormented her until Nisa's every breath was a plea for release. She murmured his name, she clutched his hair, but he didn't stop. Waves of searing pleasure scorched through her body, her legs tightened around his shoulders, her toes curled.

A wild crest of rapture crashed over her. She twisted and writhed in his grasp. Ecstasy compounded and built, unrestrained, beyond the limit of her control. She cried his name and surrendered.

The feverish currents demanded deeper fulfillment. Nisa seized Seneca's hair and pulled him up to her. Seneca chuckled, though his face was contorted with lust. "You can be so violent, maiden."

As he spoke, he entered her and Nisa kissed his mouth wildly, desperately. Her hips rose to draw him deeper, and they moved together in an ever-increasing rhythm. Her legs wrapped around his, holding him inside her as the sparkling currents built and intensified.

She squeezed tight around him, urging him to join her. All her body, all her life, seemed designed to receive him. She writhed with untamed fury, possessed and freed by primal demand. As she pleased herself with his length, his body erupted and poured deep inside her. She wrapped around him, taking all he had, giving all of herself.

The shattering currents subsided, leaving tiny aftershocks shivering between them. Nisa's breath came in small gasps, her heart pounding beneath his. Seneca kissed her forehead, then withdrew from her body. He lay back on the wide bed, and Nisa snuggled beside him.

Nisa kissed his shoulder and gazed into his face. He looked sleepy and satisfied, his damp hair hanging around his face.

"We would have done this in the holding cell. I should have come to you sooner."

"We would. But it wouldn't have meant what it means tonight, maiden. You and I were too young to know what we had together. We were selfish and demanding. We would have found other reasons to doubt each other and to fight."

Nisa settled back on his shoulder. "I suppose you're right. More likely the assassin would have arrived while we were . . . together, and killed us both."

"Maybe, but it was Fedor who installed the shackles, maiden. I suspect he knew you'd find occasion to use them. I don't believe he meant to kill you. It seems more likely he wanted you for himself."

Nisa shifted uneasily. "That is what he said. He wanted me to give his rule legitimacy to the Thorwalians who would resist an insurrection."

"There's more to it than that, Nisa. If you could see yourself as I do, you would know. A man would go to great lengths to have you. Even to usurping leadership in order to force you to mate with him."

"I can't believe Fedor did this for me."

"It was my greatest fear when I realized the potential in the Candor Moon."

Nisa sat up. "What are you talking about?"

Seneca folded his arms behind his head, still calm. "A man who loves you knows when another feels the same. From the moment I met you at the even meal table, I knew Fedor wanted you, too. I took you from him without remorse, but I knew his desire wouldn't abate. If he gained power from the conquest of Candor, the first thing he would demand would be you."

Nisa shuddered and lay back close beside Seneca. "That is a grim thought. For a long while I considered Fedor weak, but still my uncle's faithful servant. I think Helmar thought that, too. Dane never trusted him, but he was a child then, and I didn't take his warnings seriously."

"Children have good sense."

Nisa smiled. "Because they take to you?"

Seneca smiled, too. "As I said, good sense."

Nisa settled back into Seneca's arms. He fell silent, but she knew something was on his mind.

"It may be wise for you to remain here tomorrow, Nisa."

Nisa sat up again, her expression aghast. "What do you mean, remain here? I will go to Candor with you!"

"There is danger. I see no reason for you to face it."

"You're facing it!"

"I caused it."

"Not so." Nisa fought to maintain logic. "You said I bore a shield. You were right. It was guilt and fear and love, Seneca. You carry one, too. You blame yourself for actions you took when you were little older than Dane. Would you blame him for his mistakes?"

Seneca hesitated. "No, but Dane has wisely avoided taking responsibility greater than his experience warrants."

"Only because I took it first. Seneca, did you demand to become Deiaquande? Don't answer, because I already know. You didn't. You were the most brilliant mind they'd ever had; you were the best pilot. You could do everything. The old Deiaquande was a lethargic puppet to my uncle. I know, because Helmar told me so."

Seneca sighed heavily. "That is true, maiden. The old Deiaquande was my father."

Nisa's mouth dropped. "Your father?" Her voice was a small squeak. "You never told me that."

Seneca smiled at her shock. "It wasn't a point of honor for me."

"I thought your parents died."

"My parents ended their union when I was a small child. My mother took another mate, and they died on a research expedition as I told you. I had never met my real father, but when I did I knew his weak will would be disaster for Dakota."

Nisa shook her head in disbelief. "I remember him. He was soft and pudgy and all he thought about was food."

"That is how I remember him also."

"Well, obviously someone lied. That man couldn't have sired you."

"He had good qualities, albeit concealed ones. He had a quick brain, but I believed Thorwal had dominated him, ruined him. He might have been a great man, but his humiliation ran deep, even before I accused him of subverting our interests."

"You blamed us."

"I did then. I was wrong."

Nisa squirmed uncomfortably. "I'm not sure you were so wrong."

"The Dakotans have no inner strength, nothing to support our souls. We began on this sweet, balmy world with no history, no fight for survival such as the struggles that gave Akando and Thorwal strength. Nothing challenged us; nothing strengthened us. Even our basis in science seems to have evolved out of nothing. As if handed to us . . ."

Seneca stopped, his brow knitting thoughtfully. "As if handed to us from an outside source."

"Is that possible?"

"Anything is possible, maiden."

"Well, you were strong, Seneca. Whether you think so or not. When you were Motega, you were like . . ." Nisa paused and her heart filled with love and understanding. "You were like the wind, blowing up storms. And now, my sweet love, you will calm them."

Seneca stared at her in amazement. "I have heard those words before. Nodin told me this when he took me to the cliff and made me part of his clan."

Nisa kissed his shoulder and wrapped her arm over his chest. "What he gave you, you have given to Dakota. And to me. In return you deserve what you want most. You deserve peace."

Chapter Ten

Nisa rose early, but Seneca had already left their bed. Her heart pounded in fear that he might have left her behind. She dressed hurriedly, then raced out into the square. Seneca led the Dakotans through the motions of TiKay, and she closed her eyes in relief.

She watched their motions, amazed at the fluid grace of even the heaviest Dakotans. Their expressions were serene as they concentrated on Seneca's instructions. Even Dane appeared somber and controlled.

Without speaking, Nisa joined them. She moved as Seneca moved, like a mirror image. She felt him in her own limbs; she felt his strength in hers. Seneca's warm, dark eyes met hers across the square, a slight smile on his face as he led her motion like a graceful dance.

When he stopped, the Dakotans bowed, and Nisa bowed, too. Seneca returned the honor, and the Dakotans scattered to their respective tasks, leaving Nisa standing on the far side of the square, unable to move as he came to her.

Seneca took her hand and kissed it. She felt his pleasure. "I was afraid you left me behind."

"I wouldn't deny you the right to choose, maiden. For your own safety I ask you to remain here. But I ask that, knowing it is for my own peace of mind. Something tells me you won't be dissuaded in this."

"That's true. I'm coming with you."

Seneca bent and kissed her brow. "I knew you would."

"When do we leave?"

"Now."

The Dakotan party situated themselves in the rejuvenated vessel. Rather than engaging in their usual bickering, the scientists were quiet and reserved as they arranged their gear. Dane couldn't restrain his excitement, and darted around the vessel for a last-minute check of its controls.

Carob was positioned in the viewport, offering advice no one listened to. "You won't need any warm coverings on Candor. It's hot and dry."

"How can it be hot, rodent? It's farther from the sun than Thorwal by a long reach." Dane tucked his Thorwalian coat around his waist.

"The moon draws its heat from the Candor gas planet, boy. If I say it's hot, it's hot."

Dane relented and tossed his coat out the ramp. Seneca caught it as he entered. "Your family is hazardous, maiden."

"You're simply ill placed, Akandan. You must learn when to duck."

"I learned that when I took my first fateful ride in your small deathtrap."

Nisa punched his chest. "We will witness your piloting skills, and see that you haven't lost your touch."

Seneca glanced at Dane, but the boy shrugged. "I'm good for a training run, but I don't want the pressure of piloting us to Candor."

"Very well." Seneca seated himself at the helm, Dane beside him. Nisa stood behind his seat and gazed out at the waving Dakotans.

"They will miss you."

Seneca lifted his hand in a still salute to his people. "Langundo assures me they will continue their morning practice sessions, and avoid pudding at all costs until my return."

Until my return . . . Nisa's heart leaped. She had feared he would return directly to Akando after Candor, but apparently Seneca hadn't considered this possibility.

Just as her hope returned, Seneca's Akandan pack caught her eye. She saw the outline of the white sapling, and her hope faded. Seneca hadn't decided, but he kept his choices open. Nisa vowed again not to sway him in any way. But the concealed tree loomed like an enemy.

Under Seneca's gentle touch, the craft eased into life, then lifted from the landing strip. Nisa and Dane watched enviously as he guided the vessel above the trees, then maneuvered it straight through the outer atmosphere into black space.

Dane leaned forward in his seat as he marveled at Seneca's easy skill. "It never quite works this way when I do it."

Carob glanced back from the viewport. "You can say that again! Nosedive down, backspin up. Your trajectory is frightening to comprehend."

Dane ignored the rodent. "Shall I try to raise Thorwal on communications?"

Seneca studied the radar screen. "There's no need, Dane. Look." He pointed to a small blip angling fast from Thorwal. "It appears Fedor has made good progress. The course appears to be set for Candor."

Nisa examined the blip's position. "He's already a good distance away. He will pass Akando soon. If he's this far ahead how will we catch him in time?"

"There is a way. Akando has just passed its farthest orbital point. We can use its gravity for acceleration, which can be used for a quick thrust toward Candor."

Nisa shook her head. "The last pilot who tried that maneuver burned up in the sun, Seneca."

Seneca smiled. "The last pilot was Thorwalian."

Nisa clasped his shoulder. "I see Motega's arrogance hasn't entirely disappeared. You'll lose control of the vessel. We'll all be plastered to the walls from the centrifugal pull. There must be another way."

Seneca sat back in his seat. "If you can think of one, I'll be happy to consider it."

Nisa struggled with the problem, then shrugged miserably. "Nothing comes to mind."

Seneca returned to his controls, altering the course toward Akando. "Don't worry, maiden. If successful, we'll reach the Candor Moon right on Fedor's heels."

"And if not?"

"We'll do a crash landing on Akando, and hope for the best."

Nisa groaned, but the Dakotans remained silent. Dane appeared doubtful, but he accepted Seneca's decision without argument.

"If only we'd had more time to work on water suits! We could use them now. At least one, for Seneca. A water suit would diminish the effect of the pull, and you'd be able to maintain control."

"Just a theory, boy," said Manipi. "Our early tests were not promising."

Seneca remained unconcerned. "There are other ways."

"What other ways?"

"Balance, maiden. With ourselves, with each other . . . and with gravity."

"You're going to try your shield, aren't you?"

Seneca smiled. "Consider this a test of my abilities."

Carob leaned forward, then fluttered his wings.

"Here she comes! That miserable hunk of rock has to be Akando."

Seneca's dark eyes glowed. Nisa watched his expression change as he neared his world, and her heart ached. "We'll see what your power cell can do, maiden." He engaged the speed to full power, and the tiny ball of Akando grew larger.

"As soon as we enter orbit, you'll have to strap yourselves in."

"How will we help you?"

"If TiKay can't help me, nothing can."

Nisa fiddled with the scanner screen to distract herself. She couldn't know the outcome of Seneca's attempt. She had to allow fate to unfold beyond her assistance. Nothing was harder.

"We should be able to get images from the surface now." She did a scan of the area surrounding the Akandan village. "All seems peaceful. . . ." Her voice trailed as she centered on a slow-moving, solitary figure. "It appears another follows your course of the manhood trial."

Seneca's attention wavered as he examined the screen. "Increase the image."

Nisa obeyed, and a small landscape formed. Seneca rose from his seat and studied the screen. Nisa looked over his shoulder to see what caught his attention. There, on a windswept crag of ice-covered rock, a man crawled. He appeared injured, near death.

Seneca's face paled. "Carack." As he spoke, the young man dragged himself into the shelter of a ragged boulder. Nisa's hands shook, but she increased the image to full power.

The boy's tunic was bloody and torn; his pack hung at his side, limp from lack of gear. Seneca stared at the image. Pain soaked his strong features; his hand clenched. "No. You are too young for such a journey. Why?"

Nisa laid her hand on his arm, though she knew she

318

could offer no comfort. "It's not your fault." Misery gripped her and she turned away. "It's mine."

Seneca shook his head, but Nisa looked back at him, her blue eyes shimmering with unshed tears. "We must face truth. He is there because I took you away."

Seneca didn't argue, but Nisa saw no blame in the depths of his eyes. "Seneca, we can land. We can save him."

Seneca stared at Nisa in amazement. "If we land, all hope of reaching Candor is lost."

"I know."

Seneca turned back to the screen. Carack lay crouched beneath the boulder, unmoving as night raced across the frozen planet toward him, consuming him in darkness. Seneca's dark eyes welled with tears and he touched the screen. "I love you so."

With all the effort of his will, Seneca turned away and returned to the helm of the Thorwalian vessel. Nisa watched the darkening screen a moment longer, then knelt beside Seneca's seat. "We can land."

"No, Nisa. Such a rescue would dishonor Carack. He is a boy, he is too young, but it was his choice to attempt the trial. He has come this far, in winter. It is a great accomplishment."

Pain engulfed Nisa, but she accepted his word. She would have abandoned her quest to rescue his brother, no matter what the cost. She bowed her head to his knee, but Seneca gently touched her shoulder.

"Strap yourself in, maiden. It is time."

The Dakotans seated themselves side by side. Manipi held Aponi's hand in his, but no one spoke. Dane strapped in beside Seneca, his young face eager and fearless. Nisa hesitated. Tears glittered on Seneca's high cheekbones, but he didn't brush them away nor resist his pain.

Face your feelings, maiden. Nisa seated herself next to Aponi and closed her eyes.

Seneca aimed the craft straight for Akando. The

vessel's speed accelerated rapidly, until it began to rattle.

"I hope you built this craft strong enough. . . ." Manipi's words slowed as the speed increased. Everything seemed to move in slow motion.

Nisa heard Dane's voice, broken and slow. "We . . . build every . . . thing . . . strong. . . ."

Last, before the speed stopped the capacity for speech, she heard Carob's high voice. "Ex . . . cept your . . . selves . . ."

Nisa's laugh seemed to move back and through her as Akando filled the viewport. She looked for Seneca one final time, but she couldn't see him. His shield had worked.

Night came cold and bitter, more bitter than in all the days of his trial. Carack focused his fading vision on the stars. He had reached the Zaltana Mountains and found a sapling of the Lasting Trees. Though he had discarded nearly all his gear, the sapling remained untarnished by the cold.

Carack leaned against the frozen stone. There, in the sacred grove, he had found evidence of his brother's arrival. He had found the turned earth where another sapling had been uprooted.

Seneca had made it that far.

All along his journey, Carack had found evidence of his brother's passage. Unhindered, swift. As Seneca did everything else, with skill and power, his trial had progressed without delay.

Carack's own trial had faltered often; he had often strayed from the wisest course. Rather than move on toward his village, he had pursued an oren-cat across the Wastes, for the sake of revenge.

His injured pride might have cost him his life. He had veered from Seneca's trail, and he was lost. The Wastes stretched on endlessly, in every direction. The village shouldn't have been far, but Carack knew he would never complete the journey now.

Seneca wouldn't have made such a choice. Carack knew his brother's loss drove him to recklessness. Seneca was the heir to the wind. No one would follow Nodin with as much leadership ability as Seneca.

But Nodin's life faltered; he longed for release. And Seneca never returned from the trial of manhood. Carack took the quest with the hopes of finding his brother alive. He found no sign of death, but neither did he find evidence that Seneca lived.

"I have failed, brother. I cannot equal you. I should not have tried."

Carack's eyes drifted shut, but a bright, fiery light scorched across the black sky. Carack sat up, despite the pain in his wounded body. He shook his head to clear his vision, but the flaming trail remained.

"It can't be. . . ." The legends of Akando filled Carack's mind. Gods borne on fire . . . "Seneca."

Carack felt his brother, heard his voice in his mind. *I love you so.*

Carack's heart filled with fire. He rose to his feet, and he felt no pain. He shouldered his pack and followed the light.

"There it is." Dane rose from his seat, leaning forward as the huge gas planet of Candor came into view. "Amazing!" Red, yellow, and orange intermingled with purple hues, sending shimmering light through the blackness of space.

For once Carob said nothing, but his round eyes reflected Candor's brilliant light. The Dakotans gathered around the helm, relishing the first up-close view of the giant world.

Only Nisa remained unimpressed. She wanted it over with. She wanted to know what Seneca intended afterward. "Where's the moon? The civilization isn't on the gas planet."

Carob hopped to the center of the viewport. "The moon should be at the far side of Candoria. If you enter orbit, it is an easy task to adjust to the moon's field."

Dane eyed the lingbat suspiciously. "Candoria? What are you talking about, rodent?"

Carob puffed up his round chest, and his head angled back in a superior fashion. "Since you're entering their world, you might as well start using some of their terms. Candoria is the gas giant, which means 'brother of the sun' to the Candorians. The moon itself is called Candor."

Seneca considered the bat's words. "It seems strange to me that, by chance, we should have named the moon Candor, if the meaning is the same to its inhabitants."

Carob nodded meaningfully, chuckling to himself, but he offered no explanation. "Isn't it?"

Dane's fingers clenched as if squeezing the bat, but Nisa tapped his shoulder in warning. Carob turned back to look out the viewport.

Seneca guided the vessel around the giant planet. Several moons orbited the planet, but only one revealed an atmosphere. Layered rings orbited the moon, and interspersed among the rings were satellites made for human use.

Manipi leaned over Seneca's seat and whistled. "Those rings aren't natural, Deiaquande."

"No. I would say they are used as some sort of mining operation. Perhaps the Candorians build their craft in space, as Thorwal has done. But on a much larger scale."

Nisa edged in front of Manipi. "They are obviously far beyond us, whether they have defensive capacity or not. Maybe Fedor realized this and turned back."

"Greed outweighs good sense, maiden. There is his ship, in a tight orbit around the moon."

Dane adjusted the scanner screen to study Fedor's vessel. "At least he hasn't landed yet."

"He won't land," said Nisa. "He'll send a shuttle filled

with guards. Forty at the least."

Manipi shook his head, bewildered by the Thorwalian lust for conquest. "What makes him think a society this advanced can't protect itself?"

"Fedor believes the Candorians have gone unchallenged, with access to vast natural resources to aid development. He believes from our studies they are few in number, and won't be able to resist an assault."

"That's right," agreed Dane. "He thinks he can take over with ease. He has trained the guards with this in mind." A light flashed on Dane's panel. "There! Fedor's shuttle, about to land on Candor's surface."

Nisa clasped Seneca's shoulder. "What do we do?"

"Dane, try the communication system."

Dane fiddled with several dials, but received only static. "It's not working." He eyed Carob. "Well, rodent? What do we do?"

Carob's wings twitched with suppressed excitement. "I'd say you'd better land, and land fast. I warned you, the Candorians won't tolerate aggression."

Nisa looked at Seneca. "Should we? Maybe we can try signaling them first."

"We have no time. Strap in and prepare for landing. Dane, hone in on that shuttle, and set our coordinates accordingly."

Seneca guided the vessel to the rings, which consisted of tiny mineral particles. Manipi ran tests as they passed through the outer rings, and lower into Candor's atmosphere. "You're right, Deiaquande. Man, or something, made these. It's not a naturally occurring substance."

Carob chuckled, but offered no further clarification. As the vessel lowered, he positioned himself on Dane's shoulder, digging in with his claws to steady himself. Dane winced, but the bat refused to be dislodged.

"I just had a horrible thought. The Candorians, they aren't winged, are they? Say, about ankle high, subsisting on a diet of grotesque insect matter . . ."

"Lingbats are an ancient species, boy, capable of any number of wonders. But we have no need for spaceships."

Dane strapped himself in. "Good. I'm not sure I could stand that image. A nation of pompous rodents wielding insurmountable power . . . No, it is too much for the imagination to bear."

Nisa's nerves tensed. "Quiet! Both of you. Seneca needs to concentrate."

Nisa refused to sit. She clutched the back of Seneca's seat as they entered Candor's atmosphere. A brown-and-gold surface came into view, appearing mostly flat, with no obvious buildings or machinery.

Dane adjusted the viewscreen. "Fedor's shuttle landed on that flat surface. Course set."

Seneca guided the vessel down behind Fedor. "If we remain in his path, he'll pick up nothing but shuttle debris. If we're lucky he won't notice us until we've landed."

Nisa held her breath as the vessel sank toward the golden-brown earth. "Where are the buildings? I don't see any people."

Dane groaned. "I knew it. The Candorians are all hanging from their toes in tunnels this time of day."

Seneca lowered the vessel to an effortless landing just behind the Thorwalian shuttle. Dane examined the scanner. "The shuttle is empty. Fedor has already headed off."

Seneca rose from his seat and stood before his small crew. "I have taught you TiKay. Now its use becomes necessity. We will carry stun rifles, but no one is to fire without my command. We will attack no one, but use what we know for our defense. Anything else will mean our death, and the possible destruction of our worlds."

The Dakotans surrounded him, ready. "You follow your heart, Deiaquande. We will follow you."

Seneca glanced out the viewport. "This action involves risk to all who leave this shuttle. The Thorwalians are armed, and they will shoot. Our task is to disarm them, and subdue them, then leave this world undisturbed by our strife."

Nisa's heart pounded, but she positioned herself by the ramp. Seneca took her arm and drew her aside. "Maiden, it would please me if you waited here."

"Would it? Well, it would please me if you'd hide beneath your seat, with your head covered!"

Seneca smiled and kissed her forehead. "I had to ask."

"I may possibly obey your commands out there, Akandan, but you will not leave me here without you. Is that understood?"

Dane sighed. "She always was bossy." He slapped Seneca on the shoulder and lowered the ramp.

Seneca led the Dakotans from the vessel into the hot, dry air of Candor. The sky was blue, but the clouds were colored with streaks of yellow and purple.

"What an amazing place!" Dane shouldered his rifle and looked around, oblivious to possible danger. Carob sat on his shoulder, pleased with the boy's enthusiasm.

Seneca checked Nisa's reaction to the new world. She paid no attention to the brilliant sky. She held her rifle poised for battle, moving outward from Seneca as she checked the area. "Fedor's party came this way. See, there . . . . From the shuttle, they moved toward those low hills."

The Dakotans had no interest in battle. With their rifles slung at their sides, they gazed around at Candor's strange terrain. Manipi tested a handful of soil. "What do you make of the sky, Deiaquande? Cloud coverage is particularly interesting."

Nisa groaned and aimed her rifle at Manipi. "This is no time for research! Pull yourselves together!"

Seneca smiled at her combative posture. "Maiden, your Ravager queen ancestors would be proud. But Nisa is right. We can study the environment after we locate Fedor."

Dane glanced at the lingbat perched on his shoulder. "If our host would be so good as to direct us . . ."

"I wouldn't want to interfere."

Nisa turned her rifle on Carob. "I'm not in the mood for this, rodent. Start talking."

The bat's eyes widened in surprise. "Go to the left, and you might cut him off."

Nisa forced a smile, acknowledging his cooperation. "Thank you." She stomped on ahead of the rest, but Seneca stood watching her. For a moment, all time held as his heart filled with love.

"There marches a woman worth dying for."

Manipi patted Seneca's shoulder as he passed by after Nisa. "Maybe worth living for, too."

Carob directed the Dakotan party along a low hill. "Fedor chose the easier route, but it will take longer."

Nisa hurried along beside Seneca. "Where are we going?"

Carob chuckled. "You'll see."

Nisa ignored the bat and looked at Seneca. "Fedor seems to know."

"He had ample time for scanning, maiden. We had no such luxury. But he will go where he detected civilization."

"Then we follow."

Nisa picked her way along the uneven ground. Despite the heat, the Dakotans kept up a good pace. The moon turned from Candoria, and the sky darkened to red.

Manipi stopped to take in the sight. "What a world! I couldn't have imagined this from our probes."

Nisa turned to him impatiently. "Move!"

"Patience, maiden. Just over this hill." Seneca directed his group up a steep slope. Dane and Nisa kept up with him, though the others straggled behind. Nisa reached the crest and stared in wonder.

Far below stretched a deep valley dotted with structures that resembled pyramids. Nisa looked up at Seneca. "What are those?"

Dane glanced at Carob. "Temples?"

"Not exactly." Carob seemed to be grinning, and Dane jerked his shoulder.

The Dakotans joined them, marveling at the endless structures. "What do you make of it, Deiaquande?"

Seneca studied the pyramids. "I would say . . . gateways."

Carob chirped. "He's got it!"

"Look!" Dane pointed down toward the valley's entrance. "There's Fedor!"

From the lowest edge of the valley, Thorwalian guards emerged, then spread out toward the nearest pyramid. The red sky glittered on their arms.

Nisa took out a pocket telescope and surveyed the landscape. "Where are the Candorians? I see no one. No hovercraft, nothing."

"We have no time for speculation. If I guess correctly, those pyramids provide access to an inner world. And that seems to be where Fedor is heading."

Seneca started down the cliff wall. "Keep low, angling left. If we're lucky he won't notice us until we're upon him."

Dane slid straight down the cliff, though he maintained adequate balance to support Carob. "We won't catch him in time."

Nisa followed Seneca. Where he stepped, she stepped also, though her legs ached from stretching. The Dakotans kept up relatively well, though Manipi tripped and rolled partway down the hill. Aponi caught him and pulled him to his feet.

"Glad you came, woman."

"Thought you would be, old man."

327

Nisa shook her head. Here, crossing an alien desert, beneath a red sky, the Dakotans bickered and chattered. Carob taunted Dane, and her own heart centered on where Seneca would go afterward.

Nothing had changed.

They reached the bottom of the cliff and Nisa took his hand. "No matter what happens, what we are remains."

Seneca kissed Nisa's hand. "That has always been true, maiden. This love never dies."

"There they go!" Dane turned their attention back to Fedor as the Thorwalian party disappeared into the pyramid. "I suggest we run."

Seneca agreed. "Then we run."

He started off across the valley floor, Nisa beside him, running as fast as she could. Dane sprinted on ahead, but Seneca remained beside her, his stride light and effortless. As she remembered from Akando.

As she ran, Nisa realized another truth. If their lives ended here, if their quest failed entirely, some good remained. They had lived their lives to the fullest limit; they had loved and fought with all the passion in their souls. Nothing could change that now.

They reached the pyramid and stopped while the Dakotans lumbered up behind. Panting and gasping, cheeks red from exertion, the scientists still examined the entrance with full concentration.

Up close, the entrance appeared multicolored, though the colors shifted as the eye focused. "What are we waiting for?" Dane engaged his rifle. "Fedor went in."

Manipi scowled at the boy. "And he may have fallen into a lava pit for all we know. Patience, boy."

Carob seemed almost as impatient as Dane. "No fire pit. It's safe."

Seneca shrugged and stepped into the brilliant passage. Nisa gasped when he disappeared, and she jumped through after him.

Nisa stumbled, landing on her knees, facedown, looking at a finely chiseled mosaic floor. "Here, maiden. Your entrance was dramatic, but unnecessary. It's a simple doorway." He took her hand and helped her to her feet. "I suggest we step aside."

As Seneca spoke, the others crashed through the doorway with equal force. Seneca laughed and shook his head. "I lead an enthusiastic group, at least."

Nisa ignored his casual teasing and looked around at her surroundings. "It's not a room. What is this place?"

As far as the eye could see, a huge cavern opened before them. Here evidence of civilization was obvious. Delicate pictures covered every wall, combined with symbols that resembled Akandan art.

Long, wide stairs were carved from rock, leading to giant doorways. Dane gazed around, his blue eyes wide, his mouth open. "It's an underground city. Amazing!"

"Welcome to Nerotania, boy! Subterranean home of the Candorians. Not their original home, mind you. Nerotania was created by mysterious humanoids from beyond the wormhole, probably before your species walked upright."

Dane bowed his head, a pained, weary expression on his young face. "Now he starts talking."

Nisa cast a quick glance around the vast cavern, then turned to Seneca. The grandeur of Candor meant nothing. "Where's Fedor?"

"There, up ahead." Seneca pointed toward a giant archway. Fedor's party crossed beneath, searching. "Keep close to the wall, and follow."

He started ahead, moving like a hunter. Nisa followed, though her lungs burned from the previous run. The cavern wound deeper into the moon, twisting and turning beneath arches and over bridges that spanned endless ravines.

Every wall they passed was decorated in the tiniest

detail. The floor they covered was formed of flawless mosaics, unchipped, undamaged by time. Seneca slowed as the passage narrowed. He stopped and listened.

Nisa heard nothing except the Dakotans' gasps, but Seneca held up his hand, speaking quietly. "In there. I will go first. The rest of you wait for my word."

Nisa opened her mouth to object, but Seneca touched her lips to silence her. "Maiden, I will go. Wait here."

Before she could stop him, Seneca passed through the arch. "Motega!" Thorwalians shouted on the other side of the entry, and Nisa's heart held its beat.

"No . . ." Nisa sprang through the doorway after Seneca. Manipi cursed behind her, but the Dakotans didn't follow.

Nisa stopped. She stood in a wide, open room, surrounded by Thorwalians. Fedor's pale eyes glinted in triumph as he moved toward her. Nisa's hands shook, but she aimed her rifle. "Where is he?"

"Here." Seneca emerged from his shield and sighed. "Maiden, can you obey no command?"

Nisa realized her error, but too late. Fedor motioned to his guards, who moved in around her. Nisa aimed her rifle at Fedor's head. "Stay back, Fedor. I am High Councillor of Thorwal, and you are coming back with us to face a full inquisition on your insurrection."

Nisa's defiance surprised the guards, but Fedor seized a Nebulon torch and pointed it at Seneca.

"I failed the first time. But the body was burned beyond recognition. Will you know him this time, Nisa?"

Nisa hesitated. Her hands shook, but she didn't lower the rifle.

"He appears to have a shielding device. But the torch's aim is wide. Shall I make the attempt?"

Fury surged through Nisa, but she threw aside her weapon. "Curse you! You will destroy us all."

"Destroy us?" Fedor moved closer to Nisa. She saw the wild gleam in his eye, and her blood ran cold. "On the contrary, my beautiful temptress. When I take control of Candor, I will initiate Thorwal into the greatest reign in all history."

"Your lust for power and importance threatens not only your followers, but the inner planets as well. This is madness."

Seneca stepped toward Fedor, but he grabbed Nisa's hair and pulled her in front of him. "Stay back, Motega. I would prefer taking this woman as my consort, but I won't hesitate to kill her."

Seneca met Nisa's eyes. She felt his love and his strength, and her fear eased. "It should be obvious to you, Fedor, that Candor is beyond your grasp."

"Beyond my grasp? Our scanners proved how few life-forms exist on this grand world. We detect no armaments, no weapon systems, no missile defense. With forty well-armed guards, victory is assured."

Nisa struggled to free herself, but Fedor held fast. "For what purpose? What can you hope to gain by conquering this world?"

Fedor laughed. "Surely you saw the mining rings around the moon? The resources here are vast beyond even the results of our probes. When I take control I will easily subdue Thorwal, and rule as overlord. From there it will be no difficulty to gain control over Dakota."

"Don't be too sure of that!" Manipi appeared beneath the arch, surrounded by the Dakotans and Dane.

Fedor's surprise faded to laughter. "Ah, Motega! Your arrogance astounds me. Surely you can't hope to defeat me with seven fat scientists and a skinny boy."

Dane aimed his rifle, but Seneca held up his hand. "Leave this place, Fedor. While you still have time."

Fedor seemed fey to Nisa, driven by the same madness that once claimed the Ravagers. Nisa felt a tug of recognition, of sympathy. What she saw in Fedor, she had seen many times in herself.

"Fedor, don't do this. We need balance to survive, between reason and passion. Your insurrection demanded logic to succeed. Maybe you had a point. We were wasting away, afraid of everything. But vanquishing others isn't the way to strengthen what's inside ourselves. Surely you can see this effort is futile."

Here, at the edge of death, she had found her own power. For a moment Fedor hesitated, uncertain. "There is no need to seek here what we've had all along. Maybe if you listen to Seneca . . ."

Fedor's eyes flashed with hatred and his bony fingers pinched into her cheeks. "Always Motega . . . But no more, Nisa. From now on you are mine."

Fedor jerked his hand from Nisa, and she knew her effort was lost. "Kill Motega and his followers, but leave the woman to me."

The guards aimed, but Seneca didn't move. "It appears our arrival on Candor has been detected, after all."

From all corners of the room, large, globlike creatures emerged. Their shapes changed as they moved, and a sloshing sound accompanied each motion. Fedor grabbed Nisa's arm in a painful grip as they entered the room.

"You're on your own, boy." Carob fluttered from Dane's shoulder and glided across the hall, then positioned himself on the high, domed ceiling to watch.

Nisa struggled to free herself from Fedor, but he held fast. "What are they?"

"Candorians, I presume." Seneca didn't sound frightened, so Nisa tempered her own fear.

The Dakotans positioned their rifles, looking uncertainly to Seneca. "Deiaquande . . . what do we do?"

"Wait."

The globs formed a semicircle, blocking Fedor's guards, then stopped. Seneca folded his arms over his chest. "It appears you were wrong, Fedor. Candor has a defense, after all."

"Right again," sang Carob.

Fedor motioned to a guard. "We'll see about that. Fire!"

"I wouldn't do that—" The rifle blast cut off Seneca's warning. The glob sizzled, then collapsed into an eerie pool.

Fedor's laugh cut short. The other globs grew, swelling into forbidding shapes. Nisa gasped. "I feel their anger."

Fedor's pale eyes glinted. "They'll feel mine."

"Fedor, don't!"

"He's done it now." Carob clambered higher into the dome.

The globs moved toward the Thorwalians. Fedor yanked Nisa in front of him, then backed toward a side entrance. "Fire, you fools!"

The Thorwalian guards shot into the globs, but more appeared at the entrances until they filled the end of the hall. Globs fused and sizzled, but others moved forward, absorbing the fallen masses. The globs that had been shot were rejuvenated by the others, joining together to form larger globs.

A swollen glob reached a guard, then expanded as it loomed toward him. The guard fired, but the glob enveloped him. Horrifying screams followed, then gurgling, then silence. The globs moved forward, and the guard was gone.

"Hold them!" Fedor dragged Nisa away, but she struggled and fought. She jammed her elbow into his stomach, but he didn't release her.

Seneca moved like the wind. He bounded across the room, knocking Fedor aside with one kick. "Nisa, run!"

Nisa leaped aside, then ran back toward Dane. Screams filled the air as the globs enveloped one guard after another.

"Deiaquande . . . do we shoot?" The Dakotans banded together, rifles aimed in shaking hands, but none fired without Seneca's command.

"No." Seneca stood before his group, facing the oncoming globs. "Throw down the rifles."

The Dakotans obeyed. Dane tossed his rifle well to the side, then took his place beside Nisa. "Where's Carob?"

"I think he's hiding." Nisa took her brother's hand. "He'll be all right."

The globs moved in unison toward Fedor. "Throw down the torch, Fedor."

Nisa held out her hand. "Do as Seneca says, and we can still escape."

Fedor looked between Nisa and Seneca. He hesitated. His fingers twitched on the heavy weapon. "You should have been mine. This was meant for you, Motega." Hatred filled his voice. He aimed at Seneca, but Nisa jumped forward to shield him.

The globs swarmed around Fedor. He ignited the torch and blasted into their pulsing mass. The globs hissed and sparkled; many sank to the floor. Fedor reset the torch and aimed again, but the globs moved too fast.

Nisa saw the shapeless mass rise, cutting off her view of Fedor. She heard the torch fall, heard his high, cut-off scream as the globs enveloped him.

Nisa grabbed Seneca's arm. "They're coming! What do we do?"

Seneca stood immobile as the globs reformed and absorbed the matter destroyed by Fedor's torch. "Move back, maiden."

Nisa shook her head wildly. "No! I won't leave you."

Seneca met her eyes. For a timeless moment they looked at each other. "I love you."

"Seneca . . ."

"Move back." Nisa saw no fear in his warm brown

eyes. "Dane, take Nisa back to the shuttle. All of you. Go!"

Manipi's face went white, but the Dakotans obeyed Seneca's instructions as they backed toward the entrance. Dane hesitated, then took Nisa's arm.

"Don't you dare!"

"Nisa, we must do as he says."

"I will not."

Seneca shook his head, a slight smile on his face. "Defiant to the end. Maiden, do as I tell you. Leave while you still can."

"No."

The globs oozed across the floor, flattening as they moved. Seneca turned away, then walked toward them. He stopped and waited.

Nisa's blood moved like ice as the globs closed in around him. She tried to follow, but Dane held her back. "It's too late." Tears fell to the boy's cheeks. "He has his shield."

"He's not using it." Seneca would sacrifice himself to allow the others time to flee. If he died, he knew Nisa had no reason to stay. Nisa picked up a discarded rifle and started to aim. No. She dropped it at her side.

Seneca looked back. She saw no fear. He smiled gently, then turned to face the rising globs. Nisa shook, but she couldn't look away. The glob mass swelled like a rising wave, above, then over Seneca.

Dane sobbed, then turned his head, but Nisa stared. Seneca disappeared in a gelatinous cloud, and she couldn't move.

"Come, we must go." Dane's voice cracked, and he tried to pull her away. Nisa stood as if carved from stone.

"He's given us time, Nisa."

Manipi called from the entrance, "We must obey the Deiaquande's last command." He was crying, unable to leave. Nisa didn't move.

The globs formed a mountainous shape over

Seneca, gurgling and sloshing. Nisa heard no screams. Despite her own shock, she felt a change in the creatures. The anger was gone.

The globs eased down, flattening, returning to individual beings. They withdrew, and Seneca emerged from their midst. Unharmed. Untarnished. And smiling.

Relief struck Nisa so hard that she sank to her knees, weeping. Dane cried out in joy, and the Dakotans stepped tentatively forward. "Deiaquande!"

"I am uninjured. Maiden, I would have you at my side for this moment."

He sounded calm. Nisa looked up in disbelief. He held out his hand. Dane pulled her up and she went to Seneca.

"Was it your shield?"

"No."

"Then what . . . ?" As Nisa spoke, the globs formed an aisle down the hall. From the farthest entrance, several humanoid beings appeared. Both male and female wore white robes that shimmered when they moved.

Carob glided down from the ceiling and landed on Dane's shoulder. "Close, wasn't it?" he offered conversationally.

Dane glared. "Not for you. Who are these people?"

"I'll let them tell you that."

The humanoids approached Seneca without speaking, then stood in front of him, faces calm and peaceful, serene. Nisa considered their demeanor condescending despite the impassive manner.

The female who appeared to be their leader faced Seneca, her golden eyes fixed on his. She carried an orbed scepter, ringed with the vibrant colors of Candor. She looked ageless, neither young nor old, with silver-and-gold hair bound in a long twist behind her head. The men looked similar, of equal height, but with shorter twists in their hair.

"I am Kostbera, First Representative of Nerotania. Who are you, and why have you come to our world?"

"I am called Seneca. I lead the people of Dakota, the innermost planet of this system."

"You bring violence. This is not tolerated on Nerotania."

Nisa hesitated, then stepped forward. "I am Nisa Calydon, heir to the High Council of Thorwal." She glanced at Seneca. If he could sacrifice himself, she could do the same. "The men who came here to plunder were Thorwalians. Their leader was a member of our council, who desired greater power. Their intrusion is my fault. Seneca tried to stop them. And would have, if your globs hadn't interfered."

Kostbera appeared confused. "Globs? What do you mean?"

Nisa pointed at the globs. "Those . . . squishy things that attacked us."

"Those are the native Candorians, with whom we share these caverns. They act as our guards and advisers."

"Speaking of which . . ." Carob fluttered his wings, engaging Kostbera's attention. Her eyes widened when she saw him.

"Harradenai! We thought you lost!"

Dane eyed the lingbat. "What did she call you? And how . . ." Dane paused to groan. "How does she know you?"

Carob puffed up, enjoying Dane's defeated expression. "I am Harradenai on Candor, boy. It means 'valued bearer of knowledge.' Appropriate, eh?"

"Carob seems more fitting," said Dane. "It means 'chubby rat.' "

Kostbera frowned slightly. "Is this how our ambassador is treated?"

Manipi coughed. "Ambassador?"

Dane sighed, his shoulders slumping. "I was afraid of something like this."

Carob caught his wingtip deliberately in Dane's hair and gave a sharp tug. "Ambassador, boy. We took your probe as an opportunity for contact, and thought we'd check out your development. Of course, I found myself caged and drugged."

"Until we freed you," Nisa added.

Kostbera was unimpressed. "You caged our ambassador. This is not pleasing to my ear. In the two thousand years since our first contact, it appears your barbaric tendencies have not changed. You have accumulated power, and thus endanger all civilized worlds."

Seneca considered her words. "First contact?"

"Two thousand years ago, a stray comet entered the inner system of this sun. It altered the orbital patterns of the inner planets, wreaking havoc with the native life-forms."

"We know that," put in Nisa, imitating Kostbera's patronizing tone.

Kostbera smiled at Nisa without affection, and Nisa made a fist. "What you may not know is how close the most advanced world came to utter destruction."

Nisa's chin lifted. "Thorwal became colder, but my people endured the worst hardships and survived."

"I do not speak of Thorwal." Kostbera's tone grated to the limit of Nisa's patience.

Manipi's eyes brightened. "Dakota?"

"There was no Dakota two thousand years ago." Kostbera paused while the others waited for her revelation. "I speak of the world known as Akando."

Nisa sighed. "Naturally . . ." Seneca chuckled, but he made no comment.

"Akando's civilization had reached a period of great glory. Their kings ruled with benevolence and wisdom, and their cities were built into cliffsides that housed thousands. It was, altogether, an admirable society."

Seneca nodded as long-unanswered questions became clear. "The comet devastated the natural habitat. Sites of mass graves still remain undisturbed on Akando, as well as ruins of a vast culture." He paused. "The gods borne on comets . . . yourselves."

Kostbera gazed at Seneca appreciatively. "That is correct. We had studied the Akandans and admired them greatly. When the calamity struck, we decided to escort a portion of their people to a safer world."

Seneca smiled. "Dakota."

"Dakota. We didn't know the extent of the hardships on Akando, but we left a few tribes unaffected by our presence. The new inhabitants of Dakota surprised us by their eagerness to learn. They adopted much of our science, and we soon realized the danger of their advancing too fast. We abandoned them to fend for themselves, in hopes they would return to the simplicity of life on Akando."

Nisa eyed Kostbera with growing distaste. "What about Thorwal? We have no history of outside interference."

Kostbera glanced at Nisa, then returned her gaze to Seneca. "The people of Thorwal didn't interest us. They were totally without admirable qualities. Our few studies there revealed a barbaric people intent on warfare, with a savage lust for power. It appears that hasn't changed over the eons."

Nisa's fist clenched. Kostbera was about to see a firsthand view of violence. A smile flickered on Seneca's lips. He seized Nisa's fist and drew her to his side. "Thorwalians possess unmatched violence, Kostbera."

Nisa glared up at him. "We do not!"

Seneca ignored her outburst. "There was a time when I, too, scorned their history and feared their natures. Despite the facade of civilization, the Ravager soul is still much alive in Thorwalians today. You saw that here, when Fedor chose to fight rather than retreat. You will see it in this maiden's eyes. And in her brother when he aims his weapon."

Nisa's mouth opened. She was too angry to speak. Kostbera glanced between Nisa and Dane, then shook her head sadly. "Truthfully, we hoped the ice age would destroy them, and end the wanton destruction that saddened us so."

Nisa tried to snatch her hand from Seneca's, but he didn't let go. "Then you misunderstand Thorwal, Kostbera. Ice couldn't destroy them, for their souls are made of fire."

Nisa liked this image of herself. Her anger subsided. Dane smiled at Seneca's description, nodding thoughtfully.

"They fling themselves at life with unmatched courage, without knowing the outcome. Without needing to know."

Nisa eyed Seneca doubtfully, unsure if this flattered her nature or not.

Kostbera's attention fixed on their clasped hands. "It appears your people made . . . contact."

"Between the people of Dakota and Thorwal, there is a desire to join."

Nisa blushed at Seneca's reference. "We needed each other." She meant the two worlds, but this sounded even worse. Her blush deepened and Seneca grinned.

"We found in each other what our own civilizations lacked. The Dakotans built on the science they learned from you. Yet they had no drive, no power to create the structures they designed. Only contact with Thorwal brought our images into reality."

"I cannot imagine how a barbaric people such as the Thorwalian Ravagers could have aided Dakotan progress."

"By that time Thorwal had developed a central government. They had controlled themselves and their world to the point of . . . obsessive and extreme detail."

Nisa frowned, but didn't argue.

"Dakota and Thorwal found in each other what was missing in themselves. Together they formed a mutually dependent culture. And therein lies the potential for strife. What we are remains. Beneath the Thorwalian ice lies fire. That fire is creation, Kostbera. It moves them to great lengths, to glory."

Seneca glanced at Dane. "Its power might surprise you, if you're willing to see such an elemental force in action. But in the Dakotan soul, there lies an emptiness for what we lost on Akando."

"I sense no emptiness in you." Kostbera spoke in obvious admiration.

Nisa cleared her throat and muttered under her breath, "Apparently not." She wondered how old Kostbera was, and if she was mated.

"I was empty. I sought to fill the emptiness from outside myself. In the shadow of my ambition and pride, the fire of Thorwal pales. I am Motega, Deiaquande of Dakota, and this invasion of your world was caused by my own reckless arrogance."

"I see Akando in your eyes."

"I fled to Akando to plot vengeance against the woman I loved. Nothing mattered but what I wanted. Not the world I led, not Nisa's freedom, and not the people of Akando. Akando taught me to face truth, and myself."

Kostbera considered Seneca's words. Her gaze turned with distrust to Nisa. "It seems that your connection with the Thorwalians is to blame. Such ambition seems descriptive of the man who invaded us."

Seneca looked at Nisa, an unreadable expression on his face, then back to Kostbera. "Thorwalian fire both creates and destroys, Kostbera. Fedor journeyed here to increase his own worth, his own power. Yet Nisa and her brother threw down their weapons, even when your guardians threatened us all."

"Your globs don't seem particularly peaceful," Nisa

added with a defiant tilt of her chin. Kostbera ignored her.

"This fire could prove an irritation."

Seneca laughed. "It could. But the irritant is often . . . pleasurable." Nisa winced, but Seneca kissed her hand. "We may, many times, fail in our good intentions. But we will find balance between what we were and what we can be. And one day we will make this journey in peace."

Kostbera's golden eyes darkened. "I will welcome that day."

Nisa's patience faltered. "I'm sure you will. But that day is far away. I, for one, am still quite violent. So if you'll call off your globs, we will happily depart."

Kostbera hesitated. "It seems a shame. You have advanced far enough to travel beyond your worlds. Contact between us might prove valuable. Candor is a central point for many worlds beyond this system. You might be welcome as an associate to our intersystem. Perhaps you, Seneca, might remain here. There is much to learn, and you speak well for the inner planets."

Nisa braced herself for Seneca's reply. Maybe he would prefer life on this advanced world, discussing philosophy and peace with Kostbera. Nisa believed he had gone beyond her. He was wise and strong, and could teach even these ethereal Candorian beings. She, on the other hand, would sooner engage them in battle.

"My place is on another world, Kostbera. That is where I belong."

Nisa closed her eyes. Akando.

Seneca studied his group, and a slow smile grew on his face. "Leaving a representative from our worlds might be wise, however. Should any wish to remain . . ."

"I will." Dane stepped forward, his young face alive with excitement.

"You will not! Dane!" Nisa turned to Seneca, aghast at his suggestion. "You can't leave my brother here."

Dane touched Nisa's face. "I will never know on Thorwal or Dakota what you have found, Nisa. I long for adventure, for worlds beyond ours. Can you understand? You will rule Thorwal, because that is what you do best. I have no wish to rule. I long for something . . . something outside what I know. Please don't deny me this."

Tears blurred Nisa's vision. She couldn't lose her brother, too. But as she couldn't stand in the way of Seneca's happiness, she couldn't hinder Dane's, either. "What will I tell our parents?"

Dane smiled. "Tell them I'm following in your footsteps. That should please them."

"He won't be alone." Carob leaned against Dane's head fondly. "I'll be with him. It's about time I sired another litter."

Seneca kissed Nisa's hand. "I told you, didn't I, that Carob would never be far from your brother's shoulder?"

Nisa sniffed. "That is some comfort. He won't be lonely."

Dane grinned, sensing the change in his favor. "I'll be tormented, but never lonely."

Kostbera fingered her scepter. "I don't know. This boy is Thorwalian."

"All the more reason to get to know us!"

Kostbera looked at Carob. "Harradenai, if you will speak for him and be responsible for his behavior, I will agree to admit him."

Carob hesitated while Dane's eyes widened. "Just don't let him pilot anything."

"Very well. There is much this boy can learn in the city of Nerotania. He might prove useful."

"I can do anything!"

Nisa fought tears as she hugged her brother. "You will come back, won't you?"

Dane kissed her forehead. "Yes. But the next time you see me, my dear sister, I will be a man."

Seneca laid his hand on Dane's shoulder. "What you will be is within you now, Dane. There is nothing outside you don't carry within already. But I wish you adventure, where all that you are now proves its full worth."

"I will continue the TiKay. And when I return, I may have something to show you!"

"I look forward to that day."

Kostbera watched the farewell with an emotionless expression, and Nisa wondered what pleasure her fun-loving brother would find among these ethereal beings. "I hope you know what you're doing."

Dane had already turned away. Seneca leaned toward Nisa, speaking softly. "He doesn't need to know. He flings himself at life with unmatched courage, without knowing the outcome."

Nisa sighed heavily. "Without needing to know."

Carob flapped himself from Dane's shoulder, then hopped to Nisa. He waited a moment, tapping a small foot. "If you don't mind . . ."

Nisa bent and picked him up. "I'll miss you, Carob."

"You set me free. I will not forget that. The kindness in your heart does your people honor."

Nisa's eyes puddled with tears. "You saved me and my brother. I won't forget that, either."

"You're bossy, but you're kind. I'm sorry not to see Thorwal snapped to order under your hand." Carob glanced at Seneca. "Of course, you won't be alone. You've got your transformed Motega to keep you from outright tyranny."

Nisa smiled, but she ached inside. "I set you free before I realized how much freedom meant. I know now." Her voice faltered. "Please take care of my brother. He has no fear. I don't think he'd even recognize danger."

"I'll recognize it for him. He won't go anywhere

without me, I promise you."

Nisa heard Dane groan, and Carob chuckled. Nisa carried the lingbat and placed him carefully on Dane's slumped shoulder. "My heart rests easier knowing you have such a good companion."

Dane kissed Nisa's cheek. "You've watched over me all my life, my dear sister. I will make you proud."

"You always have."

Kostbera spoke quietly with one of the men at her side, then turned to Seneca. "Erihart reminds me that if you intend to leave Candor, you must do so soon. Candoria flares with each cycle, making space flight impossible for such vessels as yours."

Seneca bowed. "You do us honor by your graciousness and wisdom, Kostbera. We will not forget your generosity and kindness."

Kostbera smiled. "We will not forget you either, Seneca. You have proven our decision to rescue the Akandans was not in error."

"We are each hands of fate, are we not? Whether for good or ill. When we follow our true natures, the winds most often blow true."

"You learned much on Akando. I trust the people there thrive and prosper."

"They do. They never lost what we fight to regain. For myself, they gave me back my soul."

Seneca led the Dakotans back to their vessel, but Nisa walked in a numb blur. She knew what she had to do, but she couldn't face their ending. The Dakotans entered the vessel, but Nisa drew Seneca aside.

"It is time I took my place, Seneca. I must use Fedor's shuttle and take command of the transport he stole. It is my duty to lead Thorwal's reconstruction."

"Maiden . . ."

"I love you, Sen_ca. I have always loved you. But you don't belong with me. You have fulfilled every promise Motega made, and more."

Stobie Piel

Nisa swallowed, and she couldn't stop her tears. She took his hand and kissed it, pressing her wet cheek against his palm. "You are Akandan, Seneca. You have been all along."

Her voice caught, but she forced herself to continue. "You belong there. You have your tree. Take it, and plant it, and go back to what you were before I abducted you. But please don't forget me."

"Forget you . . ."

A harsh sob gathered in Nisa's chest. With all her courage, she repressed her misery and looked him in the eye. "A part of you will be with me always. And where you go, my heart goes also. But I can't live knowing I've taken you from the world you love. I can't."

She rose on tiptoe and kissed his cheek. She felt his tears, but she turned away. He didn't call her back as she entered Fedor's abandoned shuttle. For one instant of weakness Nisa hesitated on the ramp.

"Farewell, my sweet Ravager. I will not forget."

Seneca's soft voice echoed in her mind as Nisa closed herself in the empty shuttle. As much as she hurt, she felt strong. She had done the hardest thing in her life. She let him go.

Nisa didn't wait. She brushed aside her tears and engaged the shuttle. It lifted above the golden-brown surface of the moon. Through the viewport, she saw the Dakotan vessel below. She saw Seneca standing, his face upturned as he watched her fly away. Then he turned and entered the craft, and disappeared.

Nisa gauged her controls to rejoin with the Thorwalian transport. She had no fear about her reception on board. She was High Councillor, born to lead her icebound world. No one would defy her now.

Nisa saw Seneca's craft rise from the moon. The faster vessel lifted past her, speeding through the atmosphere toward black space. Nisa checked its position. Its course was set for Akando.

* * *

Seneca stood at the edge of the cliff, his dark hair streaming in the night wind. Far below in the savanna lands, the village of Akando slept. The opaque leaves of the Lasting Trees reflected the distant light of Candor.

Akando had just passed its farthest point from the sun. The cold season was deep upon the land. Snow and ice covered the ground; the air was still and sharp with frost.

As the orange ball of Candor rose on the horizon, Seneca saw another light, small but bright. Thorwal glittered with a final appeal to his heart, then disappeared beyond the snow-covered tree line.

Seneca found the jagged path and moved swiftly down the cliff wall. When he reached the cliff's floor, he ran with the wind's speed to the Lasting Trees. As Seneca reached the Akandan village, the first light of dawn permeated the black sky.

The pale light brought a cold glow to the opaque leaves. A small sapling, recently planted, caught Seneca's eye. For an eternal moment his gaze fixed on the new tree. Carack had returned.

Smoke rose through the roofs of the Akandan huts. It was early for morning's tasks, but a woman appeared from a hut. Elan. The woman who would have been his mate.

Elan's long black hair was bound in a ceremonial braid, decorated with shells. She seemed excited. Seneca had never seen Elan anything but calm and reasonable and wise. He watched, bemused, as she glanced furtively around the village, then crept cautiously toward the ring of trees.

From another hut, the chief's hut, a young man emerged. Seneca's heart leaped. Carack wore the chief's amulet of the wind around his neck, and was also garbed for ritual. He looked around, then followed Elan.

Seneca stood concealed in the ancient grove. Elan waited a short distance away, her hands clasped over her breast as Carack joined her. They faced each other silently, their hearts clear as Carack took Elan's hands in his own.

As he watched them, Seneca saw himself looking at Nisa when nothing stood between them, when all they had was love.

"We should not have met this way. It isn't part of the ritual." Elan giggled despite her words.

"How do we know that, Elan? Perhaps such meetings occur before every mating."

Carack pulled her closer, then gently kissed her mouth. "When I first saw you, I thought you were the most beautiful, perfect woman on all Akando. You would have been a fit mate for the greatest man I have ever known, my brother. I cannot hope to equal him, but he lives in my heart. I will care for you, Elan, and do him honor."

Elan touched Carack's cheek. "We feel him here, still."

"He isn't dead. He has gone to the gods, as our legends tell."

"Do you know what I believe, Carack? Seneca was never one of us. He was a god, thrown out from the tempests of heaven for a misdeed we cannot comprehend. He loved a goddess, and he lost her. And when he was ready, she came for him and took him back to the stars."

Carack drew Elan into his arms and kissed her forehead. "Last night I sat beside my father's bed. Before he released his life, I told him of my vision of Seneca, that I had seen a fire trail across the sky, and knew my brother rode that fire. Nodin said he had always known. He told me he had found a man inside a god, and returned him to the sky."

Seneca's eyes stung with tears, his throat tightening. For a moment he considered telling them he was no god; he was a man with many flaws. Seneca saw Nisa in his mind, her flaming blue eyes when she was angry, her wild, golden hair around her sweet face when her temper flared. Yes, the goddess was real.

Carack stroked Elan's long hair. "As he was, we can be, Elan. I was wounded; I was ready to die. I had made many mistakes in the course of my trial. But I heard my brother's voice in my mind, and I knew my fate was not determined by my mistakes nor by my victories, either. I carry my fate within."

Elan laughed, then kissed Carack's cheek. "Today your fate is me." She glanced over her shoulder and noticed more villagers emerging from their huts. "I must hurry, lest they learn we have met in secret."

She pulled away, though their fingers still touched. "When next we meet, you will be mine."

They parted, each hurrying to different ends of the village. Seneca smiled when Carack positioned himself casually by the chief's hut, as if he had just emerged.

For a long while Seneca watched the Akandans as they began the day. Women ground carth-wheat in pottery urns, laughing with Elan as she prepared for the ritual ceremony of mating. Men appeared, decorated with paint, carrying masks to be worn during the dance to follow.

What they gave him, he would have forever. Akando was a part of him. He had returned to plant the sapling in the sacred grove, in honor of his young brother's brief life. But the sapling wasn't needed on Akando. They would go on, as they always had, over tragedy and triumph, in balance and strength.

And Seneca would go on, too. He knew now what he wanted, what he had always wanted. From the time Motega had arrived on Akando, he had given away all that he cherished. Now, at last, he was free to receive.

* * *

"Will the High Councillor admit an emissary of Dakota?"

Nisa adjusted her position in Helmar's seat. "It is my wish that relations between the two worlds be open. Send the emissary in."

The guard hurried away, and Nisa waited. She fiddled with her white robe so that it fell in a dignified fashion, covering her bare knees. She had grown used to her leggings. But the High Councillor must greet guests in full Thorwalian attire.

The hall doors slid quietly open, and the guard returned. Nisa's heart skipped a beat. The Dakotan emissary was Manipi. She bit her lip, then forced an impassive calm over her features as she rose to greet him.

Manipi resisted Nisa's formality. He wore his usual Dakotan suit, though it hung looser around his waist. He flung up his arms and whirled around. "What do you think? Not so much of me as there was!"

Nisa repressed a smile. "I see that. Your progress is impressive. Why have you come?"

"We understand you've set things to rights here, and with the council. Our leader thought you might be ready to open communications with Dakota."

"That is my wish." Nisa paused. "You've chosen a new leader?"

Manipi hesitated. "Why do you ask?"

Nisa hadn't meant to bring up the subject of Seneca. It hurt too much. "You took Seneca back to Akando, didn't you?"

"We did."

A tiny grain of hope in Nisa's heart faded and died. "I see. . . . What does your new leader ask of Thorwal?"

"Well, now. We've been doing some studies over our early culture, from what we learned about Akando. Interesting, realizing we're the same people, after all."

"Yes, go on." Nisa didn't want to hear about Akando.

"Anyway, our forebears had an interesting way of solving the problem that's plagued us. As I see it, Thorwal and Dakota are just two tribes, two clans. One is bigger, but you need us and we need you. We're not much alike, but we have much to learn from each other, and it appears we're going in the same direction."

"Yes." A heavy blanket of weariness crept across Nisa's soul. She would lead her world into a new age, but she felt empty. Nothing really mattered inside.

"What the ancients did was simple—the leaders of one tribe sent a prized female to the leader of another."

Nisa's eyes narrowed. She had heard this somewhere before. "Do you mean . . . you expect me to . . ."

Manipi nodded. "We want you as mate for our leader." Nisa's mouth opened and she started to shake her head. "Now don't answer too soon. The Dakotans know you, and they've come to trust you. They also know you're the one with the power here. I don't see us accepting another, when we know you're not mated anyway."

He might have added, *and not likely to be.* Nisa frowned. "I do not intend to take a mate. Any mate."

Manipi shrugged. "It's a shame not to reestablish communications between us."

Nisa sat back in the councillor's chair. "Do you mean our negotiations hinge on my willingness to mate with a man I've never met? That's absurd!"

"Not to our way of thinking. Thorwal has always carried deep affection for you. If there's a prize female, you're it."

Nisa got up again and paced around the hall. "If you Dakotans want to return to your ancient, primitive beginnings, that's your affair. We on Thorwal—"

"Are floundering without us. One world, Nisa. Isn't that what you want?"

Nisa stopped. One world. That was Motega's

promise long ago. Why did it matter how she spent the rest of her life, or with whom? Seneca was gone. He was free and happy, returned to the peace of Akando, where he belonged.

"If you agree, we will create one world. Our Deiaquande awaits you. Will you return with me to Dakota?"

Respect and honor. Seneca had that now. He had done his duty for their two worlds. She had one more duty to perform. Nisa turned slowly. "Yes, Manipi. I will."

The Dakotan shuttle landed on the lab just as the sun faded beyond the trees. Nisa regretted her decision more and more with each passing moment. It was one thing to spend her life alone, with memories of Seneca. But how would she mate with another man, when Seneca filled her heart and her soul?

Manipi opened the ramp and held out his hand for Nisa. "Maybe I should meet with him first."

"That is not the way the ancients performed the ceremony. You will be led to him through a line of our people. They'll throw flowers at you. Apparently most such ceremonies take place during the warm months on Akando. It was meant to give the female a pleasing scent when she goes to the nuptial bed."

Nisa repressed a groan. "I do not see the necessity—"

"Ritual," Manipi interrupted. "We're trying to do things like the ancients."

Nisa nodded, but she felt sick. *Nuptial bed, indeed.* "You've told me my new mate will be hooded. I find this peculiar in the extreme. But I suppose it doesn't matter what he looks like. What do I wear?"

Manipi glanced at Nisa's Thorwalian dress. "What you've got on is fine. We want to blend Thorwalian ritual with ancient Dakotan. The gold belt, as I recall, symbolizes the shield worn in battle."

Manipi seemed to find the shield significant, but Nisa nodded impatiently. "Is there anything else I should know? I won't have to speak in some ancient language, will I?"

"The female doesn't speak. She bows in honor to her new mate." Manipi hesitated. "As evidence she is willing to do his bidding in all things."

Nisa stopped. "You didn't mention that when you coerced me into coming here!"

Manipi took her arm, easing her forward. "It's just a formality. Anyone who knows you understands you won't be doing anyone's bidding."

"Good. I trust the new Deiaquande is aware of this facet of my character, too."

"I'm sure he is."

"I won't be doing anyone's *bidding*."

Manipi sighed. "Stars know."

Manipi led Nisa into the square as the sun's final light disappeared. Torches circled the square, and the Dakotans waited in unusual silence. In the center of the square, a man knelt. Nisa couldn't gauge his size, whether tall or heavy or squat. A hood covered his head, and a long, full robe splayed out from his shoulders.

"Is that him?"

Manipi nodded. "The Deiaquande awaits."

Nisa couldn't move. "What do I do?"

"I told you this on the journey from Thorwal." Manipi patted her arm in sympathy. "I suppose you're nervous. You go up, kneel beside him, he bows, you bow."

"Does this mean he has to do my bidding also?"

Manipi chuckled. "It means he will make the wisest decisions on your behalf."

Nisa rolled her eyes, reluctant to proceed. "I don't think this is a very good idea, after all." She started to turn away, but Manipi held her back.

"One world."

Nisa sighed. "Begin the ceremony."

Stobie Piel

Manipi left Nisa standing outside the ring of torches, then went to the center of the ring. A woman, veiled and wearing a multilayered robe, appeared. Nisa recognized Aponi.

Aponi flung her arms to the sides, chanting in what Nisa assumed was old Dakotan. Aponi fumbled, then looked to Manipi, who spoke quickly. Nisa thought she heard the Deiaquande chuckle, though he didn't move from his kneeling position.

Aponi moved in a graceful circle around the kneeling Deiaquande, flinging flowers and herbs in all directions. She faced Nisa and raised both hands above her head.

Nisa wasn't sure what this gesture signified. Aponi waited, then glanced back at Manipi, who sighed in irritation. Aponi nodded meaningfully toward the ring's center. "Get in there," she hissed.

Nisa entered the ring, feeling both foolish and lost. In this bizarre ceremony she would be mated to a man she didn't know, while her heart ached for another.

Manipi motioned her to the Deiaquande's side. Nisa hesitated, then sighed heavily. She knelt, peeking over at the man beside her. His hood revealed nothing.

To distract herself, Nisa looked around for Dakotans she knew. She saw Wicasa and Hinto. Her heart flickered with warmth when she saw the three wortpigs standing solemnly by their new masters.

Nisa didn't see Langundo. She looked harder, but no one of his size stood in the ring. Nisa glanced at her new mate. She couldn't judge his size beneath his robe—a robe large enough to conceal even Langundo.

Nisa repressed a groan, then decided Langundo was a good-hearted man. Better him than some young leader bent on taking Seneca's place. Langundo would be a comfort, a friendly companion.

She had to know. Nisa leaned slightly toward him. "Langundo?"

His only response was a soft chuckle. Nisa's hopes dwindled.

Aponi was speaking, her voice low and rhythmic, then high and excited, until Manipi tapped her shoulder. Aponi motioned for Nisa and her new mate to rise. Nisa stood, sighed, then faced him.

She couldn't make herself bow. She chewed her lip as she fought her own defiance. Manipi coughed, reminding her. Aponi cleared her throat and bowed as a reminder. Nisa surrendered. She bowed, very slightly.

The Deiaquande bowed, graceful and low. Nisa knew he was smiling. Her predicament amused him. She couldn't see him, but he could see her. How irritating! She fixed her gaze on his hood and maintained a cold, imperious expression.

She turned to Manipi. "What now?"

Manipi leaned toward her and spoke in hushed tones. "Now he takes you to his quarters, and you . . . bow more."

"What?" Nisa's voice rose and she started to move away from her mate. He seized her arm, gentle but firm, and led her toward Motega's door.

Nisa looked desperately back over her shoulder. "Manipi! Isn't there a celebration or something?"

"Of course there is! We eat and drink, and try some ritual dances, too!"

"What about me?"

"You bow."

Nisa slumped. "Bow, indeed!" A cold, fierce resolve grew in her heart. "We'll just see about that."

Her mate didn't speak as he opened Motega's door and led her inside. Nisa dragged her feet over the threshold. Whoever he was, he was Dakotan and could be made to see reason. He closed the door, and Nisa eased back from him.

Nisa found herself in his arms before she saw him move. Curse Seneca for teaching the Dakotans TiKay!

355

He was carrying her—the nerve!—upstairs . . . to Motega's bedroom.

He brought her into the dimly lit room and set her on her feet. Nisa sprang away. "This has gone far enough! I agreed to this ridiculous scheme thinking we might find a balance, you and I. But naturally, as Dakotans always do, you've taken this to extreme lengths. And if you think I'm going to bow again, you're sadly mistaken!"

"I wouldn't dream of asking."

At the soft, low sound of his voice, a chill ran along Nisa's spine and into her heart. "You're not Langundo."

"No."

Nisa's heart throbbed and ached. "I won't be a good mate. I love another, you see."

"I know." He stepped closer to her. "That makes us well matched, maiden. I never forgot my first love, either."

He pulled off his hood, and Nisa sank to her knees. Emotion overwhelmed her and a harsh sob ripped from her heart. "Seneca."

He knelt before her and took her in his arms. "I am."

Nisa looked up, her face streaked with tears. "You came back."

Seneca smiled. "I never left, Nisa. I returned to Akando to deliver the sapling, to learn what became of Carack. I never intended to stay."

"Truly? But I thought that's what you wanted, to go back."

"I thought so, too. For a while. Before I realized you loved me again, that I had been wrong about you."

Nisa sniffed and dried her eyes. "Then why did you leave me? Why didn't you tell me this on Candor?"

Seneca brushed her hair from her cheek. "If I had called you back, would you have believed me? You offered me freedom. I took it, so that when I returned to you, you would know I want nothing more than a life spent with you. But I have never been more sure of our love than I was that day on a distant moon."

Nisa rested her head on his shoulder and wrapped her arms around his waist. "Did you find your brother? Did you tell him you're all right?"

"I saw him. He is now chief of the Clan of the Wind, and he has taken Elan as his mate. I suspect she is happier now than she ever would have been with me. A woman doesn't want a man who already loves a goddess."

Nisa eyed Seneca doubtfully. "Did she have to perform this ridiculous ceremony, with all the bowing and the man wearing a hood?"

Seneca laughed, a slightly guilty expression on his dark face. "As I recall, there was bowing involved in Akandan rituals. The hood, however, was my own invention. I didn't want you to recognize me so soon."

Nisa sat back. "I thought you were Langundo because I didn't see him at the ceremony."

"As it happens, Langundo led an overenthusiastic TiKay session, and sprained several muscles. He is hospitalized for his efforts."

Nisa sighed. "I am happy to be back on Dakota. But our mating would have gone easier for me if I'd known my mate was you."

"Your compliance proved to all Dakota that Thorwal can yield despite its stubborn nature. And quite frankly, the Dakotans have developed a sense of humor that rivals a lingbat's. Manipi staged the entire affair."

"I see. You had no part in it."

Seneca grinned. "I made a few suggestions here and there. But for myself, I wished to meet you here, alone. Where nothing can stop us or delay us from what we want."

"Each other."

Seneca took Nisa's face in his hands. "I love you, Nisa Calydon. I have loved you since I first saw you, when I had no idea how deep the emotion ran."

"It ran beyond our control, as love always does." Nisa slid her arms around Seneca's neck, her eyes drifting shut as he bent to kiss her.

Seneca hesitated, his lips a breath away from hers. He looked down into her face. "We don't need to control it, maiden. We'll let it run free, and see where it goes."

Nisa's insides fluttered. "I've missed you."

"I've missed you, too."

"Will we rule together?"

"One world, maiden. As I promised you long ago. We'll bring the Thorwalian fire to Dakota, and we'll bring TiKay to Thorwal. I look forward to teaching your parents the art."

Nisa giggled. "That should be interesting. They've been hiding out in a subterranean tunnel since Fedor's insurrection. It took me a while to find them. They'd befriended a group of wortpigs during their stay."

"I trust they were pleased to find you in command."

"Surprisingly, they were. They had been told that Dane was dead, and they blamed themselves. Although I'm not sure learning his true whereabouts was exactly a relief. But they didn't argue about it."

Seneca kissed Nisa's brow and ran his fingers through her loose hair. "And what of us, maiden? How will they take the knowledge you took Motega for a mate, after all?"

Nisa hesitated, but she smiled. "Well . . . I told them about you, of course. How you went to Akando, and how Fedor had tried to kill you. I believe they softened somewhat on the subject. My mother mentioned your good looks. It seems that their time in the tunnel renewed their affection for each other. I've never seen them so close and so natural together."

"I am pleased for you, maiden. Your parents were stiff, as all Thorwalians tend to be, but they raised you. There must be good in them."

"They mated for practical reasons. I think it surprised them to find they might actually love each other."

"Love is always a surprise, maiden. And you are the most surprising woman of all."

Nisa drew back, her lips curved in a seductive smile. "I've been without you too long. But that time has given me several surprising fantasies."

Seneca's warm eyes darkened. "Then you will tell me, one by one."

Nisa wet her lips. "They're not the sort of things I can tell. . . . I must show you."

Seneca's pulse quickened. "The night is young, maiden, for all you wish to show me, and more."

Nisa woke with the sun's first light. Seneca slept with his arm protectively across her, his powerful body curled around hers. Nisa turned in his arms and pressed a soft, leisurely kiss in the hollow of his throat. He smiled before he opened his eyes.

"Maiden, did you not tire me enough in the night?" Nisa felt his arousal, despite the passion of their first mated night together. She moved closer and slid her leg over his, indicating a willingness to repeat every sweet temptation he offered.

Seneca kissed her head. He glanced out the window, then got up from the bed. Nisa sighed in disappointment. "You're not thinking of leading TiKay this early, are you?" She yawned and stretched. "If so, leave quietly, but return when you're finished. I am not thoroughly sated."

Seneca laughed and seized her hand, dragging her from the bed. "Dress, maiden, but not for TiKay. I have another event planned for our first morning as true mates."

Nisa peeked at him through one eye. "What? And why can't it wait for full morning light?"

Seneca gazed thoughtfully at the ceiling. "As I recall,

you bowed last night, indicating your solemn promise to obey my every word."

Nisa frowned. "Then I rescind it!"

"There is no such option, my sweet Ravager. Come with me. You will not be disappointed."

"Oh, very well." Nisa slipped into her blue Dakotan suit. "Where are we going?"

"You'll see."

New morning was quiet and still as Seneca led Nisa through the village square. The wortpigs slept in pens, stretched on their sides. Spike was rolled over onto his back, stout legs in the air. Snoring.

Seneca laughed as they passed by the sleeping creatures. His heart was filled with happiness. Every reminder of the woman at his side sent echoes of boundless joy into the future.

Hand in hand, they walked along the river. Nisa's sleepiness faded as she breathed deeply the sweet, fragrant air.

The birds woke as they passed, fluttering from branch to branch as the morning began. "I am pleased to share this world with you, Akandan. It is a pleasant morning. Thank you for waking me."

"It pleases me also to see the morning sun on your face. But that's not why I brought you here."

Seneca brought Nisa from the path into the grove that surrounded the pond. There, in the spot where they had found each other again, grew the white sapling Seneca bore from Akando.

"Look." Seneca pointed into the sky. Just above the high canopy of trees glittered the distant light of Candor. "Only once a year does Candor shine in the morning on Dakota. This day is sacred, maiden. The Dawn Star speaks of all eternity, of hope that overcomes all ill. But today it shines for you and me."

Nisa knelt beside the small tree and touched its delicate leaves. "You brought it here. . . . Why?"

"To remind Dakota where we came from, of the strength inside us."

Nisa stood and took his hand. "A herald of the past on a world of tomorrow. I hope we can bring this same peace to Thorwal."

Seneca drew Nisa's hand to his lips and kissed her fingers. "We will travel there soon, you and I. In particular, I would like to take you, alone, to the viewsite above the lava river. There is something I've always wanted to try in that spot."

Nisa's cheeks flushed. "That pleases me." A teasing smile grew on her face. "It might be wise to repeat our ceremony, according to Thorwalian custom."

"What does Thorwalian custom involve?"

Nisa's smile deepened. "It involves a large amount of bowing. On the part of the 'prized male.' In fact, at one point, the male must kneel before the female and profess his undying obedience."

Seneca laughed, then bent to kiss her. "I wondered if I'd gone too far with that part. I was afraid you might escape before I had you properly mated."

"Too late . . . I am properly mated now."

"You are. But one thing remains. Part of the mating ritual involves a gift bestowed from the male to the female. A token representative of the future he promises her."

Nisa's eyes narrowed with interest. "What gift?"

Seneca smiled, then drew forth a remote control. He entered a code. In response a small hovercraft buzzed through the trees, then stopped in front of Nisa.

Seneca watched Nisa's face change from surprise to that strange light of unrestrained Ravager glee he had adored from the day he first met her. She reached out and touched the small craft. "It feels . . . powerful."

"Like you, maiden."

"Is it really for me?"

"It is."

"You'll let me pilot it, and not take over in the event

of some . . . unfortunate occurrence?"

Seneca hesitated, then sighed. "I will not. And it may please you to know that this small craft has the remnant of your power cell as a motivator. The speed should surpass your wildest, most dangerous dreams."

Nisa beamed, then seized the controls from Seneca's hand. "Then let us go, Akandan! There is much of Dakota to be seen before nightfall."

Nisa hopped into the craft and waited for Seneca. He climbed in beside her. "I hope my shield works at high speeds."

"Where to, Akandan?"

"It doesn't matter, my sweet Ravager. I'll just see a streak of light, anyway."

The hovercraft leaped to life and sped over the pond, leaving ripples in its wake. Far above, no longer mysterious, yet holding infinite promise, the Dawn Star cast its final light over Dakota.

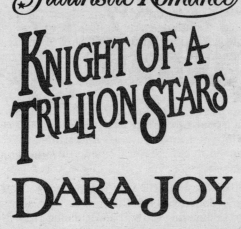

Futuristic Romance

KNIGHT OF A TRILLION STARS

DARA JOY

Fired from her job, exhausted from her miserable Boston commute, the last thing Deana Jones needs when she gets home is to find an alien in her living room. He says that his name is Lorgin and that she is part of his celestial destiny. Deana thinks his reasoning is ridiculous, but his touch is electric and his arms strong. And when she first feels the sizzling impact of his uncontrollable desire, Deana starts to wonder if maybe their passion isn't written in the stars.

_52038-9 $4.99 US/$5.99 CAN

Lady Lure — Flora Speer

"Flora Speer opens up new vistas for the romance reader!"

—*Romantic Times*

A valiant admiral felled by stellar pirates, Halvo Gibal fears he is doomed to a bleak future. Then an enchanting vision of shimmering red hair and stunning green eyes takes him captive, and he burns to taste the wildfire smoldering beneath her cool charm.

But feisty and defiant Perri will not be an easy conquest. Hers is a mission of the heart: She must deliver Halvo to his enemies or her betrothed will be put to death. Blinded by duty, Perri is ready to betray her prisoner—until he steals a kiss that awakens her desire and plunges them into a web of treachery that will test the very limits of their love.

_52072-9 $5.99 US/$7.99 CAN

NO OTHER LOVE

FLORA SPEER

Bestselling Author Of *Lady Lure*

Only Herne sees the woman. To the other explorers of the
ruined city she remains unknown. In the dead of night she
beckons him to an illicit joining, but with the dawn's light
she is gone. Herne finds he cannot forget his beautiful
seductress or her uncanny resemblance to another member
of the exploration party. Cool and reserved, Merin can pass
for the enchantress's double. Determined to unravel the
puzzle and to penetrate Merin's protective shell, Herne
begins a seduction of his own, one that will unleash a
whirlwind of danger and desire.

__51916-X $4.99 US/$5.99 CAN

Futuristic Romance

Love in another time, another place.

KATHLEEN MORGAN